THE COUNTESS DE CHARNY

"'YES, MONSIEUR,' SAID HE, 'I AM THE KING!'"

Dumas, Vol. Ten

THE WORKS OF

ALEXANDRE DUMAS

ILLUSTRATED WITH DRAWINGS ON WOOD BY
EMINENT FRENCH AND AMERICAN ARTISTS

P. F. COLLIER AND SON
MCMII

THE COUNTESS DE CHARNY.

CHAPTER I.

THE INN OF THE BRIDGE OF SÈVRES.

THE well-known manufacturing village of Sèvres lies somewhere about half-way between Paris and Versailles. At the door of the inn adjoining the bridge a personage was standing who is to play an important part in our narrative.

He was forty-five or forty-eight years of age. He was dressed as a workman, that is to say, had velvet breeches with leather facings at the pockets, like those worn by locksmiths and blacksmiths. He wore gray stockings, and shoes with copper buckles, and had on a woolen cap, like that of a lancer cut in half. A perfect forest of gray hair escaped from his cap and hung over his eyes, which were large, open, and intelligent, and flashed so wildly and so quickly that it was impossible to define their color. The other features were a nose rather large than small, heavy lips, white teeth, and a bronzed complexion.

Though not large, his figure was admirable. He had delicate limbs, a small foot, and his hand would have seemed so, too, had it not the bronze tint of that of all who work in iron.

Ascending from the hand to the elbow, and thence as far as the rolled-up sleeve suffered it to be visible, it might have been seen, in spite of the volume of muscle, that the skin was soft and fair.

This man had come an hour before from Versailles. In reply to questions asked by the innkeeper when he brought him a bottle of wine, he had said: The queen, with the king and dauphin, was coming; that they set out about noon, and they were about to occupy the Tuileries, the consequence of which would be that Paris, having in it "the baker, his wife, and the baker's boy," would not want bread.

He was waiting to see the cortège pass.

The assertion might be true, yet it was easier to see that he looked oftener toward Paris than toward Versailles.

After a few minutes he seemed satisfied, for a man clad almost as he was, and apparently of the same condition, was seen to approach the inn.

The newcomer walked heavily, like one who had made a long journey. His age might be that of the unknown man, that is to say, as people usually do, that he was on the wrong side of forty. His features betokened him to be a man of common inclinations and vulgar instincts.

The stranger looked curiously at the newcomer, as if he wished at one glance to measure all the impurity and wickedness of the man.

When the workman who came from Paris was about twenty paces from the man who awaited him, the latter poured out the first glass of wine into one of two glasses which stood on the table.

"Ah! ha!" said he, "it is cold, and the journey is long. Let us drink, and warm ourselves up."

The man from Paris looked around to see who gave him this invitation. "Do you speak to me?" said he.

"Whom else should I? There is no other person present," was the reply.

"Why offer me wine?"

"Why not?"

"Ah!"

"It is because we are of the same, or nearly the same trade."

"Everybody may be of the same trade. It is necessary, however, to know whether one be companion or master."

"Well, we will drink a glass of wine, chat, and find out which is the case."

"Very well," said the workman, advancing toward the door of the inn.

The stranger led the newcomer to the table, and gave him the glass.

"Ah!" said he, "this is Burgundy."

"Yes; the brand was recommended to me, and I do not regret that I ordered it. There is yet wine in the bottle, and other bottles in the cave."

"What are you about now?"

"I am from Paris, and await the coming of the royal cortège, which I intend to accompany to Paris."

"What mean you?"

"The king, queen, and dauphin return to Paris with the market-women, two hundred members of the assembly, and the National Guard under the command of Lafayette."

"La Bourgeois has then resolved to go to Paris?"

"He had to do so."

"So I thought, at three last night, when I left for Paris."

"Ah! I was curious to know what would become of the king, especially as I know him. This is no boast. A man who has a wife and three children must feed them, especially when there is no longer a Royal Forge."

The stranger said only, "Then business took you to Paris?"

"Yes; and on my honor, I was well paid for it." As he spoke, the man rattled several coins in his pocket. "The money, however," said he, "was given me by a servant; what is worst of all, by a German servant. That was wrong."

"Ah," said the stranger, like a man who advances slowly, but yet advances, "you are on a business which is important, and well paid for?"

"Yes."

"Because it is difficult?"

"It is."

"A secret lock—hey?"

"An invisible door."

"An invisible door! I imagine a man in a house, who finds it necessary to hide himself. Well, the bell is rung.

Where is monsieur? he is not in? No, he is; look for him. He is looked for. Good evening. I defy any one to find monsieur. An iron door with oak paneling, you understand, few can tell the difference."

"But if any one touch it?"

"Bah! just make the oak an inch thick, and no one can tell. I could not myself."

"Where made you that?"

"Aha!"

"Then you will not tell?"

"I cannot, for I do not know."

"You were then blindfolded?"

"Exactly. There was a carriage at the gate; they said, 'Are you So-and-so?' 'Yes,' said I. 'Well, we awaited you. Get in.' I did. When in, my eyes were bandaged, and the carriage was driven for nearly half an hour; at last the door of a great house was opened; I stumbled at the first step, and then went up ten steps into the vestibule. There I found a German servant, who said to the others, 'It is well! Go away; there is no longer any need of you.' The others left, and the bandage was taken from my eyes, and I was told what I had to do. I set to work, and in one hour all was done. They paid me in good louis d'or. My eyes were again blindfolded. I was put in the carriage, and taken back to the place whence I was borne."

"The bandage must have been very tight to prevent one from telling the right from the left."

"Heu! heu!"

"Come, then," said the stranger, "tell me what you really saw."

"When I stumbled I took care, in a slight degree, to derange the bandage."

"And when you had done so?" said the stranger, with equal vivacity.

"I saw a row of trees on the right, which made me think the house was on the boulevard, that is all I know."

"All?"

"On my word of honor."

"That gives little information."

"The boulevards are long, and there are many houses with wide doors on them."

"Then you would not recognize the house?"

The locksmith thought for a moment, and said, "No, I would not."

The stranger, though his face did not seem to say what he really wished to utter, appeared satisfied, and said: "Well, then, it seems there are no locksmiths, since people send to Versailles for one to make a secret door."

He then filled the glasses again, and knocked on the table with the empty bottle, that the innkeeper might bring a full one.

"Yes, there are locksmiths in Paris, but there are masters and professors."

"Ah, I see; like St. Eloi, you are one of the latter."

"I am. Do you belong to the trade?"

"Something of the sort."

"What are you?"

"A gunsmith."

"Have you any of your work about you?"

"Do you see this gun?"

The locksmith took the gun, looked carefully at it, tried the lock, and approved of the click of the springs, then reading the name on the breech, said:

"Impossible, my friend. Leclerc cannot be older than twenty-eight. Do not be offended, but you and I are close on fifty."

"True, I am not Leclerc; but I am just the same."

"How so?"

"I am his master."

"Ah! that is just as if I had said I am not the king, but his master."

"What mean you?"

"Because I am the king's master."

"Ah! have I the honor to speak to Monsieur Gamain?"

"You have, and if I could, I would serve you," said the locksmith, delighted at the effect he had produced.

"Diable! I did not know I was talking to a man of such consequence."

"Ah!"

"To a man of such consequence," repeated the stranger. "Tell me, is it pleasant to be a king's master?"

"Why?"

"I think it very humiliating for one man to be forced to call another 'your majesty.'"

"I did not have to do so. When at the forge, I called him Bourgeois, and he called me Gamain. We spoke together familiarly."

"Yes, but when dinner-time came you were sent to eat with the servants."

"Not a bit of it; a table ready served was brought to me at the shop, and at breakfast he often said: 'Bah! I will not go to see the queen, for then I will not have to wash my hands.'"

"I do not see."

"Why, when the king worked in iron as we do, his hands were like ours. That does not, however, keep us from being honest people; but the queen used to say: 'Fy, sire, your hands are dirty.' Just as if one could work in a shop and have clean hands. I tell you, he was never happy, except when in his geographical library, his study, or when he was with me. I think, though, he liked me best."

"Such a pupil as a king must have been a famous business for you."

"Not a bit; you are mistaken. I wish devoutly it was so; for though the master of Louis XVI., the Restorer of France, while all the world thinks me as rich as Crœsus, I am poor as Job."

"You poor? What on earth does he do with his money, then?"

"One half goes to the poor, the other half to the rich, so that he never has a penny. The Coigny, the Vaudreuil, and Polignac gnaw the poor fellow away. He wished to reduce Coigny's salary, and made Coigny come to the door of the shop, and after about five minutes, he came in as pale as possible, saying, 'On my honor, I thought he would beat me!' 'But his salary, sire,' said I. 'Oh, I let it stand as it is. I could not help it.' A few days afterward he sought to make some remarks to the queen about the pension of Madame de Polignac; only think, three hundred thousand francs; a nice thing."

"Bah! it was not enough. For the queen made him give her five hundred thousand. Thus, you see, these Polignacs, who a few years ago had not a sou, are about to leave France with millions. That would be nothing had they any talent, but give the whole of them an anvil and sledge, and not one can shoe a horse or make a key. They, however, like knights, as they say they are, have urged the king forward, and now leave him to get on as he can with Bailly, Mirabeau, and Lafayette; while to me, who would have given him such good advice, his master, his friend, who first put the file in his hand, he has given only fifteen hundred crowns a year."

"But you work with him, and something good falls in from day to-day."

"What! I work with him? No. It would compromise me. Since the taking of the Bastile, I have not put my foot inside of the palace. Once or twice I met him, the street was full of people, and he bowed to me. The second time was on the Satory road, and he stopped his carriage. 'Well, poor Gamain,' said he, 'things do not go on as you wish them to. This will, however, teach you. But how are your wife and children?' 'Well, very well,' said, I. 'Here,' said the king, 'make them this present for me.' He searched his pockets, and all the money he could find was nine louis. 'This is all I have,' said he, 'and I am ashamed to make you so poor a present.' You will agree with me that a king who has nine louis only, and who makes his comrade so poor a present, must be badly off."

"You did not take them?"

"Yes, I did. You must always take, for somebody else

would. It is, however, all right, for I will never go to Versailles, though he sent for me again and again. He does not deserve it; and when I think that he had ten thousand bottles of wine, each of which was worth a dozen of this, and that he never said to one of his servants, 'Take a basket to Gamain.' Ah! he preferred that his Swiss, his body-guard, and his Flemish soldiers should have it."

"Well," said the stranger, "so it is with kings; they are ungrateful. We are, however, no longer alone." At that moment two men and a fishwoman entered the room, and sat at a table near the one at which Gamain and the stranger were drinking the second bottle.

The locksmith looked at them with an attention which made the stranger smile.

The party, however, was worthy of attention.

One of the men was all torso; the other all legs. The woman it is not so easy to describe.

The torso was like a dwarf, for he was hardly five feet high. He perhaps lost an inch or two from the fact that he was knock-kneed. His face, instead of lessening his deformity, seemed to make it more apparent, for his straight and dirty hair was flattened on his head, and his badly marked brow seemed to have grown haphazard. His eyes were usually glassy, but, when irritated, flashed like those of a viper. His nose was flat, and made his high cheek-bones the more apparent. To make everything more hideous, his yellow lips covered but half a dozen black and broken teeth.

The veins of this man seemed filled with mingled blood and poison.

The second, different from the first, who had short legs, looked like a crane on stilts. His resemblance was the more striking, since humpbacked like the crane, with his head sunken between his shoulders, it was to be distinguished only by its red eyes and its long-pointed nose. Like the heron, too, it seemed to have the faculty of extending its neck at will, and picking out the eyes of any person it pleased. This, however, was nothing, for the arms seemed to have an equal elasticity, for, seated as he was, he could at once pick up a handkerchief on the floor, with which to wipe his brow.

The third was an amphibious being, the family, but not the sex, of which could be recognized. It was either a man or woman of thirty or of thirty-four years, and wore the dress of a fishwoman, with chains of gold, and earrings, lace cape, etc. Her features, as far as they could be distinguished through the coating of rouge above them, were worn and faded. When one had once seen her, one waited with anxiety until she should open her mouth, with the expectation that her voice, better than her appearance, would give some indication which might be definite. All this, though, was nothing, for her soprano voice left the examiner in equal doubt, for the ear was not more positive than the eye.

The shoes and stockings of the woman and the two men indicated that they had walked in the mud long and far.

"Strange!" said Gamain, "but I think I know that woman."

"Perhaps," said the stranger; "but, my dear fellow, when you see three persons together, be sure they have business to attend to. Let us not bore them." He took up his gun, and proposed to go.

"Do you know them?"

"Yes, by sight. I swear I have seen the woman somewhere."

"At court?"

"Bah! she is a fishwoman."

"They go to court sometimes."

"If you know them, tell me the names of the men, it may enable me to remember the woman."

"The men?"

"Yes."

"Which?"

"The crane."

"Jean Paul Marat——"

"And the hunchback."

"Prosper Vivrières?"

"Ah! ah!"

"Does that put you on the track of the woman?"

"No."

"Look again."

"I give my tongue to the dogs."

"But the fishwoman?"

"Wait a bit—no—yes."

"Yes?"

"It is—impossible."

"Yes, at first, it seems impossible."

"It is——"

"Ah, you will never name her. The fishwoman is the Duke d'Aiguillon."

At the sound of the name the apparent woman turned pale, and looked around.

The stranger placed his fingers on his lips, and left. Gamain followed him, thinking that he was mistaken. At the door, he knocked against a person, who seemed to fly, pursued by persons who shouted out: "The queen's hair-dresser!" Among these pursuers were two, each of whom bore a bloody head on a pike.

"Whε is the matter?" said the locksmith to the stranger.

"Who knows? Perhaps they wish him to curl the hair of those two heads. People in revolutionary days take strange fancies."

He mingled in the crowd, leaving Gamain, from whom perhaps he had extracted all he wished, to return to the shop at Versailles.

CHAPTER II.

CAGLIOSTRO.

The stranger was able to hide himself easily in the crowd, especially as it was large.

It was the advance-guard of the escort of the king, queen, and dauphin.

It was composed of miserable and ragged beggars, half

drunk, the floating foam of the population, like the froth which rises from water or lava.

All at once there was a great tumult. The bayonets of the National Guard and the white horse of Lafayette were seen.

The crowd shouted loudly, "Long live Lafayette!" who, from time to time, took off his hat, and saluted with his sword. "Vive Mirabeau!" too, was heard, as the latter from time to time put his head through the carriage window, in which he, with five other members of the National Assembly, sat, to get fresh air.

Thus the unfortunate king, for whom all was silence, heard the popularity he had lost, applauded. He also heard the quality in which he was deficient, praised. Dr. Gilbert, as he accompanied the king, without any immediate companion, walked on the right side of the royal carriage, that is, close to the queen.

On the two sides of the carriage of the king and queen, beyond the kind of file of footmen, who had taken that position so as to be able to aid him in case of necessity, walked, pattering in the mud, six inches deep, the men and women of the market, who seemed every moment to make a more compact array of their ribbons and gaudy colored dresses.

The king looked on with his sad, heart-broken air. He had not slept on the night before, and had eaten a bad breakfast. He had not been allowed time to readjust and to powder his hair; his beard was long, his linen rumpled, and looked wretchedly. Alas! the poor king, who was not a man for dangerous conjectures, at all crises hung down his head in dejection. Once only he looked up, and then it was when his head was about to fall upon the scaffold.

At about a hundred paces from the cabaret, the crowd halted, and the cries down the whole line were increased.

The queen looked out of the window, and the motion, which seemed like a salute, increased the murmur.

"Gilbert," said she, "what is it my people are singing? What are they crying?"

Gilbert uttered a sigh, which meant: She is unchanged. Then, with an expression of deep sadness, he said:

"Madame, the people you call yours was once really so, when, twenty years ago, an elegant gentleman, whom I now look for in vain, introduced you to them on the balcony, and shouted, 'Long live our dauphiness!' adding, madame, 'There you have two hundred thousand lovers.'"

The queen bit her lips, for she could find no fault with his answer.

"True," said she; "but it only proves that people change."

Gilbert bowed, and was silent.

"I asked you a question, Monsieur Gilbert," with an obstinacy she persisted in, even when aware that the answer would be unpleasant.

"Yes, madame; and as your majesty insists, I will reply. The people sing:

"'La Boulangère a des écus,
Qui ne lui coutent guère.'

You know who the people call the baker's wife."

"Yes, sir; I know they do me that honor. I am, however, used to nicknames. They once called me Madame Deficit. Is there any connection between the first and the last name?"

"Yes, madame; and to be assured you have only to think of one of the two verses I have repeated to you."

The queen repeated them, and said:

"Monsieur Gilbert, I do not understand."

Gilbert was silent.

The queen continued:

"Well, did you hear me? I do not understand."

"Does your majesty insist on an explanation?"

"Certainly."

"They mean your majesty's ministers, especially of finance, have been too complaisant. Monsieur de Calonne, for instance. The people knew that your majesty had only to ask that it ought to be given you, and as queens ask without much difficulty, for on asking they command, the people sing :

> " ' La Boulangère a des écus.
> Qui ne lui coutent guère.

That is to say, which scarcely cost the trouble of asking."

The queen grasped convulsively, with her white hand, the velvet of the carriage door.

"Well," said she, "that is what it signs. Now, Monsieur Gilbert, please, for you explain its thoughts well, tell me what it says."

"It says, madame, we will not want bread in Paris, for we have the baker, his wife, and the shop-boy."

"You can explain this second insolence distinctly as the first, can you not ? I hope so."

"Madame," said Gilbert, with the same kind melancholy, "if you would reflect, not on the words, but on the intention of this people, you would see that you have not so much to complain of as you think."

"Let us see," said the queen. "You know, doctor, I wish for nothing so much as for information."

"Whether correctly or not, madame, I cannot say, but it is said that a heavy trade in corn is carried on at Versailles, and that, therefore, none is brought to Paris. Who feed the poor ? The baker and his wife. To whom as father, mother, and son turn their hands, when for want of money they die ? To the baker and his wife. Whom does he beg, after that God who provides the harvests ? Those who distribute bread. Are you not, madame, the king, this august child, all distributors of bread ? Do not find fault, then, with the name, but thank God for the hope entertained, that when once king, queen, and dauphin are amid one million two hundred thousand starving people, they will cease to want."

"And should we thank the people while it shouts out nicknames before, around, behind us, for such songs and insults ?"

"Yes, madame ; and the more sincerely that this is an

expression of good-humor, for the nicknames are manifestations of hope, as its cries are an expression of desire."

"Ah! ah! The people wish prosperity to Messieurs De Lafayette and De Mirabeau?"

"Yes, madame; for if they have, being, as you see, separated from the abyss over which you hang, they may serve and preserve the monarchy."

"Is, then, the monarchy so fallen that it may be preserved by two men?"

Gilbert was about to reply, when cries of terror, mingled with bursts of laughter, were heard, and a motio of the crowd was made, which, far from separating Gilbert from the carriage, drove him close to it. He clung to the door-string, that it might be necessary for him to defend and aid the queen.

They were two heads which, after having made Leonard dress the hair, they had come to present to the queen.

At the cries and the sight of the heads the crowd opened to let them pass.

"For mercy's sake," said Gilbert, "do not look to the right!"

The queen was not a woman to obey, she knew not why, such an injunction.

She consequently looked in the direction Gilbert had told her not. She uttered a terrible cry.

All at once her eyes became detached from the horrible spectacle, as if there were something yet more awful, and became riveted, as it were, to a Medusa's head.

The queen took her hand from the door of the carriage, and placing it on Gilbert's shoulders, drove her finger-nails almost into the flesh.

The Medusa's head was that of the stranger whom we saw drinking in the inn with Gamain, who leaned with his arms folded against a tree.

Gilbert turned, and when he saw the pale, quivering lips of the queen, and her fixed eyes, he attributed her excitement to the appearance of the two heads, but he saw she was looking in a horizontal direction.

Gilbert looked in the same direction, and at the same moment, uttering a cry of surprise, as the queen had of terror, both exclaimed:

"Cagliostro!"

The man who leaned against the tree saw the queen perfectly well.

He made a sign to Gilbert, as if to say, "hither."

Just then the carriages prepared to set out mechanically, instinctively, and naturally; the queen pushed Gilbert to prevent his being hurt by the wheel.

He thought she meant him to go to the stranger.

If, too, the queen had not pushed him, he could not but have gone, for he was no longer master of himself.

Consequently, he stood still while the cortège defiled, and following the false workman, who from time to time looked back to see if he was followed, entered a narrow street, hurried at a rapid pace toward Bellevue, and disappeared behind a wall, just at the moment when the cortège was hidden from sight in the direction of Paris, being completely hidden by the mountain behind which it was.

Gilbert followed the guide, who preceded him some twenty paces, until he was half-way up the ascent. Being then in front of a large and handsome house, the stranger took a key from his pocket and opened a little door, which enabled the master to leave the house when he pleased, unseen by his servants.

He left the door half open, a direct invitation for his companion to follow him.

Gilbert did so, and carefully closed the door, which turned quietly on its hinges, and closed without any noise.

When once in, Gilbert saw himself in a corridor, the walls of which were inlaid as high as a man in the most marvelous manner with bronze plates, like those with which Ghiberti enriched the door of the baptistry of Florence.

His feet sunk in a soft Turkey carpet.

On the left was an open door.

Gilbert thought this room, too, was intentionally kept open, and entered a room hung with India satin and furniture covered with the same material—one of those fantastic birds, painted or embroidered in the fashion the Chinese are so fond of, was hung to the wall, and sustained in its beak a mirror, which, like the candelabra, was of most exquisite workmanship, and represented bunches of lilies.

There was but one single picture to ornament the room —Raphael's Virgin. Gilbert was admiring this picture, when he heard, or, rather divined, that a door opened behind him. He turned and saw Cagliostro coming from a kind of dressing-room. One moment had enabled him to efface the stains from his hands and arms, to give his dark hair the most aristocratic change, and to effect a perfect transformation.

His costume was covered with embroidery, his hands sparkled with diamonds, strangely contrasting with the black dress and simple gold ring which Gilbert had received from Washington.

Cagliostro, with an open and smiling face, advanced, and reached forth his hand.

Gilbert seized it.

"Wait a moment, dear Gilbert. Since we parted you have made such progress, especially in philosophy, that you are the master, and I scarcely worthy of being a scholar."

"Thank you for the compliment," said Gilbert; "but if I have made such progress, how do you know it? We have not met for eight years."

"Think you, dear doctor, that you are one of those men unknown because you are unseen? I have not seen you for eight years, but I can nevertheless tell you what you have been about every day."

"Indeed!"

"Will you still doubt my double sight?"

"You know that I am a mathematician."

"And therefore incredulous. Let us see. You come first to France on account of family affairs. They do not concern me, and——"

"No!" said Gilbert, who thought to annoy Cagliostro. "Tell me."

"Well, you wish to attend to the education of your son

Sebastian, and to place him at a little city eighteen or twenty leagues from Paris, and to settle matters with your agent, a good fellow, whom, contrary to his inclinations, you keep in Paris, and who for many reasons should be with his wife."

"Indeed, you are wonderful."

"Listen. You came the second time in consequence of political affairs, which brought you to France, as they have brought many others. Then you wrote various pamphlets, and sent them to Louis XVI., and as you have a little of the old man in you, you are prouder of the royal approbation than you would be of that of the master who preceded me in your education, Jean Jacques Rousseau, who, were he now alive, would be far greater than any king. You were desirous to know what the descendant of Louis XIV. and Henry IV. thought of Doctor Gilbert. Unfortunately there existed a little matter of which you had not thought, yet which caused me one day to find you all bloody, with a ball in your breast, at the Azores, where my vessel chanced to touch. This little affair had relation to a certain Mademoiselle Andrée de Taverney, who became Countess de Charny, and who esteems herself happy in being able to serve the queen. Now, as the queen could refuse nothing to Charny's wife, she asked and obtained a lettre de cachet; you were arrested at Havre, and taken thence to the Bastile, where, dear doctor, you would be yet if the people one day had not torn it down. Then, like a good royalist as you are, you took side with the king, the physician of whom you are. Yesterday, or, rather, this morning, you contributed greatly to the safety of the royal family by hurrying to awaken Lafayette, who slept like an honest man, and just now, when you saw me, thinking that the queen, who, by the bye, detests you, was in danger, you were willing to make your body a defense for your sovereign. Is not this the case? But I forgot a thing of some importance, a magnetic exhibition in the presence of the king, the withdrawal of a certain casket seized by one Ras de Loup. Have I either forgotten or mistaken aught?"

"True, you are still the magician, sorcerer, and enchanter, Cagliostro."

Cagliostro smiled with satisfaction. He was rejoiced at having, contrary to Gilbert's wishes, produced the effects which the countenance of the latter exhibited.

Gilbert continued:

"Now," said he, "as I love you certainly as much as you love me, and as my desire to know what has become of you since our separation, is very great, and equal to that which impelled you to find out where I was, tell me in what part of the world your genius and power have been employed?"

"Six months ago I was in the Castle of San Angelo, while you, three months ago, were in the Bastile."

"But I thought there was no escape from San Angelo?"

"Bah! Remember Benvenuto Cellini."

"Did you, too, then make a pair of wings, as he did, and like a new Icarus fly over the Tiber?"

"I could not by evangelical precaution. I was placed in a deep, dark dungeon."

"You did get out, though?"

"Yes; for here I am."

"You bribed the keeper?"

"Not so; I unfortunately had an incorruptible, but fortunately not immortal, jailer; chance, or one less infidel than I would say Providence, contrived that he died one day, after he had thrice refused to release me."

"Suddenly?"

"Yes. His successor was not incorruptible; the first time he brought me supper, he said eat and get strong, for before to-morrow we have a journey to take. He did not lie, for that night each of us used up three horses, and traveled a hundred miles."

"What said the government to your flight?"

"Nothing. They dressed the body of the dead jailer in my clothes, fired a pistol-ball in his face, laid the weapon beside him, and said that, having procured arms, I had killed myself. An account of my death was published, and the poor devil was buried in my place. You see,

Gilbert, at last I am dead. If I say I am not dead, they will reply by producing the magistrate's certificate to prove my burial, at least. There was no need of that, however, for it became necessary for me, for the time, to disappear. I then, as Abbé Dutille said, made a plunge, and have appeared under another name."

"And what is your name now, if I commit no indiscretion?"

"My name is Zanoni; I am a Genoese banker, and do a little discount business with princes. You know my heart and purse, as ever, are at your service. If you are ever in need of money, there is a private chest in my secretary, the other is at St. Cloud, in Paris, and if you need money and I am not at home, come hither; and I will show you the way to open the little door. Push the spring; this is the way, and you will always find about a million there."

"You are indeed a wonderful man!" said Gilbert, with a smile; "but, you know, with my twenty thousand livres a year, I am richer than the king."

"And what are you about in Paris?"

"Who knows! establishing what you contributed to in the United States—a republic."

Gilbert shook his head.

"France has no tendency to republicanism."

"We will make it so."

"The king will resist."

"Possibly."

"The nobles will appeal to arms."

"Probably."

"What, then, will you do?"

"We will not make a republic then, but a revolution."

Gilbert let his head fall on his breast.

"Know you who destroyed the Bastile, my friend?"

"The people."

"You do not understand, but take cause for effect. For five hundred years counts, lords, princes have been locked up in the Bastile, yet still it stood. One day the king, in his folly, sought to imprison thought, which needs space and extent, in that place. Thought burst through the Bastile, and the people entered by the breach."

"True!" murmured Gilbert.

"You remember what Voltaire wrote to Monsieur de Chauvelin, March 2, 1764, about twenty-six years since?"

"Tell me."

"Voltaire wrote: 'All I see announces the seeds of a revolution, which certainly will come, and which I will not be happy enough to see. The French are slow, but they always succeed. Light has been gradually diffused, and one day there will be an outbreak. There will be a fearful clatter."

"The young are very happy; they will see sights."

"What think you of things yesterday and to-day?"

"Terrible!"

"What think you of what you saw?"

"Awful!"

"Well, Gilbert, we are only at the beginning. All things in this old world march to the tomb—nobility, royalty all will find a tomb in an abyss."

"I guess the nobility may, for it has given itself to gain ever since the famous night of August 4. Let us save our royalty, which is the palladium of the nation."

"Those are fine words, dear Gilbert. Tell me if the palladium saved Troy, though. Save royalty? Do you think royalty can be saved with ease when we have such a king?"

"He is sprung from a great race."

"Yes, a race of eagles transformed into paroquets. Before Utopians like you, Gilbert, save royalty, kings must make an effort for themselves. Is the king a representative of your ideal of the scepter bearer? Think you Charlemagne, St. Louis, Philippe Augustus, Henry IV., Francis I., or Louis XIV. had those flabby cheeks, hanging lips, inexpressive eyes, and hesitating steps? They had not, but were men with nerve, blood, life beneath their royal robes, and were not bastardized by constant transmission in one strain. That is a good radical idea, which these short-sighted people have forgotten.

"To preserve animal and even vegetable life in vigor, Nature herself has prescribed the fusion of races—as the graft in the vegetable kingdom is the preserver of beauty and grace, marriage in man, between parents too closely connected, causes individuals to decay. Nature suffers, languishes, and degenerates, when several generations of the same blood succeed one another; but on the contrary, becomes revived and invigorated by the infusion of a new element. Look at the heroes who found dynasties and the sluggards who end. Henry III., the last Valois, and Gaston, the last Medici, the Cardinal of York, the last Stuart, and Charles VI., the last Hapsbourg. Going back, Louis XV., and Marie de Medici, Henry IV., is four times his ancestor, and Marie de Medici, four times his ancestress. Passing to Philip III. of Spain, and Margaret of Parma, the former is three times his ancestor, and the latter his ancestress. I, who had nothing better to do, have counted all this, and have come to this conclusion: out of the thirty-two ancestors there are, in Louis XV.'s case, six Bourbons, five Medicis, eleven Hapsbourgs, three Savois, three Stuarts, and a Danish princess. Subject the best horse or dog on earth to such treatment, and in the fourth generation you will either have a pony or a cur. How the devil can it be otherwise with us men? You are a mathematician, doctor, and how do you like my calculation?"

"I tell you, my dear wizard," said Gilbert, rising and taking his hat, "that your calculation reminds me that my place is with the king."

Gilbert advanced toward the door.

Cagliostro asked him to stop, and said:

"Hear me, Gilbert: you know I love you, and to spare you trouble, would expose myself to intense agony. Let me advise you."

"What?"

"Let the king escape and leave France, now while he

can. In three months, perhaps in six, in a year it will be too late."

"Count," said Gilbert, "would you advise a soldier to leave his post because it is dangerous?"

"Were the soldier so situated, hemmed in, surrounded, if his life, especially, compromised that of half a million of men, I would. You, even you Gilbert, will tell the king so, when, alas! it will be too late. Wait not until to-morrow, but tell him to-day. Do not wait until evening, but tell him now."

"Count, you know that I am a fatalist. What will be, will be; as long as I have influence the king will remain in France. We will meet in the contest, and perhaps rest side by side on the battle-field."

"Well, then, the world will say, no man, intelligent soever as he may be, can escape from his destiny. I sought you for the purpose of telling you this, and you have heard me. Like Cassandra's prediction, mine is vain. Adieu."

"Listen, count. Do you tell me here, as you did in America, that you are able to read the human fate in the face?"

He stood at the threshold.

"Gilbert, certainly, as you read the course of the stars, while common men fancy they stray at hazard."

"Listen; some one knocks at the door."

"True."

"Tell me who knocks at the door? When and what death he will die?"

"I will; let us admit him."

Gilbert went toward the end of the corridor, and his heart beat in a way he could not express—though he said:

"It was absurd for him to have faith in this charlatanism."

The door opened. A man of distinguished bearing, tall, and with his face impressed with an expression of great kindness, entered the room, and looked at Gilbert with an expression not devoid of anxiety.

"Good morning, marquis," said Cagliostro.

"Good morning, baron," said the stranger.

As Cagliostro saw the latter looked anxiously at Gilbert, he said:

"Marquis, this is a friend of mine. My dear Gilbert, this is one of my clients, the Marquis de Favras."

They bowed; then, speaking to the stranger, he said:

"Marquis, be pleased to await me a few moments only in that room."

The marquis bowed again, and left.

"Well?" said Gilbert.

"You wish to know how he will die?"

"Did you not promise to tell me?"

Cagliostro gave a strange look, and glanced around to see that no one was listening.

"Have you ever seen a nobleman hung?"

"No."

"Well, it is a curious spectacle, and you will be on the Place de Grève on the day of De Favras's execution."

Then, taking Gilbert to the gate, he said:

"Listen: when you wish to see me without being seen or seeing, push this knob thus," and he showed the secret. "Excuse me. Those who have not long to live should not be kept waiting."

He left, leaving Gilbert amazed at the statement which had excited his surprise, but not conquered his incredulity.

CHAPTER III.

FATALITY.

In the interim the king, queen, and royal family continued the journey to Paris.

On the way the dauphin became very hungry, and asked for bread. The queen looked around her, and nothing was more easy, for every bayonet had a loaf on its point. She looked for Gilbert. He, as we know, was with Cagliostro. Had he been there, the queen would not have hesitated to have asked for a piece of bread. She would not, however, ask one of the men of the people she hated so.

"My child," said she, "wait until evening; we have none now, but to-night may, perhaps." She wept.

The dauphin reached his little hand toward one of the loaves the people had on the points of their bayonets, and said:

"But those men have."

"Yes, my child; it is theirs, and not ours. They got it at Versailles, for they say they have had none for three days at Paris."

"For three days!" said the child. "Have they eaten nothing for three days, mamma?"

"No, my child," said the queen.

"Then," said the dauphin, "they must be very hungry."

Ceasing his complaints, he sought to sleep. Poor prince! more than once before his death he begged in vain for bread. At the barrier there was another halt, to celebrate the arrival. After about half an hour of cries, clamor, and dances in the mud, an immense hurrah was given; every gun, whether borne by man, woman, or child, was fired in the air, without any attention being paid to the fact that they were charged with ball, and after a second or two the missiles were heard falling in every direction like hail.

The dauphin and his sister wept. They were so frightened that they forgot their hunger. The march was resumed, and the Place de l'Hôtel de Ville was reached. There a square was formed to keep back all the carriages except the king's, and all but the royal household and the National Assembly, and the Hôtel de Ville was entered.

The queen then saw Weber, her confidential valet, making every effort to enter the palace. Weber was an Austrian, and had come with her from Vienna. She called to him. He came.

Seeing at Versailles that the National Guard on that day had the post of honor, Weber, to give himself an importance which might enable him to be useful to the queen, had put on the uniform of the guard, and to the dress of the private had added the decorations of the staff. The equerry had lent him a horse. Not to arouse suspicion, he had kept out of the way, with the intention, however, of approaching if the queen needed him. Being called, he came.

"Why do you seek to force the lines, Weber?" said the queen, preserving her usual familiarity with him.

"To be of use to your majesty."

"You can do nothing in the Hôtel de Ville, but elsewhere you may be very useful. On to the Tuileries, where we are not expected, and whither you must go, or we shall find neither lights, supper, nor a bed."

Bailly, one of the three popular men of the day, whom we have seen appear during the first excursion of the king, now, when bayonets and cannon displaced the bouquets of flowers and garlands, awaited the king and queen at the foot of a throne prepared for them; it was badly made, and trembled beneath the velvet that covered it. It was appropriate.

The Mayor of Paris now almost echoed his previous address.

The king replied:

"I always come with pleasure and confidence among the people of my good city of Paris."

The king spoke in a low tone, for he was faint with fatigue and hunger. Bailly repeated his words aloud, so that all might hear.

He, however, either voluntarily or not, forgot the words, "and confidence."

Her bitterness was delighted at an opportunity to give vent to itself.

She said:

"Excuse me, Mr. Mayor, you either did not hear, or your memory is bad."

"Madame," said Bailly, with that star-gazing eye which read heaven so well and earth so badly.

The queen said:

"The king's remark was that he always came with

pleasure and confidence among the people of his city of Paris. Now, as people may doubt if he came with pleasure, it is important that it be known that he came with confidence."

She ascended the steps of the throne, and sat down to hear the addresses of the electors.

In the meantime, Weber reached the Tuileries.

About ten, the wheels of the royal carriage were heard, and Weber cried out:

"Attend the king!"

The king, queen, dauphin, Mme. Royale, the Princess Elizabeth, and Andrée entered.

M. de Provence had gone to the Luxembourg.

The king looked gladly around, and as he entered the room, observed, through a half-open door, that supper was ready.

At the same time, an usher entered, and uttered the usual ceremonial phrase: "The king is served."

"Ah, Weber is a man of great resources. Madame, tell him from me I am much pleased with him."

"I will not fail to do so, sire."

When the children had supped, the queen asked leave to retire to her room.

"Certainly, madame, for you must be fatigued. As, however, you will need food before to-morrow, have some prepared in time."

The queen left with the children.

The king sat at table and finished his supper. Mme. Elizabeth, the devotion of whom not even the vulgarity of Louis XVI. could change, remained with the king, to render him those little attentions which even the best domestics neglect.

The queen, when in her room, breathed freely. She had ordered all her ladies not to leave Versailles unordered, and she was alone.

She set about finding then a chair or sofa, purposing to put the children in her own bed; but entering an adjoining room, and seeing that it was comfortably warmed and lighted, was enchanted to observe two clean beds in it.

The children being asleep, she sat down at a table, on which there was a candelabra with four lights.

The table had a red cover.

She looked through the fingers of the hand on which she rested her head, but saw nothing but the red cover.

Twice or thrice something in the red glare made her shake her head mechanically. She seemed to feel her eyes become filled with blood, and her ears to tingle.

Then, like a tempest, her past life swept before her.

She remembered that she was born November 8th, 1755, on the day of the Lisbon earthquake, when fifty thousand lives and two hundred churches were overthrown.

She remembered that the first room she slept in at Strasbourg was hung with a tapestry representing the Murder of the Innocents, and, amid the dense light of the fire, she saw the blood streaming from their wounds, while the faces of the ruffians assumed so dread and terrible an expression that she called for aid, and at dawn left a city which had given her so painful a reception in France.

She remembered that on her way to Paris she paused at the house of the Baron de Taverney, where, for the first time, she met the wretch Cagliostro. He had shown her a horrible object, an unknown and terrible machine of death, and afterward a head, her own, rolling from it.

She remembered that when Mme. Lebrun painted her portrait, she was then a young and beautiful woman; by some accident she had given her the air of the Henrietta of England, wife of Charles I. She remembered that when she first came to Versailles and placed her foot on that marble pavement, which, on the evening before, she had seen running with blood, a terrible clap of thunder had been heard, preceded by a flash, which divided the whole sky from right to left in so terrible a manner, that the Duc de Richelieu, not easily frightened, shook his head, and said, "The omen is bad."

As she saw all this, she fancied that a reddish vapor rose before her, and became every moment more dense.

The darkening of the air became so apparent that the queen looked up and saw that without any apparent cause one of the lights was out. She trembled; the light yet smoked, and she could not comprehend why it was out.

As she looked at the light with amazement, it seemed to her that the next one grew more and more pale, that the white blaze became red, and then burned blue. Then the light grew thinner and larger, and appeared about to leave the wick; at last it quivered for a moment as if under some invisible influence, and disappeared.

The queen gasped as she saw the quivering light, and insensibly her hands approached more and more near the table. She saw it go out, and threw herself back in a chair and placed her hands on her brow, which was damp with perspiration.

She remained thus for about ten minutes, and when she looked around, saw that the blaze of the third light was being bedimmed as the others had been.

At first, Marie Antoinette thought she was dreaming, or under the influence of some fearful hallucination. She sought to rise, but felt herself chained to her seat. She sought to call her daughter, whom ten minutes before she would not have awakened for the world. Her voice, however, stuck in her throat. She sought to look away, but the third expiring light seemed to fascinate her. At last, as the second had changed color, the third took different hues, floated to and fro, from right to left and went out.

The queen was so terrified that she regained her utterance, and sought, by talking to herself, to regain the courage she had lost.

All at once, without undergoing the changes of the others, as the queen was saying:

"I do not make myself uneasy about the three, but if the fourth go out, woe, woe to me!" it went out.

She uttered a cry of agony, and, rising from her seat in the dark, tossed her arms around, and fell on the floor.

As her body struck the floor, the door opened, and Andrée appeared at the entrance.

She paused for a moment, as if, in this obscurity, she saw a kind of vapor, and as if she heard the rustling of a shroud in the air.

Looking about her, she saw the queen prostrate on the floor, and unconscious.

She stepped back, as if her first intention had been to retire. Soon, however, she controlled herself, and saying nothing, and answering no question (it would have been in vain to do so), with a strength of which she might have been supposed incapable, lifted her up, and without any other light than that of the two candles, which shone from her room through the door, placed her on the bed.

Taking a flacon of salts from her pocket, she placed it to the nose of Marie Antoinette.

Notwithstanding this, the queen had fainted so completely, that not for ten minutes did she breathe.

A deep sigh announced that consciousness had returned. Andrée felt inclined to go, but, as before, a sense of consciousness retained her.

She merely withdrew her arm from the head of Marie Antoinette, whom she had lifted up, that no portion of the corrosive liquid might get on the queen's face or chest. She removed the salts also.

As soon as it was done, her head fell back on the pillow, and the queen seemed again plunged in a faint, almost as profound as the one she had just recovered from.

A shudder passed over the whole of the queen's frame. She sighed, and opened her eyes, while Andrée, cold, passionless as a statue, again attended her.

Gradually she recalled her ideas, and, seeing a woman near her, threw her arms around her neck. She cried out:

"Ah! defend—save me!"

"Your majesty, surrounded by your friends, needs no defense, and you have now recovered from a fainting fit."

"The Countess of Charny!" said the queen, when she saw whom she had embraced. She withdrew her arms and almost repelled Andrée.

Andrée did not fail to observe both the feeling and the action.

For a moment she remained in almost an impassible state.

Stepping back, she says:

"Does the queen order me to assist in undressing her!"

"No, thank you, countess," said the queen, in a tone of emotion. "I will do so alone. Return to your room; you must have need of sleep."

"I will return to my room, not to sleep, however, but to watch your majesty."

Having bowed respectfully, she retired with a step not unlike that a statue would have.

CHAPTER IV

SEBASTIAN.

On the same evening when the events we have spoken of took place, a not less strange affair took place in the college of the Abbé Fortier.

Sebastian Gilbert disappeared at about six in the evening, and, notwithstanding every effort made, could not be found.

Every one was questioned, but none could tell.

Aunt Angelique alone, as she left the church, where she had been fixing the benches, had seen him go down the little street, between the church and prison, apparently toward the fields.

This did not make the abbé less uneasy, but, on the contrary, more unhappy. He was not unaware that strange hallucinations sometimes seized young Gilbert whenever the woman he called his mother appeared. And more than once the abbé had followed him, when, under the influence of this vertigo, he seemed inclined to go too far into the fields, where he was afraid he would be lost, and on such occasions would send the best runners of the college after him.

The child had always been found panting, and almost exhausted, leaning against some tree, or resting on some bank beside some beautiful hedge.

Sebastian, however, had never had this vertigo late in

the day. No one had ever been obliged to run after him at night.

Something extraordinary, therefore, must have happened. But the abbé could not fancy what.

To be more completely satisfied than the abbé, we will follow Sebastian Gilbert, and find out whither he went.

Aunt Angelique was not mistaken. She had seen Sebastian Gilbert hurrying in the shade, and seeking as rapidly as possible to reach the park. Thence he had gone to the Pheasantry, and had proceeded down a lane which led toward Haramont.

He went to find Pitou.

But Pitou went out of one side of the village as Sebastian entered the other.

Pitou, in the simplicity of his nature, did not see the use of keeping a door closed, whether one be out or in. Sebastian knew Pitou's room as well as he knew his own. He looked for a flint and steel, lighted the candle, and waited.

Sebastian was in too great agitation, however, to wait quietly or long.

As time passed, he went to a rickety table, on which was pen, ink, and paper. On the first page were the names and surnames of the thirty-three men who formed the effective force of the National Guard of Haramont, and who were under Pitou's orders.

Gilbert carefully lifted this sheet, which was the chef-d'œuvre, of the commandant's writing, for he did not disdain, in order that things might be correctly done, to play the orderly-sergeant.

On the second sheet he wrote :

"DEAR PITOU,—I am about to tell you that eight days ago I overheard a conversation between the Abbé Fortier and the Vicar of Villers-Cotterets. It seems the Abbé Fortier connives with aristocrats at Paris, and told the vicar that a counter revolution was being prepared."

"So we heard about the queen who put on a black cockade and trampled the tricolor in the dust.

"This threat of a counter revolution, according to what we heard about the events that followed the banquet, made me uneasy on my father's account, for, as you know, he is opposed to the aristocrats. Things now, though, are far worse.

"The vicar returned to see the curate, and, as I was anxious about my father, I thought I would hear all about what I got an inkling of by accident.

"It seems the people went to Versailles, and massacred many persons, among them Monsieur George de Charny.

"Fortier added:

"'Let us speak low, lest we annoy little Gilbert. His father was there, and may have been among the victims.'

"You see, Pitou, I heard no more.

"I slipped out of my hiding-place, unseen, went through the garden to the Castle Square, and hurried to ask you to take me back to Paris, which I know you would willingly do if you were here.

"As, however, you may not be back for some time, having gone probably to fix your nets in the forest, which will keep you till morning, I am too anxious to wait.

"I will, then, go alone. Be at ease, for I know the way. Besides, I have yet two louis left of the money my father sent me, and I will take a place in the first carriage I meet.

"Your loving
"SEBASTIAN.

"P.S.—I have written a long letter, first to explain to you why I go, and, in the second place, because I hoped you would return before I finished.

"But you did not. Good-by until we meet again. If my father be unhurt, I will return.

"Make the Abbé Fortier easy about me, or, at least, do not do so until to-morrow, lest he should pursue me.

"Well, as you will not come, adieu."

As Sebastian knew how economical his friend Pitou was, he put out the candle and left.

The lad, then entirely engrossed by his undertaking, set

out for Lorgny. He passed the village and reached the broad ravine which led thence to Valenciennes, and which drains the ponds of Walue; at Valenciennes, he reached the highroad, and when in the plain, began to walk more rapidly. He did not slacken his pace or leave the center until he came to a brief eminence, where the two roads to Paris and Cressy divided.

When coming from Paris, he had not noticed the separation, and now did not remember which he should take.

He paused, undecided.

He looked around to see if anything would tell him which he should take. This he could have done by day, but it was impossible at night. Just then he heard the gallop of two horses.

He prepared to stop and ask the wayfarers, and accordingly advanced to address the first.

The latter, seeing a man leave the road-side, put his hand in his holster.

Sebastian saw him do so.

"Sir," he said, "I am not a robber, but a poor lad, whom recent events at Versailles force to go to Paris to look for his father. I do not know which road to take. Tell me, and you will do me a great favor."

The servant came up.

"Sir," he said, "do you recognize that lad?"

"No; yet it seems to me——"

"How, sir, do you not recognize young Sebastian Gilbert, who is at school with the Abbé Fortier?"

"Yes, who often goes with Pitou to the farm of Mademoiselle Catherine."

"You are right."

Turning around, he said:

"Is it you, Sebastian?"

"Yes, Monsieur Isidor," said the child, who knew to whom he spoke.

"Tell me, then, why you are here at this hour?"

"I am on my way to Paris to see if my father be dead or alive."

"Alas! child," said the gentleman, sadly, "I go for the same purpose, but am certain of all."

"Yes, I know; your brother."

"One of my brothers, George, was killed yesterday, at Versailles."

"Ah! Monsieur de Charny."

"Well, my child," said the latter, "since we go for the same purpose, we must not separate, for you, like me, must go to Paris."

"Yes, sir."

"You cannot go on foot."

"I will not go far, for to-morrow I will take a seat in the first carriage I find, and go as far as possible to Paris in it."

"But if you meet none?"

"Then I must go on foot."

"You can do something better than that; get down, Baptiste, and help Sebastian up."

"Thank you, it is useless;" and, active as a boy, he sprung up behind the count.

The three men and the two horses galloped off, and disappeared behind the hill of Grande Ville.

They continued on to Daumartin, which they reached at six o'clock.

All needed refreshments, and, besides, it was necessary to find post-horses.

After having left Daumartin at noon, they reached the Tuileries at six in the afternoon.

There a delay took place. M. de Lafayette had posted the guards, and having taken charge of the king's safety, in these troublous times, punctiliously discharged his duty.

When Charny, however, mentioned his name and his brother's he was introduced into the Swiss courtyard with Sebastian, and thence they went into the central yard.

Sebastian wished at once to go to the house in the Rue St. Honoré where he had left his father, but Charny told him that, as the doctor was now royal physician, he would be found more probably in the palace than elsewhere.

Isidor was introduced by the state staircase, and an

usher made him wait in a saloon hung with green cloth, dimly lighted by two candelabrums.

The usher went at once to ask for the Count de Charny and the doctor.

After about ten minutes he came back and said the Count de Charny was with the queen.

Nothing had happened to the doctor, and it was thought that he was with the king.

Sebastian breathed freely. He had not any occasion to dread anything, for his father was unhurt and safe.

"The Vicomte de Charny," said an usher.

"Well, I am he."

"Is expected by the queen."

"Wait for me, Sebastian, at least until your father comes. Remember, I must be responsible to him for you."

Isidor followed the usher, and Sebastian again sat down.

At ease in relation to his father's health and about himself, for he was sure he would be forgiven by the doctor for what he had done, he began to think of the Abbé Fortier and of Pitou, and of the anxiety both would feel on account of his letter.

He did not see how, after all the great delay they met with on the road, it had happened that Pitou had not overtaken them with his long legs.

By the simple association of ideas with Pitou, he thought of his usual home, of the tall trees, the many pathways, the blue horizon, and then the strange visions he so often had had beneath the old trees of the vast forest.

He thought of her he had so often seen in his dreams, and but once only, he fancied, in reality, in the wood of Satory, where she appeared and disappeared, like a cloud borne away in a calash by a magnificent steed.

He remembered the deep emotion the apparition always caused, and, half lost in that dream, murmured:

"Mother, mother, mother!"

Suddenly the door through which Isidor had gone opened again, and a female form appeared.

So perfectly was the figure in harmony with the thoughts that flitted by, that, seeing his dream realized, the lad trembled.

His feeling, however, was far more intense when he saw both the shadow and reality.

The shadow of dreamland, the reality of Satory.

He sprung at once to his feet.

His lips opened, his eyes rolled, and his pupils expanded.

He panted, but sought in vain to speak.

The woman passed proudly, majestically by, and seemed not to notice him.

She crossed the hall diagonally, opened the door opposite to that through which she had entered, and disappeared in the corridor.

Sebastian saw that he was about to lose, and hurried after her. He looked carefully, as if to be sure that she had gone from the door she had entered to the one whence she passed, and overtook her before her silken robe had disappeared.

Hearing his steps, she had walked quickly, as if she feared pursuit.

Sebastian hurried, but the corridor was long and dark. He was afraid his vision would desert him.

She, hearing his footsteps approach, hurried away the more rapidly, but looked back.

Sebastian uttered an exclamation of joy. It was indeed she.

The woman, seeing the lad follow her, she knew not why, hurried to the ladder, and rushed down the steps.

Scarcely had she descended a single story, than Sebastian stood at the top, and cried :

" Lady, lady ! "

The voice filled her heart with strange sensations ; it seemed that a blow, half pleasant, half painful, had struck her heart, and, passing through her veins, had filled her bosom with emotion.

Understanding neither appeal nor the emotion, she increased her gait, and finally ran.

The lad was, however, too near for her to escape, and

they reached a carriage together, the door of which a servant kept open. She sprung in, and sat down.

Before, however, the door could be shut, Sebastian got between her and the servant, seized her skirt, and, kissing it passionately, exclaimed :

"Ah, lady, lady!"

The woman, then looking at the child who had first frightened her, said, in a gentler tone than usual, but yet maintaining something of fear :

"Well, why do you follow me? why did you call me? tell me what you wish for me to do."

"I wish—I wish to kiss you," said our panting child; and, low enough to be heard only by her, added : "I wish to call you mother."

The young woman uttered a cry, took the head of her child in her hands, and, as if by a sudden revelation, which made her know some great mystery, pressed her burning lips on his brow.

Then, as if she feared some one would deprive her of the child she had so strangely found, she drew him into the carriage, put him on the other side of her, and closed the glass of the door, which she pulled to with her own hands.

"Drive to my house, No. 9 Rue Coq-Heron," said she, "first door from Rue Platrière."

Turning to the child, she said :

"What is your name?"

"Sebastian."

"Here, here, Sebastian, to my heart!"

Then, sinking back as if she were about to faint, she said :

"Oh, what new sensation is this? Can it be happiness?"

The whole drive was but one exchange of kisses between mother and son.

This child, for never for a moment did she doubt that it was hers, which had been taken away on that fearful night of anguish and disgrace; this child, which had disappeared without the ravisher having left any trace but the print of his feet in the snow; this child, whom she had hated and cursed, because she had not heard its first cry, its first moan; whom she had sought, besought, and asked for everywhere; whom her brother had followed with Gilbert, beyond the seas; whom for fifteen years she had regretted, and despaired ever meeting; of whom she thought no more, but as one loved and dead; at the moment she least expected, it was miraculously found, and, strange to say, himself recognized and pursued her, calling her mother, pressed her to his heart, without ever having seen her, loved her with true filial love, as she him with a mother's heart. From his lips, pure from the contamination of any kiss, she regains all the pleasures of a wasted life, and feels it when she first kisses him.

There is, then, above the head of men, something more than the void in which worlds revolve. There is in life something more than chance and fate.

She had said Rue Coq-Heron, No. 9, first door from Rue Platrière.

It was a strange coincidence that, after the lapse of so many years, brought the child to the very spot where he was born, where he drew the first breath of life, and whence he had been taken by his father.

This little house, bought by old Taverney, when some ease had been ingrafted in his family by the high favor with which the queen honored him, was kept in order by an old porter, who apparently had been bought with the house. It was a resting-place to the countess when in Paris.

Six o'clock struck as the porte-cochère opened to the driver's call, and they were at the door of the house.

Giving the driver a piece of money twice the amount of his fare, she rushed, followed by the child, into the house, the door of which she closed carefully.

At the door of the saloon she paused. It was lighted cheerfully by a light which burned in the grate, and by two candles on the mantel.

Andrée drew her son to a kind of chaise-longue, on which were concentrated the double light of the candles and of the fire.

With an explosion of joy, in which, however, there yet lingered something of doubt, she said

"My child, is it indeed you?"

"My mother!" said Sebastian, and his heart expanded into dewlike tenderness, as he leaned against Andrée's beating bosom.

"And here, here!" as she looked around, and saw that she was in the same room in which she gave birth to him, and saw with terror the door whence he had been taken.

"Here!" said Sebastian, "what means that, mother?"

"That you were born here, where we sit; and I thank the mercy of God, which, after fifteen years, has so miraculously restored you."

"Yes, miraculously. Had I not feared for my father's life, I would not alone and at night have set out for Paris. I would not have doubted which of the two roads to take. I would not have waited on the highroad and asked Monsieur Isidor de Charny. He would not have known and taken me to the Palace of the Tuileries. I would not have seen you as you crossed the green-room, and run after and joined you. I would not, in fine, have called you mother. It is a pleasant word to say."

At the words, "Had I not feared for my father's life," Andrée felt a sharp pain run through her heart. She shut her eyes, and drew back.

At the words, "Monsieur Isidor would not have known and taken me to the palace," her eyes opened, and she thanked God with them. That her husband's brother should restore her child was indeed strangely miraculous.

At the words, "I would not have called you mother. It is a pleasant word to say," she again remembered her happiness, and clasping Sebastian again to her heart, said:

"Yes, you are right; there is, perhaps, but one more so, 'My child, my child!'"

There was a moment of silence, during which she pressed her lips again and again on his brow.

Andrée suddenly started up, and said:

"It is impossible for all to be thus mysterious; you explained how you came hither, but you have not told me how and why you knew and ran after me. Why you called me mother."

"Can I tell you that?" said Sebastian, looking at Andrée with an ineffable expression. "I do not know myself. You talk of mystery; all that relates to me is mysterious."

"But, then, something told you when I passed."

"Yes, my heart."

"Your heart?"

"Listen, mother, I am about to tell something strange."

Andrée drew yet nearer to her child, and looked up to heaven in thankfulness for the child thus restored to her.

"I have known you ten years."

Andrée trembled.

"Do you not understand?"

She shook her head.

"Let me tell you. I sometimes have strange dreams, which my father calls hallucinations."

The name of Gilbert on her child's lips passed like a dagger through her heart.

"I have seen you twenty times, mother."

"How so?"

"In the dreams of which I spoke just now."

Andrée thought of those strange dreams which had endangered her life, and to one of which Sebastian owed his existence.

"Do you fancy, mother, that even when in childhood I played with village children, my impressions were like those of the rest, and related to real, palpable things? As soon as I left the village, passed the last gardens, and went into the wood, I heard by me the rustling of a robe. I reached forth to grasp it, but my fingers closed in air, and the phantom left. Then, though invisible, it gradually became distinct, and a transparent vapor, like that with which Virgil surrounds the mother of Æneas when she appeared to him in Carthage. The vapor grew dense, and assumed human form, which was that of a woman gliding rather than walking over the ground. Then a strange, unknown, and irresistible power took hold of me, and I was borne into the depths of the forest, where I followed this phantom with open hands, without its pursuing or my being able to overtake it, until it vanished away by degrees.

"It seemed to suffer as much as I did that the will of Heaven separated us, for, as the phantom left, it looked back, and when no longer sustained by its presence, I sunk exhausted on the ground."

This kind of second life of Sebastian, this waking dream, was too much like what Andrée had herself experienced for her not to recognize her son.

"Poor child!" said she, embracing him. "It was in vain that hatred separated us, God insensibly brought us together. Less happy, though, than you, I saw you neither in dreams nor in reality. When, though I passed you in the green room, a cold shudder seized me. When I heard your steps behind me, something like dizziness occupied both my heart and mind. When you called me madame, I had nearly stopped, and almost fainted when you said mother. When you touched me, I knew you."

"Mother, mother, mother!" said Sebastian, as if to console Andrée for not having heard that word for such a time.

"Yes, your mother!" said she, with a transport which it was impossible to describe.

"And now that we are met," said the child, "since you are satisfied, we will never part again."

Andrée trembled. She had seized the present, and half closing her eyes to the past, neglected the future.

"My poor child!" said she, with a sigh, "I would indeed bless you if you could work a miracle."

"Let me. I will arrange all."

"And how?"

"I do not know. What circumstances separated you from my father?"

Andrée grew pale.

"Whatever though they be, they will be effaced by my prayers, or, if need be, by my tears."

Andrée shook her head.

"Never, never!" said she.

"Listen," said Sebastian. "One day my father said,

'Child, never speak to me of your mother; and then I knew all the wrongs of the separation were on his side. Listen, my father adores me."

The hands of Andrée, which clasped her child's, were loosened. The child seemed, and probably did not notice it.

He continued:

"I will prepare him to see you. I will say how happy you have made me, and I will take you by the hand and say, 'How beautiful she is!'"

Andrée pushed him away, and rose.

The child looked on with amazement.

She was so pale that he was frightened.

"Never," said she, "never!"

The child now shrunk back, for on her face were the terrible lines with which Raphael described fallen angels.

"And why not?"

At those words, as when two clouds are driven together by the wind, the lightning fell.

"Why? You ask me why? Poor child, you know nothing."

"Yes," said Sebastian, firmly. "I ask why."

"Well," said Andrée, who found it impossible to repress the pain of the serpent's wounds in her heart, "because your father is a base villain."

Sebastian sprung from his seat, and stood erect before Andrée.

"Do you speak thus of my father, madame? Of Doctor Gilbert, who has educated me, and to whom I owe everything—whom alone I know? I was wrong, madame; you cannot be my mother."

He rushed toward the door.

Andrée made him pause.

"Listen; you can neither know, feel, nor judge."

"No, no; I fear that I do not love you."

Andrée uttered a cry of agony.

Just then a noise was heard outside, the door opened, and a carriage stopped.

Such a shudder passed over Andrée's limbs, that it was transfused to his soul.

"Wait," said she, "and be silent."

Perfectly subdued, Sebastian waited.

The door of the antechamber opened, and footsteps were heard.

Without eyes, ears, or sound, Andrée stood like a statue.

"Whom shall I announce to the countess?"

"The Count de Charny, and ask if the countess will see me."

"Ah!" said Andrée. "Go into that room, child, into that room. He must not see you, or know that you live."

She pushed the terrified boy into the next room, and shut the door.

As she did so, she said:

"Remain there. When he is gone I will tell you—no, no; I will kiss you, and then you will really know I am your mother."

Sebastian replied with a kind of sigh.

At that moment the door opened, and then the old porter appeared. The countess saw a human form behind him.

"Show the count in," said she, in as firm a tone as she could.

The old man withdrew, hat in hand; the count appeared in the room.

As he was in mourning for his brother, who had been killed two days before, the count was dressed in black.

His mourning, like Hamlet's, too, was not on his face, but in his heart, and his pale countenance attested the tears he had shed, and his suffering.

The countess saw all this at one glance. Handsome faces even looked better in tears. Never had Charny looked so well.

She shut her eyes, and threw her head back, as if to give herself time to breathe, and placed her hand on her heart, which felt as if it would break.

When she opened her eyes, but a second after she had closed them, she saw Charny in the same place.

"Pardon me, madame, but is my unexpected presence an intrusion? I am ready, and, as the carriage waits, can go as I came."

"Not so," said Andrée, quickly. "I knew you were safe, but am not the less rejoiced to see you after the terrible events that have occurred."

"Then you were kind enough to ask about me?" said the count.

"Certainly. Yesterday and this morning I heard you were at Versailles. They told me you were this evening with the queen."

"Were the last words intended as a reproach, or meant they nothing?"

It was evident that the count himself did not know what they meant, and thought for a moment.

"Madame," said he, "religious duty kept me yesterday and to-day at Versailles. I look on the duty as sacred, and that, in the queen's situation, took me, as soon as I could reach Paris, to her presence."

Andrée now sought to distinguish the real significance of his words.

Thinking that she really owed an answer to his first words, she said:

"Yes, sir, I knew the terrible loss."

"Yes, madame, as you say, the death of my brother is a terrible blow to me. You, luckily, cannot understand it, having known poor George so slightly. One thing would console me, if anything could, that poor George has died as Isidor will, as I will die, probably, doing his duty."

The words, "as I will die, probably," touched Andrée deeply.

"Alas! sir, and do you, then, think affairs so desperate that other sacrifices of blood are needed to appease divine wrath?"

"I think, madame, the final hour of kings, if not come, is near at hand, and that if the monarchy falls, it will be accompanied by all who have shared its splendor."

"True; and when the day comes, sir, believe it will find me, like you, prepared for every devotion."

"Ah! madame, you have, in by-gone days, given too strong proofs of devotion, that any, and least of all I, should doubt you in the future; and perhaps have I less reason to doubt yours than mine, which for the first time has hesitated to obey an order of the queen."

"I do not understand you, sir."

"When I came from Versailles, I received an order at once to present myself to the queen."

"Ah!" said Andrée, smiling sadly, "it is plain, like you, the queen sees the sad and mysterious future, and wishes to collect around her men on whom she can rely."

"You are mistaken, madame; not to join me to, but to remove me from her, did she send for me."

"To separate you from her," said the countess, drawing a little nearer to the count. "Excuse me," said she, seeing that the count, during the whole conversation, yet stood at the door, "but I keep you standing." She pointed to a chair.

As she spoke, she sunk back exhausted on the sofa Sebastian had left; she could stand no longer.

"Separate," said she, with an emotion not devoid of joy, as she thought the queen and Charny about to be separated. "And why?"

"To go on a mission to the Count d'Artois and the Duke of Bourbon, at Turin."

"And you accepted?"

Charny looked fixedly at Andrée, and said at once:

"No, madame."

Andrée grew so pale that Charny advanced toward her to aid her, but she recalled her strength as she saw him come.

"No," added she, "no; you said no to an order of the queen."

"I replied that at this moment I thought my presence more useful at Paris than at Turin, where any one could discharge the mission proposed as an honor to me. That I had another brother just arrived, whom I proposed to place at her majesty's service, and who is ready at once to set out in my place."

"And certainly the queen was gratified at the proposition," said Andrée, with a degree of bitterness she could not conceal, and which did not escape Charny.

"No, madame; my refusal seemed to wound her deeply. I should have been forced to go had not the king come in, and the matter been referred to him."

"And the king sustained you!" said Andrée, with an ironical smile. "The king is kind, indeed, and, like you, thought you should remain at the Tuileries."

Charny did not frown.

"The king said my brother Isidor was well calculated for the mission, especially as having come to court for the first time, and being almost unknown, his presence was not likely to be missed, and required the queen to exact me not to leave you at such a crisis."

"Leave me! The king said not leave me?"

"I repeat his own words, madame. Glancing from the queen to me, he said, 'And where, too, is the Countess Charny?'"

"'Sire,' said the queen, 'Madame de Charny left the palace about an hour ago.'

"'How?' said the king; 'the countess left the palace? But to return soon?' added the king.

"The queen replied, 'I think not.'

"'So the countess has gone. Whither, madame, do you know?'

"'I do not,' said the queen. 'When my friends leave me, I let them go, and never ask them whither.'

"'Ah!' said the king, 'some woman's quarrel. Monsieur de Charny, I would speak with the queen. Await me in my room, and present me to your brother. He will start for Turin this very evening. I agree with you, De Charny, I need you, and will keep you.'

"I sent for my brother, who had come, and who awaited me in the green saloon."

At the last word Andrée, who had almost forgotten Sebastian in her husband's story, remembered all that had passed between her son and herself, and looked sadly at the door of the room in which he was.

"Excuse me, madame," said Charny; "I annoy you,

with matters with which you do not feel interested, and you, doubtless, wonder why I am here."

"Not so, monsieur. What you have said interests me deeply; as for your presence here, after all the fear I have felt for you, in thus proving you to be safe, cannot but please me. Go on, then, sir; the king told you to await him, and you sent for your brother?"

"We went to the king, and as the mission was important he spoke of that first. (He was not ten minutes behind us.) The object of the mission was to tell their royal highnesses what had taken place. A quarter of an hour after my brother was on the road. The king walked moodily about for awhile, and then pausing in front of me, said: 'Count, do you know what has taken place between the queen and the countess?'"

"'No, sire,' said I; 'something must have taken place, for I found the queen in a terrible humor toward her, and very unjustly, too, it seemed to me.'

"'At all events,' said the king, 'if the queen does not know where the countess is, you must find out.' I said I was hardly more informed than the queen, but that I knew you had a household in Rue Coq-Heron, whither you, without doubt, had gone. 'Go thither, count. I give you leave until to-morrow, provided you bring her back with you then.'"

Charny looked so fixedly at Andrée, that, seeing she could not meet his glance, she closed her eyes.

"'Tell her,' said Charny, continuing to speak in the king's name, 'that I will have her here even if I go myself for her, and find rooms, certainly not so large as those she had at Versailles, but large enough for man and wife.' Thus it was that I came at the king's instance. You will, I know, excuse me."

"Ah, sir!" said Andrée, rising quickly, and placing her hands in his, "can you doubt it?"

Charny seized her hands, and placed them to his lips. Andrée cried out as if his lips had been hot iron, and sunk on the sofa. Her hands were locked in his, so that she could not extricate them, and, without intending it, he was beside her. Having heard some noise in the next room, she hurried to the door so rapidly that the count, not knowing to what movement to attribute the brusquerie of her conduct, arose, and again was before her.

Charny leaned on the back of the sofa and sighed. Andrée let her head rest on her hands; the sigh of Charny had touched the very depth of her heart. What then passed in the heart of the young woman is indescribable. Having been married for years to a man whom she adored, without that man, constantly occupied by another woman, being aware of the terrible sacrifice she made in marrying, she had, with the denial inspired by the double duty of a wife and subject, seen and borne all and concealed all. But for some time it had seemed to her that some words of her husband were gentler, and some glances of the queen more stern, so that the impression was not lost on her. During the days which had rolled by, the terrible days full of terror to so many, alone, perhaps, of all the terrified courtiers, Andrée had experienced some pleasant emotions; Charny seemed anxious about her, looked uneasily for her, and met her with joy; a light pressure of the hand communicated a sympathy unseen by those who surrounded them, and established a community of thought between them. These were delicious sensations, unknown to the icy frame and diamond heart which had ever experienced only the pain of love and its unrequitedness.

All at once, just as the poor creature had regained her child, and again become a mother, something like the dawn of love was awakened on the horizon of a heart previously obscure and clouded. It was a strange coincidence, and proved that true happiness was not for her. The two circumstances destroyed the effect of each other; the return of the child depriving her forever of the husband's love, and the love of the husband making that of the child impossible.

Charny could not see this when the cry escaped from Andrée's lips, when she repelled his advances, and thrust him into an abyss, from which it seemed impossible for him to extricate himself. He thought it was produced by dislike. Not so, it was the effect of fear.

Charny sighed, and renewed the conversation where it had been abandoned.

"What, madame, must I say to the king?"

At the sound of his voice she quailed; then, lifting up her clear blue eyes, she said:

"Sir, tell his majesty that I have suffered so much since I belonged to the court, that the queen has had the kindness to permit me to retire, and I do so thankfully. I was not born to live in the world, and in solitude have always found rest, if not happiness. The happiest days of my life were those I passed as a girl, in the Castle of Taverney, and later, those I spent in the Convent of St. Denis, with that pure daughter of France, known as Madame Louise. With your permission, sir, I will inhabit this pavilion, which is full of memories, which, though sad, have yet some soothing."

The permission Andrée asked was given by the count willingly, like a man not anxious to grant a prayer, but to obey an order.

"Then, madame, you have decided?"

"Yes, sir," said Andrée, gently but firmly.

Charny bowed again.

"And now, madame," said he, "I have one favor to ask you, to be permitted to visit you here?"

Andrée looked at Charny, with the clear blue eyes ordinarily cold and impassive, but now full of surprise and amazement.

"Certainly, sir," said she, "but as I see no one, when you are not required at the Tuileries, and have a few moments to spare, I shall always be happy to see you, if you will spare them to me."

Charny had never seen so much charm in Andrée's eye. He had never seen so much tenderness in her voice. Something penetrated his veins like the velvet tremor of a first kiss. Charny would have given a whole year to have sat by Andrée, though she had previously repulsed him.

Timid as a child, however, he dared not without encouragement, do so.

Andrée would have given, not a year, but an existence, to have seen the one, from whom she had so long been separated, by her side.

Unfortunately, they did not know each other, and each was motionless.

Charny was the first to break the silence, which one, capable alone of reading the heart, could have translated.

"You say you have suffered much at court, madame? Has not the king always treated you with respect amounting to admiration, and the queen almost idolized you?"

"Ah! yes, sir, the king has ever been very kind to me."

"Permit me to observe, madame, that you reply only to a part of my question; has the queen been less kind than the king?"

The lips of Andrée closed, as if they would have refused an answer. She said:

"I make no charge against the queen, and would be unjust were I to refuse to do her full justice."

"I say this, madame," said Charny, "because I see that for some time the friendship she bore you has been somewhat diminished."

"Possibly, sir, and on that account, as I had the honor to say, I wished to leave the court."

"But, madame, you will be very lonely and isolated."

"Have I not always been as a child? a girl, and as——"

She paused seeing that she was going too far.

"Go on, madame," said Charny.

"You have seen my idea, sir. I was about to say as a wife."

"Am I so happy as to have you reproach me on that account?"

"Reproach, sir," said Andrée, quickly. "What right, great God, have I to reproach you? Think you I forget the circumstances of our marriage? No; those who at the foot of the altar do not swear eternal love, but, as we did, eternal indifference and separation, have no right to reproach each other for violation of the marriage vow."

Andrée's words wrung a sigh from the heart of Charny.

"I see, madame, said he, "that your determination is fixed, but, at least, let me ask you, how you are to live here?"

Andrée smiled sadly.

"My father's household," said she, "was so poor that, compared with it, this pavilion, naked as it seems, is more luxurious than anything I have been used to."

"But the charming retreat of Trianon, Versailles."

"Ah! I knew I would have to relinquish them."

"You will at least have here all you need."

"I shall find all I am used to."

"Let me see," said Charny, who wished to form an idea of the room she was to occupy, and who was examining everything.

"What do you wish to see, sir?" asked Andrée, rising slowly and looking anxiously in the direction of the chamber.

"But if you are not very humble in your wishes, madame, this pavilion is not a home. I passed through one antechamber, and I am now in the saloon. This door" (he opened one on the side) "leads into a chamber, and that, I see into a dining-room."

Andrée rushed between the count and the door, and fancied that she saw Sebastian.

"Monsieur," said she, "I beg you not to go further."

And she closed the passage.

"Ah! I understand; this is the door of your bedchamber."

"Yes, sir," muttered Andrée, half stifled.

Charny looked at the countess, and saw that she was trembling and pale. Terror was never more evident than in the expression of her face.

"Ah! madame, I was aware that you did not love me, but was not aware that you hated me."

Unable to repress his feelings in Andrée's presence any longer, he staggered for a moment like a drunken man, and rushed out of the room with a cry of agony which reached the depth of Andrée's heart

The young woman looked after him until he had disappeared. With straining ears she listened as long as she could to hear his carriage wheels, which gradually became more indistinct, and then arousing all her power, though she felt that her heart would almost break, and that she had not too much maternal love to combat this other love, she rushed into the room, crying :

" Sebastian ! Sebastian ! "

No voice replied to her, and her cry of agony had no echo.

By the light of the lamp she looked around, and saw that the room was empty.

She could, however, scarcely believe her eyes.

She called Sebastian, again and again.

The silence was unbroken.

Then only did she see that the window was open, and that the current of air agitated the flame of the lamp.

The same window had been found open, when fifteen years before her son had first disappeared.

"True," said she, "did he not say I was not his mother ? "

Then she saw that at the moment she had regained them, she had lost both a husband and a child, and she threw herself on her bed with arms outstretched, and her fingers convulsively grasped. Her strength and resignation were exhausted.

She could but cry, weep, and appreciate her loss.

Nearly an hour passed in this state of profound annihilation, in a total oblivion of the whole world, and that wish for annihilation which the unhappy entertain. The hope that, returning to nothing, the world will, with it, bear them away.

All at once it seemed to Andrée that something more terrible than grief coursed through her veins. A sensation she had experienced but twice or thrice before, and which had always preceded great crises of her life, took possession of her. By a slow motion, independent of will, she slowly lifted herself up. Her voice died in her throat ; all her body, as if involuntarily attracted, became convulsed, and she fancied she could see that she was not alone. Her sight became fixed and clear; a man who seemed to have passed the window-sill stood before her; she wished to call, to reach out her hand to the bell-rope; she felt the same inexpressible stupor she had before experienced in the presence of Balsamo. The man who thus fascinated her was Gilbert.

Here came the father she hated, to replace the son she loved.

CHAPTER V.

WHAT BECAME OF SEBASTIAN.

THE first sentiment of Andrée, when she saw Gilbert, was not only that of profound terror, but of invincible repugnance.

Gilbert, on the contrary, entertained for Andrée, in spite of her contempt, scorn, and persecutions, not the ardent love which led him when young to crime, but the deep, passionate devotion which would have made a man do her a service, even at the peril of his life.

The reason is that he saw that all Andrée's troubles were due to him, and that he owed her a sum of happiness equal to that of which he had deprived her.

Andrée spoke first; she said:

"What do you wish, sir? How came you here, and why? What wish you?"

"I came to demand a treasure which is valueless to you, but inestimable to me. What do I wish? To know how that child was borne away by you, and know what has become of him."

"What has become of him?" said Andrée. "How do I know? He fled from me. You have taught him thoroughly to hate his mother."

"His mother!" said Gilbert. "Are you really such?"

"Ah!" said she, "he sees my distress, he hears my cries, and asks if I am really a mother!"

"You do not know where he is?"

"I tell you he fled from me. When I came to this room, in which I had left him, he was gone. The window was up, and he gone."

"My God! what will become of him? How can he find his way through Paris? It is after twelve, too."

"Oh!" said Andrée, "think you that he is in danger?"

"We will know, and from you," said he.

He stretched forth his hand.

"Monsieur!" said she, drawing back to avoid the magnetic influence.

"Madame, do not fear. I talk to a mother of her son, of the means to find him. To me you are sacred. Sleep, and read with your heart."

"I do sleep."

"Do you, with me, employ all the power of my will, or do you sleep voluntarily?"

"Will you again say that I am not Sebastian's mother?"

"As the case may be. Do you love him?"

"Can you ask if I love the child I bore? Yes, I love him deeply."

"Then you are his mother, madame, for you love him as I do."

"Yes," said Andrée, sighing.

"You will reply voluntarily?"

"Will you permit me to see him?"

"Have I not said that you were his mother, as I am his father? You love him as I do, and shall see him."

"Thanks," said Andrée, with an expression of unutterable joy, and she clasped her hands. "Now ask. I see."

"What?"

"Follow him since he left, that I may not lose track of him."

"Well, where did you see him?"

"In the green room."

"Where did he follow you?"

"Down the corridor."

"Where did he join you?"

"At the carriage."

"Whither did you take him?"

"To the next room."

"Where did he sit?"

"By me."

"How long?"

"Half an hour."

"Why did he leave you?"

"Because the noise of a carriage was heard."

"Who was in the carriage?"

Andrée hesitated.

"Who was in the carriage?" said Gilbert, in a firmer tone, and a positive expression of will.

"The Count de Charny."

"Where did you hide the child?"

"In that room."

"What did he say as he left you?"

"That I was not his mother."

"Why?"

Andrée was silent.

"Why? Speak, for I will have it so."

"Because I said——"

"What?"

"Because I said you were a vile rascal."

"Look at the heart of that poor child, madame, and see the wrong you have done."

"My God! my God! Forgive me, my child."

"Did Monsieur de Charny suspect the child was yours?"

"No."

"Are you sure?"

"Yes."

"Why did he not remain?"

"Monsieur de Charny does not live with me."

Andrée was silent for a moment. Her eyes became fixed, and she attempted to see into darkness.

"My dear!" said she, "Charny, dear Charny!"

Gilbert looked at her with surprise.

"Alas!" said she, "it was for the purpose of returning to me that he refused this mission. He loves me."

Gilbert began to read confusedly the terrible drama he first penetrated.

"And do you love him?"

She sighed.

"Why do you ask me that question?" said Andrée.

"Read my heart."

"Yes, your intention is good. You would make me forget the wrong you have done me by conferring happiness on me. I would not, however, owe happiness to you. I hate you, and will continue to do so forever."

"Poor human nature!" murmured Gilbert; "is so much happiness set aside for you that you can refuse this? You love him?"

"Yes."

"Since when?"

"Since I have known him. Since the day he came from Versailles in the carriage with the queen and myself."

"Then you know what love is?" said Gilbert, sadly.

"I do," said the young woman, "know that love is given to us, too, as a measure of woe."

"True; you are now a woman. A rough diamond you have been, set by the hands of the terrible lapidary, grief. Let us return to Sebastian."

"Ah! yes, let us do so. Do not let me think of Monsieur de Charny. The idea of him troubles my faculties, and, instead of my child, I will, perhaps, follow the count."

"True wife forget the husband, mother remember the child alone."

A half-gentle expression at once took possession of her face and whole frame, entirely displacing the one she usually bore.

"Where was he while you talked with your husband?"

"Here, at the door."

"Did he hear the conversation?"

"A part of it."

"When did he resolve to leave the room?"

"At the moment when the count——"

She paused.

"When Monsieur de Charny kissed my hand, and I cried."

"You see him, then?"

"Yes, with plaited brow, his lips fixed, and clinched hands."

"What does he do?"

"Sees if there be no door opening into the garden. Seeing there is none, goes to the window, opens it, looks out, glances at the saloon, springs out, and disappears."

"Follow him."

"I cannot."

Gilbert passed his hand in front of Andrée's eyes.

"You know that for you there is no darkness. Look."

"Ah! ah! Runs down the alley by the wall, he opens the gate unseen, and gains the Rue Platrière. He stops, and speaks to a woman."

"Listen; do you hear him?"

"I do."

"What does he ask?"

"The way to the Rue St. Honoré."

"Yes; I live there. Poor lad! he awaits me there."

"No," said she, shaking her head with an expression of great sadness. "He did not go in. He did not wait."

"Whither, then, did he go?"

"Let me follow him, or I shall lose him."

"Follow him, follow him," said Gilbert, who saw that Andrée foretold some misfortune for him.

"I see him, I see him!"

"Well?"

"He is in the Rue Grenelli; he is at the Rue St. Honoré; he crosses the Place Palais Royal at full speed; he asks the road again; he hurries on; he is in the Rue Richelieu, in the Rue des Frondeurs, the Rue New St. Roch. Stop, stop, my poor child! Sebastian, do you not see that carriage driven down the Rue Sourdière? I see, I see the horses."

She muttered a terrible cry, rose up, and maternal agony was imprinted on her brow.

"Ah!" said Gilbert, "if anything happens to him, remember it will recoil on you."

"Ah!" said Andrée, without hearing or listening to anything said by Gilbert. "Thank the God of heaven, the horse has thrown him out of the way of the wheels. I see him senseless, but not dead. No, no, not dead. He has only fainted. Help, help! My child!"

With a cry of agony, Andrée fell back again on the bed.

Great as was Gilbert's wish to know more, he granted to the trembling woman the repose she needed so much.

He feared, if he excited her too much, a fiber of her heart would break, or that she would burst a blood-vessel.

As soon, however, as he thought he could question her safely, he said:

"Well?"

"Wait, wait! There is a crowd around him. Ah! for mercy, let me go. It is my son, Sebastian. My God! is there no surgeon?"

"Oh! I will go," said Gilbert.

"Wait," said Andrée, seizing his arm; "the crowd opens; here is one. Quick, sir, quick! You see he is not dead; you must save him."

She uttered a cry of agony.

"What is the matter?" asked Gilbert.

"It is not a man, but a gnome, a dwarf, a vampire; hideous, hideous!"

"Madame, madame, do not lose sight of Sebastian."

"Ah!" said she, with a fixed expression of the lip and eye, "do not be uneasy, I will not."

"What does the man do?"

"He carries him away. He goes into the Rue Sourdière. He enters the lane of St. Hyacinthe. He approaches a low door, which is half open. He ascends a stairway, and places him on a table covered with papers, both printed and manuscript. He takes off Sebastian's coat, rolls up the sleeve, and binds his arm with ligatures, which a woman, dirty and hideous as the man, is bringing him. He takes out a lancet, and is about to bleed him. Ah! I cannot bear to see my child's blood."

"Well," said Gilbert, "look, and count the steps."

"I have. Eleven."

"Look at the door, and tell me what you see strange about it."

"A little opened; closed by a cross-bar grating."

"Well, that is all I need."

"Hurry, and you will find him there."

"Do you wish to awake at once, and to remember, or not until to-morrow, after having forgotten all?

Arouse me now. Let me remember."

Gilbert passed his hands in front of Andrée's eyes, breathed on her brow, and said:

"Awake!"

The eyes of the young woman immediately became bright, and her lips lost their rigidity. She looked at Gilbert almost without fear, and continued when awake the advice given him in sleep.

"Hurry, hurry!" said she, "and take him from that man, of whom I am afraid."

CHAPTER VI.

THE MAN OF THE PLACE LOUIS XV.

GILBERT'S anxiety required no stimulation. He remembered what Andrée had told him of his son's route, and hurried after it, and reached the lane of St. Hyacinthe.

Here he began to inspect the locality, and in the third door by the grated cross recognized Andrée's description, which was too exact to admit of a doubt. He knocked, but no one answered. He knocked again.

He fancied that he heard a timid and suspicious step approach him by the stairway.

He knocked again.

"Who is there?" said a female voice.

"Open the door; I am the father of the wounded child whom you received."

"Open, Albertine!" said another voice. "It is Doctor Gilbert."

"Father, father!" said a third voice, in which Gilbert recognized his son's.

He breathed freely.

The door was opened, and he ascended the steps, uttering his thanks as he went.

At the last step he found himself in a kind of cellar, lighted by a lamp, and covered with papers, as Andrée had said.

In the dark, and on a kind of pallet, Gilbert saw his son, who appealed to him with outstretched hands. Powerful as Gilbert's self-control was, paternal love triumphed over philosophical decorum, and he clasped his child to his breast warmly, though he took care not to wound his bleeding arm or sore chest.

After a long paternal kiss, in which all was communicated, though unuttered, Gilbert turned to his host.

He stood erect, with his legs apart, one hand resting on the table, the other on his hip, looking by the light of the lamp at the scene which passed before him.

"Look, Albertine," said he, "and thank the chance which has enabled me to be of service to one of my confrères."

As the surgeon spoke, Gilbert looked around, and for the first time looked at the shapeless being before him.

A yellow-and-green light seemed to flash from his eyes, and declare that, like one of those persons pursued by Latona, if not human, he was not a toad.

Gilbert shuddered in spite of himself. He seemed, in some dream, to have already seen this man in a sea of carnage.

He approached Sebastian, and clasped him more tenderly than before.

He soon triumphed over this feeling, and going to the stranger, pressed his hand tenderly, saying:

"Receive my thanks, sir, for the preservation of my son's life. Believe me, I speak truly, and from my heart."

"Sir," said the surgeon, "I have done only what feelings and science inspired and required. Monsieur Terence says: '*Homo sum et nihi humani abienum ameputo.*' My heart, too, is tender, and I cannot see even an insect suffer—certainly, then, I cannot see a man."

"May I ask to what philanthropist I have the honor to speak?"

"You do not know me, brother," said the surgeon, smiling with an air he wished to make insinuatory, but which was hideous. "Eh! Well—I know you are Doctor Gilbert, the friend of Washington and Lafayette." He laid particular stress upon the last name. "The men of America and France, the honest Utopians who made such magnificent theories about constitutional monarchy, addressed to His Majesty Louis XVI., which His Majesty Louis XVI. rewarded by sending you to the Bastile, directly you touched the soil of France. You wished to save him by sweeping away impediments in his future course. He sent you to prison as a reward. Royal gratitude!"

On this occasion the surgeon laughed terribly.

"As you know me, sir, it is another reason why I repeat my question, and ask your name in return."

"Ah, we became acquainted very long ago, sir. Twenty years ago, on a terrible night, you were then about as old as this child. You were brought dead, wounded, and dying as he is. You were brought to me by Master Rousseau, and I bled you on a table covered with bodies and amputated limbs. On that terrible night, it is pleasant to remember, I have, thanks to a knife that knows how far to enter, to cut, to cure, or to cicatrize, saved many lives."

"Oh!" said Gilbert, "you are Jean Paul Marat?"

In spite of him, he drew back a pace.

"You see, Albertine, that my name has its influence."

And he burst into a malicious laugh.

"But," said Gilbert, quickly, "why are you here in this cellar, lighted only by a smoky lamp? I thought you physician of Monsieur d'Artois."

"I was his veterinary surgeon. The prince, however, has emigrated, and having no horses, needs no veterinary surgeon. Besides, I resigned—I would not servė tyrants."

"Why, though, are you here, in this cellar—in this den?"

"Because I am a patriot, and denounce the ambitious in my writing. Monsieur Bailly hates me, Necker fears me, Lafayette pursues me, and has put a price on my head. The ambitious dictator! From my cavern I pursue, denounce, and brave the dictator. Do you know what has been done?"

"No," naïvely said Gilbert.

"He has had made in the Faubourg St. Antoine fifteen thousand snuff boxes with his portrait. I beg all good citizens to break them wherever they find them. It is the password, this, of a royalist plot. You do not know, that while poor Louis weeps hot tears at the follies the Austrian makes him commit, Lafayette conspires with the queen."

"With the queen?" said Gilbert, in thought.

"Yes, with the queen," said Marat, sharply. "You will not say that she does not conspire. She distributed the other day so many ribbons and white cockades, that white ribbon rose three cents a yard. The thing is certain; I heard it from one of the daughters of Madame Bertin, the queen's *marchande des modes*, her prime minister. That lady said, 'I have been all day at work with her majesty.'"

"And where do you denounce all that?"

"In my paper, a journal I have founded, 'L'Ami du Peuple,' or 'le Publiciste Parisien,' a political and impartial paper. To pay for the paper and printing of the first number, I sold even the covering of the bed on which your child lies."

Gilbert did turn, and saw that Sebastian really lay on a perfectly bare mattress, and that, overcome by fatigue and pain, he slept.

The doctor approached him, to ascertain whether or not he had fainted. Reassured, however, by his regular respiration, he returned to Marat, who inspired the same interest called forth by a wild animal.

"And who assists you?"

"Ah! ha! turkeys fly in gangs—eagles fly alone. I am assisted by my hand and head.

"See you that table? It is Vulcan's forge, where thunder-bolts are made. Every day I write eight pages, which are sold in the morning. Sometimes eight pages will not suffice, and then I write sixteen. What I begin with large type, generally ends in small. Other journalists relieve one another at intervals, and then suspend; it is not my way; 'The Friend of the People' always appears. It is not merely a name, but a person. It is myself."

"But how do you accomplish all this work?"

"Ah, that is a secret between death and myself. I have given up ten years of my life, and she grants me days that need no rest, nights that need no repose. My life is simple. I write all day and all night. Lafayette's police compels me to live in secret, and forces me to activity. At first it annoyed me, and was oppressive to me—now I like it. I like to look at society through the miserable gratings of my cavern, through my dark cage. In the depth of night I reign over the living, and judge, without appeal, science and politics. With one hand I demolish Newton, Franklin, La Place, Monge, Lavoisier; with the other, I make Bailly, Necker, and Lafayette tremble. I will overthrow all that. Yes, perhaps as Samson overthrew the temple, and buried himself beneath the ruins, I, too, may be crushed amid the fragments of the throne."

This man repeated in a cavern, and in the rags of misery, nearly what Cagliostro had, in embroidery, said in the palace.

"But," said he, "popular as you are, why have you not at least procured a nomination to the National Assembly?"

"Ah!" said Marat, almost at once, "were I sustained as tribune of the people, by some thousands of determined men, I promise you that in six weeks the constitution would be perfected, and the political machine proceed perfectly. Not a villain should dare to interfere with it

—the nation would be free and happy, and in less than one year it would become flourishing, and remain so as long as I live."

The vainglorious creature became transformed beneath Gilbert's eye. His own eyes became blood-shot, as his yellow skin shone with sweat. The monster was great on account of his ugliness, as others are on account of their beauty.

"Ah!" continued he, resuming his thought, which enthusiasm had interrupted. "I will not be tribune, I cannot find the thousands of men I need. I have though, writing materials, pen, ink, and paper. I have readers and subscribers, who look on me as a prophet and an oracle. I have the people, the friend of whom I am, and whom I lead trembling from treason, from terror. In the first number of 'L'Ami du Peuple,' I denounced the aristocrats, and said there were six hundred criminals in France, and that six hundred ropes were required. I was deceived nearly a month, for on the 5th and 6th of October I became enlightened and saw that not six hundred but ten thousand aristocrats should be destroyed."

Gilbert smiled. Fury, which had reached this point, surpassed folly.

"Take care," said he. "There is not hemp enough in France to make the ropes you think so necessary."

"I trust," said Marat, "that more expeditious means will be tried. Do you know whom I expect in ten minutes to knock at my door?"

"No."

"A person of our profession, a member of the National Assembly, whom you know by name, Citizen Guillotin."

"Yes," said Gilbert.

"Do you know what Guillotin has invented? A wonderful machine which kills without pain. Death should be a punishment, not a torture. He has invented this machine, and one these of days we will try it."

Gilbert shuddered. This was the second time he had heard of this machine. From the man in the cellar, and from Cagliostro in the palace.

"Ah!" said Marat, as a knock was just heard. "It is he. Go, Albertine, and open."

Amazed, terrified, a prey to something like swimming in the head, he went instinctively to Sebastian's side, intending to take him in his arms, and carry him home.

"Look," said Marat, mechanically, "at a machine which is self-acting, and needs but one man to put it in motion, which by changing the knife three times can cut off a hundred heads a day, without any other sensation than a slight coolness about the neck."

"Ah!" is it you, doctor?" said Marat, turning to a little man who had a box, of the form and size of those which contain children's toys, in his hands. "What have you there?"

"A model of my famous machine, dear Marat. I am not mistaken," said the little man. "Is that Doctor Gilbert I see?"

"It is," said Gilbert, bowing.

"I am delighted to see you; you are not in the way at all, and I shall be glad to have the opinion of so distinguished a man on my invention. I must tell you, Marat, I found a very skilful carpenter, Guidon, to make my large machine. He asks five thousand francs for it, but no sacrifice is too great, in my opinion, for the benefit of man. In two months it will be completed, and tried. Yes, I will, in the interim, propose the matter to the assembly, and I hope they will approve the proposition, and that you will prepare the way in your excellent journal, though, indeed, my machine recommends itself, as you are about to see. A few lines in 'L'Ami du Peuple' will do no harm."

"Be easy about the matter," said Marat. "I will not only afford you a few lines, but an entire number."

"You are very good, dear Marat, but I wish you to judge for yourself," said Guillotin.

He drew from his pocket a second box, about the size of the first, and a noise inside denoted that it contained something alive, or, rather, something anxious to get out.

This noise was observed immediately by Marat's quick ear.

"Ah, ha!" said the latter. "What is that?"

"You shall see," said Guillotin.

Marat put his hand on the box.

"Be careful not to let them escape, for we cannot retake them. They are mice, whom we are about to decapitate. What are you going to do, Doctor Gilbert? Not go?"

"Alas! yes, sir," replied Gilbert, "to my great regret. But my son, wounded this evening by being knocked down in the street, has been relieved, bled, and dressed by Doctor Marat, to whom, under similar circumstances, I am indebted for my own life, and whom I again thank. The child needs a fresh bed, rest, and care. I cannot then witness your interesting experiment."

"But you will see the great experiment we will make two months hence? Will you not? Will you not, doctor?"

"I will."

"I will remember your promise."

"Doctor," said Marat, "I need not remind you to keep the place of my concealment a secret."

"Oh, sir!"

"Your friend Lafayette, if he knew it, would have me shot like a dog, or hung as a robber."

"Shot! hung!" said Guillotin, "all that will be done away with. Shooting and hanging will disappear. There will be a quiet, easy, and instantaneous death established, A death so easy that all men disgusted with life, and who wish to die like sages and philosophers, will prefer it to a natural one. Come, look at it, dear Marat, look at it."

Without attending any longer to Dr. Gilbert, Guillotin opened the large box, and began to arrange his machine with equal curiosity and enthusiasm.

Gilbert took advantage of the opportunity to lift up Sebastian, who was yet asleep, and carry him away.

Albertine again escorted him to the gate, which she carefully closed behind him.

Once again in the street, he felt, by the cold on his face, that he was covered with perspiration, which the night wind was congealing.

"Oh, my God! what is about to befall this city, whose cellars conceal, perhaps even now, five hundred philanthropists, occupied and busy in such discoveries as that I was so near seeing just now, and which one day will burst forth beneath the light of heaven."

From the Rue de la Sourdière to the house of Gilbert, the Rue St. Honoré, was but a step.

Cold and motion had awakened Sebastian. He wished to walk, but his father would not consent, and continued to carry him.

When the doctor came to the door, he placed Sebastian on his feet for a moment, and knocked. He had not long to wait in the street.

A coarse though quick voice was heard on the other side of the door.

"Is it you, Monsieur Gilbert?" said the voice.

"That is Pitou's voice."

"Heaven be praised!" said Pitou, as he opened the door. "Sebastian is found and unhurt, I trust, Monsieur Gilbert?"

"At least, without any serious accident," said the doctor. "Come, Sebastian."

Leaving to Pitou the care of closing the door in the face of the drowsy porter, who appeared in chemise and night-cap, with Sebastian in his arms, he began to go up-stairs.

Uneasy and afraid, Pitou followed. By his muddy and stained shoes it was easy to see that he had just arrived after a long journey.

Gilbert thanked Pitou as a brave fellow should be thanked—that is, by a pressure of the hand, and as he thought that, after a journey of eighteen leagues, and anxiety for six hours, the traveler ought to have some rest, he wished him good night and sent him to his bed.

As for Gilbert, he did not wish to leave to another the care of watching and attending Sebastian. He himself examined the bruise on the breast of his child, and applied his ear to several places on his chest, and being assured that respiration was thoroughly free, he settled himself in his easy-chair near the child, who, in spite of much fever, sank quickly to sleep.

But, soon remembering the uneasiness which Andrée must feel, according to that which he had himself experienced, he called his valet, and directed him to put at once into the post, so that it should reach her address early in the morning, a letter in which were written the following words:

"Reassure yourself; the child is found, and is not injured."

CHAPTER VII.

TRUCE.

A WEEK had rolled away between the events we have just related and the day on which we again take the reader by the hand and conduct him to the palace of the Tuileries, now the principal theater of the great catastrophes about to be accomplished.

Oh, Tuileries! fatal heritage, bequeathed by the queen of St. Barthélemy, the foreigner, Catherine de Medicis, to her descendants and to her successors. Palace of giddiness, which attracts but to destroy; what fascination dwells in your gates, where all the crowned fools who wish to be called kings lose themselves; who believe themselves only really sacred so long as they are within thy walls, and whom thou castest out, one after the other; these as bodies without heads, and those as fugitives without crowns!

Without doubt, there is in thy stones, chiseled even as the works of Benvenuto Cellini, some fatal malignancy; without doubt, some fatal talisman hath found a refuge 'neath thy roof. Look back on the last kings thou hast received, and say what thou hast done with them! Of these five kings, one only has been dismissed by you to the tomb where his ancestors awaited him; and of the four others whom history claims of thee, one has been delivered to the scaffold, and the three others to exile.

One day a whole crowd wished to brave the danger and to establish itself in the place of the kings, as commissioner of the people, to station itself there, where the elect of monarchy had sat. From this moment giddiness seized it; from this moment it destroyed itself. The scaffold devoured some; exile swallowed up others; and a strange fraternity reunited Louis XVI. and Robespierre, Collot d'Herbois and Napoleon, Billeaud, Varennes and Charles X., Vadier and Louis Philippe.

Oh, Tuileries, Tuileries! mad indeed will he be who shall dare to cross thy threshold and attempt to enter where Louis XVI., Napoleon, Charles X., and Louis Philippe entered, for sooner or later he must pass out the same door as they!

And yet, gloomy palace, each of them entered into thy bosom amid the acclamations of the people, and thy double balcony has seen them one after the other smile at these acclamations, confiding in the wishes and the vows that urged them on; this has made those who sat on the royal dais, each of them severally labor at his own work, and not at that of the people; one day, the people, perceiving this, has caused them to be led to thy gates like unfaithful stewards, or has punished them like ungrateful commissioners.

It was thus that after the terrible 6th of October, in the midst of mud, blood, and shrieks, the pale sun of the morning discovered, as he rose, the court of the Tuileries filled by a people moved at the return of their king, and elated to see him.

All the day Louis XVI. received the constituted authorities; during this time the crowd waited without, sought him, and gazed through the windows; he, who thought he perceived him, raised a cry of joy, and pointed him out to his neighbor, as he said:

"Do you see him? There! there!"

At noon he showed himself on the balcony, and the cheers and the bravos were unanimous.

In the evening he descended into the garden, and there were more than bravos and cheers; there were emotions, there were tears.

Mme. Elizabeth, pious and naïve, pointed this people out to her brother, and said to him:

"It seems to me it is not difficult to rule such men."

Her lodging was on the ground floor. In the evening she caused the windows to be opened, and supped before the people.

Men and women looked on, applauded, and saluted; the women especially. They caused their children to mount the window-sills, ordering these little innocents to send kisses to the great lady, and to tell her how beautiful she was.

The little children repeated, "You are very, very beautiful, madame," and with their little dimpled hands waved numberless kisses.

Every one said:

"The revolution is over; the king is rescued from Versailles, his courtiers and counselors. The enchantment which kept him in captivity beyond his capital, in that world of automata, of statues, and box-wood forests called Versailles, is broken. Thank God, the king is restored to life, activity, and truth—to real life! Come, sire, among us; until to-day, surrounded as you were, aught but authority to err—to-day, amid us, your people, you can do good."

The two most popular men in France, Lafayette, and Mirabeau, again became royalists.

Mirabeau had said to Lafayette, "Let us unite, and save the king."

Lafayette was essentially an honest man, but had a narrow mind. He despised the character of Mirabeau, and did not comprehend his genius.

He went to see the Duke of Orleans.

Much has been said of his royal highness; even that at night, in a slouched hat hiding his eyes, he had been seen to excite, brandishing a switch, the crowd collected in the marble court, inducing them to pillage the castle, and trusting that the grand finale would be death.

To the Duke of Orleans Mirabeau was everything.

Instead of uniting with Mirabeau, Lafayette went to the duke and invited him to leave Paris. The duke hesitated, argued, contended, and became angry.

Lafayette was so much of a king that it was necessary to obey.

"And when do I return?"

"When I think proper, prince, that you should."

"But if, monsieur, I become weary, and return without your leave, what will be the consequence?"

"Then," said Lafayette, "I expect your royal highness will fight with me the next day."

The duke left, and did not return until he was sent for.

Lafayette was not much of a royalist before the 5th and 6th of October, when he really and sincerely changed his opinion. He had saved the king and protected the queen.

We become bound to persons by services we render them, not by those we receive. The reason of this is, that men are rather proud than grateful.

During the few days which passed, during which the new inmates of the Tuileries had become established and resumed their old habits, Gilbert, not having been sent for by the king, had not thought proper to visit him; at last his day of visit having come, he thought his duty would be an excuse which he did not feel his devotion would.

Louis XVI., too, knew in his own heart, in spite of the prejudices of the queen against Gilbert, that the doctor was his friend, if not absolutely the friend of royalty; the difference was unimportant.

He then remembered that it was Gilbert's day of visit, and had ordered him to be introduced as soon as he came.

Scarcely had he crossed the door of the palace, than the valet de chambre arose, went to him, and accompanied him to the presence of the king.

The king walked up and down, so immersed in thought that he paid no attention to the announcement.

Gilbert stood silent and motionless at the door, waiting for the king to observe his presence.

The object which interested him, and it was easily seen from his stopping from time to time to observe it, was the famous portrait of Charles I., by Vandyck, the same which is now at the Louvre, and which an Englishman proposed to cover with gold as its price.

Charles I. is on foot under some of those rough, hardy trees found on downs. A page holds his horse. The sea is in the distance. The head of the king is expressive of sadness. Of what did the unlucky Stuart think? His predecessor was the beautiful and unfortunate Mary of Scotland, and his successor will be James II.

Often the king paused before the picture, and with a sigh resumed the walk, which always seemed ready to terminate in one place—the picture.

At last Gilbert remembered that there are occasions when it is better to announce one's self than to stand still.

He moaned, the king trembled, and looked around.

"Ah, doctor, is it you? I am glad to see you. How long have you been here?"

"Some moments, sire."

"Ah!" said the king, again becoming pensive.

After a pause, he took Gilbert before the picture.

"Do you know this picture?"

"Yes, sire."

"Where did you see it?"

"At the house of Madame du Barry."

"Madame du Barry! Yes, that is it," said the king.

After another pause of some moments:

"Know you the history of this picture?"

"The subject, or the picture itself, does your majesty speak of?"

"I speak of the history of the picture."

"No, sire; I only know that it was painted in London about 1645 or 1646. I know no more, and am ignorant how it came into France, and how it is now in your majesty's rooms."

"How it did pass into France, I know; how it came here, I know not."

Gilbert looked at Louis XVI. with astonishment.

"Who has ordered it to be placed here? Why is it here, or, rather, why does it pursue me, doctor?" said Louis XVI. "Lurks there no fatality beneath this?"

"A fatality, certainly, if this portrait says nothing to you, sire, but a providence if it speaks to you."

"How would you that such a portrait spoke not to a king in my situation, doctor?"

"After having permitted me to speak the truth to you, will your majesty allow me to question you?"

Louis XVI. seemed to hesitate a moment.

"Question me, doctor," said he.

"What does this portrait say to your majesty, sire?"

"It tells me that Charles I. lost his head for having made war upon his people, and that James II. lost his throne for having neglected his own."

"In this case, the portrait is like myself, sire, it speaks the truth."

"Well, then?" asked the king, soliciting Gilbert with a look.

"Since the king has permitted me to question him, I will ask him what answer he will make to a portrait that speaks so loyally?"

"Monsieur Gilbert," said the king, "I give you my word as a gentleman that I have resolved nothing as yet; I shall take counsel of circumstances."

"The people fear lest the king should think of making war on them."

Louis XVI. shook his head.

"No, sir, no," said he; "I could not make war on my people without employing foreign swords, and I know the state of Europe too well to tempt me to do that. The King of Prussia offered to enter France with a hundred thousand men, but I know the intriguing and ambitious spirit of this petty monarchy, which wishes to become a great kingdom, which pushes itself into every dispute, hoping that through some dispute she may acquire a part of New Silesia. Austria, on her side, placed a hundred thousand men at my disposal, but I loved not my brother-in-law, Leopold, a doublefaced Janus, whose mother caused my father to be poisoned. My brother, D'Artois, proposed to me the assistance of Sardinia and Spain, but I put no trust in these two powers led by my brother D'Artois; he has about his person Monsieur de Calonne, that is to say, the most cruel enemy of the queen. I know all that passes down there. In the last council the question of deposing me and appointing a regent was discussed, who would probably be my other very dear brother, Monsieur le Comte de Provence; in the last one Monsieur de Condé, my cousin, proposed to enter France, and to march upon Lyons, although he might himself, ultimately, ascend the throne. As for the great Catherine, that is another affair; she limits herself to advice, she—she gives me advice which seems perfect, and is, after all, ridiculous. 'Above all, after what has passed during the last few days, kings,' says she, 'ought to pursue their way without troubling themselves with the cries of the people, as the moon pursues her path regardless of the bayings of dogs.' It seems Russian dogs are satisfied with merely barking. Oh, that she would send and ask Deshuttes and Varicourt if ours do not bite as well!"

"The people fear lest the king should think of flying, of leaving France."

The king hesitated to reply.

"Sire," continued Gilbert, smiling, "one is always wrong in taking in a literal sense a king's permission. I see that I have been indiscreet, and merely express a fear."

The king placed his hand on Gilbert's shoulder.

"Monsieur," said he, "I promised to tell you the truth, and I will. Yes, the suggestion was made, and I will tell you the whole truth. Yes, it is the opinion of many loyal subjects who surround me that I should escape, but on the night of the 6th of October, when weeping in my arms, and clasping her children in hers, and all of us expecting to die, she made me swear that I would never fly alone, that we sit, escape, and live or die together. I gave my oath, and, sir, I will keep it; now, as I do not think we could all fly together, without being taken before we reached the frontier, again and again, we will not attempt to do so."

"Sire, I am lost in admiration of the justness of your mind. Why cannot all France hear you, as I have done? How the hatred which pursues your majesty would be mollified! How all dangers would be removed!"

"Dangers!" said the king. "Think you my people hate me? Dangers! You attach too much importance to somber thoughts with which that picture filled my mind. I think I could tell you of greater dangers I have undergone."

Gilbert looked at the king with an expression of deep melancholy.

"Think you not so, Monsieur Gilbert?" said Louis XVI.

"My opinion is that your majesty is about to engage in a contest of great severity, and that the 14th oi July and the 6th of October are but the two first acts of a terrible drama to be played before the nations of the world by France."

Louis XVI. became slightly pale, and said:

"I trust, sir, you are mistaken."

"I am not mistaken, sire."

"How, on a point of this nature, can you be better informed than I, who have both my police and counter police?"

"Sire, it is true, I have neither police nor counter-police. My very profession, however, places me in contact both with the things of heaven and the earth's very core. Sire, what we have as yet experienced is but an earthquake. We have yet to face fire, lava, and the ashes of the volcano."

"You said 'face'? Had you not better say 'combat with'?'

"I did, sire."

"You know my opinion of foreign lands. I will never invite them into France. What matters my life? I will sacrifice it, unless the lives of my wife and children be in real danger."

"I thank God, sire, that you entertain similar sentiments. No, sire, we need no foreign power—what is the use of them, as long as you have not exhausted your own resources? You fear that you have been excelled by th revolution."

"I own I do."

"Well, there are two ways to save both France and the king."

"Tell me, sir, and you will have deserved well of both."

"The first is to place yourself at the head of the revolution, and to direct it."

"They will drag me on with it, Monsieur Gilbert. I do not wish to go."

"The second is to put a bit in its mouth strong enough to break it."

"What bit is that, sir?"

"Popularity and genius."

"And who shall forge that combination?"

"Mirabeau."

He looked at Gilbert as if he had misunderstood him.

Gilbert saw there was a battle to be fought.

The king turned toward the great Vandyck.

"If you felt the earth tremble beneath you, and you were told to rely on Cromwell."

"Charles Stuart would have refused, and rightly. There is no similarity between Cromwell and Mirabeau."

"I do not know how you look at things, doctor, but to me there are no degrees of treason, and I find no difference between who is, and who is slightly, a traitor."

"Sire," said Gilbert, with deep respect, but at the same time with invincible firmness, "neither Cromwell nor Mirabeau are traitors."

"What, then, are they?" asked the king.

"Cromwell is a rebellious subject. Mirabeau a malcontent gentleman."

"Why malcontent?"

"On every account. Because his father shut him up in the Château d'If and the Donjon of Vincennes. He was dissatisfied with the courts that sentenced him to death, with the king who did not understand his genius, and was mistaken in him."

"The genius of a politician, Monsieur Gilbert, is honesty."

"The reply, sire is most apt and worthy of Titus Trajan, or Marcus Aurelius. Unfortunately, experience contradicts it."

"How so?"

"Was Augustus, who divided the world with Lepidus and Anthony, and killed Anthony to have it all himself, honest? Was Charlemagne, when he placed his brother, Carloman, in a cloister, and who, to destroy Witikind, almost as great a man as himself, cut off the heads of all Saxons, longer than his sword, honest? Was Louis XI., who revolted against his father, to dethrone him, and who inspired such terror to Charles VII., of poison, that the prince died of hunger, honest? Was Richelieu, who formed plots in the alcoves and galleries of the Place de Grève, and which had their dénouement in the Place de Grève, honest? Was Mazarin, who signed a treaty with the Protector, and who refused a half million and five hundred men to Charles II., and also drove him from France, honest? Was Colbert, who betrayed, accused, and sold Foquet, his protector, and who, having sent him to die in a dungeon, occupied his scarcely warm seat, honest? Yet none of them, thank God, ever injured either kings or royalty."

"Doctor, you know very well that Mirabeau, being the friend of the Duke of Orleans, cannot be mine."

"But, sire, the Duke of Orleans being exiled, Mirabeau belongs to no one."

"Would you have me confide in a man who is in the market? How could I?"

"By buying him. Could you not pay more than any one else?"

"He is a cormorant, who would ask a million."

"If Monsieur Mirabeau, sire, sells himself for a million, he will give himself away. So you think he is worth two million less than a male or female Polignac?"

"Doctor Gilbert."

"The king withdraws his promise, and I am silent.'

"No; speak."

"I have spoken."

"Let us argue."

"I ask nothing better, sire. I know Mirabeau by heart."

"You are his friend, unfortunately. I have not that honor. Besides, Monsieur Mirabeau has but one friend who is also the friend of the queen."

"Yes; the Count de la Morck."

"I know it; we reproach him with the fact every day."

"Your majesty, on the contrary, should prohibit him, under pain of death, from ever quarreling with him."

"And of what earthly importance in politics, doctor, is a petty gentleman like Monsieur Riquetti de Mirabeau?"

"First, sire, let me tell you, Monsieur de Mirabeau is a nobleman, and not a petty gentleman. There are few nobles in France who date further back than the eleventh century; since, to have yet a few around them, our kings exacted, in requital of the honor of riding in their coaches, no proof beyond 1399. Now, sire, a man descended from the Arrighetti of Florence is not a petty gentleman, even though, in consequence of the defeat of the Ghibellines, he should establish himself in Florence. A man is not a petty gentleman because he had an ancestor engaged in trade at Marseilles, the nobility of which city, like that of Venice, is not liable to derogation for having engaged in commerce."

"A debauchee in reputation; a hangman, a gulfer of money."

"Ah! sire, men must be taken according to their natures. The Mirabeaus have always been disorderly in their youth, but ripen in old age. When young, they are unfortunately what your majesty calls them, but when they become heads of houses, they are imperious, haughty, but austere. The king who did not reward them would be ungrateful; for they have furnished the army with gallant soldiers, and the navy with daring sailors. I know their provincial spirit makes them detest all centralization, and that in their half-feudal, half republican pride, they brave from the summit of their donjon keeps all ministerial orders. I know that more than once they have placed in restraint officers of the treasury, who visited their estates, and equally disdained courtiers and clerks, farmers-general and clerks, valuing but two things on the earth, their sword and farmers' wagons. I know that one of them wrote. 'Flunkeyism is the instinct of people of the court, with their plaster hearts and faces, just as ducks love the gutters.' All this however, sire, does not make a man a petty gentleman, but, on the contrary, may be the highest token of true nobility, though not, perhaps, of the highest moral sense."

"Come, doctor," said the king, with something of mortification, for he fancied he knew men of importance better than any one else did; "you said you knew Mirabeau by heart. Go on, for I who know him not, would learn."

"Yes, sire," said Gilbert, pricked by the kind of irony evinced by the king's intonation, "and I will tell you that Bruno of Riquetti was a Mirabeau, who, when Monsieur de la Feuillade inaugurated the statue of Victory, on the square of Victory, with four chained nations, when marching by with his guards, paused and halted his regiment in front of the statue of Henry IV., taking off his hat, said, 'Let us salute this statue, for it is worth as much as the other.' Francisco di Riquetti, who, on his return from Malta, at the age of seventeen, found his mother, Anna de Poitiers, in mourning, asked her "why?" his father having been dead sixteen years, and was told because she had been insulted. 'And did you not avenge yourself?' said he. The mother said, 'I wished to, and one day I placed a pistol at his head, and said I would avenge myself, but that I have a son who will do it for me.' 'You were right, mother,' said the young man. Without taking off his boots, he asked for his horse and cap, girded on his sword, and went in search of the Chevalier de Griasque, of whom his mother complained. He challenged him, took him to a garden, locked the gates. and threw the keys over the wall. He killed him, and returned quietly home. He, too, was a Mirabeau, as also was the Marquis Jean Antoine, who was six feet high, and beautiful as Antinous, and strong as Milo ; yet to him his mother said, in her Provençal accent, 'You are no longer men, but dwarfs.'"

"Well," said Louis XVI., evidently captivated by this nervous and interesting anecdote, "you speak well," for he was evidently amazed by the recital of this and other anecdotes of Mirabeau. "You have not told me how the Marquis Jean Antoine was killed, nor how he died."

"He died at the Castle of Mirabeau, after a sad retreat. The hold was on a strong rock, defending a double gorge, on which the north wind perpetually blew. He, too, had that stern and rugged exterior the Mirabeau family ever acquire as they grow old, and educate their children, and keep them at such a distance, that the eldest said, 'I never had the honor to touch either hand, lips, or flesh of that excellent man.' This eldest son was the father of the present Mirabeau. A hazard bird whose nest was made in four turrets, and who never would Versaillize themselves, which is the reason why your majesty neither knows nor can do them justice."

"Ah, sir, I know, on the contrary, better. He is one of the chiefs of the Economical School. He took part in the revolution which is just over, by giving the signal for social reforms, and was especially guilty of his part in them, in having said, 'Every woman now gives birth to an Artaveldt or to a Massaniello.' He was not mistaken, and his own mother's womb has proven it."

"Sire, there is in the Mirabeaus something which offends and displeases your majesty. Let me tell you, paternal and royal despotism have effected this."

"Royal despotism!" said Louis XVI.

"Certainly, sire, without the king, your father, being able to prevent it. For what great crime had the scion of this lofty and ancient race committed to induce his father, at the age of fourteen, to send him to a school of correction, in which his name was registered, not Riquetti de Mirabeau, but De Buffieres? What had he done at eighteen to make him the victim of a lettre-de-cachet? What had he done at twenty, that he was made to serve in the ranks of a punishment battalion in Corsica? His father said, 'He will, on the 16th of April next, embark on the plain, which now alone is being plowed. God grant he may not reap it some day.'

"What had he done, that after a year of marriage his father should exile him to Manosque? After six months, then, why was he transferred to Joux? Why, after his escape, was he arrested at Amsterdam and imprisoned at Vincennes, where forever to him, who was being strangled when at large, paternal love and royal clemency assigned to a dungeon of ten square feet, where for five years his youth was agitated, his passion inflamed, and his mind strengthened?

"I will tell your majesty what he had done. He had won the heart of his master, Poisson, by the ease with which he learned everything. He had gnawed through political science. Having adopted the profession of arms, he wished to persevere in it. He had, when reduced to six thousand livres a year, with his wife and child, contracted debts to the amount of thirty millions. He had broken his parole at Manosque, to cane a nobleman who had insulted his sister. He had, and that is the greatest of all offenses, yielding to the charms of a pretty woman, carried her off from her old, morose, and worn-out husband."

"Yes, sir," said the king, "and afterward deserted her, so that the unfortunate Madame Monnier, left alone with her crime, committed suicide."

Gilbert looked up to heaven, and sighed.

"What have you to say to that, and how will you defend your Mirabeau?"

"By truth, sire, by truth, which rarely penetrates to kings; that you, who seek, look, and ask for it, do not find it. No; Madame de Monnier did not die for Mirabeau, who, immediately on his leaving Vincennes, visited her first, disguised as a peddler. He entered the Convent of Gier, whither she had sought an asylum. He found Sophie cold and constrained. There was an explanation, and Mirabeau saw not only that Madame de Monnier did not love him, but even that she loved another, the Chevalier de Rancourt. She, made free by her husband's death, was about to marry this other. Mirabeau had left prison too soon; his captivity had been relied on, and it will be necessary to destroy his honor. Mirabeau gives place to his happy rival, and retires. Madame de Monnier is about to marry De Rancourt, who, however, dies suddenly. The poor woman in this last passion had expended all her soul and passion.

"One day, on the 9th of September, she killed herself with charcoal. Mirabeau's enemies then alleged that she died on his account, when she died for another. Ah, history, history, thus are you written!"

"Wherefore was it," said the king, "that he received the news with such indifference?"

"How did he receive it?" said the doctor. "I can assure your majesty he never did receive it, for it never was told him—for I know who told him. Ask that person. He will not dare to lie, for he is a priest—Curé of Gier, the Abbé Vallet, and sits in opposition to Mirabeau. He crossed the hall, and sat by his side. 'What the devil are you doing here?' asked Mirabeau. Without replying, the abbé gave him a letter containing all the details. He opened it, and was long reading it, for in all probability he could not believe the fatal news. He read it again, and then grew pale, his face from time to time expressing deep emotion. He passed his hands across his brow. His countenance grew pale, he coughed, spat, and sought to restrain his feelings. At last he had to yield. He arose, and hurried out, and did not show himself again in the assembly for three days. Sire, sire, forgive my entering into these details, for let a man have but ordinary talent, he will be slandered everywhere. What, then, must be the fate of a man of genius."

"Why so, doctor? Why should any one slander Mirabeau to me?"

"Interest, sire, the interest of mediocrity to keep near the throne. Mirabeau is one who, if he enter the temple, will expel all the hucksters. Were Mirabeau near you, sire, all petty intrigues would end. Were Mirabeau near you, genius would mark out the course of honesty. What is it to you, if Mirabeau ran away with Madame Monnier? If he was unhappy with his wife? If he owe half a million of money? Pay his debts, sire, and add to these five hundred thousand francs, one, two, ten million francs —what is the difference? Mirabeau is free; do not let him escape you. Make him a counselor and minister, and listen to his powerful voice. What it says, tell back to Europe and the world."

"Mirabeau, who became a cloth merchant at Aix, to be elected by the people, cannot be false to his constituents, and desert them for the court."

"Sire, I tell you you do not know the Mirabeaus. He, like his family, is an aristocrat, noble, and a royalist. He procured an election by the people because the nobility disdained him. The Mirabeaus have that sublime want of action, by any possible means, which torments men of genius. He was elected by neither the nobility nor the people to enter parliament as Louis XIV. did, booted and spurred, arguing divine right. He will not desert the people for the court, you say. Why, then, do the two parties exist? Why do not the two coalesce? Well, Mirabeau will effect this. Take Mirabeau, sire, or else to-morrow, repelled by your disdain, he will turn against you. Then, sire, as that picture of Charles I. says, 'All will be lost.' I tell you so, sire."

"Mirabeau will oppose me, doctor. Has he not already done so?"

"In appearance, perhaps; but in fact Mirabeau is your friend. Ask the Count de la Morck what he said at the famous session of June 21st—for Mirabeau reads the future with terrible wisdom."

"Well, what did he say?"

"He wrings his hands with grief, sire, and says, 'Thus kings are led to the scaffold. These people do not see the abyss they dig beneath the steps of monarchy. The king and queen will die, and the people will clap their hands over their carcasses.' "

The king trembled, grew pale, looked at the portrait of Charles I., appeared for a moment ready to decide, but all at once said :

" I will talk of this with the queen. It may be she will decide to have an interview with Mirabeau. I will not speak to him. I like to clasp the hands of those with whom I talk, as now, Gilbert, I do yours. Not for my liberty or my throne would I clasp that of Monsieur Mirabeau."

Gilbert was about to answer, and, perhaps, might have insisted, but just then an usher entered, and said :

" Sire, the person your majesty was to receive this morning awaits you in the antechamber."

Louis XVI. looked anxiously at Gilbert.

" Sire," said he, " if I should not see the person your majesty expects, I will go out by the other door."

" No, sir, go through this. You are aware that I look on you as my friend, and that from you I have no secret. The person I expect is a simple gentleman, once attached to my brother's household, and recommended by him. He is a faithful servant, and I wish to see if something may not be done, if not for him, at least for his wife and children. Go, Monsieur Gilbert ; you know I am always glad to see you—even when you talk to me of Monsieur Riquetti de Mirabeau."

" Sire, must I, then, think I have utterly failed ? "

" I said I would speak to the queen—and think. We will meet at another time."

" Another time ? Sire, I pray it may be soon."

" Think you, then, the danger so imminent ? "

" Sire," said Gilbert, " never suffer them to take the picture of Charles I. from your room. It is a wise adviser."

Bowing, he left the room, just as the person the king expected appeared.

Gilbert uttered a cry of surprise. The nobleman was

the Marquis de Favras, whom, eight or ten days before, he had met at Cagliostro's house, when his fated and speedy death was foretold.

CHAPTER VIII.

FAVRAS.

WHILE Gilbert, left a prey to an unknown terror in relation, not of the revolution, but of the invisible and mysterious course of events, the Marquis de Favras was introduced, as we have said in the preceding chapter, to Louis XVI.

As Dr. Gilbert had done, he paused at the door; the king beckoned him to draw near.

Favras advanced and bowed, waiting respectfully to be spoken to.

Louis XVI. fixed on him that glance of anxious inquiry which seems to be a part of the education of kings, and which is measured in profundity by him that employs it.

"You are the Marquis de Favras, sir?" said the king.

"Yes, sire," said the marquis.

"You wished to be presented to me?"

"I expressed to His Royal Highness the Count de Provence my warm desire to offer the king my homage to majesty."

"My brother has great confidence in you."

"I think he has, and I wish that good opinion to be shared by your majesty."

"My brother has known you long, Monsieur de Favras."

"But your majesty does not, I understand. Interrogate me, however, but ten minutes, and your majesty will know me as well as your august brother."

"Speak, marquis," said Louis XVI., looking at the picture of Charles Stuart, which he could not entirely eradicate from his mind nor from his glance. "Speak, marquis, I listen to you."

"Your majesty wishes to know——"

"Who you are, and what you have done."

"Who I am, sire, the announcement of my name tells you. I am Thomas Mahi, Marquis de Favras. I was born at Blois, in 1745; I entered the Mousquetaires at fifteen, and served in that corps the campaign of 1761. I was then captain and aid major in the regiment of Belzunce, and afterward lieutenant of the Swiss of the guard of the Count de Provence."

"You left his service?"

"In 1775, sire, to go to Vienna to have my wife recognized as the only and legitimate daughter of the Prince of Anhalt-Schauenburg."

"Has your wife ever been presented?"

"No, sire: but at this moment she has the honor of being, with my eldest son, received by the queen."

The king made an uneasy movement, which seemed to say, "Ah! the queen has something to do with it!"

After a momentary silence, during which he walked up and down the room, and glanced again and again at the picture of Charles I., "And then?" said the king.

"Then, for three years, during the insurrection against the Stadtholder, I commanded a legion, and to a degree contributed to the re-establishment of authority. Then, as I looked at France, and saw the evil spirit which appeared to pervade it, I returned to Paris to place my life and sword at the service of the king."

"You have indeed had trouble."

"Yes, sire; I saw the sad days of the 5th and 6th of October."

"The king seemed to wish to change the subject.

"And you say, marquis," continued he, "that my brother, the Count of Provence, had such confidence in you that he confided to your care the charge of a large sum of money?"

At this unexpected question, a third person would have had his nerves severely shaken by witnessing the nervous tremor of a curtain which half closed the alcove of the room, as if some one were hidden behind it, and at the agitation of M. de Favras, like that of a man who, expecting one question, has another altogether different addressed to him.

"Yes, sire; if it be a mark of confidence to confide the charge of money to a nobleman, his royal highness has done so to me."

The king looked at Favras, as if the direction the conversation had assumed offered his curiosity a greater interest than the course it had hitherto assumed.

The marquis then continued, but like a man who has been disappointed: "His royal highness, being deprived of his revenues by the various measures of the assembly, and thinking that the time was come when, for their own safety, it was necessary for the princes to have a large sum at their disposal, his royal highness gave me the contracts."

"On which you borrowed, sir?"

"Yes, sire."

"A large sum, you say?"

"Yes, sire, two millions."

"From whom?"

De Favras hesitated to reply to the king; the conversation appeared to have assumed a scope so widely different from that he expected—looking into private rather then general interests, and sinking from politics into police.

"I asked," said the king, "who lent the money?"

"Baron Zanoni."

"Ah!" said Louis XVI., "an Italian?"

"A Genoese, sire."

"And he lives?"

"At Sèvres, just opposite the place where," said Favras, who hoped by thus spurring his horse in the face of the king to excite the foundered animal to some vigor, "where the coach of your majesty, stopped by the cut-throats under the conduct of Marat, Vevrières, and the Duke d'Aiguillon, forced the hair-dresser of the queen to dress the heads of Varicourt and Deshuttes."

He grew pale, and had he at that moment looked toward the alcove, he would have seen that the curtain was more violently agitated than it had previously been.

It was evident that the conversation annoyed him, and

that he wished he had not engaged in it. He resolved to end it as soon as possible. He said:

"It is evident, sir, that you are a faithful subject of royalty, and, when the time comes, I promise not to forget you."

He bowed, and when the princes do that, it means you may go.

Favras understood him perfectly.

"Excuse me, sire, your majesty had one other thing to ask me."

"No," said the king, as if he wondered what the matter could be, or what new question he asked; "no, marquis, this is all I wished to know."

"You are mistaken, sire," said a voice, which made both the king and marquis turn toward the alcove. "You wished to know what course the ancestor of the marquis adopted to save King Stanislaus at Dantzig, and how he escorted him in safety to the frontier."

They both uttered an exclamation of surprise. The third person, who thus suddenly mingled in the conversation, was the queen, pale, and with quivering lips, who, not satisfied with what Favras had told her, and fancying that the king, if left to himself, would dare to act decidedly, had come by the secret stairway and corridor to participate in the conversation.

Favras at once appreciated the means offered him to unfold his plan, and, though none of his ancestors had ever contributed to the escape of the Polish monarch, he hastened to bow, and replied:

"Your majesty, doubtless, refers to my cousin, General Steinflicht, who owes his illustrious name to the services he rendered his monarch; services which were doubly important, as, in the first place, he wrested him from the hands of his enemies, and, subsequently, by means of a lucky accident, made him one of your majesty's progenitors."

"That is true, sire," said the queen, eagerly; while Louis XVI. looked at the portrait of Charles I., and sighed deeply.

"Well," said Favras, "your majesty is aware that King Stanislaus, though nominally free in Dantzig, was strictly watched by the Muscovite army, and was almost lost, if he did not determine on a prompt escape."

"He was entirely—you may say entirely lost, Monsieur de Favras," added the queen.

"Madame," said Louis XVI., with severity, "Providence watches over kings, and they are never utterly lost."

"Ah, sire," said the queen, "I have as full, or as religious a faith in Providence as you have, but I think we should do something for ourselves."

"Such was the opinion of the King of Poland, sire," added De Favras, "for he publicly declared that, no longer thinking his position tenable, and knowing his life to be in danger, he wished various plans of escape to be submitted to him. In spite of the difficulty, three were proposed. I say, in spite of the difficulty, because your majesty will remark that it was more difficult for the King of Poland to escape than for yourself; for instance, if your majesty should fancy to leave Paris, with a post-carriage, if your majesty wished to do so quietly, you could, in a day or night, gain the frontier. Or, if your majesty wished to leave Paris as a king, give an order to some gentleman to collect thirty thousand men, and seize on the Tuileries—in either case success would be sure."

"Sire," said the queen, "Monsieur de Favras tells your majesty nothing but the truth."

"Yes," said the king, "but my situation is far from being desperate, as was that of my cousin Stanislaus. Dantzig was surrounded by the Muscovites, as the marquis says; the fort of Weichselmund, its last defense, had capitulated, while I——"

"While you," interrupted the queen with impatience, "are surrounded by the people of Paris, who took the Bastile on the 14th of July, and who, on the night of the 5th and 6th of October, sought to murder you, and who, on the 6th, brought you, with insults, back to Paris. Ah! it is a far better condition than that of Stanislaus."

"Yet, madame——"

"King Stanislaus was exposed only to death or imprisonment, while we——"

A glance from the king made her pause.

"But you are the master, and must decide."

She, in her impatience, sat in front of the picture of Charles I.

"Monsieur de Favras," said she, "I have seen the marchioness and your eldest son. I found them both brave and full of courage, as the wife and son of a brave nobleman should be. And in case anything befall them, they may rely on the Queen of France, who will not abandon them. She is the daughter of Marie Thérèse, and can appreciate and reward courage."

The king, as if he were excited by this boutade, said:

"You say, sir, three modes of escape were proposed?"

"Yes, sire. The first, the disguise of a peasant. The Countess Chapoka, Palatine of Pomerania, who spoke German, her native tongue, offered, confiding in a man she knew to be well acquainted with the country, to disguise herself as a peasant woman, and pass him off as her husband. This was the method I just now spoke of to the King of France, as so easy in case he wished to fly incognito, and at night."

"The second," said Louis XVI., impatiently, as if he disliked the situation of Stanislaus being compared with his own.

"The second was to take a thousand men and cut through the Muscovites; this I suggested just now to the King of France, observing that he had not thirty, but thirty thousand at his service."

"You saw how valuable those thirty thousand were on the 14th of July, Monsieur de Favras. Now for the third."

"The third, which Stanislaus decided on, was to disguise himself as a peasant, not with a woman, who might encumber him on the road; not with a thousand men, every one of whom might be killed without cutting through the enemy; but with two or three sure men who travel much. The last was suggested by Monsieur Monti, and approved by General Steinflicht."

"Was it adopted ?"

"Yes, sire ; and if a king, finding or thinking himself in the situation of the King of Poland, should determine to adopt it, and grant me the confidence your kinsman granted General Steinflicht, I think I would answer with my head that, where the roads are free as they are in France, and the king as bold a rider as your majesty——"

"Certainly," said the queen. "But on the night of the 5th and 6th of October the king swore never to form a plan of escape without me. He promised, sir, and will keep his word."

"Madame," said Favras, "that makes the journey more difficult, but not impossible ; and had I the honor of conducting such an expedition, I would promise to carry the king and queen to Montmedy, or lose my head."

"Do you hear, sire ? I think there is all to gain and nothing to lose with a man like Monsieur de Favras."

"So, too, do I, madame ; but the moment is not yet favorable."

"Very well, sire," said the queen ; "wait as he whose portrait you study so did, the sight of which I had thought would give you better counsel. Wait until we are forced into a contest, until a battle shall have been lost, until a scaffold shall have been erected beneath your window, and then, instead of saying as you do to-day, 'It is too soon,' you will say, 'It is too late.'"

"At all events, and under all circumstances, the first word of the king will find me ready," said De Favras, bowing ; for he was afraid that his presence, having brought on a kind of contest between the king and queen, fatigued the latter. "I can only offer my life to my king ; and I should not say I offer, for the right of using it is his."

"It is well, sir ; and in case of need, I renew to you the offer of the queen, made in relation to the marquise and your children."

This was a real dismissal, which the marquis was forced to take, and finding no other encouragement than a glance from the queen, he left the room.

The queen looked after until the tapestry hid him.

"Ah, sire," said she, and she pointed toward the picture of Vandyck, "when I had that picture hung in your room, I fancied it would inspire you."

Haughty, and disdaining to pursue the conversation, she advanced toward the door of the alcove; all at once pausing, she said:

"Sire, confess that the Marquis de Favras is not the only person you have seen to-day."

"Yes, madame; I saw Doctor Gilbert."

The queen trembled.

"Ah!" said she, "so I thought; and the doctor——"

"Agrees with me, that we should not leave France."

"Thinking, then, we should not leave it, he has suggested some way to enable us to live here?"

"Yes; one which, unfortunately, if not bad, is impracticable."

"What is it?"

"That we purchase the service of Mirabeau for one year."

The queen's face was deeply pensive.

"Perhaps," said she, "that might be a way."

"Yes; but it is a thing you would refuse to do, madame."

"I say neither yes nor no," said the queen, with the expression the angel of evil might assume when sure of his triumph. "My advice is to think of it." She added, in a lower tone, as she left, "And I will think of it."

The king was alone, on his feet, and for an instant motionless. Then, as if he had feared that the retreat of the queen was feigned, he went to the door through which she had gone, opened it, and looked into the corridor and antechambers.

Seeing none of the servants, he said, in a half-voice:

"François!"

A valet, who had risen when the door of the king's apartments opened, was immediately told to draw near.

"François," said Louis XVI., "do you know the rooms of Monsieur de Charny?"

"Yes, sire."

"Find Monsieur de Charny; I wish to see him."

A valet de chambre left, and closing the door behind him, went to the rooms of M. de Charny, whom he found with his head resting on his hand and his eyes gazing on that ocean of roofs which lost itself in a horizon of tiles and slates.

The valet knocked twice without succeeding in arousing the count. Charny was lost in reflection, and at last the valet determined, as the key was in the door, to enter.

The count looked round.

"Ah, Monsieur Hue, is it you? Are you come to me from the queen?"

"No, count; from the king."

"From the king?" echoed Charny, wondering what he could want with him. "Very well; say to his majesty that I obey."

The valet de chambre retired with the formula prescribed by etiquette, while the count, with that courtesy which the old and true nobility entertained for any one coming from the king, whether wearing a gold chain or a livery, went with him to the door.

When alone, Charny for a moment rested his head on his hands, as if to arrange his ideas, put on his sword, which lay on a chair, took up his hat, and went down-stairs.

He found Louis XVI. in his chamber, sitting with his back to the picture of Vandyck, and awaiting him.

The desk was covered with charts, works on geography, English papers, and journals, among which were discovered manuscripts of Louis XVI., recognized by the fact that he wrote so closely that scarcely any margin was to be seen.

Charny looked particularly at none of the objects which lay around, and waited respectfully for the king to speak.

The king, however, in spite of the confidence he had previously exhibited, seemed to experience a certain hesitation.

In the first place, and to acquire courage, he opened a drawer in his desk, and a secret in this drawer, whence he extracted several papers in envelopes, which he placed on the table.

"Monsieur de Charny," said he, "I have observed one thing——"

He paused, looking fixedly at Charny, who waited respectfully to hear what he had to say.

"On the night of the 5th and 6th of October, having to select between the care of the queen and myself, I saw that you placed her under the charge of your brother, while you remained by me."

"Sire," said Charny, "I am the head of my family, as you are the chief of the state; I had, therefore, the right to die by your side."

"This made me think," said Louis XVI., "that if I had ever a secret mission, at once secret, difficult, and dangerous, I could trust it to your loyalty as a French noble, to your devotion as a friend."

"Oh, sire," said Charny, "exalt me as high as you please, and I will ever be grateful. I cannot do more."

"Monsieur de Charny, though scarcely thirty-six, you are a thoughtful man. You have not passed through the events which are transpiring around us, without extracting profit from them. What think you of my situation, and were you prime minister, what would you suggest to improve it?"

"Sire," said Charny, with more hesitation than embarrassment, "I am a military man, a sailor; such questions I am incompetent to answer."

"Monsieur," said the king, giving Charny his hand, with a dignity which seemed suddenly to spring from the very situation in which they were placed, "you are a man, and I am another, who, thinking you his friend, asks you simply what, if you were in his situation, you would do?"

"Sire," said Charny, "in a situation not less grave than the present, the queen did me the honor, as the king does now, to ask my opinion; I speak of the capture of the Bastile. She wished to use against the hundred thousand Parisians in arms, rolling like a hydra of fire and steel along the boulevards, her eight or ten thousand foreign soldiers. Had I been less known to the queen, had she been less familiar with my devotion and respect, my reply would doubtless have made trouble between us. Alas, sire, may I not fear that my reply to-day will offend the king?"

"What did you say to the queen?"

"That, if not strong enough to enter Paris as a conqueror, you must enter it as a father."

"Well, sir, did I not follow that advice?"

"Yes, sire."

"Now it remains to see whether I have acted correctly or not. Tell me, now, have I entered Paris as a king or as a prisoner?"

"Sire," said the count, "does the king permit me to speak to him frankly?"

"Do so, sir. When I ask your advice, I also ask your opinion."

"Sire, I disapproved of the banquet at Versailles, and begged the queen not to go to the theater without you. Sire, I despaired when I saw the queen trample on the national cockade, and put on that of Austria."

"Think you, count, that was the true cause of the events of the 5th and 6th of October?"

"No, sire; it was at least the pretext. Sire, you are not unjust to the people; the people is good, and loves you, for it is royalist; the people, though, suffers; it is cold and hungry, and has in, around, and above it, bad counselors, who urge it on. It advances, urged onward, overturning everything, and is ignorant of its own power. When once loosed, once released, turned forth, and in motion, it is either a conflagration or a deluge. It either burns or overwhelms."

"But, Monsieur de Charny, suppose one wishes neither to be burned nor drowned? This is very natural; what, then, must I do?"

"Give no pretext for the inundation to burst, for the conflagration to spread. Sire, you have seen this people of Paris, so long without sovereigns, so anxious to see them again. You have seen it murdering, burning, and assassinating at Versailles, or, rather, you thought so; at Versailles you did not see the people; you saw it, I saw it, at the Tuileries, saluting beneath the balcony the queen, the royal family; penetrating into your apartments, by means of deputations, from the market, of the civic guard, of the municipal corps; those who had not the happiness of entering your apartments and exchanging words with you, pressed close around the windows of the dining-room, through which the women sent sweet kisses to their illustrious guests, the kisses of their children."

"Yes," said the king; "I saw all that, and thence comes my hesitation. I ask what is the true people, that which burns and caresses, or that which caresses and demands?"

"The last, sire—the last, sire. Confide in that which will defend you against the other."

"Count, you say to me now exactly what Doctor Gilbert said two hours ago."

"Then, sire, how, having consulted a man so profound, so learned, so grave as the doctor, can you deign to consult a mere soldier like myself?"

"I will tell you, Monsieur de Charny," said Louis XVI.; "I think there is a great difference between you. You are the friend of the king, and Doctor Gilbert is only the friend of royalty."

"I do not understand, sire."

"I mean that if the principle of royalty were deserted, he would willingly abandon the king—that is to say, the man."

"Then your majesty is right. For to me, sire you will, ever be both the king and the impersonation of royalty. Thus I wish you to use me."

"Some time, Monsieur de Charny. I wish to know to whom you would address yourself in this calm—which perhaps intervenes between two storms—to efface all memory of the past, and conjure up better prospects of the future."

"Had I the honor and misfortune, sire, of royalty, I would remember the shoutings around my carriage on the return from Versailles, and I would give my right hand to Lafayette, and my left to Mirabeau."

"Count, how can you say this, when you hate the one and detest the other?"

"Sire, feelings, now, we have nothing to do with. The fate of the king and kingdom is at stake."

"Just what Gilbert said," the king said to himself.

"Sire," said Charny, "I am happy to find so distinguished a person agree with me."

"Think you, then, count, that the union of these two men would restore the nation to calm and to peace?"

"With God's aid, sire, I would expect much from the union of these two men."

"But if I lent myself to this union, if I consented to the compact, and if, in spite of my desire, the ministerial combination should fail, what then should I do?"

"That, having exhausted all the means placed by Providence in your hands, having fulfilled all the duties imposed by your position, it is time for you to think of your own safety, and that of your family."

"Then you propose that I should fly?"

"I would advise your majesty to retire, with those of your regiments on which you think you can rely, to some strong place like Metz, Nancy, or Strasbourg."

The face of the king lighted up.

"Ah!" said he; "and among all the generals who have given me proof of devotion, tell me, Charny—for you know them all—to whom would you confide the duty of carrying the king away?"

"Sire, it is a grave responsibility to guide a king in such a choice. I, however, recognize my influence, my weakness, my impotence. Sire, I cannot."

"Well, I will place you at ease. I have already made my choice, and I wish to send you to that man. Here is the letter I wish you to give him. Any name you may suggest will have no other influence on my determination than to point out one faithful servant more, who doubtless will have an opportunity to show his fidelity. Monsieur de Charny, had you to confide your king to the prudence, valor, and fidelity of any one, whom would you select?"

"Sire," said Charny, after a moment's reflection, "not, I swear to your majesty, on account of friendship or family, which unite us, do I say this. In the army, however, there is a man known for his great devotion to the king—a man who, as governor of the Windward Isles, efficiently protected the Antilles, and even took several from the English, who since has had many important commands, and who is now, I think, governor of the city of Metz. This man, sire, is the Marquis de Bouille. If a father, I would trust my son to him; had I a father, I would confide him to Bouille; as a subject, I would confide my king to him."

So dull was Louis XVI., that he heard with evident anxiety the words of the count. One might have seen his face either lighten or become bedimmed, as he seemed to recognize or not the person of whom Charny spoke. When he heard the name, he could not repress an exclamation of joy.

"Look, count, at the address of this letter; has not Providence itself induced me to write to him?"

Charny took the letter, and read the address:

"M. François Claude-Amour,
"Marquis de Bouille,
"General Commanding,
"Metz."

Tears of joy and pride gushed from Charny's eyes. He said:

"Sire, after this, I have but one thing to say, that I will live and die for your majesty."

"And after what has passed, I will say, I do not think that I have any longer a right to keep any secrets from you, provided that you and I are placed on a good footing. Now, to you alone I will confide my own person, that of my queen and my children. Listen to me, then; this has been proposed to me, and rejected."

Charny bowed in deep attention to the king.

"This is not the first time, monsieur, that the idea of a plan like that we speak of has occurred to myself and those around me. During the night of the 5th and 6th, I had wished to effect the queen's escape; a carriage was to have taken her to Rambouillet, where I would have joined her on horseback. Thence we easily could have reached the frontier, the surveillance which now surrounds us not having, as yet, been awakened. The project failed, because the queen would not go without me."

"Sire, I was present when the pious oath was exchanged between the king and the queen, or, rather, between the husband and wife."

"Monsieur de Breteuil has since opened negotiations with me, through the Earl of Innisdale, and to-day I received a letter from Soleure."

The king paused when he saw the count was motionless.

"You do not answer, count," said he.

"Sire, I know the Count de Breteuil is in the Austrian influence, and I am afraid to disturb your majesty's legitimate sympathies with his wife, and the Emperor Joseph II., his brother-in-law."

The king seized Charny's hand, and leaning toward him, said, in a whisper:

"Do not be afraid, count; I like Austria no better than you do. This was not the only plan of escape offered me. Do you know the Marquis de Favras?"

"The old captain of the regiment of Belzunce? The old lieutenant of the guards of Monsieur? Yes, sire."

"That is it," said the king, repeating, "'the old lieutenant of the guards of Monsieur.' What think you of him?"

"Well, he is a brave soldier and a gentleman, ruined by accidents, a thing which makes him the more unhappy, and impels him to mad attempts and foolish plans. He is, however, a man of honor, and will die rather than shrink from aught he has undertaken. He is a man on whom your majesty might rely for a coup de main, but whom I would fear to make the leader of an enterprise.

"Then," the king said, with something of bitterness, "the leader is not he, but Monsieur. Monsieur, the man who makes money, prepares everything. Monsieur, who purposes to remain in France when I shall have left it?"

Charny made a movement expressive of alarm.

"Well, what mean you, count? This is not an Austrian plot, but a movement of the princes, of the noblesse, of the émigrés."

"Sire, excuse me. I doubt neither the honor, nor the courage, nor the loyalty of Monsieur de Favras. If he promised to take your majesty anywhere, he will do so or will die in your defense. Why, though, does not Monsieur go with your majesty? Why does he remain here?"

"From devotion, I tell you; and perhaps—if it should become necessary to depose one king and appoint a regent—the people, weary of the search for a king, would not have far to look for a regent."

"Sire," said Charny, "this says terrible things."

"I tell you what everybody knows, dear count, what your brother wrote yesterday. In the last council of the princes, at Turin, it was proposed to depose me and to appoint a regent; Monsieur de Condé, my cousin, proposed to march upon Lyons. You see, then, I can neither accept the offer of Breteuil nor of Favras, neither of Austria nor of the princes. This, count, I have told no one, and I wish no one, *not even the queen*, to know of it." Louis XVI. emphasized the words we have underlined. "As no one, not even the queen, has had such confidence reposed in them, you should be more devoted to me than any one else."

"Sire," said Charny, "must the secret of my voyage be kept from every one?"

It matters not, count, that the people know whither, if they do not know why, you go."

"And the object must be revealed to Monsieur de Bouille alone?"

"To him alone, and not until you shall have ascertained his feelings. The letter I give is simply one of introduction. You know my position, my fears, better than either

Monsieur Necker, my minister, my counselor. Act accordingly. I put the thread and shears in your hands. Untwine or cut."

He then gave the count an open letter.

"Read," said he.

Charny took it, and read:

"Palais of the Tuileries, Oct. 29th.

"I trust, sir, you continue to be satisfied with your position as governor of the palace of Metz. The Count de Charny, who passes through Metz, will ask you if I can serve you in any other manner. If so, it would delight me to please you, and seize the opportunity to assure you of my esteem for you.

LOUIS."

"And now, Monsieur de Charny," said the king, "go; you have full power to make any promise to Monsieur de Bouille if you think any necessary; only promise nothing that I cannot keep."

He gave him his hand again.

Charny kissed it with an emotion which made all new protestations useless, and left the room, leaving the king convinced, as was the case, that he had by this confidence won the count's heart more completely than if he had heaped on him all the riches and favors in his bestowal during his omnipotence.

CHAPTER IX.

DARK PROSPECTS.

THE Count de Charny proceeded to the royal post to have horses put to his carriage.

While they were being harnessed, he went into the house of the agent, asked for pen, ink, and paper, and wrote to the countess, which he bid the domestic who returned with his horses to give her.

The countess, half asleep on the sofa in the corner, and

having a small stand before her, was occupied in reading this letter, when Weber entered.

"Monsieur Weber," said the femme de chambre, opening the door.

The countess folded up the letter quickly, as if Weber had come to take it from her, and placed it in her bosom.

The purport of Weber's message was, that the queen wished to see the countess in the evening.

Andrée simply replied that she would obey her majesty.

When Weber was gone, the countess closed her eyes for a moment, as if for the purpose of expelling all bad ideas and every evil thought; and not until she had succeeded in perfectly recovering herself, did she think herself able to finish the letter.

When she had read it, she kissed it tenderly, and placed it on her heart.

"May God keep you, soul of my life. I do not know where you are, but only that my prayers will ascend to God."

Then, as she could not possibly know why she was sent for, without impatience and without fear, she awaited the hour for her visit to the Tuileries.

This was not the case with the queen. A kind of prisoner in the palace, under the influence of impatience, she wandered from the pavilion of Flora to that of Warsaw.

Monsieur requested her to pass an hour. Monsieur had come to the Tuileries to ascertain how the king had received De Favras.

The queen, who was ignorant of the voyage of Charny, and wished to keep his route of safety open, promised more for the king than he had promised for himself, and told Monsieur that when the time came it would be adopted.

Monsieur, too, was in high spirits. The loan he had effected from the Genoese banker amounted to two millions, of which he could only induce De Favras to accept one hundred louis, which De Favras needed to freshen the devotion of two persons on whom he could rely, and who were to aid in the royal escape.

Favras wished to inform Monsieur about these two men, but Monsieur, ever prudent, refused either to see them or to hear their names.

Monsieur was to appear to be ignorant of what was going on. De Favras had belonged to his household, and therefore he gave him the money, but he did not care what he did with it.

Besides, as we have said, in case of the king's departure, Monsieur remained, and therefore could not be concerned in the plot. Monsieur declaimed against the flight of his family, and as he had contrived to make himself very popular in France, it was probable, as Louis XVI. said to Count de Charny, that Monsieur would be appointed regent.

If the flight was abortive, Monsieur knew nothing, would deny everything, and remain in France, or with the eighteen hundred thousand francs he retained of the money he had borrowed, would join the Count d'Artois and the Prince of Condé at Turin.

The return of the baker, his wife, and the shop-boy to Paris had not had the expected effect. Flour and bread still were scarce. Every day there was a crowd around the bakers' doors, causing great disorders. How, though, was this to be prevented?

The right of reunion was provided for in the declaration of the rights of man.

The assembly was ignorant of all that. Its members were not obliged to make a part of the tail from the baker's door; and when by accident one of the members became hungry during the session, he was always sure to find within a hundred yards a nice white roll at the shop of a baker named Françcis, who lived in the Rue Marché-Palu, in the district of Notre Dame. He baked five or six times a day, and always reserved one baking for the assembly.

The lieutenant of police was communicating to Louis XVI. his fears relative to these disorders, which some day might become an outbreak, when Weber appeared at the door of the little cabinet, and in a low voice, said:

"Madame la Comtesse de Charny."

Though the queen herself had sent for Andrée, and though she expected her to be announced, she trembled in every limb at Weber's words ; she hesitated a moment, not knowing by what name she should address the white apparition which passed from the shadow of the door into the half-lighted room. At last, giving her hand to her old friend, she said :

"Welcome, Andrée, to-day as ever."

"Is it necessary for me to tell your majesty," said Andrée, adopting the question with frankness, "to say that had she always spoken to me as she just has, it would not have been necessary to send for me out of the place she dwells in ?"

"Alas !" said the queen, "Andrée, you, so chaste and pure, whose heart has been corrupted by no hatred, should know that tempest clouds often may cover and cause a star to disappear, but which, when the wind sweeps the firmament, reappears more brilliant. All women, even in the most exalted ranks, have not your serenity. I, especially, who have asked of you assistance, you have so generously granted."

"The queen speaks of things and days I had forgotten, and I fancied so had she."

"The reply is severe, Andrée," said the queen, "yet I have deserved it, and you were right to make it to me ; not, it is true, because when I was happy, I did not remember your devotion, though no royal, and, perhaps, not even divine power, could adequately reward you. You have thought me ungrateful, when, perhaps, I was only powerless."

"I would have the right to accuse you, madame, if I had ever asked you anything, and if you had opposed my wish and refused my request. How can your majesty, though, expect me to complain when I have never asked for anything ?"

"Well, let me tell you, dear Andrée, it is just this kind of indifference to the things of the world which terrifies me in you. Yes, to me you seem a superhuman being, a creature of another world, borne hither by the wind, and cast among us, like stone purified by fire, coming none know whence. The consequence is, one becomes terrified at one's own weakness when in the face of one who has never failed. They say, though, that supreme indulgence is a quality of supreme perfection. The soul must be washed in the purest stream, and in a season of deep grief, before one does as I do, seek out that superhuman being whose censure we fear, but whose consolation we long for."

"Alas! madame," said Andrée, "if you ask that of me, I fear you will be disappointed in your expectation."

"Andrée, you forget in what a terrible situation you once consoled me."

Andrée grew pale visibly. The queen, seeing her tremble and her eyes close, as if she had lost her strength, moved her arms and hands to draw her to the same sofa with herself. Andrée, however, resisted, and still stood erect.

"Madame," said she, "if your majesty would but pity your faithful servant, and spare memories she has thought she had almost forgotten; one who does not ask for consolation, for she thinks God even unable to console certain griefs."

The queen looked closely and long at Andrée.

"Certain sorrows! Then," she said, "have you any other sorrows than those you have confided to me?"

Andrée was silent.

"Let us understand each other," said the queen. "The time for a full explanation has come. You love Monsieur de Charny?"

The countess became pale as death, but was silent.

"You love Monsieur de Charny?" repeated the queen.

"Yes," said Andrée.

The queen uttered the cry of a wounded lioness. "Oh!" said she, "I thought so; and how long have you loved him?"

"Since the first time I ever saw him."

The queen drew back in terror before this marble statue, which owned that it had a soul

"Oh!" said she, "and you are dying."

"You know that, madame, better than any one else."

"How so? Because I have seen that you love him?"

"Mean you to say that you love him better than I because I have not seen anything?"

"Ah!" said Andrée, with bitterness, "you saw nothing, because he loved you."

"Yes, and you mean to say that I see now, because he loves me no more? Is that it?"

Andrée remained silent.

"Answer me," said the queen, seizing not her hand but her arm; "own that he loves me no longer."

Andrée neither spoke nor made the least expression, either with her eyes or with her hands.

"Indeed," said the queen, "this is death. Kill me though at once, by saying that he does not love me. Now he loves me not."

"The love or indifference of Monsieur de Charny are his secrets. It is not for me to unveil them."

"His secrets? They are not his alone, for I presume he has made you his confidante."

"The Count de Charny never whispered a word either of his love or indifference to me."

"Not even this morning?"

"I did not see Monsieur de Charny this morning."

The queen looked at the countess with a penetrating glance, as if she would seek the very inmost part of her heart.

"Do you mean to say that you are ignorant of the count's departure?"

"I do not."

"How could you know if you have not seen him?"

"He wrote to tell me of it."

"Ah!" said the queen, "he wrote."

As Richard III., in an important moment, exclaimed, "My kingdom for a horse!" Marie Antoinette was ready to say, "My kingdom for that letter!"

Andrée saw the queen's anxiety, but could not resist the temptation of leaving her to revel for a time in anguish and vexation.

"I am sure you have the letter the count wrote at the very moment of his departure now upon your person."

"Yes, madame; here it is."

Taking the letter, heated by the fever of her heart and embalmed by its perfume, from her bosom, she gave it to the queen.

Marie Antoinette trembled as she took it, clasped it for a moment in her fingers, and seemed to hesitate if she should read or return it. She looked at Andrée between her eyelashes, and at last, casting aside all hesitation, opened and read the following letter:

"MADAME,—I quit Paris in an hour, in obedience to the king's order.

"I cannot tell you whither I go, or why, nor how long I will be absent. These things concern you but little, yet I regret that I am not authorized to tell you.

"I at first intended to present myself to you to inform you, in person, of my departure. I did not dare to do so, however, without your leave."

The queen knew all that she wished to know, and was about to return the letter to Andrée, but the latter, as if it were her part to obey and not to command, said:

"Read, madame, to the end."

The queen resumed her reading:

"I had refused, recently, the mission to Turin, because, fool as I was, I thought something of sympathy yet existed between us, and retained me at Paris. I have proof to the contrary, and gladly accepted an occasion to tear myself from one who is indifferent to me.

"If, during my journey, I shall die, as my poor brother George did, all steps are taken to inform you, first of the blow which has stricken me, and of the liberty restored to you. Then only, madame, you will know the deep admiration which your profound devotion, so badly rewarded by him to whom you have sacrificed youth, beauty, and happiness, has excited in my heart.

"Then, madame, all I ask of God and yourself is that you will think sometimes of the unfortunate wretch who, too late, discovered the value of the treasure he possessed.

"With all the devotion of my heart,

"OLIVIER DE CHARNY."

The queen gave the letter to Andrée, who took it, and suffered it to fall by her side. She uttered a deep and almost inanimate sigh.

"Well, madame," murmured Andrée, "are you betrayed? I will not say, have I broken my promise, for I never made one, but the confidence reposed in me——"

"Excuse me, Andrée, but I have suffered so much."

"You have suffered? Dare you before me say you have suffered? What, then, shall I say? I will not say I have suffered, for I will not use a word another woman has employed to convey the same idea—no, I must have a new, unheard-of word to express, at once, the sum of all agony and torture. You have suffered, madame! You have not seen the man you love indifferent to you, turn on his knees, with his heart in his hand, to another woman; you have not seen your brother, jealous of that other woman, whom he worshiped as a pagan worships his god, fight with the man you loved; you have not heard the man you loved, and who was wounded by your brother, it was thought fatally, in his hour of delirium, calling for that other woman, whose confidante you were; you have not seen her glide, like a phantom, down a corridor, where you yourself were, to catch the accents of that madness, which proved that if mad love does not survive life, at least, it accompanies it to the tomb; you have not seen that man restored to life by a miracle of nature and science, rise from his bed to cast himself at her feet—at the feet of your rival, madame, for in love, magnitude of love is the measure of rank. In your despair you did not then, at the age of twenty-five, retire into a convent, and seek at the icy foot of the cross to extinguish the love which devoured you. One day, after a year passed in prayer, fasting, and vigils, you hoped, if not to have extinguished, at least to have repressed, the flame which devoured you; you have not seen your old friend, now your rival, who had known nothing of your feelings, seek out your retreat to ask, what?—that in the name of old friendship, which suffering had not changed, in the name of her honor as a wife, of the safety of her sovereign's ruined honor, to become, what?—the wife of the man whom for three years you had adored—become a wife without a husband, a veil between the eye of the public and another's happiness, like a pall, to hide the coffin from the public gaze. You succeeded, madame, not from pity, for jealousy is pitiless, but from duty, and knowing this, you accepted the sacrifice. You have not heard the priest ask if you would take one to be your husband, who never could be your husband; you have not felt that man press the ring over your finger, and make the symbol of eternal union an empty ornament; you did not leave your husband an hour after your marriage, never to see him again, but as the lover of your rival. Madame, the three years that have passed were three long years of agony."

The queen, with a trembling hand, felt for Andrée's.

Andrée put her own aside.

"I promised nothing, and have done all I should. You, madame," said the fair arraigner, "promised me two things."

"Andrée, Andrée!" said the queen.

"You promised me not to see Monsieur de Charny again. A promise, the more sacred as I did not ask it of you. Then you promised me, and this was in writing, that you would treat me as a sister. A promise, the more sacred because it was not solicited."

"Andrée!"

"Must I remind you of the terms of the promise you made me, of the solemn promise, when I sacrificed to you my life, my love? that is to say, my happiness in this world, and my salvation in the next. Yes, my salvation in the next; for who can say if God will forgive my mad desires and wishes? Well, madame, at the moment I was about to sacrifice everything for you, this note was handed to me. I see now every letter glaring before my eyes. It runs thus:

"'ANDRÉE,—You have saved me; I owe you my life, my honor. In the name of that honor, which cost you so dearly, I swear you may call me sister. Do so, and I will not blush.

"'I give you this note; it is the token of my gratitude; it is the dower I give you.

"'Your heart is the noblest of hearts, and will appreciate the present I give you.

"'MARIE ANTOINETTE.'"

The queen sighed sadly.

"Yes, I see; because I burned this note you fancied I had forgotten it? No, madame, you see that I have remembered every word, every letter, though you might not seem to think of it. Ah! I remember more."

"Pardon, pardon me, Andrée; I thought he loved you."

"You thought then it was a love of the human heart, that he loved another because he loved you less."

Andrée had suffered so much that she, too, became cruel.

"You also, then, have seen that he loved me less?" said the queen, with an exclamation of grief.

Andrée did not reply; she only looked at the despairing queen, and a smile played on her lips.

"But what must be done to retain this love, which is my very life? Oh! if you know that, Andrée, my friend, my sister, tell me, I beg and conjure you!"

Andrée drew back a step.

"Can I, whom he has never loved, madame, know that?"

"But he may love you. Some day on his knees he may make atonement for the past, ask your pardon for what he has made you suffer. Sufferings, too, are so soon forgotten. In the arms of one we love pardon is so soon granted to him who has made us suffer."

"Well, if such should be the case, if this misfortune befall, and it may be a misfortune to all, do you forget that before I become Charny's wife, I have a terrible secret, an awful confidence to impart, which, perhaps, will turn his love into hate? Do you forget, I must tell him what I have told you?"

"You will tell him that you were violated by Gilbert? Tell him that you have a child."

"Oh, madame, what do you take me to be, to entertain any doubt about the matter?"

The queen breathed again.

"Then," said she, "you will do nothing to attract Monsieur de Charny to you?"

"I will do no more, madame, in the future, than I have done in the past."

"You will not tell him, nor let him suspect that you love him."

"Not until he tells me that he loves me."

"And if he comes to tell you so, if you tell him that you love him, swear——"

"Madame!" said Andrée, interrupting the queen.

"Oh!" said the queen, "Andrée, my sister, my friend, you are right, and I am cruel, wrong, exacting. But, oh, when all abandon me, friends, power, reputation, I would at least wish love to remain."

"And now, madame," said Andrée, with the icy coldness which had never abandoned her, except during the few moments when she spoke of the tortures inflicted on her, "have you aught else to ask—any order to give?"

"No, thank you, none. I wished to restore you my friendship, but you reject it. Andrée, adieu, and accept at least my gratitude."

Andrée made a gesture with her hand, which seemed to repel this sentiment, as she had the offer of friendship, and left calmly and silently as a ghost.

"Oh! you are right, body of ice, heart of diamond, soul of fire, to accept neither my gratitude nor my friendship, for I feel it, and ask that God pardon me for it; that I hate you as I have hated none; for if he does not love you now, I am sure some day he will."

Then, calling Weber, she said:

"Tell my ladies that I will go to bed to-night without

them, and that, as I am suffering and fatigued, I wish to rest until ten o'clock. The first and only person I will see will be Monsieur Gilbert."

CHAPTER X.

THE FRENCH BAKER.

We shall not attempt to say how this night passed for the two women.

At nine o'clock in the morning only, we shall again seek the queen; her eyes are red with tears, her cheeks pale for want of sleep.

During some moments, although after the orders given no one dare enter her chamber, she heard around her apartment those comings and goings, those prolonged whisperings and murmurs which announced that something unusual was passing without.

In the midst of all these confused sounds, which seemed to flit along the corridor, she heard the voice of Weber, who ordered silence.

She summoned the faithful valet de chambre.

"What is it, then, Weber?" asked the queen. "What is passing in the château, and what do these sounds mean?"

"Madame," said Weber, "there is a fight on the part of the Cité."

"A fight?" said the queen; "and to what purpose?"

"No one knows as yet, madame; they merely say that it is an *émeute* on account of the bread."

At another time he would not have broached the idea to the queen that there were people who were dying of hunger; but since, during the journey to Versailles, she had heard the dauphin ask her for bread, without being able to give him any, she understood now the misery of famine and hunger.

"Poor people!" murmured she, recalling the words which she had heard on the route, and the explanation which Gilbert had given to these words, "they see well, now, that it is not the fault of either the baker or the bakery that they have not bread." Then aloud: "And do they not fear that it may become a grave matter?" she asked.

"I cannot tell you, madame. There are no two reports alike," answered Weber.

"Well," replied the queen, "run as far as the Cité, Weber; it is not far from here; see with your own eyes what is passing, and return to me here."

Weber left the château, gained the passage of the Louvre, darted over the bridge, and, guided by the shouts, and following the wave that rolled itself onward toward the archiepiscopal palace, he arrived on the Place de Notre Dame.

In proportion as he advanced toward the old part of Paris, the crowd became thicker and the shouts more vigorous.

In the midst of these cries, or, rather, of these shrieks, voices were heard, such as are only heard in the skies in days of tempest, and on the earth in the days of revolution. Voices cried out, "He is a forestaller! à mort! à mort! à la lanterne! à la lanterne!"

And thousands of voices which did not know what this all meant, and those of many women, boldly repeated, "He is a forestaller! à mort! à mort! à la lanterne! à la lanterne!"

All at once Weber felt himself struck by one of those shocks which occur in great masses of men, when a stream establishes itself, and he perceived coming up the Rue Chanoinesse a human tide, a living cataract, in the midst of which struggled an unfortunate being, pale, and with torn clothes.

It was after him that all these people hurried; it was against him that they raised their lamentations, their shrieks, their menaces.

One single man defended him against this crowd; a single man only tried to dam this human current.

This man, who had undertaken this labor of pity, in spite of ten, twenty, a hundred men, was Gilbert.

It is true that some among the crowd, having recognized him, commenced to cry out:

"It is Doctor Gilbert, a patriot, the friend of Monsieur Lafayette and of Monsieur Bailly. Listen to Doctor Gilbert!"

At these cries there was a halt for a moment, something like the calm that spreads itself over the waters betwixt two squalls. Weber profited by them to make his way to the doctor.

He accomplished this with great difficulty.

"Doctor Gilbert," said the valet de chambre.

"Ah!" said he, "is it you, Weber?"

And then he made him a sign to come nearer.

"Go," said he, in a low tone, "and announce to the queen that I shall come to her perhaps later than she expects me. I am busy saving a man."

"Oh, yes, yes!" said the unhappy hearer of these last words; "you will save me, will you not, doctor? Tell them I am innocent; tell them that my young wife is enceinte. I swear to you that I did not conceal any bread, doctor."

But, as if the plea and the prayer of the wretched one had only added fuel to hatred and anger half moldered out, the cries redoubled, and the menaces seemed about to be completed.

"My friends," said Gilbert, opposing himself to the crowd with an almost superhuman force, "this man is a Frenchman, a citizen like yourself; we must not, we cannot destroy a man without hearing him. Conduct him to the court, and afterward we'll see."

"Yes, yes!" cried some voices, belonging to those who had recognized the doctor.

"Monsieur Gilbert," said the valet de chambre of the queen, "hold your own. I will go and warn the officers of the district; the court is only a few paces off; in five minutes they shall be here."

And he slipped off and was lost in the crowd, without even waiting for the approbation of Gilbert.

Meanwhile, four or five people had come to assist the doctor, and had formed a rampart with their bodies round the unhappy one threatened with the anger of the crowd.

This rampart, weak as it was, restrained for a few moments the mutineers, who still continued to cry down the voice of Gilbert with their shouts, and those of the good citizens who had rallied round him.

Happily, at the end of five minutes, a movement was perceptible in the crowd; a murmur succeeded this, and this murmur was followed by the words:

"The officers of the district! the officers of the district!"

Before the officers of the wards the threats lessened, the crowd opened. The assassins had not as yet the word of command.

They conducted the wretched prisoner to the Hôtel de Ville. He kept fast hold of the doctor; he held him by the arm; he would not leave him.

Now, what about this man?

He is a poor baker, named Denis François, the same whose name we have already pronounced, and who furnished the rolls to the assembly.

This morning an old woman went into his shop, in the Rue du Marché-Palu, at the very moment when he was about to deliver his sixth baking of bread, and begin to knead the seventh.

The old woman asked for bread.

François said he had none, "But wait until my seventh baking, and you shall be served first."

"I wish for some directly," said the woman; "here is the money."

"But," said the baker, "it is true as I say, there is no more."

"Let me see."

"Oh!" said the baker, "enter; see for yourself; search everywhere. I should like nothing better."

The old woman goes in, seeks all over, ferrets about, opens a cupboard, and in this cupboard finds three rolls of about four pounds each, that the boys had put away for themselves.

She took one of them, went out without paying, and when the baker claimed the bread, she roused the people by crying, "that François was a forestaller, and that he had concealed half his baking."

An ancient recruiter of dragoons, called Fleur d'Epine, who was drinking in a public-house opposite, rushed out of the house, and took up the cry of the old woman.

At this double cry, the people ran together, shouting, seized him who is here now, repeated the forced cries, rushed to the shop of the baker, forced the guard of four men the police had stationed at his door, as at that of his neighbors, spread themselves about the shop, and, besides the two rasped rolls left and denounced by the old woman, found ten dozen small rolls, retained for the use of the deputies, who were holding a sitting at the archbishop's palace, that is to say, a hundred steps from there.

The wretched baker is immediately condemned. One voice, a hundred voices, two hundred, a thousand voices cried out, "down with the informer!"

There is quite a crowd, who howl, "À la lanterne! à la lanterne!"

At this moment the doctor, who was returning from making a visit to his son, whom he had again brought back to the Abbé Berardier, at the College of Louis le Grand, is attracted by the noise; he sees a lot of people who demand the death of this man, and he rushes forward to succor him.

There, in a few words, he learned from François of what he was accused. He knew the innocence of the baker, and so he had tried to defend him.

Then the crowd had pressed together, and threatened the poor baker and his defender. They anathematized both in the same words, and were ready to kill both with the same blow.

It was at this moment that Weber had arrived at the Place Notre Dame, and had recognized Gilbert.

We have seen how, after the departure of Weber, the officers of the ward had arrived, and the unhappy baker had been, under their escort, conducted to the Hôtel de Ville.

Accused, officers, and the irritated people, all had entered, *pêle mêle* into the Hotel de Ville, whose every place was immediately filled by workmen without work, and, poor devils, dying with hunger, always ready to mix themselves up in any *émeute*, and to bestow a part of the evils which they were undergoing on any one whom they suspected of being the cause of the public suffering.

Scarcely had the miserable François disappeared through the doorway of the Hôtel de Ville, than the cries were redoubled.

Some individuals, with features quite sinister, threaded the crowd, saying in a whisper:

"He is a forestaller, paid by the court! See, then, why they wish to save him!"

At these words, "He is a forestaller! he is a forestaller!" wound, serpent-like, from the midst of the angry crowd.

Unfortunately, it was still morning; and none of the men who had power over the people, neither Bailly nor Lafayette, was there.

Those who kept repeating in the crowd, "He is a forestaller! he is a forestaller!" knew this well.

At length, when they did not see the accused reappear, the cries changed into one immense hurrah, the threats into one universal howl.

These men, of whom we have spoken, slid through the door, climbed along the galleries, and penetrated even as far as the room where was the unhappy baker, whom Gilbert was defending his best.

On the other side, the neighbors of François, who had joined the tumult, persisted in declaring that he had given, since the commencement of the revolution, continual proofs of zeal; that he had kneaded as many as ten bakings a day; that as long as his brother bakers had wanted flour they had it from his own stock; and that in order to serve the public more promptly, besides his own oven, he had rented that of a pastry-cook's, whom he had made dry his wood for him.

When these depositions were at an end, it appeared that, instead of punishment, the man deserved a reward.

But on the place, on the galleries, and even in the

salon, they continued to cry, "Down with the forestaller!" and cried aloud for his death.

All at once a sudden rush was made in the saloon, opening the circle of the National Guard, which environed François, and separating him from his protectors. Gilbert crowded back to the side of the tribunal, saw twenty arms stretched out; seized, drawn, dragged by them, the accused cried for aid, for help—suppliantly stretched out his hands, but uselessly—uselessly did Gilbert make a desperate effort to rejoin him. The opening by which François had disappeared, little by little, closed upon him; as a swimmer drawn down by a whirlpool, he has struggled a moment, with clasped hands, despair in his eyes, and a voice gurgling in his throat till the waves have recovered him, and the gulf swallowed him up.

Deserted at this moment, he was lost.

Hurried down the staircase, at each step he had received a wound. When he arrived at the door, all his body was one vast sore.

It is no longer life which he begs—it is death.

In one second, the head of the unhappy François was separated from his body, and raised on the end of a pike.

On hearing the cries in the street, the rioters in the galleries and in the chambers rush out. They must see the sight to the end.

It is a curious sight, a head on the end of a pike! It is already the twenty-first, and they have never seen one since the 6th of October.

"Oh! Billot, Billot!" murmured Gilbert, as he passed from the hall, "how happy thou art to have left Paris!"

He traversed the Place de Grève, following the border of the Seine, and leaving afar off the bloody head and its howling convoy by the Bridge of Notre Dame, until he got half across the Quai Peletier, when he suddenly felt some one touch his arm.

He raised his head, uttered a cry, and would have stopped and spoken; but the man, whom he had recognized, had slipped a note into his hand, placed a finger on his mouth, and drew off, going to the side of the archbishop's palace.

Without doubt, this person wished to preserve an incognito, but a woman of the Halle, having seen him, clapped her hands, and cried :

"Ah ! it is Mirabeau."

"Vive Mirabeau !" cried immediately some five hundred voices, "vive the defender of the people ! vive our patriotic orator !"

And the tail of the cortège, which followed the head of the unfortunate François, hearing this cry, returned and formed an escort for Mirabeau, who was accompanied by a large crowd, always cheering, until he reached the archbishop's palace.

It was, indeed, Mirabeau who, returning from the sitting in the assembly, had met Gilbert, and had given him a note which he had just written on the counter of a shop, and which he supposed would make him come to his house.

CHAPTER XI.

THE ADVANTAGE OF HAVING THE DEAL.

Gilbert had rapidly read the letter just put into his hands by Mirabeau, had read it over more slowly a second time, had put it into his waistcoat-pocket, and, calling a coach, ordered himself to be driven to the Tuileries.

At the sight of Gilbert the queen uttered a cry.

A part of the coat and ruffles of the doctor had been torn in the struggle which he had maintained in endeavoring to save François, and some drops of blood stained his shirt.

"Madame," said he, "I crave pardon of your majesty in presenting myself thus before you, but I have already, in spite of myself, made you wait so long, that I was not willing that any further delay should take place."

"And this unfortunate one, Monsieur Gilbert ?"

"He is dead, madame; he has been assassinated, torn in pieces!"

"Was he in the least guilty?"

"He was innocent, madame."

"Oh, monsieur, the fruits of your revolution. After having satiated the grand seigneurs, all functionaries, the guards, see how they file themselves among one another; but there are, at any rate, means of executing justice on these assassins."

"We are silent on that head, madame. But it would be better still to prevent the murders than to punish the murderers."

"And how, my God, can that be done? The king and I would ask nothing better."

"Madame, all these evils come from a defiance of the people expressed toward the agents of the powers; put at the head of the government men who have the confidence of the people, and nothing of the like will happen."

"Ah! yes, Monsieur de Mirabeau and Monsieur de Lafayette, is it not so?"

"I had hoped that the queen had sent for me to say that she had persuaded the king not to be hostile to the combination which I had proposed to him."

"Doctor, will you tell me seriously that I ought to trust myself to a man who caused the 5th and 6th of October, and make peace with an orator, who has publicly insulted me at the tribune?"

"Madame, believe me, it was not Monsieur de Mirabeau who caused the 5th and 6th of October. It was hunger, the high price of grain and poverty, which commenced the work of the day; but it was an arm mysteriously powerful which did the work of the night. Perhaps, some day, I shall have to defend you from this side, and to struggle with this dark power, which pursues not only you, but all other crowned heads—not only the throne of France, but all the thrones of the earth. As true as I have the honor to lay my life at your majesty's feet and the king's, Monsieur Mirabeau had nothing to do with these terrible days, and he had learned at the assembly, even as others did, it might be a little time, perhaps even before the others, by a note, that the people were marching on Versailles."

"Then you believe, Monsieur Gilbert, that this man would consent to become attached to us?"

"He is quite so, madame; when Mirabeau separates himself from royalty, he is like a horse that prances, and only requires to feel the bridle and spur of his rider to return into its right road."

"But being already of the party of the Duke of Orleans, he cannot be a member of every party."

"That is your mistake, madame."

"Does not Monsieur Mirabeau belong to the party of the Duke of Orleans?" repeated the queen.

"He is so little attached to the Duke of Orleans, that when he discovered that that prince had withdrawn to England before the threats of Monsieur de Lafayette, he said, as he crushed the note of Monsieur de Lauzun, which announced the duke's departure. 'People say that I am one of the party of this man; I would not have him as a lackey.'"

"That speaks something in his favor," said the queen, trying to smile; "and if I could believe that, we could really rely upon him."

"Do you wish that I should repeat the words he said to me?"

"Yes; I shall be glad to hear them."

"Here they are, then, word for word. I fixed them in my memory, since I hoped at some time to have the opportunity of repeating them to your majesty. 'If you have the means of making yourself heard by the king and queen, persuade them that they and France are lost if the royal family does not leave Paris. I am busied with a plan to enable them to go out. At any rate, you may assure them that they may reckon upon me.'"

The queen became thoughtful.

"Then, the advice of Monsieur Mirabeau also is that we should quit Paris?"

"It was his advice at that time."

"And he has changed since?"

"Yes, if I may trust to a note received within the half hour."

"May I see this note?"

"It is intended for your majesty."

And Gilbert drew the paper from his pocket.

"Your majesty will excuse it," said he; "but it is on common paper, and was written on the counter of a wine store."

"Ah! that does not matter; paper and desk are quite in harmony with the politics of the present period."

The queen took the paper, and read:

"The events of to-day have changed the face of things.

"We can succeed well this deal.

"The assembly will be afraid, and will establish martial law.

"Monsieur de Mirabeau could sustain and carry the measure for establishing martial law.

"Monsieur de Mirabeau could advocate the giving more power to the executive.

"Monsieur de Mirabeau could attack Monsieur de Necker upon the revenue and taxes.

"In place of a Necker ministry, it would he easy to make a Mirabeau one, and Lafayette will back Mirabeau."

"But," said the queen, "this letter is not signed."

"Have I not had the honor to inform your majesty that it was Mirabeau himself who placed it in my hand?"

"What do you think of all this?"

"My opinion is that Mirabeau is perfectly right, and that the only thing that can save France is the coalition he proposes."

"Well, let Monsieur de Mirabeau send through you a list of the ministers he would support, and I will place it before the king."

"And your majesty will support it?"

"I will. Then, in the meanwhile, as a first proof of his loyalty, let Monsieur de Mirabeau support the proposition for establishing martial law and giving greater power to the executive."

"He shall do so. In return, whenever the fall of Monsieur Necker becomes likely, a Mirabeau and Lafayette ministry will not be received unfavorably?" asked Gilbert.

"By me? No. I am anxious to prove that I am quite willing to sacrifice my private feelings for the good of the state. But you must remember I cannot answer for the king."

"Your majesty will authorize me to tell Monsieur de Mirabeau that this list of proposed ministers is asked for by yourself?"

"I will permit Monsieur Gilbert to use his own discretion as to how far he trusts a man who is our friend today and may become our enemy to-morrow."

"On this point you may confide in me, madame; only, as the circumstances are of great importance, there is no time to lose; allow me, then, to proceed to the assembly and endeavor to see Monsieur de Mirabeau this very day."

The queen made with her hand a sign of acquiescence, and Gilbert then took leave. A quarter of an hour later he was in the assembly.

The assembly was in a very excited state on account of the crime committed at its very gates, and upon a man in some sense a dependent of theirs. The members hurried betwixt the tribune and their seats; betwixt their seats and the corridors. Mirabeau alone remained immovably in his place. He sat with his eyes fixed on the public tribune. His countenance brightened on seeing Gilbert.

Gilbert made a sign, which he answered by nodding his head.

Gilbert then tore a leaf from his pocket-book, and wrote:

"Your proposals are received; not by both, but by the one whom both you and I believe has the most power.

"They wish to have a list of the proposed members today.

"Cause more power to be given to the executive."

When he had folded the paper into the form of a letter and addressed it to Monsieur de Mirabeau, he called an usher and bid him carry it to its destination.

Mirabeau read it with such an expression of perfect indifference, that his nearest neighbor could not have guessed that the letter which he had just received corresponded exactly with his most ardent wishes ; and with the same indifference he traced a few lines upon a sheet of paper lying before him, and, carefully folding the paper, gave it to the usher.

"Carry this letter," said he, "to the gentleman who gave you the one you just now brought me."

Gilbert eagerly opened the paper.

It contained a few lines which would have altered the future state of France, perhaps, if its propositions had been fairly carried out.

"I will address the assembly, and assist as far as I can in carrying out your views.

"To-morrow I will send you a memoir on the present crisis, which I hope will be satisfactory.

"I send you the list of the ministers I propose ; but I should be quite willing to alter a few names if you should wish any change."

Gilbert tore a new leaf from his pocket-book, and wrote four or five lines, and gave them to the usher, who was not very far off.

"I am going to our mistress to inform her of what we wish, and to tell her on what conditions you will act ; send word to my house, the Rue St. Honoré, just below l'Assumption, just opposite the cabinet-maker Duplay's, the result of the sitting as soon as it is terminated."

Always anxious for excitement and to struggle with political feelings, the queen awaited Gilbert's return with some impatience, especially when listening to the narration of Weber.

This consisted of the terrible scene whose end Weber had arrived in time to witness.

Sent for information by the queen, he passed by one end of the Bridge of Notre Dame, while the other was occupied by the bloody cortége who bore the head of François.

Near the bridge a young woman, pale, frightened, with perspiration standing coldly on her brow, and who, in spite of a tendency to embonpoint already visible, was running at a tolerably quick pace toward the Hôtel de Ville, stopped suddenly.

This head, whose features she could not as yet distinguish, produced upon her, even at that distance, the effect of the ancient buckler.

And as the head approached her, it was easy to see by the expression of her face that she was all but changed into stone.

When the horrible trophy was not more than twenty paces from her, she uttered a cry, stretched out her hands with a desperate movement, and, as if the earth had fallen beneath her, she sunk fainting on the bridge.

It was the wife of François, already five months enceinte. They carried her away without her knowing it.

"Oh, my God!" said the queen, "it is a terrible testimony you have sent your servant to teach her that if she is unhappy there exist others still more so."

Just at this moment Gilbert entered. He did not meet a queen, but a woman—that is to say, a wife, a mother. Her state of feeling could not have been better, and Gilbert, with advice at least, came to offer the means to put an end to these murmurs.

And the queen, looking into his eyes, where tears were gathering, and on his brow, where the perspiration stood in big, heavy drops, seized Gilbert by the hands, and took from them the paper which they contained.

But before looking at this paper, important as it was, "Weber," said she, "if this poor woman is not already dead, I will receive her to-morrow; if she be really enceinte, I will be the godmother of the child."

"Ah, madame, madame!" cried Gilbert, "why cannot every Frenchman hear your voice broken with emotion, and see the hot tears run down your cheeks, as I do?"

The queen started; they were nearly the same words which, in a crisis equally critical, Charny had addressed to her.

She cast a hasty glance over the note of Mirabeau, but was too much troubled at this particular time to give an answer.

At seven o'clock in the evening, a valet without livery placed the following letter in Gilbert's hands:

"The sitting has been a warm one.

"Martial law was carried.

"Bugot and Robespierre wished to have a still higher court at law.

"I have caused it to be decreed that *lèse-nation* (a new word which we have created) shall be judged by the royal privilege of Châtelet.

"I rely with confidence for the safety of France on the royal power, and three-quarters of the assembly will support it.

"To-day is the 21st of October. I hope, even as it is, that royalty has made some progress since the 6th instant.

"Vala et me ama."

The note was not signed, but it was in the same handwriting as the one which referred to the ministerial changes, and that of the morning. It was truly the writing of Mirabeau.

Although one can easily understand all that Mirabeau had gained, and all that the royal family had conseqnently lost, we must inform our readers what the Châtelet really was.

One of its first judgments became the object of one of the most terrible scenes which occurred in the Grève in the year 1790, a scene since it is not foreign to our subject we shall find best to weave into our narrative.

Le Châtelet had been of great historical importance in history ever since the thirteenth century, and both as a tribunal and court had exercised great influence over the mighty ones during the five centuries succeeding the good King Louis IX. Another king, who was a builder, if ever there was one. He built Notre Dame. He founded the Hospitals de la Trinité, de St. Catherine, and de St. Nicholas, near the Louvre. He paved the streets of Paris. He had, in truth, a great bank to run to for all these expenses—the Jews, to wit. In 1189 he was tinctured with the follies of the time.

The folly of the time was the wish to take Jerusalem from the guardianship of the Soldan. He joined Richard Cœur de Lion, and started for the holy places. But before he went, in order that the good Parisians should not lose their time, and never dream, in their leisure moments, of revolting against him, as at his instigation they had revolted more than once, he left them a plan, and bid them execute it after his departure.

He left them a program, and bid them build one of those thick walls of the twelfth century, ornamented with towers.

This wall was the third which surrounded Paris.

It contained, within its bounds, a number of small hamlets, which were destined, eventually, to become a portion of the great whole.

These hamlets and villages, however poor and small they might be, possessed each their *justice seigneuriale*. All these *justices seigneuriales* contradicting one another, from time to time, caused great confusion in this strange capital. There was it seems, at this time, a certain *seigneur* of Vincennes, who, having apparently more to complain of these contradictions than any of the others, determined to put an end to them.

This *seigneur* was Louis IX.

As it is easy to understand that when Louis IX. distributed justice under the oak, now become proverbial, he did it as a *seigneur*, not as a king.

He ordered, however, as king, that all the causes determined by these petty *juges seigneuriales* should, by appeal, be brought before the Châtelet of Paris. The jurisdiction of the châtelet, consequently, was all-powerful.

The châtelet was then the supreme court of justice, until the parliament took upon itself to determine even the appeals of the châtelet. But the assembly was about to suspend these parliaments.

"We have buried them in a very lively fashion," said Lameth, in returning from the sitting.

And in place of parliament, upon the suggestion of Mirabeau, they were about to restore the privileges of the châtelet, and with increased powers.

This was a great triumph for royalty, since the crime of *lèse-nation* would be brought before its own courts.

The first crime that the châtelet had to take cognizance of was the one which we are going to narrate.

The very day of the promulgation of the law authorizing the power of the châtelet, two assassins of the unhappy François were hung in the Grève without any other trial than *l'accusation* and the notoriety of the crime.

Two cases remained for judgment. That of the farmer-general, Augeard, and that of the inspector-general of the Suisses, Pierre Victor de Bésenval.

These were two men devoted to the court, and for this reason they hastened to transfer their causes to the châtelet.

Augeard was accused with having furnished the funds with which the Camarilla of the queen paid in July the troops assembled in the Champs de Mars. The châtelet acquitted him without much scandal.

Bésenval's name could not have been more popular—the wrong way. He it was who commanded the Suisses at Réveillon, the Bastile, and the Champs de Mars. The people remembered these three circumstances, and were not indisposed to take their revenge.

Very precise orders were given to the court at châtelet; under any pretense, the king and queen wished M. de Bésenval to escape condemnation.

He knew there was only this double protection to save

him. As he entered the hall he was saluted, almost unanimously, with cries for his death. "Bésenval à la lanterne!" "Bésenval to the gallows!" was bellowed forth from all sides.

With great trouble silence was obtained.

One of the spectators profited by it. "I demand," cried he, in a loud strong voice, "that he be cut into thirteen pieces, and a piece sent to each canton."

But in spite of the charges brought against him, and the animosity of the audience, Bésenval was acquitted.

Indignant at this double acquittal, one of the spectators wrote four verses on a piece of paper, which he rolled into a ball and sent to the president.

The stanza was signed. This was not all; the president turned in order to seek out the author. The author, seated on the end of a bench, solicited by his gesture the attention of the president. But before him the countenance of the president fell. He did not dare to have him arrested. The author was Camille Desmoulins.

One of those who went out in the crowd, and who, to judge from his dress, was a simple bourgeois of the Marais, addressed one of his neighbors, and laying his hand on his shoulder, although he seemed to belong to a higher class, said to him:

"Well, Doctor Gilbert, what do you think of these two acquittals?"

The one whom he had addressed turned round and looked at the questioner, and seemed as if he wished to recognize the form, the tones of whose voice he had recognized.

"Of you, and not of me, my master, must that question be asked—of you, who know everything, the present, the past, the future."

"Well, then, I think, after these two shameless acquittals it will be best to pity the poor innocent fellow to be tried next in this court."

"But why do you think," asked Gilbert, "that the one who will succeed them will be innocent, and succeeding them, will be punished?"

"For the simple reason," answered the other, with some irony that seemed to be natural to him, "that it is customary in this world for the good to suffer for the bad."

Adieu, master," said Gilbert, taking his hand off Cagliostro, for even in these few words the terrible skeptic will have been recognized.

"And why adieu ?"

"Because I have something to attend to," said Gilbert, smiling.

"You are going somewhere ?"

"Yes."

"To whom ? To Mirabeau, to Lafayette, or to the queen ?"

Gilbert stopped and looked at Cagliostro with an uneasy air.

"Do you know that you frighten me ?" said he.

"On the contrary, I should reassure," observed Cagliostro.

"How so ?"

"Am I not one of your friends ?"

"I believe so."

"Be sure, and if you want any proof——"

"Well ?"

"Come with me, and I will give you information about these negotiations which you believe are so secret—information so secret that even you, who seem to be conducting them, know nothing about them."

"Listen," said Gilbert; "perhaps you will summon to you some of those influences which, with you, are familiar. But never mind, things are so dark that I think I would accept a little light even if it came from Satan himself. I will follow you or you may conduct me."

"Oh, be easy; it won't be far, and it shall be in a place where you are not known; only allow me to hail this coach that is passing; the style of dress in which I have come out prevented my bringing my carriage." And he made a sign to a coach that was on the other side of the way. The coach drew up, and both got in.

"Where shall I take you, my jolly bourgeois?" asked the cabman of Cagliostro, as if he knew, in spite of his apparently simple dress, that the latter led the other and molded him to his will.

"Where thou knowest," said Balsamo, making a kind of masonic sign.

The coachman looked at Balsamo with astonishment.

"Pardon, monseigneur," said he, "that I did not recognize you at once."

"This is never my case," said Cagliostro, in a firm, sonorous voice; "in spite of their number, I never forget any one, from the highest to the lowest of my subjects."

The driver shut the door to, mounted his box, and drove at a rapid rate to the corner of the Rue St. Claude.

The carriage stopped, and the porter saw the door open with such rapidity as showed the zeal and respect of the driver.

Cagliostro made a sign to Gilbert to get out first, and then he himself descended from the carriage.

"Have you nothing to say to me?" asked he.

"Yes, monseigneur," answered the driver; "I was to have made my report this evening, if I was lucky enough to meet you."

"Speak, then."

"That which I have to say, monseigneur, ought not to be heard or listened to by profane ears."

"Oh!" said Cagliostro, smiling, "he who listens to us is not quite one of the profane ears."

This was Gilbert, who had moved some distance.

But still he could not prevent himself looking at them and listening a little.

He saw a smile, as the driver spoke, flit across the countenance of Balsamo.

He heard the two names, Monsieur and Favras.

The report concluded, Cagliostro drew a double louis from his pocket, and wished to give it to the driver. But the latter shook his head.

"Monseigneur knows well," said he, "that it is forbidden to receive money for our reports."

"It is not for thy report I wish to pay thee, it is for the drive."

"For that I will accept it," said the driver. And, in taking the louis, he added: "Thanks, monseigneur, my day's work's done." And, jumping lightly on his box, he drove off at a round trot, and left Gilbert struck with amazement at what he had just heard.

"Come," said Cagliostro, who was holding the door open for Gilbert, who never dreamed of entering, "will you not come in, my dear doctor?"

"Yes," said Gilbert, "excuse me."

And he crossed the threshold, staggering like a drunken man.

In the antechamber he saw the same German servant whom he had met here sixteen years before. He was standing in the same place, and held in his hands a similar book; only like himself, the count and the very chamber itself, he had aged sixteen years.

Fritz guessed from his eye the passage down which his master intended to conduct Gilbert, and, rapidly opening two doors, he stopped at the third, to see if Cagliostro had any further orders to give.

This third door was that of the salon.

Cagliostro made a sign to Gilbert to enter the salon, and another to Fritz to retire. Only he said, "I am not at home until further orders." Then, turning toward Gilbert, "Now, sit down; I am quite at your service, dear doctor."

Gilbert sighed, and leaned his head on his hand. The memories of the past had mastered for a time, at least, his present curiosity.

Cagliostro looked at Gilbert as Faust might have looked at Mephistopheles, when that German philosopher imprudently let him go before him.

All at once he said:

"It seems, dear doctor, that you recognize this room again."

"Yes," said Gilbert; "and it recalls the many obligations I owe you."

"Ah! bah! trifles!"

"In truth," said Gilbert, addressing himself as much as Cagliostro, "you are a strange man, and if all-powerful reason would permit me to place any faith in the magic stories of the Middle Ages, I should be tempted to believe that you were a sorcerer like Merlin, or a melter of gold like Nicolas Hamel."

"To the world I am so, but not to you. I have never endeavored to deceive you by marvels. You know I have always made you understand everything, and if sometimes you have seen truth at my summons issue forth from her well, better dressed and clad than is her wont, it is true, Sicilian as I am, that I have a taste for tinsel. But let the events of the past sleep quietly in the past, in their tomb; let us speak of the present; let us speak of the future, if you like."

"Count, you have called me back to realities. The future! What if this future was in your hands! What if your eyes could read the indistinct hieroglyphics?"

"Let us see, then, doctor, how we are as regards these ministerial arrangements."

"Ministerial arrangements?"

"Yes; of our Mirabeau and Lafayette ministry."

"That is one of those vague rumors you, like others, have heard repeated, and you wish, by questioning me, to ascertain their truth."

"Doctor, you are the very incarnation of doubt, and if there is anything terrible, it is that you doubt not because you do not believe, but because you do not wish to believe it. It will be the best to tell you at first what you know as well as I do, and afterward I will tell you what I know better than you."

"I listen, count."

"For the last fifteen days you have spoken to thy king of Monsieur de Mirabeau as the only man who can save the monarchy."

"It is my opinion, count; hence you will easily understand the present coalition."

"It is mine, too, doctor; hence the coalition you have presented to the king will fail."

"Will fail?"

"The king, sufficiently struck by what you had told him—pardon me, but I am obliged to commence from the beginning, in order to show you that I am not ignorant of any one phase of the negotiation—the king, I say, sufficiently struck by what you had told him, has conversed with the queen concerning the combination, and the queen was less opposed to the project than the king even; she discussed with you the for and against, and finished by authorizing you to speak to Monsieur de Mirabeau. Is not that the truth, doctor?" said Cagliostro, looking Gilbert in the face.

"I must confess that to this time you have kept on the right way."

"Well, the queen yielded for two reasons; the first is, that she has suffered much, and to propose an intrigue to her is to assist her to forget; the second reason is, that the queen is a woman, and she has been told that Monsieur de Mirabeau is like a lion, a tiger, a bear, and no woman knows how to resist the wish so flattering to their vanity, to tame a bear, a tiger, a lion. She said, 'It will be curious to bring to my feet the man who hates me, and cause him to apologize on the very tribune where he insulted me. I shall see him at my knees; this shall be my reward, my vengeance. And if from this genuflexion any good results to France and royalty, so much the better.' But I tell you that Mirabeau, the man of genius, the man of wit, the great orator, will spend his life and sink into the tomb without ever arriving at what all the world would have him attain—that is to say, he will never be minister. Ah! mediocrity, after all, dear Gilbert, is a great protection."

"Then," asked Gilbert, "the king opposes the arrangement?"

"Peste! he takes care; he must discuss the matter with the queen, when he has nearly pledged his word. You know, the politics of the king consist in that one word, *nearly;* he is nearly constitutional, he is nearly philosopher, he is nearly popular. Go to-morrow to the assembly, my dear doctor, and you will see what will happen."

"Can you not tell me beforehand?"

"You shall have the pleasure of being surprised."

"To-morrow? It is a long time."

"Then do better. It is five o'clock; in another hour the Jacobin Club will open. You know these Jacobins are night-birds. Do you belong to the society?"

"No; Camille Desmoulins and Danton made me belong to the Cordeliers."

"As I said, the Jacobin Club will meet in an hour. It is a society well put together, and one in which you will not be out of place—be easy. We will dine together; after dinner we will take a carriage; we will go to the Rue St. Honoré, and then, forewarned twelve hours, you will have time, perhaps, to prepare for the blow."

"Monseigneur, dinner is served," said a valet, opening the two leaves of a door leading into the dining-room, splendidly lighted and sumptuously furnished.

"Come," said Cagliostro, taking the arm of Gilbert.

Gilbert followed the enchanter, entertaining some hope that he might gain a little light from the conversation to guide him through the dark night which seemed now to surround him.

Two hours after a carriage without liveries or emblazonries stopped before the steps of the Eglise St. Roch.

Two men, dressed in black, descended from the vehicle, and passed along the right side of the street, to the little gateway of the Convent of the Jacobins.

The two newcomers had only to follow the crowd, for the crowd was great.

"Will you go into the nave, or take a place in the tribune?" Cagliostro asked Gilbert.

"I believe," said Gilbert, "the nave is devoted solely to the members."

"Without doubt," said Cagliostro, smiling; "but do not I belong to all societies, and since I belong to them, do not my friends, too? Here is a ticket for you, if you wish; as for me, I have only to speak one word."

"They will recognize us as strangers and make us go out," observed Gilbert.

"The society of the Jacobins has been founded three months; there are already sixty thousand members in France, and there will be four hundred thousand before the year is out; moreover, my dear friend," said Cagliostro, smiling, "here is truly the Grand Orient, the center of all secret societies, and not with that imbecile Fauchet, as some think, and if you have not the right to enter here as a Jacobin, you have the right to a place as one of the Rose Cross."

"No matter," said Gilbert: "I like the tribunes best."

"To the tribunes, then," said Cagliostro. And he went to the right, up a staircase, which conducted to the improvised tribunes.

The tribunes were full, but to the first one he addressed Cagliostro had only to make a sign, and speak one word in a low tone, and two men who were seated before him, as if they had been forewarned of his intended arrival and were only there to guard the seats of himself and Dr. Gilbert, immediately rose and retired.

The sitting had not as yet commenced. The members of the assembly were spread confusedly over the nave; some formed themselves into groups, and others promenaded in the narrow space left them by their numerous colleagues, while others sat alone in the shade leaning against the massive pillars.

A few lights sprinkled here and there lessened the gloom and lighted up the countenances and figures of those who happened to be standing near them.

It was easy to see, in spite of the darkness, that in the midst an aristocratic reunion existed. Embroidered coats, and the naval and military uniforms of the officers mottled the crowd with their reflections from the gold and silver.

For the lower class there was a second salle below the first, which opened at a different hour, so that the people and the aristocracy did not elbow one another. For the instruction of the people, they had founded a fraternal society.

As for the Jacobins, they were at this time a military society; aristocratic, intellectual, and, above all, literary and artistic.

In reality, men of letters and artists were in the majority.

Gilbert cast a long look at this brilliant assembly, recognizing each and calculating in his mind all their different capacities.

Perhaps this royal assembly comforted him somewhat.

"In one word," said he to Cagliostro, "what man do you see among all these men who is really hostile to royalty?"

"Should I examine them with the eyes of all the world, with yours, or with those of Monsieur Necker, with those of the Abbé Maury, or with my own?"

"With your own," said Gilbert. "Is it not fit that they should be the eyes of a sorcerer?"

"Very well, then, there are two who are hostile to royalty."

"Oh! that's not many among four hundred men."

"It is enough, if one of these two men is to be the slayer of Louis XVI. and the other his successor!"

Gilbert started. "Oh!" murmured he, "are there here a future Brutus and a future Cæsar?"

"No less, my dear doctor."

"You will point them out, will you not, count?" with a smile of doubt upon his brow.

"Oh! unbeliever whose eyes are covered with scales," murmured Cagliostro. "I will do more if you wish; I will let you touch them with your finger; with which one will you begin?"

"I think with the renverseur. I have a great regard for chronology. Let us begin with Brutus."

"Thou knowest," said Cagliostro, becoming animated as if he were inspired, "thou knowest that men do not always pursue the same end by the same means. Our

Brutus to us will not resemble in any way the Brutus of old."

"Only another reason why I should wish to see him."

"Very well," said Cagliostro; "look at him."

And he stretched his arm in the direction of a man who leaned against the pulpit, whose head only just at this moment stood forth in the light, and the rest of whose body was in the shade.

This head, pale and livid, seemed like a head nailed in the ancient days of proscription to the tribune.

The eyes alone seemed to sparkle with an expression of hatred almost disdainful, with the expression of a viper that knows its tooth contains a mortal venom. They followed in their numerous evolutions the fiery and wordy Barnave.

Gilbert felt a chill run through his whole body.

"Really," said he, "you have warned me beforehand; there is here neither the head of Brutus nor that of Cromwell."

"No," said Cagliostro; "but it is perhaps that of Cassius. You know, my dear fellow, what Cæsar said: 'I do not fear all these fat men, these bon-vivants, who pass their days at the table and their nights in orgies; no, those that I fear are the dreamers, with their thin bodies and pale visages.'"

"He whom you have pointed out certainly fulfils these last conditions.

"Then, do you not know him?" asked Cagliostro.

"Ay," said Gilbert, looking at him with attention. "I know him, or, rather, I recognize him as a member of the National Assembly."

"You are right."

"For one of the most long-winded orators of the Left."

"You are right!"

"No one listens when he speaks."

"You are right."

"A little lawyer of Arras, called Maximilien de Robespierre."

"Quite right. Now look at his head with attention."

"I do."

"What do you see?"

"Count, I am not a Lavater."

"No, but you may be a disciple."

"I see there is an expression of hatred to genius."

"That is to say, that you, too, judge him like the rest of the world. Yes, it is true, his voice, feeble and a little sharp, his thin and sad face; the skin of his forehead, which seems drawn tightly over his skull, like yellow and immovable parchment; his glassy eye, which only now and then lets a flash of greenish light escape, and then immediately grows dull; this continual discord of the muscles and the voice; this laborious physiognomy, fatigued through its very immobility; this invariable olive-colored dress—yes, I can understand that all this ought not to make any very great impression on an assembly so rich in orators; one which has the right to be difficult to please, accustomed, as it is, to the lionlike face of Mirabeau, to the audacity of Barnave, to the sharp repartee of Maury, the warmth of Cazales, and the logic of Sieyès; but we cannot reproach him, as Mirabeau, with immorality; he is an honest man; he will not desert his principles, and if ever he deserts the law, it will be to destroy the old text with the new law."

"But then," asked Gilbert, "what is this Robespierre?"

"Well done, thou aristocrat of the seventeenth century!"

"What, then, is this Cromwell?" asked Earl Stafford, whose head the Protector cut off.

"A brewer, I believe."

"Would you have me believe that my head runs the same risk as that of Sir Thomas Wentworth?" said Gilbert, trying a smile, which froze on his lips.

"Who knows?" said Cagliostro.

"Then so much the more reason to take care," observed Gilbert.

"What is Robespierre? Well, perhaps no one in the whole of France knows except myself. I like to know whence come the elected of fate; it assists me to tell where they will go. The Robespierres were Irish ; perhaps their ancestors formed part of those Irish colonies which, in the sixteenth century, came to inhabit the seminaries and monasteries of our southern coasts. There they received from our Jesuits the good educations they were accustomed to give to their pupils. From father to son they were notaries. One branch of the family—that from which this man descends—established himself at Arras, a great center, as you know, of *Noblesse* and the Church. There were in the town two *seigneurs,* or, rather, two kings ; one was the Abbé of St. Waast, the other was the Bishop of Arras, whose palace threw one half the town into the shade. It was in this town that he whom you see there was born, in 17—. What he did as a child, what as a young man, and what he is doing at this moment, I will tell you in two words ; what he will do, I have already told you in one word. There were four children in the house ; the head of the family lost his wife ; he was *avocat aux conseils* at Arras ; he sunk into a profound melancholy ; he ceased to plead ; started for a journey, and never returned. At eleven years old, this one, the eldest, found himself at the head of the family in his turn—guardian of a brother and two sisters ; at his age—strange ! strange ! The child undertook the task, and became a man at once ; in twenty-four hours he became what he still remains. A countenance that seldom smiles, a heart that never has smiled. He was the best pupil of the college. One of the offices of the College of Louis le Grand, in the gift of the prelate, was obtained for him from the Abbé of St. Waast. He arrived alone at Paris with a recommendation to a canon of Notre Dame. In the same year the canon died ; nearly at the same time his youngest and best-loved sister died. The shadow of the Jesuits, whom they were about to expel from France, cast itself again upon the walls of Louis le Grand. You know this building, where even now your young Sebastian is studying, its courts dark and melancholy as those of the Bastile, would cloud the happiest countenance—that of young Robespierre was already pale ; they made them livid. Other children went out sometimes. For them the year had its Sundays and fête days; for the orphan, without protection, every day was the same. While the others enjoyed the air of their family, he breathed that of solitude, sadness, and melancholy. Hatred and envy grew up in his heart, and took away the flower from his soul. This hatred destroyed the child, and made him a dull young man. Some day they will not believe in the truth of a portrait of Robespierre at twenty-four, holding a rose in one hand and the other on his breast, with the device, "All for my friend!"

Gilbert sighed sadly when he looked at Robespierre.

"It is true," continued Cagliostro, "that when he took this device, and had himself painted thus, the girl swore that nothing on earth should separate their destiny; he also swore it, and he was a man to keep an oath. He traveled for three months, and returned to find her married. For the rest, the Abbé de St. Waast was still his friend; he had given the office in the College of Louis le Grand to his brother, and made him one of the judges of the criminal courts. A case to be tried—an assassin to punish—came on. Robespierre, too full of remorse to dare to take the life of a man, although guilty, gave in his resignation. He became an *avocat* because he wished to live with and maintain his young sister. The brother got on badly at Louis le Grand, but afterward succeeded better. At last the peasants begged him to plead for them against the Bishop of Arras. The peasants were right; Robespierre was convinced of this by a strict examination of the evidence; pleaded, gained the cause for the peasants, and, still warm with success, was sent to the assembly. At the National Assembly, Robespierre found himself placed betwixt powerful hatreds and profound contempt—hatred from the clergy for having dared to plead against a bishop; contempt from the nobles, since he had been brought up through charity."

"But tell me," interrupted Gilbert, "what has he done up till to-day?"

"Oh, my God! perhaps nothing too thers—enough to

me. If it did not coincide with my views, the fact of this man being poor, I would give him a million to-morrow."

"Once again I ask you, what has he done?"

"Do you remember the day when the clergy came to the assembly to pray the state, kept in suspense by the royal veto, to commence their labors?"

"Yes."

"Then read the speech made by the little lawyer of Arras on that day, and you will see that if there is not a future shadowed forth in this sour vehemence, there is at least eloquence."

"But, then?"

"Then? Ah! it is true we must skip from May to October, when, on the 5th, Maillard, the delegate of the women of Paris, came in the name of his clients, to address the assembly. Well, all the members of the assembly remained immovable and silent. This little lawyer not only showed himself more cross and sour, but more audacious than any. All the pretending defenders of the public were silent; he rose twice. The first time in the midst of a tumult, the second time in the midst of silence. He assisted Maillard, who spoke in the name of the famine, and who asked for bread."

"Yes, in effect," said Gilbert, thoughtfully; "but, perhaps, he will change."

"Oh, my dear doctor, you do not know the Incorruptible, as they called him one day; otherwise who could buy this little lawyer, who laughs at all the world? This man who, a little later—listen, Gilbert, well to what I am now saying—will be the terror of the assembly, is to-day the butt. It is agreed among the Jacobin nobles that Monsieur de Robespierre is the ridiculous man of the assembly—the one who amuses everybody, and one whom all may jeer. In the eyes of Lameth, of Cazales, of Maury, of Barnave, of Dupont, Monsieur de Robespierre is a ninny. When he speaks, all the world talks; when he raises his voice, all cry out; and when he has pronounced—always in favor of right, and often to defend a principle—a discourse to which no one has listened, the orator fixes his eyes upon some member—no matter which—and asks ironically what impression his speech has made. One only of his colleagues understands him. Guess who that is. Mirabeau. 'This man will go great lengths,' he said to me the day before yesterday, because he believes what he says'—a thing which you know well seems singular to Mirabeau."

"But," said Gilbert, "I have read the speeches of this man, and have found them flat and dull."

"Eh, mon Dieu, I never said he was a Demosthenes, or a Cicero ; a Mirabeau, or a Barnave. No ; Monsieur de Robespierre is what one chooses to call him. And then they have treated his speeches at the printer's much in the same way as in the tribune—at the tribune they interrupted him, in the printing-house they mutilated them. The journalists do not even name Monsieur de Robespierre. No ; the journalists do not know his name. They call him Monsieur B——, Monsieur N——, or Monsieur. God and myself alone, perhaps, only know what there is in that breast, in that heart. In his melancholy apartments of the Trist Marais, in his cold lodging, poor, badly furnished, in the Rue Saintonge, where he lives carefully on his salary as deputy, he is as lonely as he was in the damp courts of Louis le Grand. Until the last year his countenance still looked young. He does not leave the Jacobins, and from emotion which is invisible to all, he has suffered hemorrhage, which has left him senseless two or three times. You are a great algebraist, Gilbert, but I defy you to calculate the blood which it will cost this noblesse who insult him, these priests who persecute him, the king who ignores him, the blood which Robespierre loses."

"But why does he come to the Jacobin Club ?"

"It is that, hissed at the assembly, he is listened to at the Jacobin. Of the Jacobins Robespierre is the type ; society abridges itself in him, and he is the expression of society ; nothing more, nothing less ; he walks in the same time as society does, without following it, without being in advance. I promised you, did I not, to let you see a little instrument which has for its object the taking off a head, perhaps two, in a minute? Well, of all the people here present, the one who will give most employment to this deadly machine is the little lawyer of Arras, Monsieur de Robespierre."

"In truth," said Gilbert, "you are somewhat funereal, and if your Cæsar does not make up for your Brutus, I am capable of forgetting the cause for which I came here. Pardon, but what about Cæsar?"

"Look! you may see him down there. He speaks with a man whom he does not know as yet, but who will exert a great influence over his destiny. This man calls himself Barras; will you recollect this name, and recall it when necessary?"

"I do not know, count, whether you deceive yourself or not," said Gilbert, "but in any case you have chosen your types well. Your Cæsar has a good forehead to carry a crown on, and his eyes, though I cannot exactly catch their expression——"

"Yes, because they are cast down. It is those very eyes which point out the future, doctor."

"And what says he to Barras?"

"He says that if he had defended the Bastile, it would not have been taken."

"Then he is not a patriot?"

"Men like him do not wish to be anything, until they can be it completely."

"And so you have the pleasantry to think so much of this little sous-lieutenant?"

"Gilbert," said Cagliostro, as he stretched his hand toward Robespierre, "as surely as one shall reconstruct the scaffold of Charles I., so surely shall that one," and he pointed to the sous-lieutenant, "so surely shall he reconstruct the throne of Charlemagne."

"Then," cried Gilbert, discouraged, "our struggle for liberty is useless?"

"And who has told you that the one will not do as much for her with the throne as the other with the scaffold?"

"He will be, then, a Titus, a Marcus Aurelius, the

god of peace, coming to console the world for the age of brass."

"He will belong to the line of Alexander and Hannibal. Born in the midst of war, he will become great through war, and fall by war. I have defied you to calculate how much blood, the blood lost by Robespierre, will cost the noblesse and the clergy; take the blood which will be lost by priests and nobles, multiply them time after time, and you will not have obtained a knowledge of the river of blood, the lake, the sea of blood, which this man, with his army of five hundred thousand men, and his battles lasting three days, will spill."

"And what will be the result of all this?"

"That which results from the beginnings. Gilbert, we are charged to bury the old world; our children will see a new world born. This man is the giant who guards the door. Like Louis XIV., like Leo X. and Augustus, he will give his name to the age which he commences."

"And what is his name?" asked Gilbert, in some measure controlled by the air of conviction evident in Cagliostro.

"He is only called Bonaparte at present," replied the prophet, "but some day he will call himself Napoleon."

Gilbert rested his head on his hand, and sunk into a reverie so deep that he did not perceive at once that the séance was opened, and that an orator had mounted the tribune.

An hour had passed before the different noises of the assembly had power sufficient to draw Gilbert from his meditations; not until he felt a hand, strong and powerful, laid upon his shoulder.

He turned; Cagliostro had disappeared, but in his place he found Mirabeau.

Mirabeau's countenance was filled with anger.

Gilbert looked at him with a questioning eye.

"So!" said Mirabeau.

"What is it?" asked Gilbert.

"It is that we are played with, baffled, betrayed; it is

that the court does not wish my services; that it has taken me for a dupe, and you for a fool."

"I do not understand you, count."

"You have not heard, then?"

"What?"

"The resolution which has just been taken."

"Where?"

"Here."

"What resolution?"

"Then you have slept, have you?"

"No," said Gilbert; "I dreamed."

"Well, to-day, in reply to my motion of yesterday, which proposes to invite the ministers to assist at the national deliberation, three friends of the king demanded that no member of the assembly should be a minister during the session. Then, this combination so laboriously constructed, passed away before the capricious breath of His Majesty Louis XVI. But," continued Mirabeau, in the meanwhile, like Ajax, his finger points heavenward, "but, as sure as my name is Mirabeau, I will repay them; and if their breath can overturn a ministry, I will show them that mine can upset a throne."

"But," said Gilbert, "you will not go less to the assembly? You will struggle to the end?"

"I will go to the assembly; I will struggle to the end. I am one of those buried, but beneath ruins."

And Mirabeau, half exploding, became more beautiful and terrible from the divine furor which the thunder of his passion had stamped upon his face.

The very next day, indeed, upon the proposition of Lanjuinais, in spite of the efforts of the superhuman genius brought to bear on the question by Mirabeau, the National Assembly adopted the following motion by an immense majority: "That no member of the assembly could be a minister during the session."

"And I," cried Mirabeau, when the decree was voted, "propose an amendment, which shall alter nothing—here it is. 'All the members of the present assembly may

"HE TOOK THE PEN, AND WROTE, 'FLY! FLY! FLY!'"

Dumas, Vol. Ten

hold office and become ministers, except Monsieur le Comte de Mirabeau.'"

Deaf to this audacity, although spoken in the midst of universal silence, Mirabeau descended from his desk with that step with which he had marched to M. de Dreux-Breze, when he said to him :

"We are here by the will of the people, we shall not go out except with a bayonet in our stomach." He left the salle.

The defeat of Mirabeau resembled the triumph of another.

Gilbert had not even come to the assembly. He had remained at home, and dreamed over the predictions of Cagliostro without believing ; but meanwhile he could not banish them from his mind. The present seemed to him very little when compared with the future.

CHAPTER XII.

METZ AND PARIS.

As Cagliostro had said, as Mirabeau had foretold, it was the king who had caused all Gilbert's plans to prove abortive. The queen, who in the offers made to Mirabeau, had placed more reliance on the curiosity of a woman than the policy of a queen, saw without great regret the fall of the whole constitutional structure. As for the king, it was his policy to wait, to gain time and profit by circumstances. These, besides two foreigners, offering an escape from Paris and a retreat to some fortress. This was his favorite idea.

These two negotiations we know were those brought about on the one hand by M. de Favras, the agent of Monsieur, and that of Charny, emphatically the man of Louis XVI.

Charny had gone from Paris to Metz in two days. He had found M. de Bouille at Metz, and had given him a letter. This letter, be it remembered, was but a method of putting Charny in communication with M. de Bouille, who, though more discontented with the state of things, acted with great reserve.

Before he gave Charny an answer, Bouille, determined, under the pretext that Charny's powers were not extensive enough, to send to Paris, and communicate directly with the king. He selected his son, Count Louis Bouille.

Charny would, during these negotiations, remain at Metz. There was nothing to call him from Paris, and his almost exaggerated honor made him feel it obligatory on him to remain at Metz, as it were, a hostage.

Count Louis reached Paris about the middle of November. At this time the king was watched by M. de Lafayette, and Count Louis de Bouille was his cousin.

He went to the house of one of his friends whose patriotic sentiments were well known, and who then traveled in England.

To enter the Tuileries unknown to M. de Lafayette, was then, if not impossible, at least very dangerous to the young man.

On the other hand, as Lafayette must necessarily be in total ignorance of the communications of the king to M. de Bouille, nothing was easier than for Count Louis to call on his cousin Lafayette.

Circumstances seemed to contribute to the young officer's wishes.

He had been three days in Paris without coming to any decision, and ever thinking on a way to reach the king, and asking himself if it was not better to call at once on Lafayette, when he received a letter stating that his presence in Paris was known, and inviting him to the headquarters of the staff of the guard at the Hôtel de Noailles.

The count went to headquarters. The general was just going to the Hôtel de Ville, where he had business with Bailly. He, however, saw the general's aide-de-camp, Romœuf.

Romœuf had served in the same regiment with the young count, and though one belonged to the aristocracy and the other to the democracy, they were friends. Since then Romœuf had gone into one of the regiments disbanded after July 14th, and served only in the National Guard, where he was aide-de-camp of Lafayette. The two young men, though differing in other matters, each bore love and respect to the king. One loved him, however, as a patriot, provided he swore and maintained the constitution; while the other loved him as the aristocrats did, on condition that he would refuse the oath and appeal, if necessary, for strangers to bring the people to their senses.

Romœuf was twenty-six, Louis de Bouille twenty-two. They could not, therefore, talk politics long.

Count Louis, too, did not wish even to be suspected to have any serious idea.

As a great secret, he told Romœuf that on a simple leave he had come from Paris to see a woman he adored.

While he thus confided in the aide-de-camp, Lafayette appeared at the threshold of the door, which had remained open; though he perfectly saw the newcomer in the glass placed before him, M. de Bouille went on with his story; only, that in spite of the signs of Romœuf, which he pretended not to understand, he raised his voice, so that the general did not lose a word of what was said.

The general heard all precisely as young Bouille had intended he should.

He continued to advance behind the narrator, and put his hand on his shoulder. "Ah! ha! Monsieur de Libertin. This is the reason why you hide yourself from your relations."

The young general of thirty-two was not a very rigid monitor, for at that time he was much sought after by the women of fashion. Louis was not much afraid of the blowing up he was to get.

"I did not hide, my dear cousin, for on that very day I intended to have the honor to present myself to the most illustrious of them, and would have done so had I not been anticipated by this message."

He showed the letter he had just received.

"Well, then, do you country gentlemen say that the Parisian police is badly organized?" said the general, with an air of satisfaction, proving that on that head his self-esteem was interested.

"We know, general, that we can hide nothing from Him who watches over the people's liberty and the king's life."

Lafayette looked aside at his cousin, and with an expression at once kind, spiritual, and mixed something with raillery, which we ourselves have seen him use. He knew that the safety of the king was a great matter of interest to this branch of the family, though popular liberty was of little importance in its eyes. Hence he only answered a portion of the last speech.

"And has the Marquis de Bouille, my cousin," said he, emphatically, using a title he had renounced after the night of the 4th of August, "given his son no commission to his king relating to the safety and watch over?"

"He bid me place at his feet the greatest protestations of respect," said the young man; "if General Lafayette does not think me worthy of being presented to my king."

"Present you? and when?"

"As soon as possible, general."

"Be it so."

"I believe I have had the honor of telling you or Romœuf that I am here without a leave."

"You told Romœuf; but, as I heard it, it is all the same. Well, good actions should not be retarded. It is eleven; I see the king every day at noon, and the queen also. Eat with me, if you have not breakfasted, and I will take you to the Tuileries."

"But," said the young man, looking at his uniform, "am I in costume?"

"In the first place, my child, I will tell you that the great questioner of etiquette, your nurse, is very sick, if not dead, since you left. When I look, though, your coat is irreproachable, and your boots clean. What other costume so becomes a gentleman ready to die for his king than his uniform? Come, Romœuf, see if breakfast is ready. I will immediately after take Monsieur de Bouille to the Tuileries."

The proposition was too much in accordance with the young man's wishes for him to make any real objections, so he bowed an assent at once, and thanked his kinsman.

Half an hour afterward, the sentinels at the gates presented arms to General Lafayette and the young Count de Bouille, without suspecting that they were at once paying military compliments to both revolution and counter-revolution.

Every door was opened to M. de Lafayette. The sentinels saluted, the footmen bowed; the king of the king, the *maise* of the palace, was easily recognized, as Marat said.

Lafayette was first introduced into the rooms of the queen; the king was at his forge.

Three years had passed since M. Louis de Bouille had seen Marie Antoinette.

The queen had reached the age of thirty-four, as Michel says, a touching age, which Vandyck so loved to paint; the age of a wife, the age of a mother, and, in the case of Marie Antoinette especially, the age of a queen.

During these three years, the queen had suffered much both in body and mind, and also in self-respect. Thirty-four years seemed, therefore, to be written on the cheeks of the poor woman by those slight, changeable, and violet lines which reveal eyes full of tears and sleepless nights, which betray some deep sorrow in a woman's heart, whether she be either woman or queen; sorrow incurable until it be extinguished.

This was the age of Marie Stuart when she was in prison. It was the age of her deepest passion, when Douglas, Mortimer, Norfolk, and Babington became enamored of her, devoted themselves to, and died for her.

This sight of this royal prisoner, hated, calumniated, maligned—the 5th of October had proven those signs not vain—made a deep impression on the chivalric heart of young Louis de Bouille.

Women are never mistaken in the influence they produce; and as kings and queens have a memory of faces they have seen, this is a portion of their education; as soon as Marie Antoinette saw M. de Bouille, she recognized him; as soon as she saw him, she knew she saw a friend.

The result was, that even before the general was presented, before he was at the foot of the divan on which the queen lay, and as one speaks to an old friend who has long been absent and who is welcomed back, or to a servant on whose fidelity we may rely, she exclaimed at once, "Ah! Monsieur de Bouille."

Without paying any attention to Lafayette, she offered her hand to the young man.

This was one of the queen's mistakes, and she committed many such. M. de Bouille was hers without this favor, and by this favor, granted in the presence of Lafayette, who had never been similarly honored, she established a sign of demarkation which wounded the man of whom she had most need as a friend.

Therefore, with a politeness which he never laid aside, but with some emotion in his voice, he said:

"On my honor, dear cousin," said Lafayette, "I offered to present you to her majesty, but it seems it had been the better for you to present me to her."

The queen was so happy to meet a person in whom she could confide; the woman, so proud of the effect she seemed to have produced on the count, that, feeling in her heart one of those ways of youth she had fancied extinguished, and around her those breezes of spring and youth she thought gone forever, turned toward Lafayette, and, with one of those smiles of Trianon and Versailles, said:

"General, Count Louis is not a severe republican, as you are. He has come from Metz, and not from America; he has not come to Paris to establish a constitution, but to do homage. Do not, therefore, be surprised if I grant him, though a poor and half-dethroned queen, a favor which, to a country gentleman like him, deserves to be called so, while to you——"

And the queen flirted almost as much as a young girl would, anxious to say, "while to you, Sir Scipio, while to you, Sir Cincinnatus, such things would be ridiculous."

"Madame," said Lafayette, "I have ever been kind and respectful to the queen, though she never understood my respect or appreciated my devotion; this is, to me, a great misfortune, but perhaps is a greater one for her." He bowed.

The queen looked at him with her clear blue eye; more than once Lafayette had spoken to her thus, and more than once had she reflected on his words. It was, however, her misfortune to entertain a repulsive and intense dislike to the man.

"Come, general," said she, "be generous; excuse me, pardon me."

"I pardon you, madame! For what?"

"My enthusiasm for those good De Bouilles, who love me with all their hearts, and of which that young man is an almost electric chain; I saw his father, his uncles, when he appeared and kissed my hand."

Lafayette bowed again.

"Now," said the queen, "having pardoned me, let there be peace. Let us shake hands, general, as Englishmen and Americans do."

She gave him her hand; it was open, with the palm upward, *en carte*. Lafayette touched, with a slow and cold hand, that of the queen, and said:

"I regret that you will never remember, madame, that I am a Frenchman. The 6th of October and 16th of November, however, are not very distant."

"You are right, general," said the queen, clasping his hand; "it is I who am ungrateful."

She sunk back on the sofa, as if she were overcome by emotion.

"This should not surprise you," she said; "you know the reproach is often made by me." Then, lifting up her head, she said, "Well, general, what news from Paris?"

Lafayette had a petty vengeance to exercise; he did so, and took the present opportunity.

"Ah, madame," said he, "how sorry I am that you were not yesterday at the assembly; you would have witnessed a touching scene, which certainly would have moved your heart; an old man came to thank the assembly and the king, for the assembly, you know, is powerless without the king, for the happiness he owed to it."

"An old man?" said the queen.

"Yes, madame; and what an old man! He is one of the deans of humanity, an old peasant, subject to the capital jurisdiction of his lord, a hundred and twenty years old. He was brought from the Jura to the bar of the assembly by five generations of descendants, to thank them for the decree of August 4th. Can you fancy how a man looked who was for fifty years a serf under Louis XIV., and seventy years since?"

"And what did the assembly do for this man?"

"It rose with one accord, and made him sit down and cover himself."

"Ah!" said the queen, with the tone peculiar to herself, "it must have been very touching; I am sorry I was not there. You, however, better than any one else, know that we cannot always be where we wish to be."

The general, by his motions, signified that he had nothing to say. The queen continued, though without the interruption of a moment.

"No, I was here, and received the wife of François, whom the National Assembly suffered to be killed at its very door. What was the assembly doing then, Monsieur de Lafayette?"

"Madame, you speak of one of the misfortunes which are most distressing to representatives of France. They could not prevent the murder, but at least they punished the murderers."

"Yes; but that is a small consolation to the poor woman; she is almost crazy, and it is thought that she will give birth to a still-born child. If the child live, I have promised to be its godmother, that the people may know that at least I am not insensible to its sorrows. I ask you, dear general, would it be inconvenient to christen the child at Notre Dame?"

"Madame, this is the second time you have alluded to the captivity in which, it is pretended to your faithful servants, that I keep you. Madame, I say, before my cousin, before Paris, before Europe, before the world, I wrote yesterday to Monsieur Monnier, who laments over your captivity in Dauphiny, that you are free. Madame, I have but one request to make, that the king resume his hunting and other excursions, and that you, madame, accompany him."

The queen smiled, like a person unconvinced.

"As for becoming godmother to the poor orphan about to be born in mourning, in promising to do so, the queen has obeyed only the dictates of that excellent heart, which makes all who approach love her; when the day appointed for the ceremony shall have come, the queen can select any church she pleases; she has but to order, which will be obeyed. Now," said the general, "I await her majesty's orders for to-day."

"To-day, my dear general," said the queen, "I have no prayer to address you, but that you invite your cousin, if he remain long in Paris, to one of the circles of the Princess de Lamballe; you know she receives both for herself and me."

"I, madame," said Lafayette, "will take advantage of the invitation, both for him and myself. If your majesty has not seen me there before, I beg you believe it was because you had ceased to manifest any wish to do so."

The queen replied by a bow and by a smile. This was a dismissal. Each one understood his own part of the scene. Lafayette took the dismissal to himself; Count Louis took the smile as his.

They both retired backward; the one having acquired, from this scene, far more bitterness, and the other inspired with far more devotion.

At the door of the queen's room the two visitors found the valet de chambre of the king, Hue.

The king wished him to say to M. de Lafayette that, having begun a curious piece of locksmithing, he wished him to come to the forge.

A forge was the first thing Louis XVI. asked after, on his arrival at the Tuileries, when he learned that this necessity had been forgotten by Catherine de Medici and

Philibert de Lorraine, he selected, on the second story, just above his bedroom, a great garret, with two stair-ways, one into his room, and the other in the corridor, as his locksmith shop.

Amid all the troubles that had assailed him during the five weeks he had been at the Tuileries, Louis XVI. had not forgotten his forge. His forge had been his fixed idea, and he had himself taken charge of the arrangement, prescribing a place for the bellows, the hearth, the anvil, the the bench, and the vise. The forge being fixed sound, bastards, hooks, pincers of every variety, were soon in their places, and every other imaginable thing, which locksmiths use, was in reach. Louis XVI. had not been able to resist any longer, and ever since morning had been busy at that trade which distracted his attention so completely, and in which, if we believe Master Gamain, he would have been a proficient, had not certain idlers, like Turgot de Calonne and M. Necker, diverted him from his business by talking of the affairs of France, which Gamain might submit to, but also of the affairs of Brabant, Austria, England, America, and Spain. This is the reason why, being busy with his work, Louis XVI., instead of coming to see Lafayette, had asked the general to come to him.

Perhaps, too, having shown the commandant of the National Guard his weakness as a king, he was not unwilling to exhibit himself in his majesty as a locksmith.

At the door of the forge, the valet bowed and said, as he was ignorant of De Bouille's name :

"Whom shall I announce ?"

"The general-in-chief of the National Guard. I will present this gentleman to his majesty."

"The commander-in-chief of the National Guard," said the valet.

The king turned around.

"Ah ! ha ! is it you, Monsieur de Lafayette ? I beg you excuse me for making you come hither, but the locksmith assures you that you are welcome to his forge. A charcoal-burner told Henry IV., my grandfather, that every charcoal-burner is lord of his skin. I tell you, general, that you are master both of the smith and of the king."

Louis XVI., it will be seen, began the conversation almost in the same manner that Marie Antoinette had.

"Sire," said Lafayette, "under whatever circumstances I may have the honor to present myself to you, in whatever story, or in whatever costume I find you, to me the king is ever the king, and I, who now offer you my homage, will ever be your true and devoted servant."

"I do not doubt it, marquis. Have you, though, changed your aide-de-camp, for I see that you are not alone? Does this young officer occupy the place of either Monsieur Gouvion or of Monsieur Romœuf?"

"This young officer, sire, whom I ask permission to present to you, is my cousin, Count Louis Bouille, captain of Monsieur's regiment of dragoons."

"Ah! ah!" said the king, exhibiting a slight emotion. "Yes, Count Louis Bouille, son of the Marquis de Bouille; excuse me for not having recognized you, but I am very short-sighted. Have you been long from Metz?"

"About five days, sire; I am in Paris without any official leave, but by permission of my father, and I came to ask General Lafayette, my kinsman, the honor of being presented to your majesty."

"Monsieur de Lafayette? you did well. No one was better calculated to present you at any time, and presentation by no one would be more agreeable to me."

"Your majesty," said Lafayette, not a little annoyed how to approach a king who had received him with his sleeves turned up, with a file in his hand, and wearing a leather apron, "has undertaken an important work."

"Yes, general; I have undertaken the great masterpiece of a locksmith, an entire lock. I'll tell you what I do, so that if Marat knew I had gone to work, and should say that I forged chains for France, you might tell him you knew better. You, Monsieur Bouille, are neither locksmith nor journeyman."

"No, sire, but I am an apprentice, and if I could in any way be useful to your majesty——"

"Ah! true; my dear cousin, was not the husband of your nurse a locksmith? Your father used to say that, although no admirer of the advice of the author of 'Emilie,' that if he had to follow them with regard to you, he would make you a locksmith."

"Exactly, sir; and that is why I had the honor to tell his majesty that if he needed an apprentice——"

"An apprentice would not be without his use to me, sir," said the king; "what I want, though, is a master."

"What kind of lock is your majesty making, though?" asked young De Bouille. "Spring, double bolt, catch lock, or what?"

"Cousin," said Lafayette, "I did not know you could be a practical man; but as a man of theory you seemed to me quite *au courant du jour*. I will not say of the trade, for the king has ennobled it, but of the art."

Louis heard the young gentleman mention the different kinds of locks with visible pleasure, and said:

"No, it is simply a secret lock, known as the Benarde lock, with bolts on both sides. I feel, though, that I have overestimated my power. Ah! had I but Gamain; he used to call himself master over master, master over all."

"Is he dead, then, sire?"

"No," said the king, glancing at the young nobleman, with an expression which seemed to say, "Do you not understand? No; he is at Versailles, Rue des Reservoirs, No. 9. The old fellow would not dare to come and see me at the Tuileries."

"How so, sire?" said Lafayette.

"For fear of compromising himself. Just now a king of France is a very dangerous acquaintance, and the evidence is, that all my friends are either at London, Coblentz, or Turin. But, my dear general, if you do not think it inconvenient for him to come with one of his apprentices to give the finishing stroke, I will send for him."

"Sire," said M. de Lafayette, quickly, "your majesty knows perfectly well that you can order what you please, and send for whom you will."

"Yes, provided they submit to be felt and handled by your sentinels as if they were smugglers. Poor Gamain would think himself lost if his files were considered poniards and his sack a cartouche-box."

"I cannot, sire, excuse myself; but I answer to Paris, to France, to Europe, for the king's life, and I cannot take too much precaution to preserve that precious, life. As far as the man you speak of is concerned, your majesty may give any orders you please."

"That is well; thank you, Monsieur de Lafayette, but I shall not need him or his apprentice for ten days," added he, looking at M. de Bouille aside. "I will send my valet de chambre, Durey, who is one of his friends, for him."

"When he comes, sire, he will be admitted to his king. His name will be his passport. God protect me, sire, from bearing the reputation of a jailer, of a watch-dog, or a turnkey. No king was ever more free than you are now. I have come even to beg your majesty to resume your hunting-parties and your excursions."

"My hunting-parties? no, thank you. Besides, just now I am thinking of other matters. My excursions, you see, are different. My last one, from Versailles to Paris, has cured me of all desire to wander, at least, with so many persons."

The king again glanced at young De Bouille, who by a slight motion of the eyes showed that he understood his words.

"Sire," said young De Bouille, "in two or three days I leave Paris; not, however, for Metz, but for Versailles, where I have an old grandmother, in the Rue des Reservoirs, whom I must see. Besides, I am authorized by my father to terminate an important family affair, and eight or ten days hence I am to see the person from whom I am to receive orders. I shall not, therefore, see my father until the early part of December, unless the king wishes me at once to go to Metz."

"No, monsieur, no. Take your own time at Versailles. Attend to the business, the marquis, your father, has confided to you, and when they are done, tell him that I do not forget him, that I know him to be one of my most faithful subjects, and that some day I will recommend him to Monsieur de Lafayette, that Monsieur de Lafayette may recommend him to Monsieur du Portail."

Lafayette smiled at hearing this allusion to his omnipotence.

"Sire, I would long ago have recommended both the Messieurs de Bouille to Monsieur du Portail had I not the honor of being their relation. The fear that it should be said I used the king's favor for the benefit of my family alone has prevented me."

"The king will permit me to say that my father would regard as an unkindness, as a disgrace, almost any promotion which would deprive him of the means of serving his king."

"Oh! that is well understood, and I will not permit the position of Monsieur de Bouille to be touched, except to make it more consonant with his wishes and with mine, Let Monsieur de Lafayette and myself attend to that, and attend to pleasure, without neglecting business. Go, gentlemen, go."

He dismissed the two nobles with an air of majesty, which strangely contrasted with his vulgar dress. Then, when the door was shut, he said:

"Well, I think the young man understood me, and that in eight or ten days I will find Master Gamain and his apprentice to aid me in putting on my lock."

CHAPTER XIII.

OLD ACQUAINTANCES.

ON the evening of the day when M. Louis de Bouille had the honor to be received by the queen first, and by the king afterwards, between five and six o'clock there passed in the third and fourth story of an old, small, and somber house of the Rue de la Juiverie a scene to which we beg our readers to permit us to introduce them all.

The interior of the room is miserable; it is occupied by three persons, a man, woman, and a child.

The man wears an old uniform of a sergeant of the French guards, venerated since July 14th, when the French guards joined the people and exchanged shots with the Germans of M. de Lamberg and the Swiss of M. de Bésenval.

He has in his hand a full pack of cards, from the ace, deux, trois of the same color, to king. He tries for the hundredth, for the thousandth, and for the ten thousandth time to effect a perfect martingale. A card with as many holes as there are stars lies by him.

The woman wears an old silk dress; misery seems in her case the more terrible because it appears with the remnants of luxury. Her hair is supported by a copper comb which once was gilt. Her hands are scrupulously clean, and from that cleanliness have acquired a certain aristocratic air. Her nails were carefully rounded; and her slippers, out of shape and with holes made in them here and there, once braided with gold, were worn over the remnants of dress stockings.

Her face was that of a woman of thirty-four or five years, which, if artistically managed according to the fashion of the day, would give the wearer a right to assume any age with lustrum, as the Abbé Celle said, and even two lustra; women ever cling closely to twenty-nine. That face, however, without rouge and Spanish white, deprived of all means of concealing grief and misery, the third and fourth wings of time, seemed four years older than it was in fact.

The child is five years old; his hair is *frise au cherubin;* his cheeks are round; he has the devilish eyes of his mother, the gourmand mouth of his father, and the caprices and idleness of both.

He is clad in the remnant of an old mottled velvet habit; and while he eats a piece of bread covered with *confits* by the grocer at the next corner, tears to pieces the remnant of an old tricolored sash fringed with copper, and throws the fragments into an old gray felt hat.

The room is lighted by a candle with a huge wick, to which an empty bottle serves as a candlestick, and which, while it places the man in the light, leaves the rest of the room in total darkness.

If, after all this, explained, with our usual precision, the reader has learned nothing, listen.

The child speaks first; after having thrown down the last of his bread and butter, and thrown himself down on the bed, which is now reduced to a mere mattress:

"Mama, I do not want any more bread and preserves—puh!"

"Well, Toussaint, what do you wish?"

"A piece of barley-sugar."

"Do you hear, Beausire?" said the woman.

"He shall have some to-morrow."

"I shall have it to-night!" cried the child, with an angry yell which betokened a stormy time.

"Toussaint, my child, you had best be silent, or I will have to settle with you."

"You touch him, drunkard!" said the mother, "and you will have to settle with me!" and she stretched forth that white hand, which, thanks to the care taken of her nails, might on occasions become a claw.

"Who the devil wishes to touch him? You know very well what I mean, for though one sometimes beats the dresses of Eve, mother, one always respects the jacket of the child. Come, kiss your dear Beausire, who in eight days will be rich as a king."

"When you are rich as a king, my dear fellow, I will kiss you; but—now no, no!"

"But I tell you it is certain as if I had a million. Give me an advance, for good luck, and then the baker will trust us."

"Bah! the idea of a man who wants credit for four pounds of bread talking about millions."

"I want some barley-sugar!" cried the child, in a tone becoming more and more menacing.

"Come, now, you man of millions, give the child some barley-sugar."

"Well," said he, "yesterday I gave you my last piece of twenty-four sous."

"Since you have money," said the child, turning to her whom M. Beausire called Olive, "give me a sou to buy some barley-sugar."

"Here are two, you bad boy, and take care not to hurt yourself as you go down the steps."

"Thank you, dear mother!" said the child, leaping up with joy, and now reaching her his hand.

The woman, having looked after the child until the door closed on him, glanced at the father, and said:

"Ah! Monsieur de Beausire, will your intelligence extract us from our miserable condition? Unless it do, I must have recourse to mine."

She pronounced these last words with the finnikin air of a woman who looks in a glass and says, do not be alarmed; with such a face one does not die of hunger.

"You know, dear Nicole, that I am very busy," said M. de Beausire.

"Yes, in shuffling cards and pricking a piece of pasteboard."

"But since I have found it?"

"Found what?"

"My martingale."

"There you begin again! Monsieur de Beausire, I warn you that I shall go among my old acquaintances, and see if I can find no one who has influence, and who will be kind enough to lock you up as a madman at Charenton."

"But I tell you it is infallible."

"Ah! If Monsieur de Richelieu were not dead!" murmured the woman, in a low voice.

"What do you say?"

"If the Cardinal de Rohan were not ruined!"

"What then?"

"One might find resources, and one would not be forced to share the misery of an old rector like this!"

With the gesture of a queen, Mlle. Nicole Legay, called Mme. Olive, pointed disdainfully at Beausire.

"But I tell you," said the man, "to-morrow we shall be rich."

"Worth millions?"

"Worth millions."

"Monsieur Beausire, show me the first ten louis of your millions, and I will believe the rest."

"Well, you shall see this evening the first ten louis d'or. That is exactly the sum promised me."

"And you will give them to me, dear De Beausire?" said Nicole, eagerly.

"I will give you five to buy a silk dress for yourself and a velvet jacket for the young one. And with the other five I will win the millions."

"You are going to play again?"

"Yes. I have found my martingale."

"Yes, like that one with which you lost the sixty thousand livres left of your Portuguese business."

"Money illy earned never lasts," said Beausire, sententiously. "I always thought that from the manner that money was acquired it would do us no good."

"Then this comes to you by inheritance? You had an uncle who died in the Indies, I presume, and he has left you these ten louis?"

"These ten louis, Mademoiselle Nicole Legay," said Beausire, with an air of great superiority, "will be gained honestly, do you understand? even honorably. The more so, as it is a cause in which I and all the nobility in France are interested."

"You are, then, noble, Monsieur Beausire?" said Nicole, mockingly.

"Say *De* Beausire, if you please, Madame Legay—De Beausire," added he, "as the certificate of your child's birth in the register of the Church of St. Paul, which your servant Jean Baptiste Toussaint signed when he gave the boy his own name."

"A very pretty present," murmured Nicole.

"And my fortune," added De Beausire, emphatically.

"If you grant him nothing else, the poor child is certain to die in the almshouse or hospital."

"Indeed, Nicole," said the man, "this is insupportable; you are never satisfied."

"Then do not bear it," said Nicole, letting loose the dike of her long-repressed wrath. "Eh! good God, who asks you to bear it? Thank God, I am not anxious either for myself or for my child, and am ready this very evening to seek my fortune elsewhere."

Nicole took three steps toward the door.

Beausire advanced to the same door, which he barred with his arms.

"But when you are told that this fortune——"

"Well?" said Nicole.

"Will come this evening. Even if the martingale be lost, which is impossible after all my calculations, we will have lost five louis. That is all."

"There are moments when five louis are a fortune, Mr. Spendthrift. You do not know that you have wasted the whole of our income."

"That, Nicole, proves my merit. If I did waste, I wasted what I had gained. Besides, there is a God who watches over adroit people."

"Ah, yes; down there, perhaps."

"Nicole," said Beausire, seriously, "are you an atheist?"

Nicole shrugged her shoulders.

"Do you belong to the school of Voltaire, which denies a Providence?"

"Beausire, you are a fool."

"There is nothing astonishing in the fact that one sprung like you from the people should have such ideas; but I inform you that they do not suit my social caste and my ideas of right and wrong."

"Monsieur de Beausire, you are insolent."

"I—do you understand me, madame?—have faith, and if any one should say that my son, Jean Baptiste Toussaint de Beausire, who went downstairs with two sous to buy a piece of barley-sugar, will come up with a purse of gold in his hand, I would say, certainly, if it be the will of God."

Beausire lifted his eye piously to heaven.

"Beausire, you are a fool."

Just then the voice of the young heir was heard on the stairway, shouting lustily: "Papa! mama!" and the nearer he came, the louder he bellowed.

"What has happened?" said Nicole, as she opened the door anxiously, as even the worst mothers do for their children's sake. "Come, child, come."

"Papa! mama!" said the voice, coming closer and closer, like that of a ventriloquist imitating sounds from the depth of a cave.

"I would not be surprised," said Beausire, "if the miracle were accomplished, for the child's voice is so joyous that he may have found the purse spoken of."

Just then the child appeared at the top step of the stairway, and rushed into the room, having in one hand a stick of sugar candy, clasping a bundle of candy to his breast, and showing in his right hand a louis d'or, which in the dimness of the candle shone like the star Aldebaran.

"My God!" said Nicole, suffering the door to close itself. "What has happened?"

She covered the gelatinous face of the young vagabond with such kisses that nothing makes disgusting, for they are a mother's.

"This is," said Beausire, adroitly taking possession of the gold louis d'or, "good, and is worth twenty-four livres."

He then said to the child, "Tell me, my son, where you found this, for I wish to look for the others."

"I did not find it, papa," said the child. "It was given to me."

"Who gave it to you?" said the mother.

"A gentleman who came into the grocer's while I was there;" and as he spoke, the young scamp crushed the barley-sugar in his teeth, "a gentleman——"

Beausire echoed the words, "A gentleman."

"Yes, papa, a gentleman, who came into the grocer's while I was there, and said 'Monsieur, do you not now serve a nobleman named De Beausire?"

Beausire looked up proudly, and Nicole shrugged her shoulders.

"What said the grocer, my son?" asked Beausire.

"He replied, 'I do not know if he be noble or not, but his name is Beausire.' 'Does he not live near here?" asked the gentleman. 'Here in the house next door to the left, on the third story, at the head of the staircase. This is his son.' 'Give all sorts of good things to this child,' said he, 'I will pay.' He then said to me, 'Here, my lad, is a louis to buy more when they are gone.' He then put the money in my hand, the grocer gave me this package, and I left, very well satisfied. Where is my louis?"

The child, who had not seen the sleight-of-hand by which Beausire took possession of his louis, began to look around for it everywhere.

"Awkward fellow!" said Beausire, "you have lost it."

"No, no, no!" said the young one.

The discussion might have been serious but for an event we are about to relate, and which necessarily terminated it.

While the child, though evidently in doubt himself, was hunting everywhere on the floor for the money, which was snugly ensconced in Beausire's pocket, while Beausire admired the intelligence of young Toussaint, manifested by his relating the story we just told, while Nicole partook of her husband's admiration of the precocious eloquence, and asked who the bestower of bonbons and giver of gold possibly could be, the door opened, and a voice of exquisite softness exclaimed:

"*Bon soir,* Monsieur de Beausire. *Bon soir,* Toussaint. *Bon soir,* Mademoiselle Nicole."

All turned to the place whence the voice came.

At the door, smiling on this family picture, was a man elegantly dressed.

"Ah! the gentleman who gave me the bonbons!" exclaimed Toussaint.

"Count Cagliostro!" said Nicole and Beausire.

"You have a charming child, Monsieur de Beausire, and you should be proud of him."

After these gracious words of the count, there was a moment of silence, during which Cagliostro advanced to the middle of the chamber, and looked around him, without doubt, to form an idea of the moral and pecuniary condition of his old acquaintances.

"Ah! monsieur, what a misfortune! I have lost my louis!" exclaimed Toussaint.

Nicole was about to tell the truth, but she reflected that if she held her tongue the child might get another louis, which she would inherit.

Nicole was not mistaken.

"You have lost your louis, my poor child?" said Cagliostro. "Here are two more; try and not lose them this time."

"Here, mama," said he, turning to Nicole, "here is one for me, and another for you."

The child divided his treasure with his mother.

Cagliostro had remarked the tenacity with which the false sergeant followed his purse. As he saw it disappear in the depth of his pocket, the lover of Nicole sighed.

"Eh! what, Monsieur de Beausire," said Cagliostro, "always melancholy."

"Yes, count; and you always a millionaire."

"Eh, my God! You, who are one of the greatest philanthropists I ever knew in all modern times and in antiquity, should be aware of an axiom, honored in all, times, 'Money does not bring happiness.' I have seen you comparatively rich."

"Yes, it is true. I had a hundred thousand francs. But what are a hundred thousand francs to the huge sums you expend?"

"Now tell me," said Cagliostro, "would you change your position, even though you have not one louis, except that you took from the unfortunate Toussaint?"

"Monsieur!" said the old bailiff.

"Do not let us quarrel, Monsieur de Beausire; we did so once, and you had to look on the other side of the window for your sword. You remember? See what a thing it is to have memory. Well, I ask you now, would you change your position, though you have only the unfortunate louis you took from poor Toussaint," on this occasion the allegation passed without any recrimination, "for the precarious position from which I have sought to extricate you?"

"Indeed, count, you are right; I would not change. Alas! at that time I was separated from Nicole."

"And slightly pursued by the police, on account of your Portugal affair, Monsieur de Beausire? It was a bad affair, as far as I can recollect."

"It is forgotten, count," said Beausire.

"Ah! so much the better, for it must have made you uneasy. Do not, however, be too confident that such is the case. Rude divers are found in the police, and it matters not how deep the waters of oblivion be, some of them might reach the bottom; a great crime is found as easy as a rich pearl."

"But, count, for the misery to which we are reduced——"

"You would be happy. You only need a thousand louis to be completely happy."

The eyes of Nicole glittered; those of Beausire seemed a jet of flame.

Beausire said, "With the half we would buy, that is to say, had we twenty-four thousand livres, we would buy a farm, with the other, some little rent, and I would become a laborer."

"Like Cincinnatus."

"While Nicole would devote herself entirely to the education of her child."

"Like Cornelia. Monsieur de Beausire, this would be beautiful; but you do not expect to earn that money in the affair you are at present engaged in."

Beausire trembled. "What affair?"

"That in which you are to figure as a sergeant of the guards: the affair for which you have a rendezvous tonight under the arches of the Place Royale."

Beausire became pale as death. "Count!" said he, clasping his hands in a supplicating manner.

"What?"

"Do not ruin me."

"Good! you digress already; am I a policeman?"

"Now I told you," said Nicole, "that you were engaged in some wicked business."

"Then you, too, Mademoiselle Legay, know about this business?"

"No, count, only this: whenever he conceals anything from me, the reason is that it is bad, and I cannot be quiet."

"Everything has a good and a bad side; good for some, bad for others; any operation cannot be good for all or bad for all. Well, it is important to be on the right side."

"Well, and it appears that I am not to be on the right side."

"Not at all, Monsieur de Beausire, not at all; I will add even that if you engage in it on this occasion, not your honor, but your life will be in danger; besides risking your fortune, you will certainly be hung."

"Monsieur," said De Beausire, trying to keep his countenance, but wiping away the sweat from his brow, "noblemen are not hung."

"That is true; but to obtain the honor of decollation, it will be necessary to prove your pedigree, which probably is so long that the court would become weary, and order you to be hung. But perhaps you will say, when the cause is good the mode matters little:

"'Tis not the ax that brings disgrace, but crime

as a great poet has said."

Yet, more and more terrified, De Beausire said:

"Yes; one is not so much devoted to his opinions as to shed one's life for them. Diable! 'one can live but once,' as a great poet has said, not so great as the first, however, but who yet had something of reason about him. Count, in the course of the little intercourse I had with you, I have observed that you have a way of talking which makes a man's hair stand erect, especially if he be a timid man."

"Diable! that is not my intention," said Cagliostro; "besides, you are not a timid man."

"No," said Beausire, "not if it be necessary to be otherwise, but under certain circumstances."

"Yes, I understand; when the galleys for theft are behind a man, and before him a gallows for high treason, *lèse-nation* now, as it used to be called *lèse-majesté.* It would be now *lèse-nation* to carry away the king."

"Monsieur!" said Beausire, with terror.

"Unfortunate man!" said Olive. "Was it on this carrying away that you built all your hopes of gold?"

"And he was not altogether wrong, my dear, except as I had the honor just now to tell you; everything has a good and a bad side. Beausire was stupid enough to kiss the bad faces, to side with the wrong parties; he has but to change, and all will be right."

"Has he time?"

"Certainly."

"Count," cried Beausire, "what must I do?"

"Fancy one thing, my dear sir," said Cagliostro.

"What?"

"Suppose your plot fails, suppose the accomplices of the masked man, the man with the brown cloak, be arrested and condemned to death; suppose—do not be offended by supposition after supposition, we will ultimately arrive at a fact—suppose yourself one of those accomplices, suppose the rope around your neck, and in reply to your lamentations you were told, for in such a situation a man always laments, more or less, be he ever so brave——"

"Go on, count, go on, for mercy's sake. It seems to me I am already strangled."

"Pardieu! it is not surprising, I suppose, to you to feel the rope around your neck, eh? Well, suppose they were to reply to all your lamentations, my dear Monsieur de Beausire, 'It is your own fault!'"

"How so?" said Beausire.

"'How is this?' the voice will say; 'you might not only have escaped from the unpleasant fix in which you are, but also have gained a thousand louis, with which you could have bought the pretty house in which you were to have lived with Mademoiselle Olive and little Toussaint, with the income of five hundred louis, derived from the twelve thousand not expended in the purchase of the house, you might live, as you say, like a farmer, wearing slippers in summer and wooden shoes in winter. Instead of this charming picture, however, we have before our eyes the Place de Grève, planted with two or three ugly-looking scaffolds, from the arm of the highest of which you hang. Pah! De Beausire, the prospect is bad.'"

"How, though, could I escape this evil exit? How else could I have gained the thousand louis, and assured the tranquillity of Nicole and Toussaint?"

"You still will ask questions. 'Nothing will be more facile,' the voice will reply. 'You had Count Cagliostro within two feet of you.' 'I know him,' you will say; 'a foreign nobleman, living in Paris, and who is wearied to death when news is scarce.' 'That is it; well, you had only to go to him, and say, "Count."' 'I did not, though, know where he lived—I did not know that he was in Paris—I did not even know that he was alive.' 'Then, my dear Monsieur de Beausire,' the voice will answer, 'he came to you for the very purpose, and from that time confess that you had no excuse. Well, you had only to say to him: "Count, I know you are always anxious for news." "I am." "I have something rare; Monsieur, the brother of the king, conspires——" "Bah! yes." "With the Marquis de Favras." "Not possible." "Yes, I speak advisedly, for I am one of his agents." "Indeed! what is the object of the plot?" "To carry away the king, and carry him to Peronne. Well, count, to amuse you I will go every day and every hour to inform you of the state of affairs." Then the count, who is a generous nobleman, would have answered: "Monsieur de Beausire, will you really do this?" "Yes." "Well, as every trouble deserves a salary, if you keep the promise you have made, I have, in a certain place, twenty-four thousand livres, which will be at your service; I will put them on this risk, that if you inform me of the day when the king is to be taken away by Monsieur de Favras, you will come to tell me, and, on my honor as a gentleman, the twenty-four thousand livres will be given you, as are these ten louis, not as a loan to be repaid, but as a simple gift."'"

At these words, Cagliostro took the heavy purse from his pocket, and took ten louis, which, to tell the truth, Beausire advanced an open hand to receive.

Cagliostro put aside his hand.

"Excuse me, Monsieur de Beausire, but I suppose we can return to suppositions."

"Yes, but," said M. de Beausire, whose eyes shone like two pieces of burning coal, "did you not say, count, that, from supposition to supposition, we would gradually reach the fact?"

"Have we reached it?"

Beausire hesitated; let us say that it was not poverty, fidelity to a promise, nor conscience which caused this hesitation. No; he simply was afraid that the count would not keep his word.

"My dear Beausire, I know what is passing in your mind."

"Yes, count, you do; I hesitate to betray a confidence reposed in me."

Looking up to heaven, he shook his head, like a man who says, "Ah, it is very hard!"

"No, that is not it, and you are another proof of the truth of the proverb, 'No one knows himself.'"

"What, then, is it?" asked Beausire, a little put out by the facility with which the count read every heart.

"You are afraid that, after having promised, I will not give you the thousand louis."

"Oh, count!"

"All is natural enough; but give me a security. For though I proposed the matter, I should be safe."

"Security? The count certainly needs none."

"A security which satisfies me, body for body."

"What security?" asked De Beausire.

"Mademoiselle Nicole Olive Legay."

"Oh!" said Nicole, "if the count promises, it is enough. It is as certain as if we had it, Beausire."

"See, monsieur, the advantage of fulfilling our promises scrupulously. One day, when Mademoiselle Legay was much sought after by the police, I made her an offer to find a refuge in my house. She hesitated. I promised, and in spite of every temptation I had to undergo—and you, sir, can understand them better than any other—I kept my promise, Monsieur de Beausire. Is not that so, mademoiselle?"

"Yes, by our little Toussaint, I swear it!"

"Do you think, then, Mademoiselle Nicole, that I will keep my word to Monsieur de Beausire, to give him a thousand louis if he will inform me of the king's flight, or De Favras's arrest, without taking into consideration that I now loose the knot being woven around his neck, and you be forever removed from danger of the cord and gallows? Apropos of that old affair, I do not promise for the future; for the moment let us talk. There are vocations."

"For my part, monsieur," said Nicole, "all is fixed as if the notary had already set his seal on it."

"Well, my dear lady," said Cagliostro, as he arranged on the table the ten louis which he had not yet parted with, "infuse your convictions into the heart of Monsieur de Beausire, and all is decided." He, by a gesture, bid her talk to Beausire.

The conversation lasted only five minutes, but it is proper to say, was very animated.

In the interim, Cagliostro looked at the pierced card, and shook his head, as if he recognized an old acquaintance.

"Ah, ha!" said he, "it is the famous martingale of Monsieur Law, which you have discovered again. I have lost a million on it."

This observation seemed to give a new activity to the

conversation between Beausire and Nicole. At last Beausire decided. He advanced to Cagliostro, open-handed, like a man who had just made an indissoluble contract.

The count drew back his hand, and said:

"Monsieur, among gentlemen, a word passes. I have given you mine, give me yours."

"By my faith, sir, it is settled."

"That is enough, sir," said Cagliostro.

Taking from his pocket a watch enriched with diamonds, on which was the portrait of King Frederick of Prussia, he said:

"It wants a quarter of nine, Monsieur de Beausire; at nine exactly you are expected under the arches of the Place Royale, on the side of the Hotel Sully; take these louis, put them in your vest-pocket, put on your coat, gird on your sword; you must not be waited for."

Beausire did not wait to be told twice. He took the money, put it in his pocket, put on his coat, and left.

"Where shall I find you, count?"

"At the Cemetery of St. Jean, if you please. When one wishes to talk such things without being heard, it must not be among the living."

"And when?"

"As soon as you be disengaged. The first will wait for the second."

CHAPTER XIV.

ŒDIPUS AND LOT.

It wanted but a few minutes of midnight, when a man, coming from the Rue Royale into that of St. Antoine, followed the latter to the Fountain of St. Catherine, and at last reached the gate of the Cemetery St. Jean.

There, as if his eyes had feared to see some specter start from the ground, he waited, and with the sleeve of his coat, the uniform of a sergeant of the guards, he wiped the heavy drops of sweat from his brow.

Just as the clock struck twelve, something like a shadow appeared to glide amid the ivies, box-trees, and cypresses. This shadow approached the gate, and by the grating of the key in the lock one might see that the specter, if such it was, not only had the privilege of leaving the tomb, but when once out, of leaving the cemetery.

When he heard the key turn, the soldier drew back.

"Well, Monsieur de Beausire," said the mocking voice of Cagliostro, "do you not know me, or have you forgotten our rendezvous?"

"Ah! is it you?" said Beausire, breathing like a man, the heart of whom is relieved from a heavy burden. "So much the better. These damned streets are so dark and deserted that one does not know if it be better to travel alone or to meet anybody."

"Bah!" said Cagliostro, "for you to fear anything, at any hour, either of the day or night! You cannot make me believe that of a brave man who travels with his sword by his side. There," said Cagliostro, "follow this little path, and about twenty paces hence we will find a kind of ruined altar, on the steps of which we will be able to talk at ease of our affairs."

Beausire hurried to obey Cagliostro; but after a moment of hesitation, said:

"Where the devil is the path? I see only briers, which wound my elbows, and grass, which reaches to my knees."

"The fact is, the cemetery is in worse order than any I know of, but that is not surprising. You know that none are buried here but criminals executed in the Grève, and no lady takes an interest in these poor devils. Yet, my dear Monsieur de Beausire, we have many illustrious characters here. If it were day I could show you where the Constable de Montmorency lies. He was executed for having fought a duel; the Chevalier de Rohan, for having conspired against the government; the Count de Horn, who was broken on the wheel for having assassinated a Jew; Damiens, who was quartered because he sought to kill Louis XV., and who knows who else? You are wrong to speak ill of the Cemetery of St. John. It is not kept well, but it is very full. However," said Cagliostro, pausing near a kind of ruin, "here we are!"

Sitting on a broken stone, he pointed out to Beausire a stone, which seemed designated by the first to spare Cinna the trouble of removing his seat to the side of that of Augustus.

"Now we are at our ease and able to talk, my dear Monsieur de Beausire," said Cagliostro, "tell me what took place this evening under the arches of the Place Royale; was the meeting interesting?"

"Ma foi," said Beausire, "I own, count, that my head just now is a little bothered, and indeed I think each of us would gain, if you adopted the system of questions and answers."

"So be it," said Cagliostro; "I am easy, and provided I obtain my end, do not care what means be adopted. How many were you under the arches of the Place Royale?"

"Six, with myself."

"Six, with yourself, dear Monsieur de Beausire; let me see if they are the men I think? In the first place, yourself?"

Beausire uttered a sigh, which indicated that he wished there was a possibility of doubt.

"Then, there was your friend Trocarty. Then, a royalist, named Marquée, ci-devant sergeant in the Royal French Guards, and now sous-lieutenant in a company of the center?"

"Yes, count, Marquée was there."

"And Monsieur de Favras?"

"And Monsieur de Favras."

"Then, the masked man?"

"Then, the masked man."

"Can you give me any information about this masked man, Monsieur de Beausire?"

"Well," said Beausire, "I think it was Monsieur——"

"Monsieur who?" said Cagliostro, sharply.

"Monsieur—Monsieur, the brother of the king."

"Ah! dear Monsieur de Beausire, the Marquis de Favras

has a deep interest in creating the impression that, in all this affair, he has touched the prince's head. That may be so; but a man who cannot lie cannot conspire. But, that you and your friend Trocarty, two recruiting officers, used to measure men by the eye, by feet, inches, and signs, is very improbable. Monsieur is five feet three high, the masked man was five feet six."

"True, count, so I thought; but who was he?"

"Pardieu! my dear Monsieur de Beausire, will I not be prettily engaged in teaching you, when I expected to be taught by you?"

"Then," said Beausire, who gradually recovered his presence of mind, as he returned, little by little, to reality, "you know who this man is?"

"Parbleu!"

"Is there any indiscretion in asking?"

"His name?"

Beausire nodded that was what he wished.

"Do you know the play of Œdipus?"

"Not well; I have seen the play at the Comedie Française; but toward the end of the fourth act I sunk to sleep."

"I will, then, briefly tell you the story:

"I knew Œdipus; it was foretold that he would be the murderer of his father, and the husband of his mother. Now, believing Polybius his father, he left him and set out, without assigning any reason, for Phocis. As he set out, I advised him, instead of taking the highroad from Dantes to Delphi, to take a mountain-path I was acquainted with. He, however, was obstinate, and as I could not tell him why I gave him this advice, all exhortation was vain. From this obstinacy resulted exactly what I expected. At the forks of the road, from Delphi to Thebes, he met a man followed by five slaves. The man was in a chariot, which crowded the whole road; all difficulty would have been obviated had the man in the car consented to have turned a little to the right and Œdipus to the left; each, however insisted on the center of the road. The man in the chariot was choleric and Œdipus not very patient. The five slaves rushed, one after the other, before their master, and, one after the other, were slain. Œdipus passed over six dead bodies, one of which was his father."

"The devil!" said M. de Beausire.

"He then went to Thebes; now, on the road to Thebes was Mount Pincior, and in a yet more narrow road than that in which he had slain his father, a strange animal had a cavern. This animal had the wings of an eagle, the head and heart of a woman, the body and claws of a lion."

"Oh! ho!" said Beausire, "are there any such monsters, in your opinion?"

"I cannot possibly affirm their existence, since, when I went to Thebes, a thousand years afterward, and traveled the same road, during the time of Epaminondas, the Sphinx was alive. At the time of Œdipus it was one of the passions of the Sphinx to place himself by the roadside, proposing enigmas to the passing travelers, and devouring all who could not answer them. Now, as this lasted for more than three centuries, travelers became more and more rare, and the Sphinx's teeth rather long. When he saw Œdipus, he placed himself in the center of the road, and lifted up his paw, to bid the young man stop. 'Traveler,' said he, 'I am the Sphinx.' 'Well, what then?' asked Œdipus. 'Well, destiny has sent me to earth to propose an enigma to men. If they do not guess it, they are mine; if they do, I am Death's, and I must throw myself into the abyss where I have thrown the fragments of the bodies of those I have devoured.' Œdipus looked over the precipice and saw the white bones. 'Well,' said the young man, 'the enigma?' 'It is this: "What animal walks on four legs in the morning, on two at noon, and on three at night?"' Œdipus thought for a moment, with a smile of disdain, which could not but make the Sphinx uneasy. 'If I guess it,' said Œdipus, 'will you precipitate yourself into the abyss?' 'Yes,' 'Well,' said Œdipus, 'that animal is man.'"

"How so? Man!" interrupted Beausire, who became interested in the conversation, as if it related to something contemporary.

"Yes, man, who in his childhood, that is to say, in the morning of life, crawls on his feet and hands; who in the age, that is to say, at the noon of life, walks erect, and in the evening, that is to say, in old age, uses a staff."

"Ah!" said Beausire, "that is true. Fool the Sphinx was!"

"Yes, my dear Monsieur de Beausire, so foolish that he threw himself into the cavern, without using his wings, and broke his head on the rocks. As for Œdipus, he pursued his journey, came to Thebes, found Jocasta a widow, married her, and thus fulfilled the oracle, that he would kill one parent and marry the other."

"But, count," said De Beausire, "where is the analogy between the story of Œdipus and the mask?"

"Great! you desired to know his name just now?"

"Yes."

"And I told you that I was about to propose an enigma. True, I am of better material than the Sphinx, and will not devour you if you do not answer. Attention! I am about to lift up my hand. 'What part of the court is the grandson of his father, the brother of his mother, and the uncle of his sisters?'"

"Diable!" said Beausire, relapsing into a quandary great as that of Œdipus.

"Think, sir; study it out," said Cagliostro.

"Assist me a little, count."

"Willingly; I asked you if you knew the story of Œdipus?"

"You did me that honor."

"Now we will pass to sacred history. You know what is said of Lot——"

"And his daughters?"

"Exactly."

"Parbleu! I know. Wait, though; do you know what was said of Louis XV. and his daughter, Madame Adelaide?"

"You know, my dear sir."

"Then the masked man was Count Louis."

"Well?"

"It is true," murmured Beausire; "the grandson of his father, the brother of his mother, the uncle of his sisters, is Count Louis de Nar."

"Attention," said Cagliostro.

Beausire interrupted his monologue, and listened with all his ears.

"Now we no longer doubt who the conspirators are, either masked or not. Let us proceed to the plot."

Beausire nodded, as if to say that he was ready.

"The object is to convey the king away?"

"That is it exactly."

"To take him to Peronne?"

"To Peronne."

"What at present are the means?"

"Pecuniary?"

"Yes."

"Two millions."

"Lent them by a Genoese banker. I know him. Have they none other?"

"I do not know."

"They have money enough, but they need men."

"Monsieur Lafayette has authorized the raising of a legion, to aid Brabant, which has revolted against the empire."

"Oh! kind Lafayette, I see your hand clearly there."

Then aloud: "So be it; but not a legion, an army is needed for such an enterprise."

"There is an army."

"Let us see what."

"Two hundred horse will be collected at Versailles, and on the appointed day will leave Versailles at eleven P. M. At two o'clock in the morning they will reach Paris in three columns."

"Good!"

"The first will enter Paris at the gate of Chaillot, the second at the Barrière du Roule, the third at Grenelle. The latter will murder Lafayette, the first Monsieur Necker, and the other Bailly, the maire of Paris."

"Good!" said Cagliostro.

"The blow being struck, the guns will be spiked. They will meet at the Champs Elysées, and a march will be made on the Tuileries, which are ours."

"What, yours? and the National Guard?"

"There the Brabanconne column will act, joined to four hundred Swiss, and three hundred people from the outside of Paris. Thanks to confederates in the palace, they will hurry to the king, and say: 'Sire, the Faubourg St. Antoine is in a state of insurrection. A carriage is ready harnessed. You must go.' If the king consent the thing will all be right; if he do not, he will be carried forcibly, seized, and taken to St. Denis."

"Good!"

"There are twenty thousand infantry. They will set out on the appointed day, at eleven at night, with twelve hundred cavalry; the Brabanconne legion, the Swiss, the people from out of Paris, and ten or twenty thousand royalists, will escort the king to Peronne."

"Better and better; and what will be done at Peronne?"

"At Peronne are expected twenty thousand men, from the Flemish border, Picardy, Artois, Champagne, Burgundy, Lorraine, Alsace, and Cambresis. They are in treaty for twenty thousand Swiss, twelve thousand Germans, and twelve thousand Sardinians, who, joined to the royal escort, will form an effective force of one hundred and fifty thousand men."

"A nice army."

"With these one hundred and fifty thousand men it is purposed to march on Paris, to intercept water communication above and below the city, and cut off all supplies. Paris will be starved out, and will capitulate. The National Assembly will be dissolved, and the king restored to the throne of his fathers."

"Amen!" said Cagliostro. Arising, he said: "My dear Monsieur de Beausire, you have a most agreeable knack of conversation; the case with you is like that of all great orators—when you have said all, there is nothing more to be said."

"Yes, count, at the time."

"Then, my dear Monsieur de Beausire, when you need ten other louis, always on this condition, be it understood, come to my house at Bellevue."

"At Bellevue, and will I ask for Count Cagliostro?"

"Cagliostro? No, they would not know whom you mean. Ask for Baron Zanoni."

"And now," said Cagliostro, "whither, Monsieur de Beausire, do you go?"

"Whither go you, count?"

"In the direction you do not go."

"I go to the Palais Royal, count."

"And I go to the Bastile, Monsieur de Beausire."

CHAPTER XV.

IN WHICH GAMAIN SHOWS THAT HE IS REALLY MASTER OF MASTERS, MASTER OF ALL.

THE wish the king had expressed to Lafayette in the presence of the Count de Bouille, to have his old master, Gamain, to assist him in an important piece of locksmithing, will be recollected. He had even added, and we think it not unimportant to give the detail, that an apprentice would not be unimportant in the work. The number three, in which the gods delight, was not displeasing to Lafayette, and he therefore gave orders to admit Master Gamain and his apprentice freely, and that whenever they came they should be taken to the king.

It will not, therefore, surprise our readers to see M. Gamain, accompanied by an apprentice, in their working-dress, present themselves at the gate of the Tuileries. After their admission, to which no objection was made, they went round the royal apartments by the common corridor, and up the stairway to the door of the forge, where they left their names with the valet de chambre.

Their names were Nicolas Claude Gamain and Louis Lecomte.

Though the names were not at all aristocratic, as soon

as he heard them Louis XVI. himself went to the door, and said :

"Come in !"

"Here ! here ! here !" said Gamain, appearing, not only with the familiarity of a fellow-workman, but of an apprentice.

"Ah ! Gamain, is it you ? I am glad to see you, for I thought that you had forgotten me."

"And that is the reason why you took an apprentice ? You did well ; you were right, for I was not here. Unfortunately," said he, with a wry expression, "the apprentice is not a master."

"What else could I do, poor Gamain ?" said Louis XVI. "They told me you wished to have nothing to do with me under any circumstances, for fear of compromising yourself."

"Ma foi, sir, you might have learned at Versailles that it is not a safe thing to be one of your friends, for I saw, in the little inn of the Pont de Sèvres, the heads of two guardsmen, who grinned horribly, dressed by Monsieur Leonard. They were killed because they chanced to be in your antechamber when you received the visits of your Parisian friends."

A cloud passed over the king's face, and the apprentice bowed his head.

"They say, though, that since your return to Paris things are much better, and that you now make the Parisians do all you wish. That is not wonderful, for the Parisians are such fools, and you and the queen have such winning ways about you."

Louis XVI. said nothing, but a faint blush passed over his cheeks.

"Now," said Gamain, "let us look at that famous lock, for I promised my wife to return to-night."

The king gave Gamain a lock three-quarters done.

Gamain pointed out a great many alterations, and the king said :

"But it will take a day's hard work to effect all this, Gamain."

"Ah, yes, to another; but two hours will be enough for me; only, you must not annoy me with questions, and say, 'Gamain this, and Gamain that;' leave me alone. The shop seems to have tools enough, and in two hours—yes, two hours—come back, and all will be complete," said Gamain, with a smile.

This was exactly what the king wished. The solitude of Gamain would enable him to talk alone with Louis.

"If you want anything, Gamain——"

"If I do, I will call the valet de chambre, provided he be ordered to bring me what I wish."

The king went to the door. "François," said he, as he opened it, "remain here, I pray you; Gamain, my old master, has come to correct a mistake in a lock I began. Give him all he wants, especially two or three bottles of excellent Bordeaux."

"Will your majesty please to remember that I like Burgundy best, sire? Damn Bordeaux; it is like drinking warm water!"

"Ah, yes, true; I forgot, we have often *trinquered* together, my poor Gamain. Burgundy, you understand, Volnay."

"Ah, yes," said Gamain, wetting his lips, "I remember."

"And did it make the water come to your lips?"

"Do not talk to me about water; I do not know of what earthly use it is, except to temper metal with; all who use it for any other purpose divert it from its true destination."

"Be easy; as long as you are here you will not hear water mentioned, and lest by accident the word escape from our lips, we will leave you; when you have done, send for us. The drawer for which this lock is intended——"

"Ah! that is the kind of work which suits you. Wish you joy."

"So be it," said the king.

Bowing familiarly to Gamain, the king left with the apprentice, Louis le Comte, or le Comte Louis, whom the reader has had sufficient perspicuity to have recognized as the son of the Marquis de Bouille.

Louis XVI. did not go from the shop by the outer stairway, but by the private one intended for him alone. This led to his study. The table was covered by a vast map of France, which proved that the king had already studied the shortest and most feasible way to leave his kingdom.

Not until at the foot of the staircase did Louis XVI. appear to recognize the young apprentice, who, with his hat in his hand, and his jacket over his arm, followed him. He then looked carefully around the room, and said :

"Now, my dear count, that we are alone, let me compliment you on your address, and thank you for your devotion. But we have no time to lose ; all, even the queen, are ignorant of your business here ; none have heard us, and tell me quickly what brings you."

"Did not your majesty do my father the honor to send an officer to his garrison ?"

"Yes, the Count de Charny."

"Yes, sire, that is the name ; he had a letter."

"Which meant nothing in words, and which was but an introduction to a verbal message."

"This verbal message, sire, he delivered, and that its execution might be certain, at my father's order, and with the hope of seeing your majesty, I set out for Paris."

"Then you know all ?"

"I know that the king wishes, at a certain given moment, to be able to quit France."

"And thinks the Marquis de Bouille able to second him in his plan.'

"My father is proud and grateful for the honor you have done him."

"But to the point, what says he of the plan ?"

"That it is hazardous, demands great precaution, but is not impossible."

"In the first place," said the king, "that the co-operation of Monsieur Bouille may have such full effect as his loyalty and devotion promise, would it not be better that the governments of several provinces were united to his command at Metz, especially the government of Franche Comte?"

"So my father thinks, sire, and I am happy that your majesty has yourself first expressed the idea. The marquis feared your majesty would attribute it to personal ambition."

"Go, go! do I not know your father's personal abnegation? Come, tell me, did he explain himself to you as to the course to be adopted?"

"That is what my father proposes to your majesty."

"Speak," said the king, looking over the map of France, to follow the different routes the young count was about to propose.

"Sire, there are many points to which the king can retire."

"Certainly, but I prefer Montmedy, which is in the center of your father's command. Tell the marquis that my choice is made, and that I prefer Montmedy."

"Has the king resolved upon the attempt, or is it but a project?" the young count dared to ask.

"My dear Louis," replied Louis XVI., "nothing is as yet determined on. If I see the queen and my children exposed to new dangers, like those of the night of the 5th and 6th of October, I will decide; tell your father, my dear count, when I shall once have made up my mind, it will be irrevocable."

"Now, sire," said the young count, "if it were permitted to me to express an opinion in relation to the manner of the voyage, may I mention to your majesty my father's advice?"

"Go on, go on."

"He thinks that the dangers would be diminished by dividing them."

"Explain."

"Sire, your majesty should start with Madame Elizabeth and Madame Royale, while the queen, with the dauphin—so that——"

"It is useless, my dear Louis, to discuss this point.

In a solemn moment, we decided, the queen and I, not to separate. If your father wishes to save us, he must save us all together, or not at all."

The count bowed.

"Another thing, sire; there are two roads to Montmedy. I must ask your majesty which you will take, in order that it may be examined by a competent engineer.

"We have a competent engineer, Monsieur de Charny, who is devoted to us. The fewer persons we put in the secret, the better. In the count we have a servant intelligent and tried, and will make use of him. As I chose Montmedy, the two roads are marked out on this map."

"There are three, sire," said De Bouille, respectfully.

"I know—that from Paris to Metz, which I left beyond Verdun, to take the Stenup road along the Meuse, from which Montmedy is but three leagues distant."

"There also is Rheims, l'Isle de Retter, and De Stenay," said the young count, anxious that the king should select that.

"Ah! ha!" said the king; "it seems that is the route you prefer."

"Sire, it is not my opinion, but my father's, and is founded on the fact that the country it passes is poor and almost a desert; consequently, fewer precautions are required. He adds that the Royal German, the best regiment in the service, the only one, perhaps, which has remained completely faithful, is stationed at Stenay, and can be your escort from Isle de Retter. Thus the danger of an observing suspicion by too great a movement of troops would be avoided."

"Yes," said the king, "we would have to pass Rheims, where I was crowned, and where the first-comer might recognize me. No, my dear count, on that point I am resolved."

The king pronounced these words in so firm a voice that Count Louis did not even dare to make another suggestion.

"Then the king is resolved?"

"On the road from Chalons to Verdun there are troops

in the little cities between Montmedy and Chalons. I do not see any inconvenience," added the king, "even if the first detachment met me in this last city."

"Sire, when there it will be time enough to decide how far the regiments can venture. The king is, however, aware that there is not a post-station at Varennes."

"I am glad, count, to see that you are so well informed; it proves that you have seriously studied our plan. Do not be afraid, though, for we will contrive a way to find horses, both above and below that town—our engineer will decide on the spot."

"And now, sire, that nearly all is decided, will your majesty permit me to quote in my father's name a few lines from an Italian author, which seemed to him so appropriate to the situation in which the king is that he bid me commit them to memory, that I might repeat them to you?"

"What are they, sir?"

"These: 'Delay is always injurious, and there is no circumstance entirely favorable in any undertaking; he who waits an opportunity perfectly favorable will never undertake anything—or, if he does, it will turn out badly.'"

"Yes, sir, the author is Machiavelli. I will pay attention, you may be sure, to the advice of the ambassador of the magnificent republic. But, eh! I hear steps on the stairway. It is Gamain. Let us go to meet him, that he may not see that we have not been busied with aught but the drawer."

As he spoke, the king opened the door of the stairway.

It was high time, for with the lock in his hand Gamain stood on the last step.

CHAPTER XVI.

A PROVIDENCE WATCHES OVER DRUNKEN MEN.

On that day, about eight o'clock P. M. a man clad as a workman, and keeping his hand carefully on his vest-pocket, as if on that night it contained a sum of money larger than workmen usually carry, left the Tuileries by the turning bridge, and inclining to the left, went entirely down one of the long aisles of trees, which toward the Seine prolong that portion of the Champs Elysées formerly called the marble post, or the stone post, and now called Cours la Reine.

At the first cabaret on the road, the man seemed to undergo a violent mental contest, whence he emerged victorious. The *res in lite* was whether he would enter the cabaret or not. He passed on.

The temptation was renewed at the second, and at this moment a man who followed him like a shadow, though unseen, might have fancied he was about to yield, so much did he deviate from the straight line, and incline toward that temple of Bacchus.

This time, also, temperance triumphed, and it is probable that if a third cabaret had not been met with, that he would have had to return to break a vow he seemed to have made. He continued his route, not fasting, for he seemed already to have taken a decent quantity of liquor, but yet had sufficient self-control for his legs to bear him in a line sufficiently straight for all ordinary purposes.

Unfortunately, however, there was not only a third, but a fourth, fifth, and twentieth cabaret. The result was that the temptation was too often renewed, and the force of resistance not being in harmony with the power of temptation, he gave way at the third test.

True it is that by a kind of transaction with himself the workman who had so long and so unfortunately combated the demon of wine, as he entered the cabaret, stood erect at the counter, and asked for but one chopin.

The demon of wine, with which he had so long contended, seemed to be victoriously represented by the stranger who had followed him in the distance, taking care to remain unseen, but, however, never losing sight of his quarry.

It was, without doubt, to enjoy this particularly agreeable prospect that he sat on the parapet, just opposite the tap, where the man drank his chopin, and set out just five minutes after the latter had drunk his chopin and crossed the door to resume his journey.

Who, however, can say when the lips once dampened by wine will be dried ; and who have never seen, as drunkards always do, that nothing excites them so much as drinking ? Scarcely had the *ouvrier* gone a hundred paces, than he felt such a thirst that he had to stop again, and on this occasion called, not for a chopin, but for a half bottle.

The shadow that followed him did not seem at all dissatisfied at the delay caused by this quenchless thirst, but stopped at the angle of the wall of the cabaret, and though the man sat down at his ease, and drank a whole quart to settle the half bottle and chopin, the benevolent shadow exhibited no impatience, contented when he came out to follow him as he had done before.

About a hundred paces further on, he had a new temptation, and a ruder test to submit to ; the *ouvrier* made a third halt, and this time, as his thirst continued to increase, he again asked for a bottle.

The argus had again to wait half an hour, a thing he did with the greatest patience.

Certainly, these five minutes, this half hour, successively lost, awakened something of remorse in the heart of the drinker. He took the precaution, before he set out again, to provide himself with an uncorked bottle, as he evidently did not wish to halt, but to continue on his journey drinking.

It was a prudent resolution, and which did not delay

him much, taking into consideration the curves and zigzags which were the result of every approach of the bottle to his lips.

By an adroitly combined curve, he passed the barrier of Passy without any trouble ; vessels carrying liquids, it is well known, not being liable to any *octroi* out of Paris.

A hundred paces from the barrier our man had occasion to congratulate himself on the ingenious precautions, for from that place cabarets became rarer, until at last there was none.

What was that to our philosopher ? Like the sage of old, he carried about with him, not only his fortune, but his joy.

We say his joy, since after getting half through his bottle, our traveler began to sing, and no one will deny but that song and laughter are the great means by which man exhibits joy.

The shadow appeared fully satisfied with the music, which it seemed to repeat in a low tone, and the expression of pleasure which it seemed to take great interest in. But, unfortunately, the joy was ephemeral and the song short. The joy lasted just as long as the wine did, and the empty bottle was pressed again and again, to no purpose. The song at last changed into growls, which, becoming more and more deep, ended in imprecations.

These imprecations were addressed to unknown persecutors, of whom, as he staggered, our traveler complained.

" Base people," said he, " to give poisoned wine to an old friend and to a master-workman ! Pah ! let him but send to me to fix his locks, and I will tell him : '*Bon soir*, your majesty, let your majesty fix your own locks.' Sir, if you make a lock as easy as you can a decree ; catch me doing any such thing again. I care nothing about your keys, springs, and tumblers, only catch me there again, that is all. The villain ! They certainly have poisoned me."

Having spoken these words, he was overcome by the force of the poison, and fell headlong three times on the road, which, fortunately, was covered with a soft cushion of mud.

Our friend, on the two first occasions, arose without assistance. The operation was difficult, but was accomplished safely. The third time, after desperate efforts, he was forced to confess that the effort was beyond his power, and with a sigh, not unlike a groan, he seemed determined for that night to sleep on our common mother, earth.

Doubtless, at this point of discouragement and weakness, that the shadow which had accompanied him from the Place Louis XV. with so much perseverance, for he had, in the distance, witnessed his abortive efforts to rise, and which we have sought to describe, approached him, went around him, and called a fiacre which chanced to pass.

"My friend," said he to the driver, "my companion is ill; take these six livres, and put the poor devil inside your carriage, and take him to the inn at the Pont de Sèvres. I will ride with you." There was nothing strange in one of the two riding with the driver, as both seemed very common men. Therefore, with the touching confidence people of that class have in one another, the driver said, "Six francs, where are they?"

"Here they are, my friend," said the other, who did not seem the least annoyed, and at the same time giving the coachman a crown.

"All right, sir," said the automaton, softened by the sight of the king's effigy.

"Take up this poor devil, put him inside, shut the doors carefully, and try to make your two nags last until we reach the Pont de Sèvres, and we will act then as you act to us."

"Very well," said the driver; "that is the way to talk. Be easy; I know what is what. Get on the box and keep our peacocks from cutting up capers. Damn! they already smell the stable, and are anxious to get into it."

Without making any remark, the generous stranger did as he was directed, and the driver carefully as he could lifted up the drunken man and placed him between the seats, shut the door, got on the box, whipped up the horses, who at the melancholy gait hack horses acquire so easily, passed the little hamlet of Pont de Jour, and in an hour reached the inn of the Pont de Sèvres.

In the interior of this inn, after ten hours or minutes, devoted to the unpacking of Gamain, whom the reader has doubtless recognized before now, we will find the worthy locksmith, master over masters, seated at the same table with the same armorer we described in the opening of this history.

The host of the cabaret of the Pont de Sèvres had gone to bed, and the least ray of light passed through the blinds, when the first knock of the philanthropist who had rescued Gamain sounded on the door.

The blows were so long and frequent that there was no possibility for the inmates of the cabaret, sleepy as they were, to resist so violent an attack.

Sleepy, and slumbering, and growling, the keeper of the house came to open the door himself, and in his own mind determined to give them a pretty scolding for so disturbing him. For, as he said, "the game was not worth the candle."

It seemed, however, that the game was worth the candle, for at the first word spoken by the man who knocked so irreverently, the latter took off his cap, and bowing in a most reverent, and in his costume, most ridiculous manner, introduced Gamain and his escort into the little room, where we previously have seen him sipping his favorite vin de Burgogne.

Both driver and horses had done as well as they could; the one using his whip, and the others their legs, which the stranger rewarded with a twenty-four sous piece for drink, in addition to the six livres he had already given them.

Having seen Gamain firmly deposited in a chair, with his head on a table in front of him, he hastened to make the innkeeper bring two bottles of wine, a pitcher of water, and to open the blinds for the purpose of purifying the mephitic air of the house.

The host, after having himself brought two bottles of

wine and a pitcher of water, the first promptly but the latter after some delay, had retired, and left his two guests together.

The stranger we have seen had taken care to renew the air; then, before the window was closed, had placed a flacon beneath the dilated nostrils of the locksmith, who snored as men do in that state of drunkenness, and who, could they hear themselves, would certainly be cured of that mad love of wine. The sovereign wisdom of the Most High does not, however, permit drunkards to hear themselves.

"The wretch, he has poisoned me—he has poisoned me!"

The armorer was pleased to see that Gamain was still under the influence of the same idea, and placed the flacon again beneath his nostrils, which, restoring some strength to the worthy son of Noah, permitted him to complete the last phrase, by adding to the words he had already pronounced, the two last words, which were the more horrible, as they signified a total abuse of confidence and want of heart.

"To poison a friend—a friend."

"Fortunately," said the armorer, "I was there with the antidote."

"Yes, indeed," murmured Gamain.

"But as one dose is not enough for such a person," continued the stranger, "take another."

He poured into half a glass of water four or five drops of the fluid in the flacon, which was only a solution of ammonia.

He then placed the glass close to Gamain's lips.

"Ah!" said he, "this is to be drunk with the mouth; I like it better than with the nose."

He swallowed the contents of the glass. Scarcely had he done so, however, than he opened his mouth wide and sneezed violently twice.

"Robber! what have you given me? Puh! puh!"

"I have given you a liquid which will save your life."

"Ah!" said he, "if it saves my life, you were right to

give it me. But if you call it liquor, you are damnably mistaken."

He sneezed again, opening his mouth and expanding his eyes, like a work of old Greek tragedy.

The stranger took advantage of this pantomime to shut, not the window, but the blinds.

This was not without advantage, for Gamain began to open his eyes for the second or third time. During this movement, convulsive as it was, Gamain had looked around him, and with this sentiment of profound remembrance, which drunkards have of the walls of a room, he recognized these.

In fact, in the many trips he was obliged to make to Paris, it was rare that Gamain did not stop at the Pont de Sèvres. This pause might also be considered a necessity, the cabaret being half-way. This recollection had a great effect. It restored the confidence of the locksmith by proving to him that he was in the company of friends.

"Ah, ha!" said he, "I am half-way, it seems."

"Yes, thanks to me," said the armorer.

"How, thanks to you?" said Gamain, looking from inanimate to living things—"thanks to you? Who are you?"

"My dear Gamain, that proves to me that you have a bad memory."

"Wait a bit, wait a bit; it seems to me that I have seen you before. But where was it? That is the thing."

"Where? Look around you and the objects may, perhaps, arouse some recollections. When, is another thing. Think, or it may be necessary to administer to you another dose of the antidote to enable you to tell me."

"No, I thank you, I have had enough of your antidote, and since I am saved a little, I will be content with that. Where did I see you? Where did I see you? Why, here."

"All right."

"When did I see you? Wait; on the morning when I came from doing some work in Paris. It really seems I have luck with those enterprises."

"Very well; and now what am I?"

"What are you? a man who paid for my liquor. Consequently, you are a good fellow. Give me your hand."

"With especial pleasure, as between a master locksmith and a master armorer there is but one step."

"Ah, well! there it is. I remember now. Yes, it was on the 6th of October, on the day of the king's return to Paris. We even talked of him on that day."

"And I found your conversation was interesting, Master Gamain; on that account I am anxious to enjoy it again, and since memory has returned to you, if I am not indiscreet, tell me what you were doing about an hour ago, stretched at your length in the street, within twenty feet of a carriage, which would have cut you in two if I had not passed by. Have you any troubles that you wish thus to commit suicide?"

"I commit suicide? My God! what was I doing there in the middle of the road? Are you sure I was there?"

"Parbleu! look at yourself."

Gamain looked around him. "Ah!" said he, "Madame Gamain will scold not a little. She told me not to put on my new coat. 'Put on your old jacket. It is good enough for the Tuileries.'"

"How the Tuileries?" said the stranger; "did you come from the Tuileries when I saw you?"

Gamain scratched his head, as if to rake up his ideas, which were not yet in order.

"Yes, I came from the Tuileries. What of that, though? Everybody knows I was the king's master. All know I served Monsieur Veto."

"How Monsieur Veto? Whom do you call Monsieur Veto?"

"Ah, good! you know they give that name to the king. Where did you come from, anyhow? From China?"

"Bah! I attend to my business, and do not attend to politics."

"You are very lucky. I do busy myself in politics; or, rather, I am forced to do so." Gamain looked up to heaven, and sighed.

"Bah!" said the stranger. "Have you been called to

Paris to do some work for the person of whom you spoke when we first met ?"

"Exactly. Only at that time I did not know whither I was going, for my eyes were bandaged ; but now I went with them opened."

"You had no trouble, then, in recognizing the Tuileries ?"

"The Tuileries !" said Gamain, echoing his words. "Who told you I went to the Tuileries ?"

"You just now. How do I know you came from the Tuileries ? Why, you told me so yourself."

"True," said Gamain, speaking to himself. "How could he know, unless I told him myself ?"

Then, speaking to the stranger, he said :

"Perhaps I was wrong to tell you ; but, ma foi ! you are not everybody. Well, since I told you so, I will not contradict it. I do not contradict it. I was at the Tuileries."

"And," said the stranger, "you worked with the king, who gave you twenty-five louis ?"

"Here, I have twenty-five louis now, in my pocket."

"Have you got them still ?"

Gamain put his hand in his pocket, and pulled out a handful of gold, mingled with silver and some copper.

"Wait a bit—five, six, seven—good ; and I forgot all this. Twelve, thirteen, fourteen ; just twenty-five louis. This is a sum which, as times go, is not found in the road. Twenty-three, twenty-four, twenty-five. Ah !" continued he, breathing with more liberty, "thank God, all is right. How did you know I had this money ?"

"My dear Monsieur Gamain, I have already had the honor to tell you that I found you asleep across the road, about twenty feet from a carriage which was passing. I took down one of the lanterns of this carriage, and by its means saw two or three louis on the ground. As they must have come from your pocket, I put them back again, and in doing so felt some twenty more. The coachman then said, shaking his head, 'No, monsieur, I cannot take that man ; he is too rich for his dress. Twenty-five louis in a cotton-velvet jacket will make a man smell a gallows a mile off.' 'How, think you he is a robber?' It seems the word struck you. 'Robber! robber! I, a robber?' said you. 'Certainly; or how else would you have twenty-five louis in your pocket?' 'I have, because my pupil, the King of France, has given them to me,' said you. In fact, at these words, I fancied that I knew you. I placed the lantern close to your face. 'Ah!' said I, 'all is explained; it is Gamain, the locksmith of Versailles. He has been at work with the king, who has given him twenty-five louis for the trouble. Come, I will answer for him.' As soon as I said I would do so, the driver made no more difficulty. I then placed in your pocket the louis d'or which had escaped. You were placed in the carriage and brought hither. I got on the seat and brought you here, where you have nothing to complain of, except the desertion of your apprentice."

"What, I spoke of an apprentice, and of his desertion?" said Gamain, more and more amazed.

"Now, only look; he no longer remembers what he has said!"

"I?"

"How, did you not say so just now: It was the fault of that fellow?—I do not just now remember his name."

"Louis Lecomte."

"That is it. Now, did you not just now say it was the fault of that fellow, Louis Lecomte, who promised to return with me to Versailles, and who, instead, merely burned me up with politeness?"

"Well, I might have said all this, but it yet is true."

"Well, since it is true, why should you deny it? Do you know, my fine fellow, that it might be dangerous to talk in this way to another than myself?"

"Yes, but with you," said Gamain, fawning on the count.

"With me? what does this mean?"

"It means to say, with a friend."

"Ah, yes; you show great confidence to a friend. You

say, 'It is true,' and then, 'It is not true.' The meaning of it is, that the other day you told me a story."

"What story?"

"The story of the secret door you had been sent to fix at the house of some great lord, the address of whom even you had forgotten."

"Well, you may believe me if you please, but on this time I also had to do with a door."

"At the king's?"

"At the king's; only, instead of the staircase, it was the door of a bureau."

"And you mean to say that the king, who is curious about locksmiths, sent for you to close a door for him. Bah!"

"Yet that is the truth. Poor man! he thought he could do without me, but it was of no use."

"He then sent for you, by some confidential valet? By Hue, Durey, or Weber?"

"Now you are exactly wrong. To assist him, he had employed a young man who knew less than he did. So that one day that fellow came to Versailles, and said: 'Look here, Master Gamain, the king and I wish you to make a lock. The damned thing will not turn.' 'What do you wish me to do?' I replied. 'Come and correct it,' said he. When I said, 'It is not time, you are not sent by the king, and you wish to get me into some scrape,' he said, 'Very well, the king has sent you these twenty-five louis to remove all suspicion. He gave them to me.'"

"Then these are the twenty-five louis he gave you?"

"No, not these; these are others. The first twenty-five were only on account."

"Peste! Fifty louis for mending a toy? There is something beneath all that, Master Gamain."

"That is what I say. Besides, you see, the other."

"What other?"

"Well, he looked to me like a pretender. I should have questioned him, and asked him details about his tour to France, etc."

"Yet you are a man to be deceived, when an apprentice offers himself."

"I do not say he was a deceiver. He managed the file and chisel well enough, and I have seen him cut a hot bar of iron by a single blow, and with a rat-tail file cut a hole, just as if he had a bit and brace. But you see, he was more theoretical than practical. He had no sooner finished his work than he washed his hands, which at once became white; would the hands of a true locksmith like myself ever become white?"

Gamain put forth two hard, callous hands, which really would seem likely to defy all the almond paste ever made.

"But," said the stranger, leading the locksmith back to the matter under consideration, "what did you do when you saw the king?"

"At first it seemed as if we were expected, for we were taken to the forge; there the king gave me a lock begun wrong, and which would not work. Few locksmiths, you see, are able to make a lock with three beards, and no king can. I looked at it, I saw the joint, and said, 'Just leave me alone for an hour, and in that time I will fix it.' Then the king said, 'Well, Gamain, as you please; you are in your own shop; here are your files, pincers; work, my lad, work; we will go and fix the bureau for which the lock is intended.' He left with the apprentice."

"By the great stairway?" asked the count, carelessly.

"No; by the little secret stairway which opens into the king's study; when I had finished, I said, 'The bureau is a humbug, and they are shut up concocting some plot.' I sought to descend softly; I said to myself, 'I will open the door of the library, when I will see what they are about.'"

"What were they about?"

"Ah, they probably heard me; you know I am no dancing master; tread lightly as I could, the infernal stairway would crack. They heard me, and came to me, and just as I was about to put my hand on the door, 'crack,' it opened."

"Then you know nothing?"

"Wait a bit. 'Ah, ha! Gamain,' said the king, 'is it you?' 'Yes, I have done.' 'And so, too, have we,' said he. 'Come, I now intend to give you another job.' He pushed me through the library, but not so quickly that I did not see, on the table, a great map of France, for it had fleur-de-lis at one of the corners."

"You observed nothing particular on this map of France?"

"Yes; three long rows of pins stuck in, each at some distance from the other, reaching toward the sides of the map. One might have fancied them soldiers advancing by three different routes to the frontier."

"My dear Gamain, your perspicuity is so great that nothing escapes it. And you think, instead of attending to the doors of the drawer, the king and his companion were busied with the map?"

"I am sure of it," said Gamain.

"How so?"

"It is simple enough; the pins had wax heads, some were black, others red; well, the king held in his hand, though he paid no attention to it, and occasionally picked his teeth with a pin with red wax on its head."

"Gamain," said the armorer, "if I ever discover any new system of locksmithing, I will not bring you into my room, nor will I suffer you even to pass through it. If I want you, I will bandage your eyes, as was done on the day you were taken to the great lord's. On that day, though, did you not perceive that the front entrance had ten steps, and that the house was on the boulevard?"

"Wait a moment," said Gamain, enchanted with the eulogium heaped on him; "you have not come to the end yet. There really was an armoire in question."

"Ah! ha! where?"

"Ah! just guess; inserted in the wall, my friend."

"What wall?"

"The wall of the interior corridor, which leads from the king's bedchamber to the dauphin's room."

"Do you know that fact is, to me, peculiarly interesting? Was that armoire open?"

"Not a bit; I looked around on all sides, and saw nothing, and said, 'Well, where is that armoire?' The king then looked around, and said, 'Gamain, I always had confidence in you, and therefore wished no one else to know my secret.' As he spoke while the apprentice held the light for us, for the corridor was dark, the king moved a panel of the wood-work, and I saw a round hole about two feet across; as he saw my surprise, he said, 'See you that hole, my friend; I had it made to hide away money. This young man has assisted me during the three or four days he has been in the castle; now I must put the lock on in such a manner that the panel will resume its place, and hide it as it hides the hole. Have you any need of assistance? this young man will assist you, as he assisted me. If not,' said he, 'I will employ him elsewhere.' 'Ah,' said I, 'you know that when I am at work, I never want anybody with me. There are four hours' work here for a competent man, and as I am a master, all will be done in three. Go about your business, young man, and do you go about yours, sire. If you have anything to conceal, come back in three hours, and all will be done.' The king must have had something for the young man to do, for I never saw him again. After about three hours, the king came back, and said, 'Eh! Gamain, how do we get on?' 'So, so, sire; it is done,' and I showed him the panel moved perfectly well, so well that it was a pleasure to hear it. There was not the least noise, and the lock worked like one of Vaucanson's automatons. 'Come, said he, 'Gamain help me to count the money I place within there.' Then I counted one million, and he another, after which there were twenty-five over, he said to me, 'There, Gamain, are twenty-five louis;' as they came very convenient to a poor man, who has five children, and not much out of the way when he had counted a million, I took them. What do you say now?"

The stranger moved his lips. "The fact is, he is mean."

"Wait, that is not all. I took the twenty-five louis

and put them in my pocket. 'Thanks, sire,' said I, 'but with all this, I have eaten nothing to-day, and am dying of hunger and thirst.' I had scarcely spoken, when the queen came in by a masked door, so suddenly that all at once I found her in front of me. She had in her hand a salver, on which was a glass of wine and a biscuit. 'Gamain,' said she, 'you must be hungry and thirsty, take this.' 'Ah,' said I to the queen, 'you need not have put yourself out for me; it was not worth while.' Tell me what you think of that? To give a glass of wine to a man who is thirsty, and a biscuit to one who is hungry? What was the queen about? Anybody might know that, were I hungry and thirsty, one glass of wine, one biscuit—pah!"

"Then you refused it?"

"It would have been better if I had. No, I drank it. As for the biscuit, I wrapped it up in a handkerchief, and said, 'What is good for the father, is good for the children.' I then thanked her majesty and set out for Versailles, swearing they would never catch me at the Tuileries again."

"Why do you say it would have been better for you to have refused the wine?"

"Because they had put poison in it—scarcely had I passed the turning bridge than I felt thirsty—and so thirsty—it was just where the river is on one side, and the wine merchants on the other. Then I saw the bad properties of the wine they had given me. The more I drank, the more I wanted to drink, and thus it was until I lost all consciousness. They may rest assured, if ever I am called upon to give testimony against them, I will say they gave me twenty-five louis for working four hours and counting a million, and then, fearing lest I should tell where they hid the money, poisoned me like a dog." *

"And I, my dear Gamain," said the armorer, rising, for he now knew what he wished, "I will rely on your evi-

* This was really the accusation made to the convention by this ungrateful wretch on the occasion of the trial of the queen.

dence, as it was I who gave you the antidote which, thank God, saved your life."

Then Gamain, taking the hands of the stranger between his own, said:

"Henceforth we are friends to the death."

Refusing, with almost Spartan sobriety, the glass of wine which had been three or four times offered him by the man to whom he swore eternal fidelity, Gamain, on whom the ammonia had produced the double effect of instantaneously sobering him and of disgusting him for three or four days of wine, resumed the route to Versailles, which he reached at four or five in the morning, with the king's louis and the queen's biscuit in his pocket.

Having remained in the cabaret, the false armorer took his tablets from his pocket; they were inlaid with gold, and wrote:

"Behind the alcove of the king, the dark corridor leading to the dauphin's room. Iron armoire. To ascertain if Louis le Comte, a locksmith's apprentice, be not Count Louis, son of the Marquis de Bouille, who came eleven days ago from Metz."

CHAPTER XVII.

THE MACHINE OF M. GUILLOTIN.

Two days after, thanks to the strange ramification Cagliostro possessed in all classes of society, and even in the royal service, he ascertained that Count Louis, son of the Marquis de Bouille, had come on the 15th or 16th of November, had been discovered by his cousin, Lafayette, on the 18th, and on the same day introduced himself to the king. That he had offered himself to the locksmith as an apprentice on the 22d; had remained three days with him, and on the fourth day had gone to the Tuileries and been introduced to the king without any difficulty; that he had left the king two hours after Gamain, and having gone to the lodging of his friend Achille du Chastillon, had immediately changed his dress, and on the same evening returned to Metz.

On the other hand, on the day after the nocturnal conference in the Cemetery of St. John, between Beausire and Cagliostro, the former hurried out of breath to Bellevue, the house of the banker Zanoni. As he came from the gaming-table at seven in the morning, after losing his last sou, in spite of the certain martingale of Law, Beausire found the house empty, and that Olive and Toussaint had disappeared.

He then remembered that Cagliostro had refused to leave with him, saying that he had something confidential to say to Olive. This opened the door to suspicion. Cagliostro had carried Olive off. Like a good dog, Beausire put his nose on the track, and went to Bellevue, where he left his name, and was at once admitted to Baron Zanoni, or to Count Cagliostro, as the reader pleases to call him, if not the principal personage, at least the one on whom all the drama hinges.

Being introduced into the saloon with which we are already acquainted, from having seen Dr. Gilbert, Cagliostro and the Marquis de Favras, Beausire when he saw the count hesitated. The count appeared such a great lord that he dared not even demand his mistress.

As if though he read the heart of hearts of the old bailiff, Cagliostro said:

"Beausire, I have observed that you have two real passions: gaming and Mademoiselle Olive."

"Ah! count, you know what I came for?"

"Yes, to ask Mademoiselle Olive of me. She is in my house. Yes, at my house in the Rue St. Claude, where she has her old rooms, and if you be prudent, and I am satisfied with you, and you bring me news which amuse me, some day, Monsieur de Beausire, we will put twenty-five louis in your pocket to enable you to play the gentleman in the Palais Royal, and a good coat on your back, to enable you to play the lover in the Rue St. Claude."

Beausire had a great desire to talk loudly, and to demand

Mlle. Olive, but Cagliostro had said two words about that unfortunate affair of the Portuguese embassy, which always hung over his head like the sword of Damocles. Beausire said nothing.

Some doubt having been manifested by him as to whether Mlle. Olive really was at the house in the Rue St. Claude, the count ordered his carriage, and returned with Beausire to the house on the boulevard, where he introduced him into the *sanctum sanctorum*, and displacing a picture, showed him, by a skilfully contrived opening, Mlle. Olive dressed like a queen and lolling in a chair, while she read one of the bad books, which at the time were so common, and which, when she was fille de chambre of Mlle. de Taverney, she was so happy to get hold of. M. Toussaint, her son, was dressed like a prince, with white hat, rôle Henry IV., with plumes, and sky-blue pantaloons, sustained by a tricolored sash fringed with gold and magnificently embroidered.

Beausire felt his paternal and marital heart dilate. He promised all the count wished, and the count permitted him every day as soon as he had brought him his news, and received his ten louis d'or, to enjoy the luxury of love in Olive's arms.

All progressed according to the count's wishes, and we may say almost according to Beausire's, when toward the end of the month of December, at a strange hour for that season, that is to say, at six in the morning, Dr. Gilbert, who had already been three hours at work, heard three knocks at his door, and from their peculiar intonation recognized a brother mason. He opened—Count Cagliostro stood on the other side of the door. Gilbert never met this mysterious man without something of terror.

"Ah!" said he to the count, "is it you?" Then, making an effort over himself, and giving him his hand, he said, "You are welcome whenever you come, or for whatever purpose."

"What brings me, dear Gilbert, is to enable you to be present at a philanthropical experiment, of which I have already spoken to you."

Gilbert sought to recollect, but in vain, and finally said: "I do not remember."

"Come, though, dear Gilbert; I do not disturb you for nothing. Besides, you will meet many acquaintances of yours. Go with me."

"Dear count, I will go anywhere that you please to take me. The place and persons are but secondary considerations."

"Then come, for we have no time to lose."

Gilbert was dressed, and had only to lay aside his pen and put on his hat and cloak. A carriage was waiting. They entered it.

The carriage was driven rapidly away, there being not even an order given. The driver evidently knew whither he was going.

When he got out of the carrige, Gilbert saw that he was in the court of a prison, and at once recognized the Bicetre.

It was nearly a quarter after six; the worst hour of the twenty-four, for even the most vigorous constitutions then suffer from cold.

A small misty rain fell diagonally, and stained the gray walls. In the middle of the court five or six carpenters, under the direction of a master-workman, and a little man clad in black, who seemed to direct everybody, put up a machine of a strange and unknown form.

Gilbert shuddered; he had recognized Dr. Guillotin, whom he had met at Marat's. The machine was the one a model of which he had seen in the cellar of the editor of "L'Ami du Peuple."

The little man recognized Cagliostro and Gilbert.

"Good baron," said he, "it is kind in you to come first and to bring the doctor. You remember I invited you at Marat's to come and see the experiment. I forgot, however, to ask you for your address. You will see something curious, the most philanthropic machine ever invented."

All at once, turning to the machine, which to him was a perfect hobby, he said:

"Eh! Guidon, what are you about? You are putting it hind part before."

Rushing up the ladder, which two men had placed at one of the sides, he stood for a moment on the platform, when in a few moments he gave directions for the correction of an error which the workmen had committed, they being ignorant as yet of the secrets of this novel machine.

"There," said Dr. Guillotin, seeing with satisfaction that under his direction all went right, "things go straight. It is now only necessary to put the knife in the groove."

"Guidon, Guidon!" said he, with an expression of terror, "why is not the groove faced with copper?"

"Doctor, I thought well-seasoned oak quite as good as copper," said the carpenter.

"Ah, that is it!" said the doctor. "Petty economy! economy, when the progress and good of humanity is concerned! Guidon, if the experiment fails to-day, I hold you responsible. Gentlemen," said he to Cagliostro and Gilbert, "I call you to witness that I wished the grooves for the knife to be faced with copper. Therefore, if it stick or do not slide easily, it is not my fault, and I wash my hands of it."

Notwithstanding this difficulty, however, the machine was erected, and certainly had a kind of homicidal air which delighted its inventor, but which horrified Dr. Gilbert.

This is the form of the machine:

A platform reached by a simple staircase. It was fifteen feet square, and on two of the parallel sides of this platform, ten or twelve feet high, arose two uprights. In them was the famous groove, the copper facing of which M. Guidon had sought to save, and which had evoked the lamentations of the philanthropic Guillotin. Down these grooves, slid, by means of a spring, which, when opened, suffered it to fall freely, from its own weight, and much more, fastened to it, a kind of crescent-shaped knife. A little opening was made between the two beams, through which a man's head could be passed, and which was contrived to seize the head as if it were a collar. A framework, long as the stature of an ordinary man's size, moved up and down on a hinge, and when let fall was exactly level with the opening.

All this, it will be seen, was very ingenious.

While the carpenters, Master Guidon, and the doctor were finishing their work, while Cagliostro and Gilbert were discussing the novelty of the instrument, the invention of which, by Dr. Guillotin, the count disputed by showing much that was analagous in the Italian *mannaya,* and the *doloire* of Toulouse, with which the Marshal Montmorency was executed, new spectators began to come, called together, doubtless, by a desire to witness the experiment, and filled the courtyard.

As the rain continued to fall, not so intensely, perhaps, but more steadily, Dr. Guillotin, who doubtless feared lest "bad weather" should deprive him of some of his spectators, hurried to the most important group, which was composed of Gilbert, Cagliostro, Dr. Louis, and the architect Giraud, and, like a manager aware of the impatience of the public, said :

"Gentlemen, we await only one person, Doctor Cabanis ; when he comes we will begin."

He scarcely finished these words, when a carriage entered the yard, and a man of thirty-eight or forty years, with an open face and intelligent expression of features and eye, dismounted. It was Dr. Cabanis, the person they had waited for. He bowed affably to all, as a philosophic physician should do, gave Guillotin his hand, who from his platform exclaimed, "Welcome, doctor ; we waited for no one but you." He then joined the group in which Gilbert and Cagliostro were.

"Gentlemen," said Guillotin, "all being here, we will begin."

At a motion of his hand a door was opened, and two men, clad in a kind of gray uniform, were seen to leave it, bearing on their shoulders a sack, in which the outline of a human body was vaguely seen.

Behind the glass of the windows the pale faces of the

criminals were seen, looking with an expression of terror, though uninvited, at a terrible spectacle, the object and reason of which they could not understand.

On the evening of the same day—that is to say, on the 24th of December, Christmas Eve, there was a reception at Flora's pavilion.

The queen did not wish to receive company herself, so the Princess de Lamballe received for her, and was doing the honors of the circle when the queen arrived.

In the course of the morning, the young Baron Isidor de Charny had returned from Turin, and immediately after his arrival he had been admitted to the king, and then at once had an audience of the queen.

He had been received with great courtesy by both ; but two reasons rendered this courtesy on the part of the queen remarkable.

In the first place, Isidor was the brother of Charny, and since Charny was absent, the queen experienced some pleasure in seeing his brother.

And then Isidor brought despatches from M. le Comte d'Artois and M. le Prince de Condé, which were quite in accordance with her own wishes.

The princes recommended the project of M. de Favras to the queen, and begged her to profit by the devotion of this generous gentleman, to fly and rejoin them at Turin.

He was further charged to express to M. de Favras all the sympathy which they felt for his project, as well as the wishes they entertained for its success.

The queen kept Isidor more than an hour with her, invited him to join the evening circle of Mme. de Lamballe, and would not even then have allowed him to go if he had not himself asked leave, in order to acquit himself of his commission to M. de Favras.

The marquis had been forewarned of everything direct from Turin ; and knew on whose behalf Isidor came.

The message which the queen had intrusted to the young man completed the joy of the conspirator. Everything in fact seconded his hopes ; the plot was getting on wonderfully.

One thing only made the marquis uneasy. This was the silence of the king and queen on his account. This silence the queen had attempted to break through the intervention of Isidor, and however vague might be the expressions which Isidor brought with him from the queen for M. and Mme. de Favras, they were of great importance, since they came from royal lips.

At nine in the evening the baron went to Mme. de Lamballe's.

He had never been presented to that princess. She did not know him; but, forewarned by the queen in the course of the day, when his name was announced, the princess rose and welcomed him with a charming grace, and took him at once into her own little circle.

Neither the king nor the queen had yet arrived. Monsieur, who seemed sufficiently uneasy, was talking in a corner with two gentlemen of the most intimate of his acquaintances, M. de la Chatre and M. de Avaray. Count Louis de Narbonne went from group to group with the ease of a man who feels himself to be one of the family.

When the ushers had announced the king and queen, all conversation and bursts of laughter at once gave place to a respectful silence. Mme. de Lamballe and Mme. Elizabeth joined the queen. Monsieur walked straight up to the king to pay his respects, and, bowing to his majesty, said:

"Brother, cannot you manage to get up a private game of whist, composed of yourself, the queen, me, and some one of your intimate friends, so that under the appearance of play, we may be able to enjoy some private conversation?"

"Willingly, brother," replied the king; "go and arrange the matter with the queen."

Monsieur approached Marie Antoinette, to whom Charny was tendering his respects, and saying, quite low, "Madame, I have seen Monsieur de Favras, and I have some communication of the utmost importance to make to your majesty."

"My dear sister," said Monsieur, "the king wishes us to

make up a party of four for whist ; we challenge you, and beg you to choose your partner yourself."

"Very well," said the queen, who, herself, doubted that this game of whist was but a pretext, "my choice is made. Monsieur le Baron de Charny, you shall join our game, and while we are playing you shall tell us the news you have brought with you from Turin."

"Ah ! you have just come from Turin, baron ?" said Monsieur.

"Yes, monseigneur ; and in returning from Turin I passed through the Place Royale, where I saw a man who is entirely devoted to the king, the queen, and to your royal highness."

Monsieur colored, coughed, and passed on. He was a man of considerable circumspection.

He beckoned to M. de la Chatre, who approached him, and receiving his orders in a low voice, left at once. During this time the king addressed and received the ladies and gentlemen who still continued to visit the Tuileries.

The queen went and took him by the arm to lead him to the whist-table. They played two or three hands, only speaking when necessary.

But after playing some time, and after observing that respect kept the crowd from the royal table, "Brother," hazarded the queen to Monsieur, "the baron has told you that he has only just arrived from Turin ?"

"Yes," said Monsieur, "he said something about it."

"He has told you, has he not, that Monsieur le Comte d'Artois and Monsieur le Prince de Condé advise us strongly to go and join them ?"

The king seemed impatient.

"Brother," whispered Mme. Elizabeth, with the sweetness of an angel, "do listen, I beg."

"And you, too, sister," said the king.

"I more than anybody, my dear Louis, for I love you, and am more uneasy than any one else."

"I was about to add," hazarded Isidor, "that I passed through the Place Royale, and that I stopped nearly an hour at No. 21."

"At No. 21?" said the king. "What is there?"

"At No 21," replied Isidor, "there lives a gentleman entirely devoted to your majesty, ready, as we are, to die for you, but who, more active than all of us put together, has managed a project for your safety."

"What is it, monsieur?" questioned the king, raising his head.

"If I could believe that I am displeasing the king, by repeating to his majesty what I know of this matter, I would at once be silent."

"No, no, monsieur," said the queen, quickly; "speak; sufficient people form projects against us; it is well that we should know those they make for our advantage. Monsieur le Baron, tell us what they call this gentleman?"

"Monsieur le Marquis de Favras, madame."

"Ah!" said the queen, "we know him; and you have faith in his devotion, Monsieur le Baron?"

"Of his devotion, yes; madame, I not only believe in it, but I am sure of it."

"Take care, monsieur," observed the king; "you promise much."

"Heart judges heart, sire. I answer for the devotion of Monsieur de Favras, as for the value of his project, and the chance of its succeeding, is another thing. I am too young, and while he is working for the safety of the king and queen, I am too prudent to dare to force my own opinions into the water."

"And this project. What may it be?" said the queen.

"Madame, it is ready for execution; and if it pleases the king to say a word, or make a sign this evening, tomorrow at the same hour he shall be at Peronne."

The king was silent.

"Sire," remarked the queen, addressing her husband, "did you hear what the baron said?"

"Certainly," said the king, "I heard."

"Well, brother," asked Monsieur, "is not what the baron proposes very tempting?"

The king turned very quickly toward Monsieur, and fixing his look firmly on his countenance, said:

"And if I go, will you go with me?"

Monsieur changed color; his lips trembled, agitated by an emotion which he could not master.

"I?" said he.

"Yes, you, my brother," said Louis XVI., "you who wish me to quit Paris, you, I ask, if I go, will you go with me?"

"But," lisped Monsieur, "I am not prepared, not having been forewarned, nothing is, consequently ready."

"What, you were never forewarned?" said the king; "and it is you who have furnished the money necessary to Monsieur de Favras. None of your preparations are made, and yet you have known, from hour to hour, how the conspiracy got on!"

"The conspiracy!" repeated Monsieur, looking very pale.

"Without doubt, the conspiracy; for it is a conspiracy, a conspiracy so real, that if it is discovered, Monsieur de Favras will be imprisoned, conducted to the châtelet, and condemned to death!—at least, unless, by means of money and promise, you manage to save him, as we contrived to save Monsieur de Bésenval."

"But if the king saved Bésenval, surely he will also rescue Monsieur de Favras."

"No; because what I have done for one, I may not be able to do for another. Monsieur de Bésenval was my man, just as Monsieur de Favras is yours. Let each one save his own, and then we shall each do our duty."

And as he uttered these words, the king rose.

The queen seized the skirt of his coat.

"Sire," said she, "whether you accept or refuse, you must send an answer to Monsieur de Favras."

"I must?"

"Yes; what reply shall the Baron de Charny make in the name of the king?"

"He will answer," said Louis XVI., as he loosened his dress from the hands of the queen, "he will answer that the king cannot permit himself to be carried off."

And he went away and left them.

"What he wished to say," continued Monsieur, "is, that if the Marquis de Favras carries the king off without any permission on his part, he will be heartily welcome, provided, always, the affair succeeds, because, if it does not succeed, he will seem a fool, and, in politics, fools deserve double punishment."

"Monsieur le Baron," said the queen, "run to Monsieur de Favras this very evening without losing an instant, and tell him the very words of the king: 'The king cannot consent that they carry him off.' It is for them to understand them, or for you to explain them. Go!"

The baron, who rightly regarded the answer of the king and the recommendation of the queen as a double acquiescence, seized his hat, and jumping into a carriage, ordered the driver to go to Place Royale, No. 21.

When the king arose from the whist-table he went toward a group of young men whose joyous laughter had excited his attention before he entered the saloon. They were silent at his approach.

"Ah, gentlemen," said he, "is the king so unfortunate as to bring sadness with him wherever he goes?"

"Sire!" murmured the young men.

"You were very lively and laughing gaily when the queen and I entered just now."

Then, shaking his head, "Unhappy are the kings," said he, "before whom others will not laugh."

"Sire!" said M. de Lameth "the respect——"

"My dear Charles," said the king, "when you leave your prison on Sundays and Thursdays, and I make you come, for amusement, to Versailles, does my being there ever prevent you from laughing? I have just now said, 'Unhappy are the kings before whom they all dare not laugh!' I now say, 'Happy indeed are the kings before whom all do laugh.'"

"Sire," said M. le Castries, "perhaps the subject which excites our laughter might not seem in any way comical to you."

"Of what are you talking, then, gentlemen?"

"Sire, it was apropos to the National Assembly."

"Oh! ah! gentlemen, there were good reasons to become grave then on seeing me. I really cannot allow any one in my house to laugh at the National Assembly. It is true," added the king, though he did not mean what he said, "I am not at home, but at the place of the Princess de Lamballe, so that whether you laugh any more at the assembly, there can possibly be no harm in your telling me what it really was that made you laugh so loudly?"

"Does the king know what they have been discussing at the assembly throughout the day's sitting?"

"Yes; and I have been very much interested. Has there not been a discussion about a new machine for executing criminals? Proposed by Monsieur Guillotin—and offered to the nation?"

"Yes," said Suleau.

"Oh! oh! Monsieur Suleau, and you jest with Monsieur de Guillotin—with a philosopher, a philanthropist? It's all very well, but you forget I am a philanthropist myself."

"But, sire, there are two sorts of philanthropists. There is, for example, a philanthropist at the head of the French nation—a philanthropist who has abolished the question—him we respect, him we venerate; we do more—we love him, sire."

All the young men bowed at once.

"But," continued Suleau, "there are others who, being already physicians, who, having in their hands a thousand means, both good, bad, and indifferent, to put the sick out of this world easily, endeavor to discover a means equally as satisfactory to them, to carry those in good health off too—and, by my word! I beg your majesty will abandon them to me."

"And what will you do with them, Monsieur Suleau? Not behead them without pain?" asked the king, alluding to the declaration of M. Guillotin; "or shall they take their departure, feeling an agreeable freshness about their necks, eh?"

"It is just what I wish them, but it is not what I will promise them," replied Suleau.

"What," said the king, "is it that you wish them?"

"Yes, sire, I like the people who invent this kind of machine to try them. I do not complain much of Master Aubriot trying the walls of the Bastile, nor Sir Enguerraud de Marigny trying the gibbet at Montfaucon. Unhappily, I have not the honor of being king—unhappily, I have not the honor of being a judge, it is probable, then, I shall be obliged to keep myself opposed to this very respectable doctor, and what I have promised him I have already commenced to carry out."

"And what have you promised him?" asked the king.

"It has come into my head, sire, that this great benefactor of humanity ought to be one of the first to experience its advantages. So, to-morrow morning in the 'Actes des Apotres,' which we shall print in the course of the night, the baptism shall take place. It is only that the daughter of Monsieur de Guillotin, recognized this very day in the National Assembly by her father, should be known by his name, and called Mademoiselle Guillotine."

"I believe an experiment has already been made—this very morning, in fact; were any of you there? The experiment was at Bicetre."

"No, sire; no, no, no!" said a dozen of them, all at once.

"I was there," said a grave voice.

The king turned and recognized Gilbert, who had entered during the discussion, and who was the only one who could answer the king.

"Ah! you were there, doctor, were you?" said the king, turning toward him.

"Yes, sire."

"And how do you think it succeeded?" asked his majesty.

"Perfectly on the two first, sire; but, although the vertebræ of the third was cut, they were obliged to finish the cutting off of the head with a knife."

The young men listened with open mouths and open eyes.

"How, sire," said Charles Lameth, speaking evidently for the rest as well as for himself, "have they executed three men this morning?"

"Yes, gentlemen," said the king; "only the three men were three dead bodies furnished by the Hôtel Dieu. And your opinion, Gilbert?"

"Upon what, sir?"

"On the instrument."

"Sire, it is evidently an improvement upon all machines invented for the purpose of depriving our fellow-creatures of life; but the accident which happened to the third body proves that this machine requires perfecting."

"And how does it act?" asked the king, in whom the genius of mechanism began to rise.

Gilbert then attempted to give an explanation; but as the king could not catch an exact idea of the instrument from the description of the doctor, he said:

"Come, come, doctor; here is a table, pen, ink, and paper. You draw, I think?"

"Yes, sire."

"Well, then, you shall make me a sketch; I shall understand it better."

And as the young men, restrained by respect, did not like to seek to mate the king:

"Come, come, gentlemen," said Louis XVI.; "questions like this interest the whole of humanity."

"And who knows," said Suleau, half aloud, "but one of us is destined to have the honor of marrying Mademoiselle Guillotine? Come, gentlemen, let us be made acquainted with our bride."

And all of them, following Gilbert and the king, collected round the table, at which Gilbert seated himself, in order to more conveniently make his sketch at the invitation of the king.

Gilbert commenced a sketch of the machine, while Louis XVI. traced each line with great attention.

Nothing was wanting, neither platform nor the steps which conducted to it, nor the little window, nor anything else.

He had nearly finished the last details, when the king interrupted him.

"Parbleu!" said he, "there is nothing astonishing that it should have failed, especially at the third experiment."

"How so, sire?" asked Gilbert.

"That has the form of a hatchet," said Louis XVI. "It is not necessary to know much of mechanics to be able to tell that the shape of anything intended to cut, when falling from a height, ought to approach to that of a crescent."

"What form would your majesty then give the knife?"

"A very simple one, that of a triangle."

Gilbert tried to alter the design.

"No, no, not so," said the king, "just lend me your pencil."

"Here is the pencil, sire," said Gilbert.

"Wait, wait," said Louis XVI., carried away by his love of mechanics. "Look—thus and thus—and thus—and I will undertake that you shall cut off some five-and-twenty heads, one after another, without the edge twisting at all."

He had scarcely said these words when a piercing cry, one of terror as much as grief, was uttered just behind him.

He turned quickly, and saw the queen fall fainting into Gilbert's arms.

Urged, like the rest, by curiosity, she had approached the table, and leaning on the chair of the king, she had, looking over his shoulder, at the very time he was engaged in correcting its details, recognized the machine that Cagliostro had made her look at twenty years before in the Château de Taverney Maison Rouge.

At this sight she had only strength to utter the cry, and life seemingly had abandoned her, as if the fatal machine itself had operated on her; she had, in fact, fallen completely insensible into Gilbert's arms.

One can easily understand that after such a circumstance the evening was soon brought to a close.

Her majesty had been laid upon a bed at once and taken to the bedroom of the princess, who with that peculiar intuition belonging to females, guessing there was some mystery, watched with the king, until, thanks to the skill of Dr. Gilbert, the queen recovered her senses.

But it was evident that life was going to awake before reason; for some moments she looked about the room with that vague and indifferent look with which people regard everything when they do not know where they are and what has happened? But soon a slight trembling ran through her body; she uttered a short, shrill cry, and covered her eyes with her hand as if to shut out some painful sight.

She was coming about.

But the crisis was passed. Gilbert was about to depart, when the queen, as if she had already understood he was going, stretched out her hand, and in a nervous voice, accompanied by gesture as well, "Remain!" said she.

Gilbert stopped, quite astonished. He did not ignore the little sympathetic feeling the queen entertained for him.

"I am at the orders of the queen," said he, "but I believe it will be the best to calm the excited feelings of the people in the saloons, and if your majesty will permit——"

"Thérèse," said the queen, addressing herself to the Princess de Lamballe, "go and announce to the king that I am rapidly recovering, and say that I wish to talk to Doctor Gilbert."

The princess obeyed with that sweet passiveness which was the characteristic of her temper, and even of her physiognomy.

The queen followed her with her eyes and waited anxiously for her finishing her commission. She was free now to talk with Dr. Gilbert. She turned round, and fixing her eyes upon him, she said:

"Doctor, what do you think caused this to happen?"

"Madame," said Gilbert, "I am a man of science; have the goodness to put the question in a more precise form."

"I ask you, sir," said the queen, "whether the fainting fit I have experienced has been caused by one of those nervous crises to which we poor women, through feebleness of our constitutions, are particularly liable, or if you suspect the accident has been brought on by any cause more serious ?"

"I shall answer your majesty, that the daughter of Marie Theresa, the woman whom I saw so calm and courageous during the night of the 5th and 6th of October, is not an ordinary woman, and consequently is not capable of being moved by what ordinarily affects a woman."

"You are right, doctor. Do you believe in presentiments ?"

"Science herself repulses all these phenomena which have a tendency to change the common course of things."

"I ought to have said, 'Do you believe in predictions ?'"

"I believe that Providence has concealed the future from us with an impenetrable veil. Some, by severely studying the past, are able to lift the corner and catch some idea of the future. But these instances are very rare, and since religion has abolished fatality, since philosophy has put limits to faith, prophets have lost fully three-quarters of their mystical powers. And yet——" added Gilbert.

"And yet ?" replied the queen, looking thoughtful.

"And yet, madame," continued he, as if he were making an effort over himself, to avoid coming in contact with questions which he considered to lie within the region of doubt. "And yet, madame, there is a man——"

"A man ?" said the queen, who followed Gilbert's words with great interest.

"He is a man who has often confounded all my arguments by most unaccountable deeds."

"And this man is—— ?"

"I dare not name him before your majesty."

"This man is your master, is he not, Gilbert ? the man all-powerful ! the immortal, divine Cagliostro."

"Madame, my only true master is Nature ; Cagliostro

is only my saviour. Pierced by a ball, which had traversed the whole length of my breast, and which, after having studied medicine for twenty years, I considered incurable, thanks to a salve, with whose composition I am still ignorant, he cured me in the course of a few days—hence my gratitude; I had almost said my admiration."

"And this man has predicted to you things that have come to pass?"

"Strange, incredible things! Madame, this man walks so firmly through the present, that it is to easy to believe he has some knowledge of the future."

"How far, if this man had predicted a certain thing to you, would you believe in its coming to pass?"

"I should act at least as if I expected it to be realized."

"If he had foretold that you would meet a terrible, premature, infamous death, would you prepare for such a death?"

Gilbert looked profoundly at the queen, and said:

"After having tried all possible means to escape from such a death, I should certainly prepare myself for it."

"To escape from it? No, doctor, no; I see well I am condemned," said the queen. "This revolution is a whirlpool which will swallow up the throne, this people is a lion which will devour me."

"Ah, madame," said Gilbert, "it only depends upon you, and you may see this very lion, so terrible now, come and lie at your feet like a lamb."

"Did you not see this lion at Versailles?"

"Have you not seen it at the Tuileries? It is like an ocean, madame, which beats incessantly—until it has destroyed it—against any rock which opposes itself to its strength; but it caresses the bark which trusts to it."

"Doctor, all connection between this people and me has been broken for a long time now; they hate me, I despise them."

"Because you do not really understand each other. Cease to be their queen—be their mother. Forget that you are the daughter of Marie Theresa, our ancient foe, the sister of Joseph II., our false friend. Be French, and you shall hear the voice of this people rise only to bless you, and you shall see the arms of this great people stretching out but to bless you."

Marie Antoinette shrugged up her shoulders.

"Yes, I know that; yesterday the people blessed, to-day they caress, and to-morrow they would strangle those they have blessed—those they caressed."

"Ah! madame," cried Gilbert, "be not deceived; it is not the people that would rebel against the king and queen; it is they have rebelled against the people, who continue to address them in a language full of the privileges of royalty, when they ought to speak the words of fraternity and love. Yes; Italy, Poland, Ireland, Spain will look at this France, born yesterday, and cry, stretching forth their hands chained—chained: 'France, France, we are free in thee!' Madame, madame, there is yet time; take the young one, born yesterday, take it into your lap and be its mother."

"Doctor," said the queen, "you forget that I have other children, children of my womb, and that I should disinherit them by adopting this little strange child."

"If it be so, madame," said Gilbert, in a tone of great sadness, "wrap these children up in the royal mantle, in the mantle of war, of Marie Theresa, and carry them away from France, for you spoke truly when you said the people would devour you; but there is no time to lose; you must be quick, madame, very quick!"

"And you will not oppose this departure?"

"Far from it," answered Gilbert, "now I know your intentions. I will assist you."

"That is well," said the queen, "for there is a gentleman quite ready to devote himself to this object."

"Ah, madame," said Gilbert, with alarm, "do you not mean Monsieur de Favras?"

"Who told you his name? who revealed his project to you?"

"Oh, madame, take care! A fatal prediction follows him too."

"And from the same prophet?"

"Yes, madame."

"And, according to this prophet, what fate awaits the marquis?"

"A terrible death! premature! infamous! such a one as you spoke of just now."

"Then you indeed spoke the truth; there is no time to lose in order to prevent the fulfilment of the prophecies."

"You have sent to announce to Monsieur de Favras that you accept his assistance?"

"Some one is with him now. I am expecting his answer every moment."

At this moment, as Gilbert, frightened at the circumstances in which he found himself, passed his hand over his face to shut out the light, Mme. de Lamballe entered, and whispered one or two words in the ear of the queen.

"Let him come in," said the queen, "let him come in, the doctor knows all. Doctor," continued she, "Monsieur Isidor de Charny brings me the answer of Monsieur le Marquis de Favras. To-morrow the queen will have left Paris; after to-morrow, the queen will be out of France. Come, baron, come. Great God! what's the matter? and why are you so pale?"

"Madame la Princesse de Lamballe has told me that I may speak before Doctor Gilbert," observed Isidor.

"Yes, yes, speak; you have seen the Marquis de Favras? The marquis is ready—we accept his offer; we leave Paris—we leave France?"

"The Marquis of Favras was arrested an hour ago in the Rue Beaurepaire, and carried to the châtelet," said Isidor.

The eyes of the queen crossed those of Gilbert; they were luminous, desperate, full of anger. But all the strength of Marie Antoinette seemed to be exhausted by this flash.

Gilbert approached her, and in a tone expressive of great pity, said:

"Madame, if I can be of any use to you, dispose of me

as you like; my intelligence, my devotion, my life, I lay at once at your feet."

The queen raised her eyes slowly toward the doctor.

Then, in a voice gentle and resigned:

"Monsieur Gilbert," said she, "you, who are a learned man, and have assisted at the experiment of this morning, can you tell me whether the death caused by this frightful machine is as easy as the inventor declares it to be?"

Gilbert heaved a sigh, and covered his eyes with his hands.

At this moment Monsieur, who knew all he wished to know, for the news of M. de Favras's arrest spread like wildfire through the palace—at this moment Monsieur ordered his carriage in a loud voice, and took his departure without taking leave of the king.

Louis XVI. stopped up the passage before him.

"Brother, I suppose you are not," said he, "in such a hurry to enter the Luxembourg as not to be able to give me some counsel. What ought I to do, in your opinion?"

"You would ask what, if I were in your place, I should do?"

"Yes."

"I should abandon Monsieur de Favras, and swear fidelity to the constitution."

"What, would you recommend me to swear fidelity to a constitution which is not made as yet?"

"So much the greater reason," said Monsieur, with a cunning look, "so much the greater reason, my dear brother, you should do so, for then there is no occasion to keep the oath."

The king stood thoughtfully for a moment.

"Let it be so," said he; "that will not prevent my writing to Monsieur de Bouille that our project still holds, but is adjourned, put off. This delay will allow the Count de Charny to collect together all who should follow us."

CHAPTER XVIII.

MONSIEUR DISAVOWS FAVRAS, AND THE KING TAKES THE OATH OF THE CONSTITUTION.

On the morning of the arrest of M. de Favras, this singular paper circulated through Paris:

"The Marquis de Favras (Place Royale) has been arrested, together with his wife, during the night between the 24th and 25th, for a plan which he had of raising thirty thousand men to assassinate Lafayette and the mayor of the city.

"Monsieur, brother to the king, was at the head.

"(Signed) Barauz."

One can easily understand the strange revolution such a paper made in the Paris of 1790. A train of powder fired could scarcely have produced a flame more rapid than that which passed along with this circular. At length it was in the hands of all. Two hours afterward every one knew it by heart.

On the evening of the 26th, the Mandataires de la Commune were reassembled at the Hôtel de Ville in council, when an usher announced that Monsieur demanded to be admitted to them.

"Monsieur!" repeated the good Bailly, who presided over the assembly, "what Monsieur?"

"Monsieur, brother of the king," replied the usher.

At these words the members of the Commune looked at one another. The name of Monsieur had been in everybody's mouth since break of day.

Bailly cast an inquiring glance round the assembly, and, since the silent answers he gathered from the faces of his companions were unanimous, he said:

"Go, announce to Monsieur that, however much astonished at the honor he is conferring upon us, we are ready to receive him."

Some moments after Monsieur was introduced.

He was alone ; his face was pale, and his walk, generally slovenly, this evening was more so than usual.

By good luck for Monsieur, the lights were so placed as to leave a small space partially in the dark. This circumstance did not escape the observation of Monsieur. As yet, he looked timidly on this immense reunion, where he found, at least, respect if not sympathy, and, with a voice trembling at first, but which acquired firmness by degrees :

"Gentlemen," said he, "the desire to contradict a vile calumny has brought me among you. Monsieur de Favras was arrested by your Committee of Inquiry, and they spread the report to-day that I was leagued with him."

Some smiles flitted across the faces of his auditors.

He continued :

"In my quality of citizen of the city of Paris, I thought it was my duty to let you know from myself the relations in which I stand to Monsieur de Favras."

As we may easily imagine, the attention of messieurs the members of the Commune redoubled ; they were about to hear, from the very lips of Monsieur himself, what relations his highness had with Monsieur de Favras.

His highness continued in these terms :

"In 1772 Monsieur de Favras entered my Swiss Guard ; he left them in 1775. I have never spoken to him since that time."

A murmur of incredulity passed through the audience, but a glance of Bailly repressed this murmur, and Monsieur remained in doubt as to whether his speech was approved or disapproved.

Monsieur went on : "Deprived now for many months of the enjoyment of my revenues, rendered uneasy by certain payments which I have to make in January, I wished to be able to meet my engagements without having to apply to the public treasury. I had resolved, consequently, to obtain money on mortgage. Fifteen days ago M. de Favras was pointed out to me by M. de la Chatre as a man likely to be able to effect it through a banker of Genoa. I therefore signed a bill for two millions, the sum necessary to meet my engagements at the beginning of the year, and to pay for my house. This matter was purely a financial one. I told my steward to look after it. I have not seen Monsieur de Favras. I have not written to him. What he has done in other matters is wholly unknown to me."

A sneer passed through the ranks of the Commune, which showed that they were not disposed to believe, on Monsieur's word alone, that he had placed bills for two millions in the hands of another without seeing him, and through an agent, and, above all, that agent one of his old guard.

Monsieur blushed, and, without doubt, urged on by the consciousness of being in a false position, he said, in a lively manner:

"And yet, gentlemen, I heard that there was distributed yesterday throughout the capital a paper conceived in these terms."

And Monsieur read—this was useless, since all there knew it by heart—the letter which we but just now quoted.

At the words, "Monsieur, brother of the king, was at the head," all the members of the Commune bowed.

Did they wish to imply that they were of the same opinion as the circular? Did they simply mean they were listening?

Monsieur continued:—"You do not expect that I should defend myself against a charge like this; but at a time when calumnies, of which every one must see the absurdity, may easily confound the best citizens with the enemies of the revolution, I have thought it my duty, gentlemen, both to the king, to you, and myself, to enter into the details which you have just heard, in order that public opinion may recognize the truth at once. Since the day when, in the second assembly of great men, I declared myself on our great questions, which still cause some division of opinion, I have not ceased to believe that a great revolution was ready, that the king, through his virtues and superior rank, ought to be at the head, since it could not be an advantage to the nation without being equally so to the monarch."

Although the sense was not very clear in these last expressions, yet the habit they had acquired of applauding some forms of words, caused them to applaud these.

Encouraged by this, Monsieur raised his voice, and added, addressing the assembly with a little more assurance :

"Until they can bring forward one of my actions, one of my speeches, which contradicts, in any way, the principles I have professed, until they can show that the happiness of both king and people has not been my constant thought, my every wish, I have the right to be believed. I have changed neither sentiments nor principles, and I never shall change."

The mayor of Paris replied :

"Monsieur, it is a matter of great satisfaction to the representatives of the Commune of Paris to see among them the brother of a cherished king, and of a king who is the restorer of French liberty. August brothers, the same sentiment unites you. Monsieur showed himself the first citizen ready to vote for the Third Estate in the second assembly ; he was nearly the only one of this opinion, save a few friends of the people. Monsieur, then, is the first author of civil equality. In coming to mix with the representatives of the Commune, he has shown to-day that he only wishes to be known through his patriotic sentiments. These sentiments consist of the explanation which Monsieur has just made to the assembly. The prince comes before public opinion, and citizens value the opinion of their fellow-citizens. I offer, Monsieur, then, in the name of the assembly, the tribute and respect which it owes to the sentiments and the presence of his royal highness, and particularly to the value he attaches to men being free."

Then, when Monsieur understood without doubt that in spite of the praise bestowed on his conduct by Bailly it would be differently judged afterward, he replied, with that paternal air which he knew so well how to assume whenever he thought it would answer :

"Gentlemen, the duty I have just fulfilled has been a painful one for a virtuous heart; but I am sufficiently compensated by the sentiments which the assembly has so kindly expressed toward me, and my mouth ought only to be opened to ask pardon for those who have offended me."

Monsieur had performed, then, his part of the counsel which he had given to his brother, Louis XVI.

He had thrown off M. de Favras, and, as we have seen, owing to the praises of the virtuous Bailly, the scheme had been successful.

Louis XVI., recollecting all this, determined, on his side, to swear fidelity to the constitution.

One fine morning the usher came and told the president of the assembly, who on this day was M. Bureaux de Pusey, just as the usher had reported Monsieur to the mayor, that the king, with one or two ministers and three or four officers, knocked at the door of the Manege as Monsieur had knocked at the door of the Hôtel de Ville.

The representatives of the people looked astonished. What could the king have to say to them, who for this long while had been separated from them ?

They caused Louis XVI. to be introduced, and the president gave him up his armchair.

All at once the saloon resounded with acclamations. All France, except Petion, Camille Desmoulins and Marat believed that it was once more loyal.

The king had wished to come and felicitate the assembly upon what it had effected, to praise this beautiful division of France into departments; but what he could no longer suppress was the great love he entertained for the constitution.

The commencement of the discourse caused some uneasiness, the middle was gratifying, but the end—the end brought out all the enthusiasm of the assembly.

The king could not resist expressing his love for this little constitution of 1791, which was not as yet even born ; what would he do then when he saw it some day full grown ?

We cannot give the discourse of the king ; there are six pages of it ; it is quite enough to have quoted that of Monsieur. As much as there is, however, Louis XVI. did not seem too wordy to the assembly, which was often moved to tears.

When we say that it was moved to tears, we do not say so metaphorically ; Barnave, Lameth, Dupont, Mirabeau, Barrere, all wept. It was quite a deluge.

The king left—but the king and the assembly could not part so ; it came out after him and hastened to the Tuileries, where the queen received it.

The queen, the stern daughter of Marie Theresa, was no enthusiast ; she did not weep ; she presented her son to the deputies of the nation.

"Gentlemen," said she, "I share all the sentiments of the king. Here is my son. I shall not neglect to teach him in good time to imitate the virtues of the best of fathers, to respect public liberty, and to maintain the laws, of which I hope he will be the most firm pillar."

Now there was a real enthusiasm. They proposed to take the oaths that very instant. They formed themselves into a sitting of the assembly. First of all, the president pronounced the following words :

"I swear to be faithful to the nation, and to uphold with all my power the constitution decreed by the National Assembly, and accepted by the king."

And all the members of the assembly accepted the oath at once, and raising his hand, each in turn said, "I swear!"

For the ten days following the peace Paris expended itself in balls, fêtes, and fireworks. From all parts came news of oaths being taken ; all over they were busy swearing ; people swore on the Grève, at the Hôtel de Ville, in the churches, in the streets, in the public squares ; altars were erected to La Patrie ; to these they conducted all scholars, and they took the oath, just as if they had been men and understood what was meant by it.

The assembly directed a Te Deum to be sung, and there, on the altar, before God, they renewed their oath.

The king only was not present at Notre Dame, and so did not swear again.

His absence was remarked, but all were so pleased, so confident, that they were quite satisfied with the first excuse he pleased to give them.

"Why have you not been to the Te Deum? why have you not sworn like the rest, on the altar of God?" the queen asked, ironically.

"Because," was the answer of Louis XVI., "I wish to lie well, and not to forswear myself."

The queen breathed. Until then, like the rest, she had believed in the good faith of the king.

CHAPTER XIX.

A GENTLEMAN.

THIS visit of the king to the assembly took place on the 4th of February, 1790.

Twelve days later, that is to say, in the course of the night of the 17th of the same month, in the absence of the governor of the châtelet, who had leave to go to Soissons, where his mother was dying, a man presented himself at the gate of the prison, bearing an order signed by the lieutenant of police, authorizing the visitor to speak, without a witness, to M. de Favras.

We cannot say whether the order was a forgery or not; but at any rate, the sub-governor, whom they awoke in order to submit it to him, considered it was all right, and directed him, in spite of the lateness of the hour, to be admitted into the cell of M. de Favras.

After having issued the proper orders, he returned to his bed to complete the night's rest which had thus been broken.

The visitor, under the pretense that in drawing the order from his pocket-book he had dropped an important paper, took the lamp, and looked on the floor, just as he saw M. le Sous-directeur of the châtelet enter his apartment. Then he said he believed he had left it on his dressing-table, and he begged them, in any case, to give it to him before his departure.

Then, giving the lamp to the chief turnkey, he invited him to conduct him to the cell of M. de Favras.

The turnkey opened a door, allowed the unknown to pass, and in his turn followed, and shut the last door behind him.

He seemed to look at the unknown with curiosity as he attended him.

They descended twelve steps, and found themselves in a subterraneous corridor.

Then a second door presented itself; it was opened and relocked like the first, by the jailer.

The unknown and his guide found themselves now on a kind of landing, having before them a second flight of steps to descend. The unknown stopped, gazed into the dark corridor, and when he was assured that the obscurity was as solitary as silent:

"You are the chief turnkey, Louis?" asked he.

"Yes," replied the jailer.

"A brother of the American lodge?"

"Yes."

"You have been placed here for these last eight days by a mysterious hand to effect something unknown?"

"Yes."

"You are ready to accomplish this work?"

"I am ready."

"You were to receive your orders from a man?"

"Yes, of the anointed."

"How were you to recognize this man?"

"By three letters embroidered on a plastron."

"I am that man; look at the three letters."

On saying these words, the visitor opened his coat, and showed embroidered on its breast the three letters, L. P. D.

"Master," said the jailer, bowing, "I am at your service."

"Very well; open the cell of Monsieur de Favras, and be ready to obey me."

The jailer bowed without answering, and passing on in front, in order to light the way, he stopped before a door

"This is it," he murmured, in a low voice.

The unknown made a sign with his head; the key, already in the lock, turned twice, and the door stood open.

In spite of taking every precaution to prevent the prisoner's escape, by putting him in a cell twenty feet under ground, they had not been careless of his accommodations. He had a good bed with white curtains. Near this bed was a table covered with books, pens, ink, and paper, intended, no doubt, to assist him to prepare his defense.

A lamp crowned all.

Upon a second table, in a corner, glittered the articles of the toilet, such as had been taken from the dressing-case of the marquis himself.

M. de Favras slept so soundly that the door was opened, the unknown approached his bed, and a second lamp placed on the table by the jailer, who withdrew at a gesture of the visitor, without awaking him.

For a moment the unknown regarded the sleeping man with a profound melancholy, and then, as if remembering that time was precious, he shook the sleeper by the shoulder.

The prisoner turned, and was at once thoroughly awake with eyes wide open, like those who are in the habit of sleeping always expecting to be waked to hear bad news.

"Be composed, Monsieur de Favras," said the unknown, "it is a friend."

For an instant M. de Favras looked at the visitor with an air of doubt, which expressed his astonishment that any friend should come to seek him at some eighteen or twenty feet under ground. Then all at once recalling his recollections:

"Ah! ha!" said he, "the Baron Zanoni."

"Myself, dear marquis."

Favras smiled, and looking round him, pointed out a

stool with his finger, which held neither books nor clothes. "Will you sit down?" said he to the baron.

"My dear marquis, I come to propose a thing that admits of no long discussion, and since we have no time to lose——"

"What are you going to propose, my dear baron?"

"You know they will try you to-morrow."

"Yes, I have heard something like that," replied Favras.

"You know that the judges before whom you will appear are the same as those who acquitted Augeard and Bésenval?"

"Yes."

"Do you know that neither was acquitted except through the intervention of the court?"

A third time Favras replied, "Yes," without there being any perceptible alteration in his voice.

"Without doubt, you hope the court will do for you what it has done for your predecessors?"

"Those who have had the honor to assist me in relation to the enterprise that has brought me here ought surely to do something for my sake, Monsieur le Baron. Let what they do be well done."

"They have already determined what to do; and I can instruct you as to what course they intend to pursue."

Favras did not exhibit any curiosity to know.

"Monsieur," continued the visitor, "has presented himself at the Hôtel de Ville and declared that he did not know you now; that in 1772 you had entered into the guards, and that in 1775 you had left them, and since that time he had never seen you once."

Favras bowed his head as a token of acquiescence.

"As far as regards the king, he not only no more thinks of flying, but on the fourth of the present month he went to the National Assembly and swore to the constitution."

A smile passed over Favras's lips.

"Do you doubt the truth of this?" asked the baron.

"I did not say so," said Favras.

"Then you will see at once, marquis, that it will not do to reckon on monsieur, nor on the king either."

"Right, Monsieur le Baron."

"You will go before the judges."

"You have told me so before."

"You will be condemned."

"It is very likely."

"And to death."

"It is very possible."

And Favras stretched himself out like a man about to receive the last stroke.

"But," said the baron, "do you know to what death, my dear marquis?"

"Are there two kinds of death, dear baron?"

"There are ten; there are the wheel, hanging, pieces, etc., and for more than a week there has been one which combines them all; as you say, there is but one now—the gallows!"

"The gallows!"

"Yes; the assembly having proclaimed equality before the law, have found it but just to proclaim equality in death. Nobles and peasants must now go out of the world through the same gate. You will be hung, my dear marquis."

"Ah!" said Favras.

"Condemned to death, you will be hung; a very disagreeable thing, I am sure, to a gentleman who does not fear death but only dislikes the mode of it."

"Monsieur le Baron," said Favras, "have you only come here to inform me of this bad news, or have you something else better left to tell me?"

"I came to tell you that all is ready for your escape, and to assure you that in ten minutes, if you wish, you can be out of your prison, and in twenty-four hours out of France."

Favras reflected a moment without letting the baron see that it caused him any emotion, then addressing his questioner:

"Does this offer come from the king or his royal highness?"

"No, sir; it comes from me."

Favras looked at the baron.

"From you, sir," said he, "and why from you?"

"From the interest I take in you, marquis."

"What interest can you have in me?" asked Favras; "you have seen me but twice."

"One does not require to see a man twice in order to know him, my dear marquis. True gentlemen are rare, and I wish to save one, I will not say for France, but for humanity."

"You have no other reason, then?"

"There is another reason. Having negotiated a bill of two millions for you, money which has been spent in promoting the affair which brought you here to-day, I feel myself implicated in your death, that I have contributed to it."

Favras smiled. "If you have not committed a worse crime than that, you may sleep easily," said Favras. "I pardon you."

"What!" cried the baron, "you refuse to fly?"

Favras stretched out his hand to him. "I thank you from the bottom of my heart, Monsieur le Baron," replied he, "I thank you in the name of my wife and children, but I refuse."

"Because, perhaps, you think our measures ill-taken, and you are afraid to trust to an escape, which, if discovered, would aggravate your offense?"

"I believe, sir, that you are a prudent man. I will say more, that you are adventurous, since you yourself come to propose this escape to me; but I repeat, I do not wish to fly."

"Without doubt, you think, monsieur, that, forced to fly from France, you will leave your wife and children in misery there. I have foreseen this, and offer you this pocket-book, in which you will find one hundred thousand francs in bank-notes."

Favras looked at the baron with a kind of admiration. Then, shaking his head:

"It is not that, monsieur," said he; "upon my word, and without your having had to offer me this pocket-book, if it had been my intention to leave France, I should have fled. But once more my mind is made up; I will not fly."

The baron looked at him who gave him this firm refusal, as if he doubted whether he possessed his senses.

"This astonishes you," said Favras, with a singular degree of serenity, "and you ask yourself, without daring to ask me, whence arises this strange determination to wait to the end, and to meet death, if necessary, whatever that death may be."

"I confess so, monsieur."

"I will tell you. I am a royalist, monsieur, but not of that kind who emigrate, or remaining, dissimulate at Paris. My opinion is not founded upon a sordid calculation of interest; it is a faith, a religion, and kings are no more to me than a bishop, or a pope; that is to say, it is of the visible representatives of this faith, this religion, I am speaking of now. If I fly, it will be said that the king or Monsieur have caused me to escape; if they let me escape, they were my accomplices. Religions fall, my dear baron, when there are no longer any martyrs; I will rouse up mine by dying for it. This shall be a reproach cast upon the past, an advertisement offered to the future."

"But think of the kind of death which awaits you," urged the baron.

"The more infamous the death, the more meritorious will be the sacrifice. Christ died on a cross between thieves."

"I could understand that, monsieur," said the baron, "if your death would have the same influence on royalty as that of Christ had on the world. But the sins of kings are so great that, so far from thinking that the blood of a simple gentleman will wash them away, I do not think that even the blood of a king can do it."

"That will be as God pleases, Monsieur le Baron; but at a time when so many are wanting in their duty, I shall die with the consolation of having fulfilled mine."

"Ah! no, monsieur," said the baron, with an air of impatience, "you may die with the simple regret that your death is of no use."

"When the disarmed soldier will not fly, when he awaits the enemy, when he braves death, when he receives it, he knows perfectly well that his death is useless, he can only say that flight was cowardly, and that he had rather die."

"Monsieur," said the baron, "I cannot stay to argue."

He drew out his watch; it was three o'clock in the morning.

"We have yet one hour," continued he. "I will sit at this table and read for half an hour; during this time, reflect. In half an hour you will give me a definite answer."

And taking a chair, he sat down against the table, his back turned to the prisoner, and began to read.

"Good night, monsieur," said Favras.

And he turned his face to the wall, without doubt to reflect more undisturbedly.

The reader two or three times drew his watch from his pocket; more impatient than the prisoner, when the half-hour was gone, he rose and went toward the bed. But he had waited in vain. Favras did not turn.

The baron leaned over him, and discovered from his regular and calm breathing that the prisoner slept.

"Allons!" said he, speaking to himself, "I am conquered; but judgment is not as yet pronounced; perhaps he still doubts."

And not wishing to awaken the unhappy marquis again, he seized a pen and wrote upon a sheet of white paper the following:

"When sentence is passed, and Monsieur de Favras is condemned to death, when he has no hopes either in the judges or Monsieur, should he change his opinion, Monsieur de Favras has only to call the jailer, Louis, and say to him: 'I am decided to fly,' and means will be provided to assist his flight.

"When Monsieur de Favras is in the fatal wagon, when

Monsieur de Favras begs pardon in front of Notre Dame, when Monsieur de Favras traverses, with naked feet and bound hands, the short space that separates the steps of the Hôtel de Ville from the gallows on the Grève, he has only to pronounce the words : 'I wish to be saved!' and he shall be saved.

"CAGLIOSTRO."

When he had written the above, the visitor took the lamp, and advanced to the bed a second time to see if he still slept. He then regained the door of the cell, but not without returning several times, behind which, with the imperturbable resignation of those adepts who are ready to sacrifice everything to gain their end, Louis, the jailer, was standing immovable.

"Well, master," he asked, "what shall I do?"

"Remain in the prison, and do whatever Monsieur de Favras commands thee."

The jailer bowed his assent, took the lamp from the hand of Cagliostro, and walked respectfully before him, as a valet who lights his master.

The same day, the chief jailer, about an hour after midday, descended with four armed men into the prison of M. de Favras, and announced to him that he must prepare to appear before his judges. M. de Favras had been forewarned of this during the night by Cagliostro, and at nine in the morning by the sub-lieutenant to the châtelet. The general hearing of the trial had commenced at nine, and was still proceeding at three o'clock. Since before nine in the morning the salle had been crowded with persons curious to see him whose sentence was about to be pronounced.

Forty judges were arranged in a circle at the end of the salle, the president upon a daïs, a painting representing the crucifixion of our Saviour immediately behind him, and at the other end of the hall, just opposite, was the portrait of the king.

A number of the grenadiers of the National Guard

guarded the Hall of Justice, both within and without. Four men kept watch at the door.

At a quarter to three the judges ordered the accused to be brought.

A detachment of a dozen grenadiers, who waited in the middle of the salle for this order, immediately marched off.

After this, every head, even including those of the judges, was turned toward the door through which M. de Favras would enter.

At the end of about ten minutes, four of the grenadiers reappeared. Behind them marched the Marquis de Favras. The other eight grenadiers followed after him.

The prisoner's face was perfectly calm; his toilet had been attended to with evident care; he wore an embroidered coat, a white satin vest, a culotte of the same material and workmanship as his coat, silk stockings, and buckled shoes, with the Cross of St. Louis in his hat. His hair was carefully dressed and powdered.

During the short time it took M. de Favras to pass from the door to the place which the prisoners generally occupied, every breath in the hall was suspended. Some moments elapsed between the arrival of the accused in his place, and the first word addressed to him. At last the judges made with their heads their useless but habitual sign—for silence.

"Who are you?" asked the president.

"I am the prisoner," answered Favras, with the greatest calmness.

"What is your name?"

"Thomas Mahi, Marquis de Favras."

"Where do you come from?"

"From Blois."

"What is your station?"

"Colonel in the service of the king."

"Where do you live?"

"Place Royale, No. 21."

"How old are you?"

"Forty-six."

"Sit down."

The marquis obeyed.

Then only did respiration return to the spectators, and it seemed like a respiration of vengeance.

The prisoner looked round him; every eye was full of hate, every finger threatening; one felt that he must fall.

In the midst of all these angry countenances, the accused recognized the calm face and friendly eye of his visitor on the previous night. He saluted him with an imperceptible nod, and continued his review.

"Accused," said the president, "be ready to answer."

Favras bowed. I am at your orders, Monsieur le President," said he.

Then he commenced the second examination, which the prisoner went through as calmly as he had done the first.

Then the witnesses were summoned. Favras, who refused to save his life by flight, wished to do so by discussion and argument; he had summoned fourteen witnesses to answer the charge. The witnesses to prove the charge were heard, and he expected his own to be brought forward now, when, all at once, he heard the following words pronounced by the president:

"Gentlemen, the case is closed."

"Pardon, monsieur," said Favras, with his habitual courtesy, "you have forgotten one thing, of little importance, it is true, but you have forgotten to examine the fourteen witnesses summoned at my request."

"The court," replied the president, "has decided that they will not hear them."

A slight cloud passed over the face of the accused. "I thought I was to be tried at the Châtelet of Paris," said he, "but I was wrong—I am tried, it appears, by a Spanish Inquisition."

"Remove the prisoner," said the president.

Favras was reconducted to his prison. His calmness, courtesy, and courage had made some impression upon those spectators who had come to this trial without prejudice. But these were but a small number. The departure of Favras was accompanied with cries, menaces, and howls.

"No pardon, no pardon!" cried five hundred voices, as he passed along.

Such cries accompanied him from the court to prison.

Then, as if speaking to himself, he murmured:

"See what it is to plot with princes!"

As soon as the prisoner had gone, the judges commenced their deliberations.

At his usual hour Favras went to bed. Toward one in the morning somebody entered his prison and awoke him—this was the turnkey, Louis. He had seized the opportunity to bring a bottle of wine to the marquis.

"Monsieur de Favras," said he, "the judges have this moment pronounced your sentence."

"My friend," said the marquis, "was it simply to tell me that you awoke me? You might have let me sleep."

"No, monsieur; I roused you to inquire whether you had nothing to say to the person who visited you last night."

"Nothing."

"Reflect, Monsieur le Marquis, when judgment is pronounced, you will be more strictly guarded, and however powerful that person may be, yet he may not afterward be able to effect your escape."

"Thanks, my friend," said Favras, "but neither now, nor at any time, shall I have to ask him for anything."

"Then I am sorry," said the jailer, "that I disturbed you; but you would have been roused in another hour's time."

"Well," said Favras, "according to your opinion, it's scarcely worth while going to sleep again, then?"

"Listen," said the turnkey; "judge for yourself."

There was a great noise in the corridors above; doors opened and shut—arms were presented.

"Ah! ha!" said Favras, "all this bother is for me, then?"

"They are coming to read the sentence, Monsieur le Marquis."

"Diable! they must give me time to dress."

The jailer immediately went out, fastening the door behind him.

During this time M. de Favras hurriedly dressed himself.

He was still at his toilet when the door opened.

He looked well, his head thrown back, his hair half dressed, his lace shirt open at the breast.

At the moment of the clerk of the court entering his cell he was turning down the collar of his shirt on to his shoulders.

"You see, monsieur," said he to the clerk, "I am prepared for you, and ready for the combat."

And he passed his hand over his uncovered neck, ready for the aristocratic sword or plebeian cord.

"Speak, monsieur," he said; "I listen."

The clerk read, or, rather, lisped out the sentence.

The marquis was condemned to death; he was to make the *amende honorable* in front of Notre Dame, and immediately be hung at the Grève.

Favras listened with the greatest calmness, and did not even raise an eyebrow at the word hung—a word that grates on the ear of a gentleman.

He said only, after a minute's silence, and looking the clerk in the face:

"Oh, monsieur, how sorry I am you have been compelled to condemn a man upon such slight proof!"

The clerk avoided answering.

"Monsieur," said the last, "you are aware that there is no hope for you, except what religion offers—shall I send you a confessor?"

"A confessor at the hands of those who are about to assassinate me? No, sir; I should be suspicious of him. I am quite willing to give you my life, but I set some value on my safety hereafter. I should like to see the priest of St. Paul's."

Two hours afterward this venerable priest was seated with the Marquis de Favras.

A tumbril, surrounded by a numerous guard, was waiting at the gate of the châtelet. A lighted torch was in the tumbril. When they saw the condemned, the multitude clapped their hands. Since six in the morning the sentence had been known, and the people had been collecting together ever since.

Favras got into the tumbril with a firm step. He sat down on the side where the torch was, for he knew that the torch was meant for him. The priest of St. Paul's got in directly afterward, and sat on the left. The executioner mounted last, and sat behind him. Before sitting down, the executioner passed the rope around Favras's neck. He held the other end in his hand.

Just as the tumbril commenced to move, there was a movement in the crowd. Favras naturally turned his head and looked in that direction. He saw some people pushing their way into the front rank, and getting better places. All at once he started, in spite of himself; for, in the first rank, and in the midst of five or six of his companions, who were about to make a rush through the crowd, he recognized the visitor who had said that to the very last moment he would watch over him.

The condemned made him a sign with his head, one only, a sign of acknowledgment.

The tumbril continued on its way, and did not stop until it reached Notre Dame. The road through the middle of the crowd was open, and the principal altar, brilliantly lighted by wax-candles, could be seen for some distance.

"It is necessary to descend here in order to make the *amende honorable,*" said the executioner.

Favras obeyed without answering.

The priest descended first, then the prisoner, and lastly the executioner—always retaining the end of the cord in his hands.

His arms were bound at the elbows; this left the hands of the marquis free. In his right hand they placed the torch, in his left the judgment. He then walked to the porch of the church, and knelt down.

In the front rank of those that surrounded him, he recognized the same men who had startled him when he first mounted the tumbril. This perseverance seemed to touch him, but no word escaped from his mouth.

A jailer of the châtelet seemed to be waiting for him there.

"Read, monsieur," said he, in a loud voice. Then, in a low tone, he added: "Monsieur le Marquis, you know if you wish to be saved, you have only one word to say."

Without answering, the condemned began reading.

He read in a loud voice, and nothing in tone or manner showed the least emotion. When he had done reading, he addressed those around him:

"Ready to appear before my God," said he, "I pardon the men, who against their conscience, have found me guilty. I love my king, I die faithful to him. I am setting an example which I hope will be followed by other noble hearts. The people ask for my death; they want a victim. I had rather that the fatal choice should fall upon me than upon another, who might not be able to undergo unmerited punishment without despair. And now, if there is nothing else to be done, let us be proceeding, gentlemen."

And so they went on.

It is not very far from the porch of Notre Dame to the Place de Grève, and yet the tumbril took a full hour to go there.

And with a firm step Favras descended and walked toward the scaffold.

At the very moment that he placed his foot on the first step, a voice cried out:

"Jump, marquis!

The grave and sonorous voice of the criminal replied:

"Citizens, I die innocent; pray for me!"

At the eighth step, that is to say, the one from which he would be thrown, he repeated a third time:

"Citizens, I die innocent; pray for me!"

But one of the assistants or the hangman immediately said:

"Then you do not wish to be saved?"

"Thanks, my good friend," said Favras. "God will reward you for your good intentions."

Then, raising his head toward the hangman, "Do your duty," said he.

He had scarcely pronounced the words, before the hangman pushed him off, and his body hung in the air.

CHAPTER XX.

THE MONARCHY IS SAVED.

Some days after the execution which we have narrated, a horseman slowly paced the Avenue of St. Cloud.

This slowness could neither be attributed to the fatigue of the rider nor the weariness of the horse; both had taken it gently. The foam, made by the champing of the bit, showed the horse had been restrained.

The deep thought into which the rider had fallen seemed to retard him, or else he was taking care to arrive only at a certain hour which had not yet struck.

He was a man of about forty, whose powerful lineaments did not want character; his head was large, his cheeks puffed out; his face was covered with little wrinkles; he had two quick, sharp eyes, and a mouth always ready to express satire. Such was the man who, at first sight, one felt must occupy a high position and make a great noise in the world.

Arrived at the top of the avenue, he leaped, without any hesitation, over the gate leading to the court of the palace.

Betwixt two buildings to the right another man was waiting. He made a sign to the cavalier to come on. A door was opened and the cavalier, always following the other, found himself in a secret court. There the man stopped. He was dressed in black. Then, looking round him, and observing that the court was empty, he approached the cavalier, hat in hand.

The cavalier, by leaning over the neck of his horse, brought himself, in some measure, opposite him.

"Monsieur Weber," said he, in a low tone.

"Monsieur le Comte de Mirabeau," answered the latter.

"The same," said the cavalier. And more lightly than one could have supposed, he alighted on the ground.

"Enter," said Weber; "but will you wait a moment until I put the horse in a stable myself?"

At the same time he opened the door of a saloon whose windows and other door opened upon the park.

Mirabeau entered into the saloon, and employed the few moments he was left alone by Weber in taking off the large boots which had preserved him from the mud during his ride.

Weber, as he promised, entered in the course of five minutes.

"Come, Monsieur le Comte," said he, "the queen expects you."

Weber opened a door opening on the garden, and plunged into a labyrinth of alleys, which led to the most solitary part of the park. There, in the midst of gloomy trees, appeared a pavilion, known by the name of the kiosk. The Venetian blinds of this pavilion were closed, with the exception of two, which, just resting one against the other, allowed a small quantity of light to illumine the interior. A great fire was burning on the hearth, and two branches were lighted on the chimney-piece.

Weber caused him whom he accompanied to enter the chamber, after he had said, on opening the door of the kiosk, "Monsieur le Comte Riquetti de Mirabeau."

And he drew aside to allow the count to pass him.

If he had listened, as the count passed him, he might have heard the beating of his heart against his large chest.

When the presence of the count was announced, a woman in the most distant corner of the kiosk rose and advanced toward him with some hesitation and even terror.

This woman was the queen.

Her heart also beat violently. She had before her this hated, decried, fatal man—this man who was accused of having caused the 5th and 6th of October; this man toward whom they had turned for a moment, but who had been repulsed by the court, and who, since then, had made them feel the necessity of treating with him again, by two flashes of lightning, as it were, which had even approached the sublime.

The first was his apostrophe to the clergy.

The second was the speech in which he explained how it was that the representatives of the people had constituted themselves into a National Assembly.

Having advanced a few paces, he bowed and waited.

The queen spoke, and said :

"Monsieur Mirabeau, Monsieur Gilbert assures us it is your disposition to join us."

Mirabeau bowed in assent.

The queen continued :

"Then an overture was made, to which you replied by proposing a ministry ?"

Mirabeau bowed again in assent.

The queen continued :

"It is not our fault if this do not succeed."

"I think so, madame, especially your majesty's. It may, however, be the fault of the people, who say they are devoted to the monarchy."

"Alas ! count, that is one of the perils of our position. We can neither choose our friends nor our foes, and we are often forced to accept these unfortunate friendships. We are surrounded by men who wish to serve, but who ruin us. Their conduct in keeping members of the present from the next legislature is a fair instance. Shall I quote one ? You would scarcely believe it ; but one of our most devoted friends, a man who, I am sure, would die for us, took to our public dinner the widow and children of Monsieur de Favras, all in mourning. My first emotion, when I saw them, was to rise, hurry to them, and place the family of a man who died for us by my side, for I am not of those who forget their friends. Every eye was fixed on me ; all waited to see what we would do. Know you who stood behind my chair ? Santerre, the man of the faubourg. I sank back weeping with rage, and did not dare to look at the widow and orphans. The royalists will blame me for not having noticed the widow and children ; the revolutionists will be furious because they will think they came with my permission. Monsieur," said the queen, shaking her head sadly, " one can but perish when one is attacked by men of genius, and defended by people who certainly are very estimable, but who have no idea of our position."

The queen sighed, and placed her handkerchief to her eyes.

" Madame," said Mirabeau, touched by this great misfortune, which he was not ignorant of, and which, either by the shrewd skill of the queen, or from her womanly weakness, exhibited to him her tears and sufferings, " when you speak of men who attack you, I trust you do not refer to me. I professed monarchical principles when I saw nothing but weakness in the court, and when I knew nothing of the heart and feelings of the august daughter of Marie Theresa. I fought for the rights of the throne when my every step excited suspicion, and every act was misrepresented and maligned ; I served the king when I knew that, just and august as he was, I had from him to expect neither honor nor reward ; what will I not do now, madame, when confidence sustains my courage, and gratitude for your majesty's reception make obedience a duty ? It is late, madame, I know, very late," said Mirabeau, shaking his head ; " perhaps, in proposing to me to save monarchy, you propose to me to perish with it. Had I reflected, I would, perhaps, have chosen another time than one immediately preceding that on which his majesty is about to deliver the famous red book, that is the honor of his friends, to the chamber."

" Ah, sir," said the queen, " think you the king is an accomplice of this treason, and are you ignorant how that occurred ? The red book was surrendered to the committee by the king, only on condition that they would keep it strictly secret. The committee caused it to be printed, thus breaking their words. They, not the king, are guilty."

" Alas ! madame, you know what made them determine on the publication of that, which, as a man of honor, I disapprove. At the very moment when the king was swearing fidelity to the constitution, he had a permanent agent at Turin, amid the mortal enemies of the constitution. At the hour he spoke of pecuniary reforms, and seemed disposed to accept those proposed to him by the assembly, there was, at Treves, paid and sustained by him, his grand and petty stable, under the orders of the Prince de Lambesq, a person so peculiarly obnoxious to the Parisians, that every day they demand that he be hung in effigy. To the Count d'Artois, to the Prince de Condé, to all the emigrés, vast pensions are paid, in violation of a decree passed several months since suppressing pensions. True, the king forgot to sanction this decree. For two months, madame, there has been an attempt to discover what became of sixty millions of money; yet none can tell. The king was begged, besought to explain what had been done with it; he refused to reply, and the committee felt itself relieved of its promise, and printed the book. Why does the king put arms into the hands of others to be used so dangerously against him?"

"Ah, sir!" said the queen, "were you of the king's counsel, you would not recommend him to adopt the follies which, with which—I must speak the word—he dishonors himself."

"Had I the honor, madame, of being the king's counselor, I would be the defender of royal powers regulated by law, and the apostle of liberty guaranteed by monarchical power. This liberty, madame, has three enemies—the clergy, the nobility, and the parliament. The clergy does not belong to this century and was crushed by Talleyrand; the nobility belongs to all centuries, and I think we must put up with it, for there can be no monarchy without a nobility; it must, however, be repressed, and this can only be done by making it a link of union between the people and royalty. Royalty can never coalesce with the people, so long as parliament exists, for the latter keep the nobility in hope that the old order of things will be restored. Then it is necessary, after the annihilation of the clergy, the destruction of parliaments, to revive the executive, to regenerate royal power, and make it accord with liberty. That, madame, is the sum of my politics. If it is that of the king, let him adopt it; if not, let him reject it."

"Count!" said the queen, amazed by the light shed at once over the past, present, and future, by the radiation of the mind of Mirabeau, "I do not know if the king will agree with you, but had I the power, it would be my course. Tell me, then, count, what means are to be adopted to attain this course? I listen, I do not say with attention, but with thanks."

Mirabeau glanced rapidly at the queen with that eagle eye, which sounded her very heart, and saw, if he had not convinced, he had made an impression on her.

This triumph over so superior a woman as Marie Antoinette flattered in the highest degree Mirabeau's vanity.

"Madame," said he, "we have nearly lost Paris; we yet have in the country, however, vast masses disposed to serve us, of whom we can make fascines. I advise, madame, that the king leave Paris, not France; that he join the army at Rouen, and thence publish orders more popular than the assembly's decrees; then there will be no civil war, for the king will have surpassed the revolution."

"But is not this revolution, whether exceeded or followed, a thing to be feared?" asked the queen.

"Alas! madame, better than any one else, I know something must be thrown to it. I have already told the queen that it surpasses human power to rebuild the monarchy on the basis that this revolution has shattered. All France has consented to this revolution, from the king to the peasant, either by act or by omission. I do not, madame, seek to defend the ancient monarchy, but to modify and regenerate it; to establish a form of government more or less like that of England, which led that country to its apogee of power and glory. After having, as Gilbert tells me, beheld and studied the prison and scaffold of Charles I., will not the king be satisfied with a throne like that of William III. or George I.?"

"Oh, count," said the queen, to whom what Mirabeau had said recalled with shuddering horror the vision of the Castle of Taverney and the design of Guillotin's instrument, "restore us the monarchy, and you will see we are not ungrateful, as they call us."

"Well," cried Mirabeau, "that, madame, is what I will do. Let the king sustain and the queen encourage me, and here at your feet I swear, as a gentleman, to keep the promise I make your majesty, or die!"

"Count, count! do not forget that not a mere woman, but a dynasty of five centuries, hears your oath. Seventy kings of France, from Pharamont to Louis XV., sleep in their tombs, and will be dethroned with us when we fall!"

"I know the engagement I take, madame; it is immense, I know, though it is not great as my will is, or stronger than my devotion. Let me but be sure of the confidence of my king and queen, and I will to the task."

"If that be all, Monsieur de Mirabeau, I promise you both the one and the other."

She bowed to Mirabeau with the serene smile which seemed to conquer every heart.

Mirabeau saw that the audience was over.

The politician's pride was satisfied; something, however, was needed to satisfy the vanity of the noble.

"Madame," said he, with a respectful and bold courtesy, "when your august mother, Marie Theresa, admitted one of her nobles to her presence, he never left her until he had the honor of kissing her hand."

He stood erect and waited.

The queen looked at the chained lion, who asked only to be permitted to cast himself at her feet, and with a smile of triumph on her lips gave him slowly her beautiful hand, which was white as alabaster and almost as transparent.

Mirabeau knelt, kissed her hand, and looking up proudly, said: "Madame, this kiss has saved the monarchy."

He left the room, moved, excited, and joyous, thinking himself, poor man, that his genius would enable him to maintain and to fulfil the prophecy he had made.

Mirabeau had commenced the struggle, trusting in his own powers, not ever dreaming that after so many imprudences and three intercepted plots the struggle had become impossible.

Had Mirabeau—and this would have been more prudent

—been able to have worked beneath a mask for some time longer, it might have been different, but the day after he had been to the queen, on entering the assembly, he saw groups of people and heard cries.

He approached these groups, and listened to the cries.

They handed little pamphlets about.

From time to time some one cried: "The great treachery of Monsieur de Mirabeau! The great treachery of Monsieur de Mirabeau!"

"Ah! ah!" said he, drawing a piece of money from his pocket, "methinks this concerns me. My friend," continued he to the one distributing the pamphlets, and who had several in his baskets, which an ass carried quietly wherever he wished him to go, "how much for 'The great treachery of Monsieur Mirabeau?'"

The seller looked Mirabeau in the face. "Monsieur le Comte, I give it away for nothing." And then he added, in a lower tone: "And the pamphlet has already reached a hundred thousand."

Mirabeau withdrew thoughtfully.

"This pamphlet had reached a hundred thousand. This pamphlet they gave for nothing! This colporteur, who knew him?"

But without doubt this pamphlet was one of those stupid publications, of which such numbers appeared at this time.

Mirabeau cast his eye on the first page, and turned pale.

The first page contained a list of the debts of Mirabeau, and strange, the list was correct. Two hundred and eight thousand francs.

Below this list was the date of the day when these sums had been paid to the different creditors of Mirabeau by the almoner of the queen, M. de Fontanges.

Then came the amount of the sum paid him monthly by the court. Six thousand francs.

And lastly, an account of his interview with the queen.

This was difficult to be understood; the anonymous pamphleteer had not mistaken a single sum, one might almost say he had not mistaken one word.

What terrible enemy, skilled in his secrets, could follow him thus, and through him the monarchy?

The colporteur who had spoken to him, who had recognized and addressed him as M. le Comte, struck Mirabeau as if he had seen him before. He retraced his steps. The ass, with his basket three parts empty, was still there, but the first colporteur had disappeared, and another had taken his place. This one was wholly unknown to Mirabeau. He did not follow up their distribution with less eagerness.

It so happened that at this moment Dr. Gilbert, who went nearly every day to listen to the debates in the assembly, above all, when the debates were likely to be of any importance, passed by the place where the colporteur was stationed.

Preoccupied, as he generally was, he would not, perhaps, have stopped, but Mirabeau, with his usual audacity, went straight to him, took him by the arm, and led him to the distributor of the pamphlets, who did the same to Gilbert as he had done to the others, that is, he stretched out his hands toward him, saying:

"'The great treachery of Monsieur de Mirabeau,' citizen?"

But at the sight of Gilbert his tongue and arms stopped as if paralyzed. Gilbert looked at him in his turn, and letting the pamphlet fall with disgust as he turned away, said:

"This is villainous work you are at, Monsieur Beausire!"

And taking the arm of Mirabeau, he continued his way to the assembly, which had removed from the Episcopal Palace to the Manege.

"Do you know this man, then?" asked Mirabeau.

"I know him as I know such people," said Gilbert; "he is a gamester—everything; he is ready as a calumniator, or anything."

"Ah!" murmured Mirabeau, putting his hand where his heart had been, but where there was now only the pocket-book containing the money of the château. And gloomily the great orator went on his way.

"What," said Gilbert, "are you so little of a philosopher as to let such a little attack as this dash you?"

"I?" cried Mirabeau. "Ah! doctor, you do not know me. They say I am bought, when they should simply say I am paid. Well, to-morrow I purchase a hotel; to-morrow I have a carriage, horse, servants; to-morrow I have a cook and well-covered table. And how do the popularity of yesterday and the unpopularity of to-day concern me? Is there not the future? No, doctor, what dashes me is, that I have promised what I may not probably be able to keep; these are the faults, I had better say treacheries, of the court on my account. I have seen the queen, have I not? She seemed full of confidence in me. For a moment I dreamed; mad dream with such a woman. For a moment I dreamed, not of being minister to the king, as Richelieu was, but the minister; but let us say better—and the policy of the world would not have been worse conducted. The lover of the queen, like Mazarin. Well, what did she do? On the very day she left me, I have proof that she wrote thus to her agent in Germany, Monsieur de Flachlanden: 'Tell my brother Leopold I am of his opinion; that I make use of Monsieur de Mirabeau, but there is nothing serious in my relation with him.'"

"Are you sure?" asked Gilbert.

"Positive. But this is not all; you know what the discussion is about to-day in the chamber?"

"I know it is on a question of war, but I am badly informed of the cause of this war."

"Oh, mon Dieu!" said Mirabeau, "it is very simple. The whole of Europe is split into two parties; Austria and Russia on one side, England and Prussia on the other; swayed by the same hatred—hatred of revolutions. For Russia and Austria the manifestation is not difficult, it is their own true opinion; but it requires time for liberal England and philosophic Prussia to pass from one pole to the other, and to avow themselves what they are in reality—enemies to liberty. For her part, England has seen Brabant stretch out her hand to France; this has hastened her decision. Our revolution, my dear doctor, is contagious ; it is more than a national revolution, it is a revolution of mankind. Burke, a pupil of the Jesuits of St. Owen, a bitter enemy of Pitt, is about to attack France in a work which he has been paid for in good gold by Pitt. England will not make war on France. No, she dare not yet ; but she abandons Belgium to the Emperor Leopold, and she is going to the end of the world to pick a quarrel with our ally, Spain. Louis XVI. made known to the assembly yesterday that he was arming fourteen vessels on this account ; there will be a great discussion to-day. To whom does the initiative of the war belong ? This is the question. The king has already lost the Interior, the king has already lost Justice ; if he loses the war, what will become of him ? On the other side, let us frankly, between you and me, doctor, touch on what we dare not mention in the chamber. On the other side the king is mistrusted ; the revolution can only be completed, and I have contributed to this more than any one ; the revolution can only now be completed by breaking the sword in the hands of the king ; of all the powers the most dangerous to leave in his hands is that of making war. Well, faithful to the promise I have made, I must go and ask them to leave him this power. I risk my popularity, my life, perhaps, in supporting this demand. I am about to ask them to adopt a decree which will make the king victorious, triumphant. And now what has the king done ? He has caused the whole formulas of protestation to be fetched from the archives of the parliament, doubtless to issue a secret protestation against the assembly. See the evil, my dear doctor, of doing so many things secretly, instead of frankly, openly, publicly ; and learn why I wish, I—Mirabeau—do you hear ? that they should know what I am to the queen, to the king, since I am so. You told me that this infamy against me vexed and troubled me, not so, doctor, it assists me ; with me, as with the storms, it is necessary there should be dark clouds and contrary winds. Come, come, doctor ; and you shall see a good sitting, I promise you !"

Mirabeau was not wrong ; his courage was tried as soon

as he entered the assembly. Every one cried out, "Treachery!" and one showed him a rope, another a pistol.

Mirabeau shrugged his shoulders and passed on.

The cries followed him to the hall, and he seemed to call forth new cries. Scarcely had he appeared, before a hundred voices exclaimed, "See! see! the traitor!"

Barnave was at the tribune. He was speaking against Mirabeau; Mirabeau looked fixedly at him.

"Yes," said Barnave, "it is you I call a traitor; against you I speak."

"Then," said Mirabeau, "if you are speaking about me, I'll take a walk round the Tuileries. I shall be back before you've done."

And with his head high, and a threatening air, he walked through the midst of the howlings and imprecations, reached the terrace, and descended into the Tuileries.

A third of the way from the great alley, a young woman, holding a sprig of vervain in her hand, was collecting a circle round her. A place on her left was empty; Mirabeau took a chair and sat himself down.

The half of those who surrounded her got up and left. Mirabeau watched them go, and smiled. The young woman gave him her hand.

"Ah, baronne," said he, "you are not afraid of catching the plague?"

"My dear count," replied the young woman, "they say you have left our side. I draw you to us."

Mirabeau smiled, and talked three-quarters of an hour with the young woman, who was no other than Anne Louise Germaine Necker, Baronne de Staël.

At the end of that time, taking out his watch, "Ah, baronne," said he, "I ask your pardon; Barnave was speaking against me; he had spoken an hour when I left the assembly, and for three-quarters of an hour I had the pleasure of conversing with you; my accuser, consequently, has been talking for nearly two hours; his discourse ought to be near its end. I must answer him."

"Go!" said the baronne, "answer him, and with good courage."

"Give me, madame, this sprig of vervain; it shall serve me as a talisman."

"Take care, my dear count, the vervain at funerals!"

"Give it, nevertheless; it is good to be crowned as a martyr when one descends into the circle."

"The fact is," said Mme. de Staël, "it is impossible to be more stupid than the assembly yesterday was."

"Ah, baronne," said Mirabeau, "why do you put the date?"

And as he took the sprig of vervain from her hands, which she gave him without doubt for this last speech, Mirabeau saluted her gallantly, mounted the steps which conducted to the terrace, and regained the assembly.

Barnave descended from the tribune in the midst of acclamations which filled the salle; he had pronounced a discourse of that kind which pleased all parties.

Mirabeau was scarcely in the tribune before a complete hurricane of cries and imprecations was showered upon him.

But, raising his powerful hand, and profiting by one of those intervals of silence which there always are in storms and émeutes:

"I know well," said he, "that it is but a step from the Capitol to the Tarpeian rock."

Such is the majesty of genius, that this single sentence made the most irritated silent.

From the moment when Mirabeau had obtained silence, his victory was half gained. He demanded that the initiative of the war should be given to the king; this was asking too much—they refused. Then the struggle commenced on the amendments. The principal motion had been negatived. It was necessary to recover himself by partial changes. He ascended the tribune five times.

Barnave had spoken two hours; during three hours Mirabeau spoke, and at length obtained the following:

That the king had the right to make the preparations and direct the forces as he wished; that he should propose war to the assembly, and the latter should do nothing until sanctioned by the king.

At the end of the sitting Mirabeau escaped being cut in pieces.

Barnave was carried in triumph by the people.

Poor Barnave! the day is not distant when you shall hear the cries in your turn:

"Great Treachery of Monsieur Barnave!"

CHAPTER XXI.

THE ELIXIR VITÆ.

MIRABEAU left the assembly; when he found himself in the face of danger, the strong athlete neither thought of danger nor his strength.

When he reached home, he laid himself down on cushions in the midst of flowers.

Mirabeau had two passions—women and flowers.

Since the commencement of the session his health had altered perceptibly; although of a vigorous temperament, he had suffered so much both physically and morally from his persecutions and imprisonments, that he was never in a perfect state of health.

This time it seemed to be something more than ordinary, and he only feebly resisted his valet, who spoke of going for a physician, when Dr. Gilbert rang, and was immediately admitted.

Mirabeau gave his hand to the doctor, and drew him down on to the cushions where he lay in the midst of flowers.

"So, my dear count," said Gilbert, "I thought I would not go home without congratulating you; you promised me a victory; you have succeeded better than that, you gained a triumph."

"Yes, but see, it is a triumph like that of Pyrrhus; another such victory as that, and I am lost!"

"In fine," said he, "you are ill."

Mirabeau shrugged his shoulders.

Gilbert looked at Mirabeau.

"That is to say, to do as I do, any one else, like me, would have died a hundred times; I have two secretaries; they are always at work, and are ill; Pelline, above all, who has to copy my manuscripts—and he is the only one who can read and understand my illegible scrawl—has been in bed these three days. Doctor, tell me, then, I do not say something that will make me live, but something that will give me strength as long as I live."

"What do you want?" said Gilbert, after having felt his pulse; "for an organization like yours there is no advice to give; advise repose to a man who puts all his strength into motion; temperance to a genius which glories in excess. You have made a necessity of flowers, and their absence makes you suffer more than their presence, and yet they disengage oxygen in the day and carbonic acid gas at night. Should I tell you to treat the women as the flowers, and keep away from them, especially at night, you would tell me you would rather die. Live, then, my dear count, as you have lived; only contrive to have flowers without any perfume, and amours without any passion."

"In this last particular, my dear doctor, you are admirably served. Amours of passion have succeeded too poorly for me to commence any again. Three years of imprisonment, a condemnation to death, and the suicide of the woman I loved, and that, too, for another, have cured me of these kind of amours. For a moment, I have told you, I dreamed something great; I had dreamed of the alliance of Elizabeth and Essex, of Anne of Austria and Mazarin, of Catharine II. and Potemkin; but it was a dream. I have not seen the woman again for whom I struggle, and probably never shall. Believe me, Gilbert, there is no greater burden than to feel that on us depends the success of great projects, the prosperity of a kingdom, the triumph of its friends, the abasement of its enemies, and that by an unfortunate roll of the dice, by a caprice of fate, all may escape us. Oh! how the follies of my youth make me expiate them as they will expiate themselves! But why do they defy me? But have I not, on two or three occasions, been completely for them and for them to the end? Was I not for the absolute right of veto when Monsieur Necker even was only for the suspending veto? Was I opposed to the 4th of August, a night in which I took no part, when the noblesse were deprived of their privileges? Did I not protest against the declaration of the rights of man? Not because I did not believe in it, but because I thought the day for them had not arrived. To-day, to-day, indeed, have I not served them more than they could have hoped? Have I not obtained for them, at the expense of honor, popularity, and life, more than any man, be he minister or prince, could have gained? And when I think—reflect well, thou great philosopher, on what I am going to tell you, for the fall of the monarchy perhaps lurks in this—and when I think that I, who ought to esteem it a great favor—so great that I have only been allowed once—have seen the queen; when I remember that my father died through the taking of the Bastile; that if decency had not forbid me pointing this out on the day after the day on which Lafayette was named general of the National Guard, and Bailly mayor of Paris, that I should have been named mayor in the place of Bailly! Oh! and things changed; the king found it necessary to enter into connection with me; I inspired him with other ideas; I obtained his confidence, and I brought him, before the evil had become too great, to pursue decisive measures; instead of a simple deputy, a man mistrusted, feared, hated, they have driven me from the king, calumniated me with the queen! Do you believe one thing, doctor? when she saw me at St. Cloud, she turned pale. Ah! it is quite simple; they made her believe that it was I who caused the 5th and 6th of October. During this year I have done all they have tempted me to do; and to-day—ah! to-day, for the health of the monarchy as well as my own, I have much fear that it is too late."

And Mirabeau, with a expression of suppressed pain over his whole countenance, seized with his hand the flesh of his breast above his stomach.

"Are you in pain, count?" asked Gilbert.

"As a damned one! There are days, on my honor,

when what they do to my character with calumny, I believe they do to my body with arsenic! Do you believe in the poisons of Borgia, in the *aqua tofano* of Perouse, doctor?" asked Mirabeau, smiling.

"No; but I believe in the ardent flame that burns the furnace in this blazing lamp which cracks the glass."

Gilbert drew from his pocket a small crystal bottle containing perhaps two teaspoonfuls of a green liquid.

"Here, count," said he, "we will try an experiment."

"What?" said Mirabeau, looking at the bottle with curiosity.

"One of my friends, whom I should like, too, to be yours, and who is very skilled in the natural sciences, nay even pretends to a knowledge of the occult ones as well, has given me the recipe of a beverage which is almost like the elixir vitæ. Often when I am troubled with those sad thoughts which lead our neighbors in England to melancholy, spleen, and even death, I take a few drops of this liquid, and I ought to tell you that the effect has always been salutary and prompt. Will you taste a little in your turn?"

"From your hands, doctor, I would receive anything, even the hemlock, much more the elixir of life. Is there any preparation, or must one drink it pure?"

"No; for this liquid in reality possesses great power. Order your valet to bring you a few drops of brandy or spirits of wine in a cup."

"Diable! brandy or spirits of wine; do you want to dilute your potent? it must be a fire-liquid. I do not know a man who could drink it, unless Prometheus came on earth again. I will tell you, however, that I do not believe my servant will find six drops of brandy in the whole house. I am not like Pitt, and I do not seek my eloquence in the bottle."

The servant, however, returned a few moments afterward with a cup holding the five or six drops of brandy necessary.

Gilbert added to the brandy an equal quantity of the liquor in the vial; when the two liquids combined, the mixture became the color of absinthe, and Mirabeau, seizing the cup, drank what it contained.

"Morbleu! doctor," said he to Gilbert, "you did well to warn me that your drug was strong; it seemed literally like a draught of lightning."

Gilbert smiled, and seemed to await its effects with confidence.

Mirabeau remained an instant as if burned up by jets of flame; his head lay on his chest, and his hand holding his stomach; but all at once raising his head:

"Ah! doctor," said he, "that is indeed an elixir vitæ you have given me to drink."

Then he rose, his respiration clear, his forehead bright, his arms extended.

"Overset the monarchy now," said he. "I feel I am myself able to sustain it."

Gilbert smiled.

"You feel better, then?" he asked.

"Doctor," said Mirabeau, "tell me where they sell this liquid, and if I must pay for such a drop with a diamond as large, if I must renounce every luxury but that of strength and life, I tell you I will have that liquid flame, and then I shall look on myself as invincible."

"Count," said Gilbert, "promise me never to take this liquid more than twice a week, and to address yourself only to me to provide you with more, and this vial is yours."

"Give it to me," said Mirabeau, "and I promise you all you wish."

"There," said Gilbert. "But now this is not all. You are going to have horses and a carriage, are you not?"

"Yes."

"Well, live in the country. These flowers that vitiate the air of a chamber make the air of a garden pure. The drive which you will have to Paris every day will do you much good. Choose, if possible, a residence near a height, in a wood, or near a river, Bellevue, St. Germaine, or Argenteuil."

"Argenteuil!" replied Mirabeau; "I have just sent a

servant to take a house there. Teisch, did you not say you had found something there that would suit me?"

"Yes, Monsieur le Comte," replied the valet, who had assisted the cure that Gilbert had effected; "yes, a charming house, which my compatriot Fritz mentioned to me. He has inhabited it, it seems, with his master, who is a foreign banker. It is empty, and Monsieur le Comte can have it when he will."

"Whereabouts is the house?"

"Beyond Argenteuil; it is called the Château of the Marais."

"Oh, I know it," said Mirabeau, "very well, Teisch. When my father drove me from him with his curse and beatings with his cane—you know, doctor, my father lived at Argenteuil?"

"Yes."

"Well, I said, when my father drove me from him, I used often to go and promenade round the exterior walls of this beautiful habitation, and to say, like Horace, pardon me if the quotation is false, '*O rus quando te aspiciam?*'"

"Then, my dear count, the moment has come when you can realize your dream. Go, visit the Château of the Marais—transport your family there—the sooner the better."

Mirabeau reflected an instant, and then, turning himself toward Gilbert, "It is your duty, doctor," said he, "to watch over the patient you have restored to health; it is only five o'clock, and we are in the long days of the year; it is very fine, so let us get into a carriage and go to Argenteuil."

"Let it be so," said Gilbert; "when one undertakes to cure a health so valuable as yours, one ought to take every care. Come, let us see your future country-house."

Mirabeau had not kept house as yet, and therefore kept no carriage. A servant went to fetch a hackney-coach.

Why had Mirabeau chosen Argenteuil? Was it, as he had just told the doctor, that certain souvenirs of his life attached him to this little town

It was at Argenteuil that his father, the Marquis of Mirabeau, died on the 11th of July, 1789, as became a true gentleman to die who would not assist at the taking of the Bastile.

At the foot of the bridge of Argenteuil Mirabeau directed the carriage to stop.

"Are we there?" asked the doctor.

"Yes and no; we are not quite at the Château of the Marais, which is a quarter of a league beyond Argenteuil. But what we are making to-day, doctor—I had forgotten to tell you—is not a simple visit, but a pilgrimage—a pilgrimage to three stations."

"A pilgrimage!" said Gilbert, smiling, "and to what saint?"

"To St. Riquette, my dear doctor, a saint whom you do not know, but one whom men have canonized. It is certain that here is buried St. Riquette, Marquis of Mirabeau, friend of man, put to death like a martyr by the agitations and debaucheries of his unworthy son, Honoré Gabriel Victor Riquette, Comte de Mirabeau."

"Ah! it is true," said the doctor; "it was at Argenteuil that your father died. Pardon me, my dear count, that I had forgotten that. And where did your father live?"

At the very moment Gilbert put this question, Mirabeau stopped before the gate of a house situated on the quay, in front of the river, from which it was separated by a lawn of perhaps some three hundred paces and a cluster of trees.

An enormous dog of the race of those of the Pyrenees, on perceiving a man stop before the gate, darted out and growled, and, thrusting his head between the bars, tried to catch hold of Mirabeau's flesh, or at least the lapel of his coat.

"Pardieu, doctor!" said he, "nothing is changed, and they receive me here as if my father were living."

While he spoke, a young man appeared on the steps, silenced the dog, called it to him, and advanced toward the strangers.

"Pardon, gentlemen," said he, "many promenaders stop before this house, which was inhabited by the Marquis de Mirabeau, and as poor Cartouche does not understand the historic interest which is attached to the house of his humble masters, he growls eternally. To your kennel, Cartouche!"

The young man made a threatening gesture, and he went, still growling, and hid himself in his kennel, through whose opening bars there soon passed two paws on which he leaned his head.

During this time Mirabeau and Gilbert exchanged a look.

"Gentlemen," exclaimed the young man, "there is nothing now behind this gate but a host ready to open it and receive you, if your curiosity is not satisfied with the exterior."

Gilbert nudged Mirabeau as a sign that he would willingly visit the interior of the mansion. Mirabeau understood him; moreover, his wishes coincided with those of Gilbert.

"Monsieur," said he, "you have fathomed our thoughts. We knew that this house had been inhabited by the friend of mankind, and we were curious to visit it."

"And your curiosity will redouble, gentlemen," said the young man, "when you know that two or three times, while the father lived here, it was honored by the presence of his illustrious son, and who, it is said, was not always received as he deserved to be, and as we would receive him if he should take it into his head ever to have the same curiosity as yourselves." And bowing, the young man opened the gate to the two visitors, and walked before them.

But Cartouche did not seem disposed to let them thus enjoy the hospitality which had been offered to them; he darted again out of his kennel, growling horribly.

The young man threw himself betwixt the dog and that of one of his guests against whom the animal seemed principally irritated.

But Mirabeau drew the young man aside with his hand.

"Monsieur," said he, "both dogs and men have

growled at me; men have bit me sometimes, dogs never. They say that the human eye is all-powerful in its influence on animals. Let me, I beg, make an experiment."

"Monsieur," said the young man, quickly, "Cartouche is bad-tempered. I must beg you to be very careful."

"Never mind, monsieur," Mirabeau replied, "I have to do with worse subjects than he is every day, and to-day even with one quite as savage."

"Yes, but to this savage," said Gilbert, "you could talk, and no one will deny the power of your eloquence."

"Doctor, I believe you are an adept at magnetism."

"Without doubt; what then?"

"Then you ought to know the power of the eye. Let me magnetize Cartouche."

"Do so," said Gilbert.

"Oh, monsieur," said the young man, "do not run any risk."

"Not the slightest," answered Mirabeau.

The young man bowed his consent, and drew off to the left while Gilbert went to the right, as do the witnesses of a duel.

The young man ascended two or three of the steps leading to the door, and held himself ready to stop Cartouche, if the word and eye of the unknown should prove not to be sufficient under the circumstances.

The dog turned his head to the right and left as if to see whether he against whom he seemed to have an implacable hatred was really without help. Then, seeing him without arms and assistance, he came slowly out of his kennel, more like a serpent than a quadruped, and all at once sprang forward, and at the first bound cleared one third of the distance between his adversary and himself.

Mirabeau crossed his arms, and with that look which made him the Jupiter Tonans of the tribune, fixed his eye upon the animal.

At the same time all the electricity that his body seemed capable of containing mounted to his face. His hair stood up like the mane of a lion, and if it had been midnight instead of day, without doubt each one of his hairs would have shown a feeble electric light. The dog stopped short and looked at him. Mirabeau stooped, and taking a handful of sand, threw it in his face. The dog growled, and took another bound, which brought him within three or four paces of his antagonist; but now it was the latter that walked toward the dog.

The animal remained a moment immovable as the stone dog of the *chasseur céphale*, but, made uneasy by the approach of Mirabeau, he seemed to hesitate between fear and rage, and threatening with his teeth and eyes, retreated backward. At last, Mirabeau raised his arms with a threatening gesture, and the dog, conquered and trembling in every limb, recoiled, and turning round, hastily entered his kennel.

Mirabeau joyously turned round.

"Ah! doctor," said he, "old Monsieur Mirabeau was right when he declared that dogs were candidates for humanity. You have seen this insolent, cowardly fellow, now you see him servile as a man."

And then, with a tone of command, he said:

"Cartouche, come here!"

The dog hesitated, but, with a gesture of impatience, he pushed his head a second time out of the kennel, fixed his eyes upon Mirabeau, and bounded across the space separating them, and arrived at the feet of his conqueror, raised his head slowly and timidly, and with his tongue licked Mirabeau's hand.

"Good dog!" said he, "to kennel."

He made a gesture, and the dog went and laid himself down.

Then, turning to Gilbert, while the young man, half frozen with fear and mute with astonishment, stood on the steps.

"Do you know what I was thinking of, my dear doctor," said he, "as I was acting this folly which you have just witnessed?"

"No; but tell me, you did not do it by simple bravado."

"I thought of the famous night of the 5th of October. Doctor, doctor! I would give the life left me, if the king,

Louis XVI., had seen this dog dart upon me, return to the kennel, and then come and lick my hand."

Then he added to the young man:

"You will pardon me, monsieur, I hope, for having so humiliated Cartouche? Come, let us see the house of the Friend of the People, since you are so kind as to show it us."

The young man drew aside to let Mirabeau pass, who, for that matter, did not seem to require a guide, but appeared to know the house as well as if he had been there before.

Without stopping on the ground floor, he mounted the staircase quickly, and with his usual dominating habit, Mirabeau, from a mere spectator, became an actor, from a simple visitor, master of the house. Gilbert followed him.

During this time the young man went to call his father—a man of fifty or five and fifty—and his two sisters—young girls of fifteen to eighteen—to tell them what a strange guest they were about to receive.

While he was narrating the history of the taming of the dog, Mirabeau occupied himself with showing Gilbert the working-room, chamber, and saloon of the late Marquis de Mirabeau, and each room made him tell anecdote after anecdote in that pleasing manner which belonged especially to him.

The proprietor and his family listened to this eloquent cicerone, who told them the history of their own house, with open ears.

The rooms above having been visited, and seven o'clock ringing from the church tower of Argenteuil, Mirabeau, who doubtlessly feared to be too late to accomplish his object, pressed Gilbert to descend, setting the example by jumping down the first four steps.

"Monsieur," said the proprietor of the house, "you who know so much of the history of Monsieur de Mirabeau and his illustrious son may be able to relate of these first four steps a story which will be equally curious as those you have already narrated."

"I intended that to have remained untold," said Mirabeau.

"And why so, count?" asked Gilbert.

"I'faith, you shall judge. When Mirabeau left the dungeons of Vincennes, where he had been eighteen months, he came to see his father. There were two reasons why Mirabeau was badly received in the paternal mansion: Firstly, he left Vincennes against his father's wishes; and secondly, he came to ask for money. It happened that the marquis was engaged in giving the last touch to a philosophical work, and raising his eyes, he saw his son, and at the first words about money which he pronounced, he darted on his son with his cane. The count knew his father well, and yet he thought that his age, thirty-seven, would save him from the threatened correction. The count soon found he was wrong, as the blows showered down upon him."

"What, blows with the cane?" asked Gilbert.

"Yes, and good heavy blows, too—not such as those which are administered at the Comedie-Française in Molière's plays."

"And what did the Count Mirabeau do?" asked Gilbert.

"Parbleu! he did what Horace did in his first battle—he fled. Unfortunately, he had not, like Horace, a shield to throw away, so he ran at once, and jumped down the first four steps, as I did but just now—but a little quicker, perhaps. Arrived there, he turned about, and raising his walking-stick in his turn, 'Stop, sir; we are no longer relations!' It was but a poor reply. 'Ah!' said he, 'what a pity the seneschal is dead. I could have written out that for him.' Mirabeau," continued the narrator, "was too good a strategist not to make his retreat at once. He ran down the rest of the steps almost as fast as he had descended the first four, and, to his great grief, never entered the house again. This Count Mirabeau was a beggarly fellow, don't you think so, doctor?"

"Oh, monsieur," said the young man, approaching Mirabeau, with clasped hands, as if he asked pardon of his guest for entertaining a different opinion, "rather say a very great man."

Mirabeau looked the young man in the face.

"Ah! ha!" said he, "then there are people who do think so of the Count Mirabeau?"

"Yes, sir," said the young man; "and at the risk of displeasing you, I among the first."

"Oh!" replied Mirabeau, smiling, "you need not say so so loudly in this house, lest the walls fall in upon you."

And then, saluting the old man and the two girls respectfully, he passed through the garden, making a friendly sign to Cartouche.

Gilbert followed Mirabeau, who ordered the coachman to drive into the town and pull up opposite the church.

At the corner of the first street he stopped the carriage, and drawing a card from his pocket: "Teisch," said he to his servant, "take this card to the young man, who is not aware that I am Monsieur de Mirabeau."

Then, with a sigh: "Ah, doctor," said he, "there is one who has not yet read 'The Great Treachery of Monsieur de Mirabeau.'"

Teisch returned. He was followed by the young man.

"Oh, Monsieur le Comte," said the latter, with an accent of great admiration, "allow me the honor, as you have already permitted Cartouche, allow me the honor of kissing your hand."

Mirabeau opened both his arms and pressed the young man to his breast.

"Monsieur le Comte," said he, "I am called Mormais; if ever you want any one that is ready to die for you, think of me."

Tears came to the eyes of Mirabeau. "Doctor," said he, "such are the men who will succeed us. I think, on my honor, they will be better than us."

The carriage stopped opposite the church.

"I have told you that I have never been at Argenteuil since my father struck me; I was mistaken. I was here when I placed his body in this church."

And Mirabeau descended from the carriage, and with hat in hand, and slow and solemn step, entered into the church.

Gilbert followed a few steps after him. He saw Mirabeau traverse all the church, and near the altar of the Virgin go behind a column whose Roman capital seemed to denote that it was of the twelfth century.

Bending his head, he fixed his eyes upon a black tablet in the center of the chapel.

The doctor's eyes followed those of Mirabeau and read the following inscription :

Here rests
Françoise de Castellane, Marquise de Mirabeau,
A model of purity and virtue ; a happy wife
And happy mother.
She was born in Dauphine in 1681, and died at Paris in 1769;
First buried at St. Sulpice,
And then transported here to be re-united with her worthy son in the same tomb.

Victor Riquette, Marquis de Mirabeau,
Surnamed the Friend of Man.
Born at Pertuis, in Provence, 4th of October, 1715,
Died at Argenteuil, the 11th of July, 1789.
Pray for their souls!

The religion of death is so powerful that Gilbert bent his head, and sought in his memory for a prayer, in order to obey the invitation which the sepulcher addressed to every Christian beholder.

But if Gilbert had ever, in his infancy, known the language of humility and faith, doubt and philosophy had written in its place sophisms and paradoxes.

Finding his heart hard and his lips dumb, he raised his eyes and saw two tears coursing down the cheeks of Mirabeau.

These two tears of Mirabeau seemed strange to Gilbert: he went and took him by the hand.

Mirabeau understood him.

The tears wept by Mirabeau in remembrance of the father who had imprisoned and tortured him would seem incomprehensible or trivial.

He would not, consequently, express the true cause of his sensibility to Gilbert.

"This Françoise de Castellane, mother of my father, was a worthy woman," said he. "When all the world declared me hideous, she was satisfied to find me ugly. When all the world hated me so, she loved me still. But what she loved was his son, and so, you see, my dear Gilbert, I have united them. Who will bury me with them? By whose bones will mine be laid? I have not even a dog to love me!" And he laughed bitterly.

"Monsieur," said a voice, with something of reproach which only belongs to devotees, "people never laugh in a church."

"Monsieur," he replied, with unusual sweetness, "are you the priest that serves this chapel?"

"Yes—what would you?"

"Have you many poor in your parish?"

"More than there are people to give."

"You know some charitable hearts, however—some philanthropists?"

The priest began to laugh.

"Monsieur," observed Mirabeau, "I thought you had done me the honor of informing me that no one laughed in churches."

"Monsieur," said the priest, half angrily, "has the pretension to give me a lesson?"

"No, monsieur; I only wished to show you that the people who think it their duty to correct others are not so rare as you thought. Now, monsieur, I am going, in all probability, to inhabit the Château Marais. Well, every man wanting work shall find it there, and good pay; every hungry old man there shall find food; every sick man, whatever his politics, whatever his religion, shall there meet with assistance; and, monsieur, to commence to-day, I beg your acceptance for charitable uses of a thousand francs per month

And, tearing a leaf from his pocket-book, he wrote with a pencil:

"Good for the sum of twelve thousand francs, for which Monsieur le Curé of Argenteuil can draw on me, being one thousand francs per month, to be employed by him in good works; to commence from the day I take possession of the Château Marais.

"Written in the Church of the Marais, and signed on the altar of the Virgin.

MIRABEAU, Senior."

Mirabeau wrote this letter of credit and signed it on the altar. Written and signed, he gave it to the curé, stupefied before he saw the signature, more so afterward.

He then left the church, making a sign to Dr. Gilbert to follow.

The carriage followed the principal street to the end; then it left Argenteuil and turned into the road leading to Besons. It had not gone a hundred yards before Mirabeau descried, through the trees of the park, the pointed gables of the château and its dependencies.

This was Marais.

Five minutes afterward, Teisch rang the bell at the gate of the château.

Mirabeau, as we have already said, knew it of old; but he had never had the opportunity of examining it so closely as he did now.

The gate opened, he found himself in the first court, which was nearly square. To the right was a place inhabited by the gardener, to the left was a similar lodge.

Heliotropes and fuchsias were climbing about the windows, and a bed of lilies, cactus, and narcissus spread the whole length of this court. It seemed to be covered by a carpet worthy of being woven by the hand of Penelope.

In looking at the lodges, lost almost among the roses and other flowers, Mirabeau uttered a cry of joy.

"Oh!" said he to the gardener, "is this little place to let or sell?"

"Without doubt, monsieur," he replied, "since it

belongs to the château, which is either to be let or sold. It is let just now, but as there is no lease, if monsieur takes the château, it will be easy to arrange the matter."

"And who is the inhabitant?" asked Mirabeau.

"A lady."

"Young?"

"Of thirty or so."

"Beautiful?"

"Very beautiful."

"Well," said Mirabeau, "we will see; a beautiful neighbor is never in the way. Let me see the château, mon ami."

The gardener went before Mirabeau, crossed a bridge which separated the first court from the second, and which was built over a small river. The gardener stopped.

"If monsieur," said he, "should not wish to disturb the lady in the pavilion, it will be very easy, as this river separates the garden round the pavilion from the rest of the park of the château, and thus she would be by herself, and monsieur alone, too."

"Good! good!" said Mirabeau, "and the château is here."

And he slowly ascended the five steps leading to it.

The gardener opened the principal door.

This door opened into a vestibule in stucco, with niches containing statues and vases on columns, according to the fashion of the time.

A door at the end of this vestibule, and opposite the entrance-door, let into a garden.

To the right were the billiard and dining-rooms.

To the left two saloons, a large and a small one.

This first arrangement pleased Mirabeau, who otherwise seemed impatient and uncomfortable. They passed on at the first floor. It consisted of a great saloon, admirably adapted for a study, and three or four bedchambers. The windows of the saloon and the chambers were shut. Mirabeau went and opened one of them himself. The gardener would have opened the others. But Mirabeau made a sign with his hand. The gardener stopped.

Just below the window which Mirabeau had opened, at the foot of an immense weeping willow, sat a woman reading, while a child of some five or six years played among the flowers.

Mirabeau understood at once that this was the lady of the pavilion. It was impossible to be dressed more gracefully and elegantly than this lady. Her hands were small and long; her nails beautiful.

The child dressed entirely in white satin, wore a strange mixture—but sufficiently common at that time—a hat à la Henri IV., with one of those three-colored bindings which were called national ribbons.

Such was the costume that the young dauphin wore the last time he had appeared on the balcony of the Tuileries with his mother.

The sign made by Mirabeau expressed his wish not to disturb the fair reader.

It was the lady of the pavilion aux fleurs. It was, indeed, the queen of the garden of lilies, cactus, and narcissus; it was, indeed, the beautiful neighbor that chance might give to the voluptuous Mirabeau.

Immovable as a statue, he watched this charming creature for some time, ignorant as she was of the ardent gaze fixed on her. But whether by accident or some magnetic influence, she left off reading and looked up to the window.

She perceived Mirabeau, uttered a slight cry of surprise, called her child, and taking him by the hand, walked off, but not without turning her head two or three times, and disappeared among the trees between the intervals of which Mirabeau watched her appear from time to time, for her white dress was easily distinguished in the twilight, which had already commenced.

To the beautiful unknown's cry of surprise, Mirabeau answered by one of astonishment.

This woman had not only the royal step, but as her lace veil flew aside, her features seemed those of Marie Antoinette.

The child increased the resemblance; he was just the age

of the second son of the queen. The gait, the countenance, the least movement of the queen had remained so firmly fixed in the mind of Mirabeau, ever since his first and last interview, that he believed he should have been able to have recognized her if she had come surrounded by a cloud similar to that which encircled Venus when she visited her son Æneas near Carthage.

How strange, that in the park of the house Mirabeau was about to rent there should be a woman, who, if she were not the queen, was so nearly her living portrait!

Next day Mirabeau bought the château.

CHAPTER XXII.

THE LODGE IN LA RUE PLATRIÈRE.

We shall now introduce the reader to the masonic lodge in the Rue Platrière.

A low door was surmounted by three letters in red chalk, which doubtless indicated the place of a meeting, and which before morning will be effaced.

These three letters are L. D. P.

The low door seems an alley-way; a few steps are descended, and a dark passage threaded.

Certainly the second indication would confirm the first, for after having looked at the three letters, Farmer Billot descended the steps, counting them as he went, and at last stepped from the eighth; he then went boldly down the alley.

At the extremity of this alley burned a pale light, before which sat a man pretending to read a paper.

Billot advanced, and as he did so, the man arose, and with one finger pressed on his chest, waited for him to speak.

Billot made the same answer, and then placed his finger on his lip.

This was probably the passport expected by the mysterious porter, who at once opened a perfectly invisible door, and when it was shut, showed Billot a stairway with narrow, coarse steps leading yet further below the ground.

Billot entered, and the door rapidly but silently closed behind him.

On this occasion the farmer counted seventeen steps, and when he had reached the eighteenth, in spite of the dumbness to which he seemed to have condemned himself, said :

" Good ! here I am ! "

A curtain hung a few steps before the door to which Billot went straight ; he lifted it up and found himself in a vast circular hall, in which some fifty persons were already collected. The walls were hung with red and white curtains, on which were worked the square and compass and level. A platform, which was ascended by four steps, was prepared for the orators, recipiendaries, and on this platform, in the part nearest the wall, was a solitary desk and chair for the president.

In a few moments the hall was so filled as to make motion impossible. The crowd was composed of men of every rank and condition, from the peasant to the prince, who came one by one as Billot had done, and who, without knowing each other, took their places as chance dictated or according to their sympathies.

Each of these men bore under his coat his ovat, the apron of the craft, if he was a simple mason, or, if he was one of the illuminati also, both the apron and the scarf of the higher order.

A single lamp hung from the roof cast one circle of light around, but which was not sufficient to suffer those who wished to be unknown to be seen.

Three men alone did not wear the scarf of the illuminati, but only the masonic apron.

One was Billot ; the other a young man scarcely twenty ; the third was a man about forty-five, and who, from his manners, appeared to belong to the higher classes of society.

A few seconds after the last had entered, and no more attention was paid to him than to the simplest member of the association, a masked door was opened, and the president appeared bearing the insignia of Grand Orient and of Grand Cophte.

He slowly ascended the platform, and turning toward the assembly, said:

"Brethren, to-day we have two things to do. I have to receive three new members. I have to render you an account of my work, from the day I began to the present time; but it becomes every hour more difficult. You must know if I am yet worthy of your confidence. Only by receiving light from you and diffusing it can I march on the dark and terrible journey I have undertaken. Let, then, the chiefs of the order alone remain in this hall, that we may proceed to the reception or rejection of the three members who present themselves before us. These three members, being accepted or rejected, all will enter the hall, from the first to the last, for to all, not alone to the Supreme Circle, do I wish to exhibit my conduct and to receive praise or censure."

At these words, a door opposite to the one already unmasked opened. Vast vaulted rooms, like the crypts of an ancient basilica, became open, and the crowd passed into them, like a procession of specters, through dimly lighted arcades, in which lamps of copper were placed here and there, barely sufficient, as the poet says, "to make darkness visible."

Three men alone remained — the recipiendaries. It chanced that they leaned against the wall, almost equal distances apart. They looked curiously at one another, but did not discover who and what they were.

At that moment the door through which the president had entered again reopened, and six masked men appeared and placed themselves three on each side of the president.

"Let Nos. 2 and 3 disappear for a moment. None but the Supreme Chiefs may know the secrets of the reception or rejection of a masonic brother into the Order of the Illuminati."

The young man and the man of aristocratic bearing withdrew to the corridor whence they had entered.

Billot remained.

"Approach," said the president, after a brief silence, during which the others had withdrawn. Billot drew near.

"How are you known among the profane?"

"Francis Billot."

"Among the elect?"

"Force."

"Where saw you the light?"

"In the lodge of the Friends of Truth of Soissons."

"How old are you?"

"Seven years."

Billot made a sign to show that he was a master of his order.

"Why do you wish to ascend a degree, and to be received among us?"

"Because I have been told that it is a step toward universal light."

"Have you sponsors?"

"I have none but him who came to me alone and unsolicited and offered to receive me."

Billot looked fixedly at the president.

"With what feeling will you tread the path that shall be opened to you?"

"Hatred to the powerful, and love of equality."

"Who will answer to us for your love of equality and hatred of oppression?"

"The word of a man who never has broken his word."

"What inspires you with this love of equality?"

"The inferior condition of my birth."

"What inspires you with hatred of the powerful?"

"That is my secret; that secret you know. Why make me utter aloud what I would not even whisper?"

"Will you advance according to your power and make all around you advance toward equality?"

"Yes."

The president turned toward the chiefs in masks.

"Brothers," said he, "this man speaks the truth. A great sorrow unites him to our cause, by the fraternity of hatred. Already he has contributed much to the revolution, and may do much more. I am his sponsor, and will be answerable for him in the present, past, and future."

"Let him be received," said the six, unanimously.

"You hear? Are you ready to take the oath?"

"Dictate, and I will repeat it."

The president lifted up his hand, and with a slow, solemn voice said:

"In the name of the crucified Son, I swear to break the carnal bonds which unite me yet to father, mother, brothers, sisters, wife, kindred, friends, mistresses, kings, benefactors, or any one else, or to any being to whom I have promised faith, obedience, gratitude, or service."

Billot repeated, in a firmer voice even than the president, the same words.

"Good!" said the president. "Henceforth you are freed from oaths to your country and your law. Swear to reveal to the new chief you have recognized all you shall hear, learn or guess, and even to seek and spy out what may not come before your eyes."

"I swear!" said Billot.

"Swear," continued the president, "to honor and respect poison, steel, and fire, as prompt, pure, and necessary means to purge the globe by the death of those who seek to defile truth and wrest it from our hands."

"I swear!" repeated Billot.

"Swear to avoid Naples, Rome, Spain, and every accursed land. Swear to avoid the temptation to reveal aught you may hear in our assemblies, for thunder is not more prompt than the invisible knife to reach and slay you wherever you may be."

"I swear!" repeated Billot.

"Now," said the president, "live in the name of the Father, Son, and Holy Ghost."

A brother hidden in the dark opened the door of the crypt where, until the triple reception, the brothers waited. The president made a sign to Billot, who bowed and joined those to whom the oath he had taken had assimilated him.

"No. 2!" said the president, in a loud voice; and the closed door opened again, and the young man appeared.

"Draw near," said the president.

The young man did so.

We have already said he was a young man of twenty or twenty-two, who, thanks to his fine white skin, might have passed for a woman. The huge cravat worn at that time might induce one to believe that the dazzling transparency of that skin was not to be attributed to purity of blood, but, on the contrary, to some secret and concealed malady. In spite of his high stature and great cravat, his neck was short, his forehead low, and the whole front of the head depressed. The result was that his hair, without being longer than it was usually worn at that time, touched the shoulders behind, and in front hung over his forehead. There was in the whole bearing of this man, as yet on the threshold of life, something of automatic harshness which made him look like an envoy of the other world—a deputy from the tomb.

The president looked for a moment at him with attention, and then began to question. His glance, though exceedingly fixed, could not make the young man look away. He waited and listened.

"Your name among the profane?"

"Antoine St. Just."

"Among the elect?"

"Humility."

"Where saw you light?"

"In the Lodge of the Humanitarians of Laon."

"How old are you?"

"Five years old."

The recipiendary made a sign to show that he was a free and accepted mason.

"Why do you wish to ascend a degree and to be one of us?"

"Because it is man's nature to aspire to elevations, and that on the heights the air is purer and the light more brilliant."

"Have you a model?"

"The philosopher of Geneva, the man of nature, the immortal Rousseau."

"Have you sponsors?"

"Two."

"Who are they?"

"The two Robespierres."

"With what feeling will you march in the path we open to you?"

"With faith."

"Whither will that faith conduct France and the world?"

"France to liberty, the world to freedom."

"What would you give to have France and the world reach that liberty?"

"My life is all I have, my fortune I have already given."

"Then, if received, you will advance, with all your force and power, and cause all around you to advance in the path that leads to liberty and freedom?"

"I will, and urge all others."

"Then, in proportion to your power, you will overturn every obstacle you meet within your journey?"

"I will."

"Are you free from all obligation, or if any obligation contrary to our laws has been assumed by you, will you break it?"

"I am free."

"Brothers, have you heard him?"

"Yes," said they.

"Has he told the truth?"

"Yes," said they again.

"Are you ready to take the oath?"

"I am."

And the president repeated the same oaths he had administered to Billot.

When the door of the crypt had closed on St. Just, in a loud tone the president called:

"No. 3!"

This was, as we have said, a man of forty or forty-two, flushed in the face, almost bloated, but very tall and in every lineament showing an aristocratic air, which at the first glance detected Anglomania. His dress, though elegant, bore something of that simplicity just begun to be adopted in France, the true origin of which was the relations we had with America.

His step, though it did not tremble, was not firm like St. Just's, nor heavy like Billot's.

"Draw near."

The candidate obeyed.

"Your name among the profane?"

"Louis Philippe, Duke of Orleans."

"Your name among the elect?"

"Equality."

"Where saw you the light?"

"In the Lodge of the Freemen of Paris."

"How old are you?"

"I have no age."

And the duke made a masonic sign, showing that he had reached the dignity of Rose Cross.

"Why do you wish to be received by us?"

"Because, having till now lived with the great, I now wish to live with men. Because, having ever lived with my enemies, I would now live with my brothers."

"Have you sponsors?"

"Two."

"How call you them?"

"Hatred and disgust."

"With what feeling will you walk the path we will open to you?"

"The desire to avenge myself."

"On whom?"

"Him who mistook, and on her who humiliated me."

"Are you free from all engagement, or will you renounce any engagement contrary to our laws?"

"Every engagement was broken yesterday."

"Brothers, have you heard?" said the president, turning to the masked men.

"Yes."

"You know him who presents himself to finish the work with us?"

"Yes."

"And knowing, will you receive him in our rank?"

"Yes, if he swear."

"Do you know the oath you have to take?"

"No; but repeat it and I will pronounce it."

"It is terrible, especially to you."

"Not more terrible than the outrages I have received."

"So terrible, that when you shall have heard it, we declare you at liberty to depart, if you feel unable to keep it rigidly."

"Tell it me."

"The president fixed his piercing eye on the recipiendary; then, as if he wished to prepare him for the bloody promise, inverted the order of the paragraphs, and began by the second instead of the first.

"Swear," said he, "to honor poison, steel and fire, as sure means to purge the earth by the death of those who seek to defile truth or wrest it from our hands."

"I swear," said the prince, firmly.

"Swear to break the carnal links which bind you yet to father, mother, brother, sisters, friends, wife, mistress, kings, benefactors, and all persons whatever to whom you have promised faith, obedience, and gratitude."

For a moment the duke was silent, and a pearly sweat stood on his brow.

"I told you the oath," said the president.

Instead of simply saying, "I swear," the duke repeated every word of the oath.

The president looked toward the masked men, who looked at one another, and the twinkling of their eyes was seen behind their masks.

Then, speaking to the prince, he said, "Louis Philippe Joseph, Duke of Orleans, from this moment you are free from every obligation you have taken to your country and to the law. Forget not, though, one thing, that if you betray us, thunder will not be so quick to strike, than will be, wherever you be concealed, the inevitable and invisible knife. Now live in the name of the Father, Son, and Holy Ghost."

The president pointed to the crypt, which opened before the prince.

He, like a man who has thrown down a burden too heavy for him, passed his hand over his brow, breathed deeply, and moved away.

"Ah!" said he, as he rushed into the crypt, "how I will avenge myself!"

When alone, the president and the six masked men exchanged a few words.

He then said aloud:

"Admit all; I am ready, as I promised, to receive my account."

The door opened, the members of the association, who were in the crypt walking and talking, entered the hall, filling it again.

Scarcely was the door shut behind the last of the affiliated, than Cagliostro, reaching forth his hand like a man who knows the value of time, and is unwilling to lose a second, said aloud:

"Brothers, some of you, perhaps, were present at the reunion which took place just twenty years ago, five miles from the Rhine, two miles from the village of Danenfels, in one of the caverns of Donnensberg; if any were there, let those venerable supporters of the great cause we have embraced lift up their hands and say, 'I was there.'"

Five or six hands were lifted. Five or six voices repeated as the president had asked, "I was there!"

"This is all that is needed. The rest are dead or dispersed over the surface of the globe, toiling at the common work which is made holy by the fact that it is the work of humanity. Twenty years ago this work, the different periods of which we are about to trace, was scarcely begun. Then the day which illumines us had scarcely broken, and the firmest eyes could not see through the clouds which inwrapped the future. At this meeting I will explain by what miracle death, which to man is only an oblivion of past times and ages, does not exist for me

—or, rather, that thirty-two times I have slept in the tomb during twenty centuries, without the ephemeral heirs of my immortal soul having known Lethe, the only death.

"I have, then, been able to follow through centuries the development of Christ's word, and seen people pass slowly but surely from savage life to serfdom, and thence to that state of aspiration which is the forerunner of liberty. Like the stars of the night who hurry, and even before the setting of the sunshine in the sky, we have seen at various times various small people of Europe attempt liberty. Rome, Venice, Florence, Switzerland, Genoa, Pisa, Lucca, and Arezzo—those cities of the south where the flowers open first and the fruits ripen soonest, at an earlier day established republics, one or two of which yet exist, and brave the line of kings; but all were so sullied with original sin that some were aristocratic, others oligarchic, and others despotic. Genoa, for instance, one of those which survive, is a marquisate, and the inhabitants, though simple citizens within the walls, are all noble beyond them. Switzerland alone has democratic institutions, but its imperceptible cantons, lost amid the Alps, are neither an example nor an assistance to humanity. This was not what we needed. We required a great country, not to receive, but to give, an impulse which would so rotate that Europe, like a blazing planet, might light up the world."

A murmur of approbation pervaded the whole crowd.

"I asked of God, Creator of earth, Author of all motion, for that country, and He showed me France. In France, which, from the second century, had been Catholic, national from the eleventh, Unitarian from the sixteenth, France, which the Lord himself called His eldest daughter, doubtless had the right, in this line of great devotion, to place herself at the foot of the cross of humanity, as she did at that of Christ. In fact, France, having used every form of monarchical, feudal, seignorial, and aristocratic government, seemed most apt to feel and submit to our government, and we decided, conducted like the Jews of old by the celestial ray, that France should first be free. Consider what France was twenty years ago, and you will see the sublime audacity, or, rather, sublime faith, which induced us to undertake so much. France, twenty years ago, was within the weak hands of Louis XV. The France of Louis XIV., that is to say, the great aristocratic kingdom, where all rights belonged to the noble, all privileges to the rich. At its head was a man who, at one and the same time, was the exponent of all that was lofty and base, great and petty—of God and the people. A word of this man could make you rich or poor, happy or miserable, free or captive, living or dead. He had three grandsons called to succeed him. Chance decided that he whom nature called to the throne was the one the people prayed for. He was said to be good, just, disinterested, well informed, and almost a philosopher. To crush forever the disastrous wars kindled in Europe by the fatal succession of Charles II., the daughter of Marie Theresa was selected for his wife. The two great nations which are the counterpoise of Europe, France on the Atlantic, and Austria on the Black Sea, were indissolubly united. This had been foreseen by Marie Theresa, the deepest politician of Europe. At that time France, sustained by Austria, Spain, and Italy, was about entering into a new reign, and we selected it, not to make it the first of kingdoms, but the first of nations. The only question asked, though, was, who will enter the lion's den? What Christian Theseus, guided by the light of faith, would thread the Dædal labyrinth and face the Minotaur? I said, 'I will.' Then, as some ardent minds, some uneasy organizations, asked me how much time would be required to complete the first portion of my work, I replied, 'Twenty years.' They objected. Listen to me. These men had for twenty centuries been serfs, but objected when I proposed to free them in twenty years."

Cagliostro glanced for a moment around the assembly, whom his last words had provoked into an ironical smile.

He continued: "At last I obtained these twenty years; I gave my followers the famous device: *Lilia pedibus destrue*, and set to work, advising all to follow my example.

I entered France in the midst of a triumph. Laurels and roses made one long pathway of flowers from Strasbourg to Paris. All cried, 'Long live the dauphiness!' 'Long live our future queen!' The hopes of the kingdom hung on the fecundity of the marriage. I do not wish to take to myself the credit of the attempt, nor the glory of the effect. God was with me, and I saw His divine hand held the reins of His car of fire. God be praised! I removed the stones from its road—I bridged the rivers—I leveled precipices, and the car rolled on. That was all. Now, brethren, see what has been accomplished in twenty years.

"Parliaments are gone.

"Louis XV., called the well-beloved, is dead, amid general contempt.

"The queen, after seven years of sterility, bore children, the birth of whom is contested. She was openly attacked by charges of the dauphin's illegitimacy, and was dishonored as a mother on account of the diamond necklace.

"The king, under the title of Louis, the long-wished-for, is powerless in politics as in love, and has rushed from Utopia to Utopia, to bankruptcy, and from minister to minister, to Monsieur de Calonne.

"The nobility and clergy have been overpowered by the Third Estate.

"The Bastile has been taken.

"The foreign troops driven from Paris and Versailles.

"The 14th of July, 1790, exhibited the unity of the world in France.

"The princes have been depopularized by emigration and Monsieur by De Favras's trial.

"In fine, the constitution has been sworn to on the altar of the country. The president of the National Assembly sits on a throne high as that of the king; the law and the nation are above them. All Europe hangs over us with anxiety, and is silent and applauds, or if not, trembles.

"Brothers, was I not right when I said that France would be a glowing planet to illuminate the world?"

"Yes! yes!" cried every voice.

"Now, my brothers," said Cagliostro, "do you think the work far enough advanced for us to leave it to itself? Do you think we can trust in the oath taken by the king to maintain the constitution?"

"No, no!" cried every voice.

"Then," said Cagliostro, "the second revolutionary period of the great work is to come. In your eyes, as in mine, I see with joy that the federation of 1790 is not at an end, but a halt. So be it. The halt is made, the rest is taken, the court has begun the work of counter-revolution. Let us gird up our loins, and set out again. Without doubt, timid hearts will have moments of misgiving and terror; the ray which lights us will often seem almost ready to fail, the hand which guides us will tremble and seem to desert us. More than once during the long period which remains for us to fulfil, the party will seem lost, almost destroyed, by some fortuitous accident; all will appear to go wrong. Unfavorable circumstances, the triumph of our enemies, the ingratitude of our fellow-citizens. Many, and perhaps the most conscientious of you will ask yourselves, after so much real fatigue and so much apparent impotence, if they have not followed the false road and engaged in a bad way. No, brothers, no, no! I tell you now, and let my words sound eternally in your ears, in victory like a trumpet, in defeat like a tocsin of terror. No, the people who lead the way have a holy mission, the accomplishment of which Providence watches over to fulfill. The Lord who guides them, in His mysterious way, revealing Himself only in the splendor of their fulfilment, often by a cloud is hidden from our sight, and thought absent. Often an idea draws back and seems to retreat, when, like the ancient knights in the tourneys of old, it simply gains ground to place its lance in rest, and rush again on the adversary, refreshed and more ardent. Brothers, brothers, the end to which we tend is a beacon lighted on a lofty mountain. Twenty times during every journey the inequalities of the ground hide it from our view, and we think it extinguished. Then the weak halt, murmur, and complain, saying, 'We have no guide and will advance no more in the night; let us remain where we are. Why lose ourselves?' The strong continue smiling and confident, and the beacon reappears, to fade and vanish again, each time more bright and visible, because it is nearer. Striving and persevering thus, believing especially the elect of the world will reach the foot of the beacon, the light of which will some day not only light up France, but all other nations, let us swear, then, brothers, for ourselves and our descendants—for sometimes the eternal principal uses many generations—let us swear, for ourselves and our descendants, not to pause until we have established on earth the holy device of that Christ of which we have already conquered the first part—liberty, equality, fraternity!"

The words of Cagliostro were followed by loud applause. Amid, however, all these cries and bravos, falling on the general enthusiasm like drops of water dripping from a rock of ice on a sweating brow, these words were heard, pronounced by a harsh and piercing voice:

"Let us swear; but first tell us how you understood these words, that we, your apostles, may understand you!"

A piercing glance of Cagliostro overran the whole crowd like a light refracted from a mirror, and lighted up the pale face of the deputy from Arras.

"So be it!" said he. "Hear, Maximilien!"

Then, raising both his hands and voice, he said:

"Listen, all of you."

Then one of those solemn silences pervaded the assembly. Such silences are the measures of the importance attached to the measures under discussion.

"Yes, you are right to ask what Liberty is, what Equality is, what Fraternity is. I will tell you. Let us begin with liberty. Above all, my brothers, do not confound liberty with independence. They are two sisters who resemble each other; they are two enemies who hate each other. Almost all nations inhabiting mountains are independent. I do not know one, excepting Switzerland, that is free. None will deny that the Corsican, the Calabrian, and the Scot are independent. None will dare to call them free. Let the Calabrian be wounded in his whims, the Corsican in his honor, and the Scot in his interests, the Calabrian who cannot appeal to justice, for there is no justice in oppressed lands, he will appeal to his dagger, the Corscian to his stiletto, the Scot to his dirk. He strikes, and his enemy falls. The mountain offers him a refuge, and instead of the liberty he vainly invoked by the men of cities, he finds independence in the dark caverns, the deep woods, and high places in the mountains—that is to say, the independence of the fox, chamois, and eagle. The eagle, chamois, and fox, however, are impassible, invariable, indifferent spectators of the great drama of life unfolded before them, and are animals devoted to instinct and to solitude. Primitive, ancient, and maternal civilization, such as that of India, Egypt, Etruria, Asia Minor, Greece, and Latium, by a union of their sciences, like a wreath of lights shining over the world to lighten in its cradle and development modern civilization, have left the foxes in their holes, the chamois on their cliffs, and the eagles in their clouds. To them time has passed, but been unmeasured; the sciences have flourished, but there has been no progress. To them nations have arisen, flourished, and decayed, and taught nothing. Providence has restricted all their faculties to individual preservation, while God has given man the knowledge of good and evil; the sentiment of the just and unjust, a horror of isolation, and a love of society. Thus it is that man, born solitary like the fox, wild like the chamois, isolated like the eagle, has collected into families, agglomerated into tribes, and formed peoples. The individual who isolates himself, as I told you, my brethren, has only a right to independence. Men in communities have a right to liberty.

"*Liberty!*

"This is not a primitive and universal substance like gold, but a fruit, an art, a production. Liberty is the right every one has to follow his own interests, satisfaction, amusement, glory, everything that does not injure another. It is the relinquishment of a portion of individual independence to establish a fund of general liberty, into which each one contributes an equal quota. Liberty, in fine, is more than all this; it is an obligation assumed, in the face of the world, not to close the path of progress, light, or privilege in one egotistic circle of one race or nation; but, on the contrary, to spread them openly, either as individuals or as a society, to any who are needy and ask them of you. Fear not to exhaust this treasure, for liberty has this privilege, that it multiplies itself by very prodigality, like the urn of those immense streams which water the earth, and which are at the fountain pure in proportion to the volume they emit. Such is liberty, a heavenly manna in which all have a right, and which the chosen people for whom it falls must share with all nations who ask their portion. Such is liberty as I understand it," said Cagliostro. "Now, let us pass to equality."

A murmur of approbation filled the room, inwrapping the orator in that caress which is certainly most grateful to the pride, if not to the heart of the man—popularity.

Used, though, to orations of this kind, he reached forth his hand to command silence.

"Brothers, time passes, time is valuable; every minute we lose is used by the enemies of our holy cause, and digs an abyss for us, or raises an obstacle in our way. Let me then tell you what equality is."

At these words there were many cries of "Silence," amid which the voice of Cagliostro arose clearly and distinctly.

He began by stating that none would think that he promulgated the idea of absolute equality, but only social and legal. It would be as vain to seek by a decree to level Himalaya and Chimboraza to the grade of the Pontine Marsh, as to lift all men to the intellectual superiority of Dante, Shakespeare, and Homer. He would speak of social equality.

"*Equality!*

"It is the abolition of all privileges transmissable from father to son. Free access to all offices, to all grades, to all ranks. A reward to merit, genius, and virtue, and not the appanage of a caste. Thus the throne, supposing even the throne remain, is not, or rather, will be only an exalted position to be reached by the most worthy; while the inferior degrees, according to their merit, will hold those worthy of secondary posts, without being in the least anxious for kings, ministers, councillors, judges, as far as the source whence they come is concerned. Thus royalty or magistracy, the monarchical throne or president's chair, will not be inherited as the appanage of a family. Election to the council, to the army, to the bench, will do away with family privilege. Aptitude: Thus science and art will no longer depend on patronage. Rivalry: This is social equality. Slowly, and as education advances, which shall not only be gratuitous and in every one's reach, but compulsory, ideas will increase, and equality will advance with them. Equality, instead of remaining with its feet in the mud, will ascend the loftiest summits, and a great nation like France can recognize either an equality which exalts, but not that which degrades. The latter is not that of the Titan, but of the Bandit—it is the Procrustean bed, the Caucasian couch of Prometheus."

Such a definition could not fail to unite all approbation amid a society of men of exalted ideas, every one of whom, with a few exceptions, saw the degrees of his own elevation. Hurrahs, bravos, and clappings followed, proving that even there and then there were some in the assembly who, when the time came, would put a different interpretation on equality from Cagliostro, yet, as a theory, accepted it, and the powerful genius of the strange chief interpreted it.

Cagliostro, who was more ardent, more enlightened, and more resplendent, asked again for silence in a voice which gave the token of no fatigue or of any hesitation.

"Brothers," said he, "we have now come to the third word of the device, to that which men will be the last to understand, and which, for that reason, has doubtless been placed last. We have come to

"Fraternity!

"Great word when understood; God keep me from saying that he who takes it in its narrow sense, and applies it to the citizens of a village, town, or kingdom, has a bad heart. No, brother, he has but a weak mind. Let us pity the poor souls, and try to strip their feet of the sandals of the lead of mediocrity. Let us unfold our wings and sail above all vulgar ideas. When Satan wished to tempt Jesus, he transported Him to the loftiest mountain of the world, and showed Him all the kingdoms of the earth, not to the mountain of Nazareth, whence he could see but the petty cities of Judea. Brothers, the word fraternity must not be applied to a kingdom, but to the world. Brothers, a day will come when this word, to us when now seems sacred, country, when that which seems holy, nationality, will disappear like the canvas scenes which are let down for the time being to enable carpenters and painters to prepare others. Brothers, the day will come when those who conquered the world will conquer fire and water, when the elements will be subjected to man's will, and when, thanks to rapidity of communication, all nations will be as brothers. Then, brethren, a magnificent sight will be unrolled in the face of God. Every ideal frontier will disappear: every limit of space will disappear; the rivers no longer will be an obstacle, and the mountains a hindrance; people will clasp one another's hands across mountains, and on every mountain-top the altar of Fraternity will arise. Brothers, brothers, I tell you, this is the true fraternity of the apostle.

"Christ died to ransom all the nations of the world. Do not, therefore, make these three words, Liberty, Fraternity, and Equality simply the device of France. But write it on the *labarum* of humanity as the device of the world.

"Now, my brethren, go. Your task is great, so great that through whatever valley of tears and blood you pass, your children will envy your holy mission, and like the Crusaders, who always become numerous and anxious to view the Holy Land, they will not pause, though they find their road by bleaching bones on the wayside. Courage, then, apostles, pilgrims, soldiers! Apostles, make contests; pilgrims, onward; soldiers, fight!"

Cagliostro paused, but not until general and universal applause had interrupted him.

Thrice the applause hushed, and thrice arose again beneath the arches of the vault, like the sound of the tempest,

The six masked men then bowed before him, kissed his hand, and retired.

Each of the brothers then bowed before the platform, where, like another Peter the Hermit, a new apostle preached the crusade of liberty, and passed away uttering the words, "Lilia Pedibus Destrue."

The last lamp went out, and Cagliostro remained alone in silence and darkness, like those Indian gods at the mysteries of whom he pretended to have been initiated in a thousand years before.

CHAPTER XXIII.

WOMEN AND FLOWERS.

A FEW months after the events we have related, toward the end of March, 1791, a carriage coming rapidly from Argenteuil to Besons made a détour of a quarter of a league from the latter city, and advanced toward the Castle of Marais, the gate of which opened before it, and stopped in the inner courtyard immediately in front of the door.

The clock in front of the building announced the hour to be 8 A. M.

An old servant, who seemed to await the carriage's arrival most anxiously, went to the door of the carriage, which he opened, and a man dressed in black got out.

"Ah! Monsieur Gilbert, here you are at last."

"What is the matter, Teisch?"

"Alas! sir, you will see."

Going before the doctor, he took him through the billiard room, the lamps of which, doubtless lighted at a late hour of the night, yet burned. Thence to the dining-room, the table of which, covered with flowers, uncorked bottles, fruits, and pastry, betokened that supper had been prolonged later than usual.

Gilbert looked at this scene of disorder, which showed how his prescriptions had been followed, with sadness. He then shrugged his shoulders with a sigh, and went up the stairway which led to Mirabeau's room.

"Count," the servant said, "here is Monsieur Gilbert."

"What, the doctor?" said Mirabeau. "You did not go for him for such a trifle?"

"Trifle!" said Teisch. "Judge yourself, doctor."

"Doctor," said Mirabeau, rising from his bed, "believe me, I am sorry that, without my consent, you have been so disturbed."

"Count, I am never disturbed when I have an opportunity to see you. You know that I only attend a few friends to whom I belong entirely. Tell me what has happened; above all, have no secrets from your physician. Teisch, draw the curtains aside and open the window."

This order having been obeyed, light shone on Mirabeau. The doctor was able to see the change which a month had wrought in the celebrated orator.

"Ah! ah!" said he, involuntarily.

"Yes," said Mirabeau, "am I not changed? I am going to tell you why."

Gilbert smiled sadly. But as a skilful physician always profits by what his patient says, even though he lied to him, he listened.

"You know what question was considered yesterday?"

"Yes, the mines."

"The matter is not at all understood or measured; the interests of the owners and of the government are not sufficiently distinct. The Count de la Marck, my intimate friend, is very deeply interested in the matter, and the half of his fortune depends on it. His purse has always been mine, and I must be grateful. I spoke, or, rather, I charged three times; at the last charge I routed the enemies but was myself taken a little aback. When I came home, I resolved to celebrate the victory. I had a few friends to supper, and we laughed and jested until three in the morning. At five I was taken with a violent pain in my bowels, and I cried like an imbecile. Teisch, like a fool, became terrified, and sent for you. Now you know as much as I do. Here is my pulse, here is my tongue, cure me if you can, for I tell you I know nothing of the matter."

Gilbert was too shrewd a physician not to be able to see, without looking at pulse or tongue, the danger of Mirabeau's condition. He seemed in danger of suffocation, and his face was swollen from the stoppage of blood in his lungs. He complained of excessive cold in the extremities, and from time to time pain wrung from him a sigh or a cry. His pulse was convulsive and intermittent.

"Come," said Gilbert, "this time it will be nothing; but, my dear count, I came just in time."

He took his book from his pocket with the rapidity and calmness which are the distinguishing traits of true genius.

"Ah! ha!" said Mirabeau, "you are going to bleed me?"

"At once."

"In the right or left arm?"

"In neither. Your lungs are too full. I intend to open a vein in the foot, and Teisch must go to Argenteuil for mustard and cantharides. You must be blistered. Take my carriage, Teisch."

"Diable!" said Mirabeau, "then you were just in time."

Gilbert at once bled him, and soon black, thick blood, which at first did not flow freely, gushed from the patient's foot. He was relieved instantly.

"Morbleu! doctor," said he, "you are a great man."

"And you are worse than a fool to risk a life so valuable to your friends and to all Frenchmen for the sake of a few hours of false enjoyment."

Mirabeau smiled sadly, almost ironically.

"Bah! doctor, you exaggerate the number of my friends and the condition of France."

"On my honor, great men always complain of the ingratitude of others, but it is they who really are ungrateful. Be really sick, and to-morrow all Paris will be beneath your window. Die the next day, and all France will wear mourning."

"Do you know, doctor, what you say is very consoling?" said Mirabeau, with a smile.

"The reason that I say this is, that you may see the one case without risking the other. You need some great demonstration to reinstate you in a moral point of view. Let me take you back to Paris in two hours; let me but tell the policeman at the first corner that you are sick, and you will see."

"Think you I could go to Paris?"

"Yes, at once. Where do you suffer?"

"I breathe more freely, my head is clear, the mist before my eyes is gone, but my bowels——"

"Ah! the blisters will correct that. The bleeding was well, and the blisters will do their duty. Ah! here is Teisch."

The valet came in with the ingredients he had been sent for. In a quarter of an hour the improvement the doctor had predicted was perceptible.

"Now," said Gilbert, "sleep for an hour, and then I will take you to Paris."

"Doctor," said Mirabeau, "suffer me not to leave until evening, and give me a rendezvous at my hotel in the Chaussée d'Antin, at eleven."

Gilbert looked at Mirabeau. The patient saw that his physician saw why he wished to delay.

"Why," said Mirabeau, "I have a visit to receive."

"My dear count, I saw many flowers on the table of your dining-room. You did not give a supper yesterday merely to your friends."

"You know I cannot do without flowers, it is a passion."

"Yes, but you had not flowers alone."

"Dame! if flowers be required, I must at least submit to their consequences."

"Count, you will kil yourself."

"At least, doctor, in a pleasant manner."

"I leave you for to-day."

"Doctor, I have given you my word, and will not break it."

"You will come to Paris this evening?"

"I told you I would expect you at eleven. Is that enough?"

"Not quite."

"Have I not made a conquest of Juliet, Tulma's wife? Doctor, I feel perfectly well."

"Then you drive me off."

"Oh! fy! fy!"

"Well, you are right. Live in the Quartier des Tuileries."

"Ah! ha! you will see the queen?" said Mirabeau, growing moody.

"Probably. Have you any message for her?"

"Why?"

"Because she will ask if I have saved your life as I promised to, for I will have to say it was more your fault than mine. You do not wish me to say that your labor and toil are killing you?"

Mirabeau reflected for an instant.

"Yes," said he, "say that; make me, if you please, sicker than I really am."

"Why?"

"Nothing. Curiosity. To say something."

"So be it."

"Do you promise me this, doctor?"

"I do."

"And you will tell me what she says?"

"Her very words."

"Adieu, then, doctor; a thousand good wishes."

He gave his hand to Gilbert.

Gilbert looked fixedly at Mirabeau, whom his glance appeared to disturb.

"Apropos; before you go, your prescription."

"Warm, soothing drinks. No wine; not a drop. And, above all——"

"What?"

"No nurse under fifty. Do you understand, count?"

"Doctor, rather than violate your orders, I will take two of twenty-five."

At the door Gilbert met Teisch. The poor lad wept.

"Monsieur," said he, "why do you go?"

"Because, my dear Teisch, your master has driven me away," said Gilbert, smiling.

"All this is for a woman," said the old man; "and because the woman looks like the queen. A man, who, they say, has so much genius. My God! must he be a brute?"

He opened the door to Gilbert, who got in, saying:

"What on earth has he to do with that woman who is so like the queen?"

He took Teisch by the arm, as if to question him, but let it go, saying:

"What was I about to do? It is Mirabeau's secret, not mine. Driver, to Paris."

Gilbert scrupulously discharged the promise he had made to Mirabeau. As he entered Paris, he met Camille Desmoulins, the living journal, the incarnation of a newspaper. He told him of the illness of Mirabeau, which he did gravely as possible, for he did not know if Mirabeau might not commit some new indiscretion, though he thought him then in no danger.

He then went to the Tuileries and informed the king of Mirabeau's condition. The king said:

"Poor count! Has he lost his appetite?"

"Yes, sire."

"Then he is in a bad way," said the king.

His majesty then talked of other matters.

Gilbert left the king, and went into the queen's apartments, where he said what he had told the king. The haughty Austrian brow was lighted up, and she said :

"Why was he not thus attacked on the day he made his fine address about the National tricolor?"

Then, as if she regretted having suffered these words to escape her—expressive as they were of hatred to French nationality, she said :

"It matters not. It would be most unfortunate for us and for France if he should be really sick."

"I had the honor to tell the queen that he was not indisposed, but ill."

But you will cure him, doctor?"

"I will do my best, madame."

"Doctor, I rely on you. You know—to give me news of Monsieur Mirabeau."

She spoke of other things.

That night, at the appointed hour, Gilbert went to Mirabeau's hotel. Mirabeau was waiting for him, and sat on a couch. As the doctor had been made to wait a moment, under the pretext of informing the count of his presence, he had an opportunity to look around the room into which he was shown. The first thing that met his eyes was a cashmere shawl.

As if to divert Gilbert's attention, or because he attached great importance to the first words interchanged between himself and the doctor, Mirabeau said :

"Ah! is it you? I know you have already kept a portion of your promise. Paris knows that I am sick, and for two hours poor Teisch has had, every ten minutes, to tell somebody how I am. That was your first promise; now about the second."

"What mean you?"

"You know."

Gilbert shrugged his shoulders to say he did not.

"Have you been to the Tuileries?"

"Yes."

"You saw the king?"

"Yes."

"The queen?"

"Yes."

"And you told them they would soon be rid of me?"

"I told them you were dangerously ill."

"What said they?"

"The king asked how your appetite was."

"You told him it was gone?"

"And he pitied you sincerely."

"Kind king! Like Leonidas, he will say, when he dines to-night, 'he sups with Pluto.' But the queen——"

"Pitied and asked kindly after you."

"How though?" asked Mirabeau, who evidently attached much importance to the question.

"Kindly."

"You promised to repeat her words verbatim."

"I cannot."

"Doctor, you have not forgotten one syllable."

"I swear——"

"Doctor, you gave me your word! you would not have me treat you as a faithless man."

"You are exigeant, count."

"I am."

"Do you insist that I repeat what the queen said?"

"Verbatim."

The doctor repeated the conversation between himself and the queen. Gilbert looked at Mirabeau, to see the influence it had on him.

"Kings are ungrateful," said he. This speech sufficed to make her forget the civil list of eighty millions for the king over her dower of four millions.

Mirabeau ran over the long series of his triumphs in the cause of the queen, and sunk back in his chair exhausted.

Ten minutes after, Mirabeau was in a bath, and, as usual, Teisch escorted Gilbert down.

Mirabeau arose from his bath to look after the doctor, and when he was out of sight listened to hear his footsteps. He then stood motionless until he heard the door open and close.

He then rang violently, and said:

"Jean, have a table fixed in my room, and ask Mademoiselle Olive if she will sup with me."

As he left, Mirabeau said :

"Flowers ! flowers ! You know how I love them."

At four o'clock, Dr. Gilbert was awakened by a violent ringing of the bell.

"Ah !" said he. "I am sure Mirabeau is worse."

The doctor was not wrong. After supper, Mirabeau had sent Jean and Tiesch to bed. He had then closed all the doors, except the one which admitted the unknown woman he called his evil genius. The servants, however, did not go to bed, for Jean slept in the ante-chamber, in a chair, and Teisch kept awake.

At a quarter before four the bell rang violently. Both rushed to Mirabeau's room. The doors were fastened. They went round to the room of the unknown woman, and thus reached his bed-chamber. Mirabeau on the floor, half fainting, held this woman in his arms, doubtless to keep her from calling for aid. She had rung the bell on the table, being unable to get hold of the bell-rope. When she saw the servants, she begged them to assist her as well as Mirabeau. In his convulsions Mirabeau was strangling her. Thanks to the efforts of the two servants, the dying man's grasp was torn apart. Mirabeau fell on a chair, and, all in tears, she entered her room.

Jean had gone for Dr. Gilbert, while Teisch attended to his master.

Gilbert did not wait to harness up or to send for a carriage. It was not long from his house to the Chaussée d'Antin, and in ten minutes he was at Mirabeau's house.

Teisch was in the vestibule.

"Ah, sir !" said he, "that woman—that cursed woman ! You will see, you will see !"

Something like a sob was heard. Gilbert was at the foot of the stairway, and a door opposite Mirabeau's opened. A woman, in a white veil, appeared and fell at the doctor's feet.

"Gilbert, Gilbert !" said she, folding her arms, "for mercy's save, save him !"

"Nicole!" said Gilbert, "is it you?"

Gilbert paused a moment. A terrible idea flitted across him.

"Ah!" murmured he, "Beausire sells pamphlets against him, and Nicole is his mistress. All is lost, for Cagliostro's finger is visible."

He hurried into Mirabeau's room, being aware that there was not a moment to be lost.

It is not our intention to follow all the various phases of this terrible decease. On the morning of this day a report of it got into the city, and this time more seriously than before. He had a relapse, it was said, and this relapse threatened death.

It was then that one would judge of the great space occupied by one man in the midst of a nation. All Paris was moved as if a general calamity threatened the community. All the day, as before, the street was guarded by the people, in order that the noise of carriages might not disturb him. From hour to hour the groups assembled under the windows asked the news. Bulletins were issued, which passed at once from the Chaussée d'Antin to the extremities of Paris. The door was besieged by citizens in every station, of every opinion, as if every party, however opposed to one another, had something to lose in losing Mirabeau. During all this time the relations and particular friends of the great orator filled the hall and chambers without him knowing anything about the matter.

On the evening of this first day of the relapse, a deputation, with Barnave at the head, came from the Society of the Jacobins to inquire as to the health of their ex-president.

Dr. Gilbert never quitted Mirabeau for twenty-four hours. On Wednesday evening, he was sufficiently well for Gilbert to consent to seek a few hours' repose in a neighboring chamber.

Before going to bed, the doctor ordered that at the least change he should be called at once. At break of day he awoke; no one had disturbed his sleep, and yet he rose, half afraid ; for he thought it impossible some change had not taken place.

On going downstairs, Teisch announced to the doctor, with his eyes full of tears, that Mirabeau was worse, but had forbidden any one disturbing Dr. Gilbert.

The patient had suffered severely ; the pulse had become bad again, the pains had developed themselves with greater ferocity—in fine, the spasms had returned.

"My dear doctor," he said to Gilbert, "I shall die today. When one is as I am, one has nothing to do but to perfume and crown one's self with flowers, so as to enter on the last sleep as agreeably as possible. May I do as I like ?"

Gilbert made a sign, implying that he was his own master.

He then called his two domestics.

"Jean," said he, "get me the most beautiful flowers you can find, while Teisch dresses me as well as he can."

Jean seemed to ask permission with his eyes of Gilbert, who nodded his head in assent. He went out. As for Teisch, who had been very ill from watching, he began to shave and dress his master.

When Jean, on whom, as he left the hotel, everybody rushed to learn the news, had said that he was going to fetch flowers, men rushed down the streets calling for flowers for M. de Mirabeau ; and every door opened, each offering what he had, whether in the house or conservatory. By nine o'clock in the morning M. de Mirabeau's chamber was transformed into a beautiful bed of flowers, and Teisch had finished his toilet.

"My dear doctor," said Mirabeau, "I ask you for a quarter of an hour to bid good-by to some one who ought to leave the hotel before I do. If any one should wish to insult this person, I recommend her to your care."

Gilbert understood. "Good !" said he ; "I will leave you."

"Yes, but you will wait in the adjoining chamber, and this person once gone, you will not leave me until death ?"

Gilbert signed his assent.

"Give me your word," said Mirabeau.

Gilbert gave it, sobbing. This stoic was quite astonished to find himself in tears; he had believed himself, through force of philosophy, to be insensible. He then went toward the door. Mirabeau stopped him.

"Before going out," said he, "open my secretary and give me the little casket you will find there."

Gilbert did as Mirabeau wished. This casket was heavy. Gilbert thought it contained gold. Mirabeau made him a sign to put it on the toilet-table. He then gave him hold of his hand.

"You will have the goodness to send Jean to me," said he, "Jean, not Teisch. It fatigues me to call or ring."

Gilbert went out. Jean was waiting in the next chamber, and entered as Gilbert left. Gilbert heard the door bolted behind him. The half-hour that followed was employed by Gilbert in giving information to those who were in the house. A carriage stopped before the gate of the hotel. For a moment his idea was that a carriage of the court had been allowed to pass. He ran to the window. It would have been a sweet consolation to the dying man to know that the queen had thought of him. It was a hackney-coach that Jean had been to fetch. The doctor guessed for whom. In fact, some minutes afterward, Jean came out, conducting a lady veiled in a large mantle. The lady got into the carriage. The crowd, without troubling themselves as to who the lady was, respectfully retired. Jean went into the hotel.

A moment after the door of the chamber opened, and the feeble voice of the invalid was heard inquiring for the doctor. Gilbert ran to him.

"Look!" said Mirabeau. "Put this casket in its place, my dear doctor." Then, as he seemed astonished to find it as heavy as at first, "Yes," said Mirabeau; "it is curious, is it not? Where the devil will disinterestedness come to at last?"

In approaching the bed, Gilbert found a handkerchief

on the ground, embroidered and trimmed with lace. It was wet with tears.

"Ah!" said he to Mirabeau, "if she has not taken anything, she has left something."

Mirabeau took the handkerchief, and feeling it was wet, applied it to his forehead.

"Oh," murmured he, "she is the only one who has a heart!" And he fell back on his bed, and his eyes closed as if he were already dead; but the rattle in his chest showed that he was still on his way to the grave.

From this time the few hours that Mirabeau had still to live were painful and agonizing. Gilbert had his word, and remained near his bed to the last minute.

He took a glass, poured in a few drops of that green liquid of which he had already given a vial to Mirabeau, and without mixing it this time with any brandy, he put it to the lips of the invalid.

"Oh, dear doctor," said the latter, smiling, "if you wish the elixir to have any effect upon me, give me a glassful, or the whole vial."

"Why so?" asked Gilbert, looking fixedly at Mirabeau.

"Do you believe that I, who have abused every treasure through life, would have this in my hands and not abuse it, too? No; I caused your liquor, my dear sir, to be analyzed, and I learned that it was drawn from the root of the Indian hemp; and I have taken it, not by drops, but by glassfuls—not to live alone, but to dream."

"Unhappy one!" murmured Gilbert, "I may well doubt having poisoned you!"

"Sweet poison, dear doctor, by whose aid I have doubled, quadrupled, the last hours of my existence—by which, in dying at forty-two, I have lived the life of a century. Oh, doctor, doctor! do not repent, but rather be glad. God gave me but a life, sad, discolored, unhappy, deserving of little regret, and which man ought always to be ready to give up. Doctor, do you know I doubt whether I ought to thank God for my life, but I am sure I ought you for presenting me with your poison. Fill the glass, doctor, and give it me."

The doctor did as Mirabeau wished, and presenting him the liquid, he drank it with pleasure.

"Thanks!" murmured he. And he sunk again on his pillow.

This time Gilbert no longer doubted his death. The abundant dose of hashish which Mirabeau had taken, like the effects of the voltaic pill, had given the invalid, with speech, the play of his muscles; but now that he had ceased to speak, the muscles grew stiff, and death already began to show itself in his face.

During three hours his cold hand remained between Gilbert's. During these three hours, that is, from four to seven o'clock, the agony was calm—so calm that one could easily have thought he slept.

But toward eight o'clock Gilbert felt his cold hand start in his. The starting was violent. He could no longer deceive himself.

"Allons," said he, "now the struggle, the true agony commences."

And indeed the face of the invalid was covered with sweat. He madė a motion as if he would drink. They hastened to offer him brandy, orangeade, water; but he shook his head. He wished for none of these. He made a sign, and they brought him pen, ink, and paper.

He took the pen, and in a scarcely legible hand wrote:

"Fly! fly! fly!"

He would have signed it, but he could only write the first two or three letters of his name, and stretching his arms toward Gilbert, "For her," he murmured. And he fell back on his pillow without a motion, without a look, without a groan. He was dead.

Gilbert came to his bedside, looked at him, felt his pulse, put his hand on his heart, then, turning to the spectators of this last scene, "Gentlemen," said he, "Mirabeau no longer breathes."

And putting his lips for the last time on the forehead of the dead, he took the paper, whose destination he only knew, folded it carefully, put it in his breast, and went, not thinking it right to preserve a single instant longer than necessary to go from Chaussée d'Antin to the Tuileries the commendation of the illustrious departed.

Some seconds after the doctor left the chamber of death a great clamor was raised in the street. This was the report of the death of Mirabeau, which was beginning to spread.

Soon a sculptor entered ; he was sent by Gilbert to preserve for posterity the features of this great orator. Some minutes of eternity had already given serenity to these features. Mirabeau was not dead. Mirabeau seemed to sleep—a sleep full of life and pleasant dreams.

The grief was immense—universal. In one moment it spread from the Chaussée d'Antin to the barriers of Paris. It was eight o'clock in the morning. The people raised one terrible cry. They ran to the theaters, they tore down the affiches, they shut the doors.

A ball had taken place the same evening in a hotel of the Rue Chaussée d'Antin. They went to the hotel, dispersed the dancers, and broke the instruments.

The loss which had just happened was announced to the National Assembly by the president.

Barrère immediately ascended the tribune and demanded the assembly should record, in the minutes of the day, its regret for the loss of this great man, and insisted, in the name of the country, that all the members of the assembly should assist at his funeral.

The next day, the 3d of April, the department of Paris presented itself to the National Assembly, and demanded and obtained that the Church of Ste. Geneviève should be erected into a pantheon, and consecrated as a sepulcher for great men, and that the first one buried there should be Mirabeau.

Let us give here the magnificent decree of the assembly :

ARTICLE I. The new edifice of Geneviève shall be destined to receive the ashes of great men, and date from the epoch of French liberty.

ARTICLE II. The legislature shall decide to whom this honor shall be decreed.

ARTICLE III. The honored Riquette Mirabeau is judged worthy of this honor.

ARTICLE IV. The legislature cannot confer this honor on one of its members; it can only be bestowed by the following one.

ARTICLE V. The exceptions for those great men, who died before the revolution, can only be determined by the legislature.

ARTICLE VI. The directory of the city of Paris shall be charged to put the edifice of Ste. Geneviève into a proper state for this object, and cause to be engraved on the front these words:

"Our country dedicates this to her great men."

ARTICLE VII. Meanwhile, the body of Riquette Mirabeau shall be deposited by the side of the ashes of Descartes, in the vaults of the Church of Ste. Geneviève.

The next day, at four in the evening, the National Assembly left the salle of the Manége, and went to the hotel of Mirabeau. It was attended by the directors of the department, by all the ministers, and two hundred thousand people.

But of these two hundred thousand people, no one had come on behalf of the queen.

The cortége commenced to move.

Lafayette marched at its head, as commander-general of the National Guard. Then the president of the National Assembly—Tronchet. Then the ministers. Then the assembly, without any party distinctions; Sieyès, giving his arm to Charles de Lameth. After the assembly the Jacobin Club, like a second assembly, had decreed eight days of mourning, and Robespierre, too poor to buy a dress, had hired one, as he had already done for the death of Franklin. And, lastly, came the entire population of Paris.

A funeral march, in which, for the first time until then

unknown instruments were heard—the trombone and the tomtom marked the time for this numerous cortége.

When they reached Ste. Eustache, it was eight o'clock. The funeral oration was pronounced by Cerutti; at the last word ten thousand National Guards discharged their muskets.

They continued their route with flambeaus. Darkness had fallen, not only on to the streets, but on to the hearts that passed through them.

The death of Mirabeau, in effect, was a political obscurity. Mirabeau dead—who knew whither things would tend? All felt that he had carried with him something that was wanting in the assembly. The spirit of peace watched even in the midst of war, the goodness of the heart lay concealed under the violence of the mind. All the world had lost by his death; the royalist no longer had a rallying point, the revolutionists no curb. Besides, the carriage would roll more rapidly, and the descent be longer. Who could say toward what it rolled—whether to triumph or an abyss?

Three years afterward, on a dark day in autumn, not in the salle of the Manége, but in the salle of the Tuileries, when the convention, after having killed the king, killed the queen; after having killed the Girondists, after having killed the Jacobins, the Montagnards; after having killed itself, had nothing left to kill—it killed the dead. This was, when with a savage joy, it declared that, in the judgment it had rendered to Mirabeau, it had been mistaken, and that in its eyes corruption could not be pardoned by genius.

A new decree was made which excluded Mirabeau from the Pantheon.

An usher came, and from the steps of the Temple read the decree which declared Mirabeau unworthy to share the sepulcher of Voltaire, Rousseau, and Descartes, and summoned the guardian of the church to deliver up the body.

Then a voice more terrible than that which will be heard in the valley of Jehosophat cried:

"Pantheon, deliver up the dead!"

The Pantheon obeyed. The body of Mirabeau was handed over to the usher, who caused it, as he said, to be taken and deposited in the usual place of burial.

The usual place of burial was Clamart, the cemetery of the executed.

And without doubt to render the punishment which pursued him even after death more terrible, he was buried without cross, stone, or inscription.

CHAPTER XXIV.

THE MESSENGER.

On the same morning of the 2d of April, an hour, perhaps, before Mirabeau breathed his last, a superior officer of the marine, clothed in the full uniform of a captain, and coming from the Rue St. Honoré, hastened toward the Tuileries.

Arrived there, he ascended, like a man who was familiar with the way, a little staircase, which communicated by a long winding corridor with the apartments of the king.

On perceiving him, the valet de chambre uttered a cry of surprise, almost of joy; but he, putting a finger on his mouth, asked:

"Can the king receive me at once?"

"The king is with Monsieur the General Lafayette, to whom he is giving the orders of the day," answered the valet; "but as soon as the general has gone——"

"You will announce me," said the officer.

"Oh! that is useless. His majesty expects you; since yesterday evening orders were given that you should be introduced as soon as ever you arrived."

At this moment a bell rang in the cabinet of the king.

"There!" said the valet de chambre, "the king is probably ringing to inquire about you."

"Go, then, Monsieur Hue, and do not lose any time if the king is at liberty to see me."

The valet de chambre opened the door, and almost immediately—proof that the king was alone—announced, "Monsieur le Comte de Charny."

"Oh, let him come in! let him come in! I have waited for him since yesterday."

Charny advanced quickly and approached the king.

"Sire," said he, "I am, as it seems, late by some hours, but I hope that when I have informed your majesty of the causes of this delay, you will pardon me."

"Come, come, Monsieur de Charny, I was expecting you with impatience, it is true, but I agreed at once that it could only be something of importance that could make your journey less rapid than it has been—so now you are welcome." And he gave the count his hand, which the latter kissed respectfully.

"Sire," continued Charny, who saw the impatience of the king, "I received your order the day before yesterday in the middle of the night; I left Montmedy yesterday, at three o'clock in the morning."

"How did you come?"

"By post."

"That explains the few hours you are late," said the king, smiling.

"Sire," said Charny, "I could have come on horseback, it is true, and in this way I should have been here by ten or eleven o'clock in the evening, and even sooner, by taking the direct route; but I wanted to know the chances, good and bad, of the route your majesty has chosen, what posts were well or badly served. I wished to know, too, the time to a minute, almost to a second, it took to go from Montmedy to Paris, and consequently from Paris to Montmedy. I have noted all, and am now able to answer all your questions."

"Bravo, Monsieur de Charny," said the king; "you are an admirable servant; only let me tell you how we are here, and then you shall tell me how you get on down there at Montmedy."

"Oh, sire," said Charny, "if I may judge by what I have already seen, things go on very badly."

"To such a point that I am a prisoner in the Tuileries,

my dear count. I just now said to this dear Monsieur Lafayette, my jailer, I should like better to be King of Metz than King of France; but, happily, you see me."

"His majesty will do me honor by putting me *au courant* with the situation things are in."

"Yes, in two words. You have heard of the flight of my aunts?"

"Like all the world, sir; but without any details."

"Ah, mon Dieu! it is very simple. You know that the assembly would only allow us sworn priests. Well, the poor women got frightened at the approach of Easter. They believed they were risking their souls by confessing to a priest of the constitution, and on my advice, I admit, they started for Rome. There was no law against this journey, and they could not be afraid that two poor old women could strengthen the party of the emigrants much. Narbonne arranged the whole matter, but I do not know how he managed; everything was ready when they were visited on the evening of their departure, at Bellevue, in the same way that we were at Versailles on the night of the 5th of October. Fortunately they got out of one door while all the *canaille* arrived by another. Do you understand? No carriage was ready. Three ought to have been there near the stables. They were obliged to go to Meudon on foot; there they found carriages at last, and started. Three hours afterward there was a great uproar in Paris. Those who had wished to stop this flight had found the nest warm but empty. The press was very fierce next day. Marat declared they had run off with millions, Desmoulins that they had taken the dauphin away. Nothing of all this was true; the poor women had some three or four hundred thousand francs in their purse, and they were troubled enough with this, without having to take care of a child that would have at once betrayed them. As it was, they were recognized; first at Moret—they let them pass; then at Arnay le Duc, where they were stopped. I wrote of this to the assembly, and in spite of my letter, they were discussing the matter the whole day. At last, however, they were permitted to proceed, but on the condition that a committee presented a law against all such emigration."

"Yes," said Charny, "but I thought, that owing to a magnificent speech of Monsieur de Mirabeau, the assembly had rejected the law proposed by the committee."

"Without doubt it was rejected. But alone, with this little triumph there was a great humiliation. Some devoted friends—and I have more than I thought, my dear count—when they saw the racket which the departure of the two ladies made, hastened to the Tuileries and offered me their lives. Soon a rumor spread that there was a plot on foot to carry me off. Lafayette, whom they had sent to the Faubourg St. Antoine, under the pretense that the Bastile would be attacked, furious at being duped, returned to the Tuileries, entered it with sword and bayonet, and arresting our poor friends, disarmed them. Some had pistols, some small swords. Each had taken whatever he could lay his hands on. Good! the day will be known in history under a new name; it will be called 'La Journée des Chevaliers du Poignard' ('The Day of the Knights of the Dagger')."

"Oh, sire, sire! what dreadful times we live in!" said Charny, shaking his head.

"But listen. We go every year to St. Cloud. Day before yesterday we ordered the carriages; we descended; we found fifteen hundred persons around the carriages. We got in; it was impossible; the people, seizing the reins, declared that I wished to fly. After trying uselessly for an hour, we were obliged to return. The queen wept with anger."

"But was not General Lafayette there to maintain order, and make them respect your majesty?"

"Lafayette! Do you know what he did? He caused the tocsin at St. Roch to be rung; he ran to the Hôtel de Ville, and asked for the red flag to declare the country in danger. The country in danger, forsooth! because the king and queen wished to go to St. Cloud. Do you know who refused to give him the red flag, who tore it from his hands?—Danton. He then pretended that Danton was bought—that I had given him a hundred thousand francs. You see now, my dear count, how we are fixed, letting alone that Mirabeau is dying, nay, at this very moment may be dead."

"So much the more reason that we should quicken our movements, sire."

"That is what we will do. Let us see what you have determined with Bouillé? The affair at Nancy has given me the opportunity of increasing his command, of putting new troops under his orders."

"Yes, sire; but unfortunately the orders of the minister of war have run counter to yours. He has withdrawn a regiment of hussars, and he has refused any of the Swiss Guards going there. It has been with great trouble only that Bouillé has been able to keep the regiment of Bouillon infantry."

"Then he is still doubtful?"

"No, sire; there are a few chances less; but no matter. In such enterprises we must always stand the hazard of the die, and we have still, if the enterprise is well conducted, ninety chances out of the hundred."

"Well, then, let us see."

"Sire, your majesty is still determined to follow the route through Chalons, Ste. Menehould, Clermont, and Stenay, although this route is at least twenty leagues further than the other, and there is no post at Varennes?"

"I have already told Monsieur Bouillé the reason why I prefer this road?"

"Yes, sire, and on this subject he has transmitted us the orders of your majesty. After these orders the route was thoroughly examined by me, bush by bush, stone by stone; the result ought to be in the hands of your majesty."

"And it is a model of clearness. I know the road as well as if I had made it myself."

"Now, sire, see what the researches of my last journey have added to the rest."

"Speak, Monsieur de Charny, I listen; and for greater clearness, here is the map drawn by yourself." And saying these words, the king drew a map from a portfolio, which he spread out on the table. This map was not traced, but designed, by the hand, and, as Charny had said, scarce a tree, a stone, was wanting, it was the result of more than eight months' labor.

Charny and the king leaned over the map.

"Sire," said Charny, "the real danger will commence at Ste. Menehould, and terminate at Stenay. It is over these eighteen leagues which we must station our detachment."

"Could we not let them come nearer Paris, Monsieur de Charny—as far as Chalons, for instance?"

"Sire," said Charny, "that would be difficult. Chalons is too strong a town for forty, fifty, a hundred men even, to effect anything for your majesty's safety, if that safety were menaced; and besides, all that Monsieur Bouillé can do is to place a detachment at Pont de Someville, here, your majesty, at the first post after Chalons." And Charny pointed with his finger to the place on the map.

"Let it be so," said the king; "in ten or eleven hours we can be at Chalons. How many hours has it taken you to come the eighty-six leagues?"

"Thirty-six hours, sire."

"But in a light carriage, where there was only you with a single servant."

"Sire, I lost three hours in examining whereabouts at Varennes the relay should be placed, whether on the side of the town near Ste. Menehould, or on the other near Dun. These three hours will compensate for the extra weight of the carriage. My opinion is that your majesty can go from Paris to Montmedy in thirty-five or thirty-six hours."

"And what have you decided about the relay at Varennes? It is an important point—we must never want horses."

"Yes, sire; and my advice is that the relay ought to be placed beyond the town, near Dun."

"On what do you found your opinion?"

"Upon the situation of the town itself, sire."

"Explain to me this situation, count."

"This thing is very easy, sire. I have passed five or six times through Varennes since I left Paris, and yesterday I was there three hours. Varennes is a little town of about six hundred inhabitants, divided by a river into two parts; one the High Town, the other the Low Town; these communicate with each other by a bridge over the River Aire. This bridge is commanded by a high tower. There the least thing could stop the passage. It would be better then to cross the bridge with the horses coming from Clermont than to run the risk of your majesty being recognized while we changed. The bridge could be barred by three or four men."

"You are right, count," said the king; "besides, in case of hesitation, you will be there."

"This will be at once a duty and an honor, if the king should deem me worthy."

The king again stretched his hand toward Charny.

"So," said the king, "Monsieur de Bouillé has already marked the stages and chosen the men to superintend my route?"

"If your majesty approves—yes, sire."

"Have you made any note on the subject?"

Charny took a folded paper from his pocket and presented it to the king.

"It seems good," said the king, after having read it. "But if these detachments should be obliged to stay three or four days in these towns and villages, what excuse will be made?"

"Sire, the excuse is already formed. They will have to attend on an escort bearing money from the minister to the Army of the North."

"Allons," said the king, with lively satisfaction, "all is foreseen."

Charny bowed.

At this moment the door opened. The king turned round quickly, for the opening of this door was an infraction of the rules of etiquette, which was a great insult if it was not excused by a great necessity.

It was the queen; she was pale, and held a paper in her hand. But at the sight of the count she uttered a cry of astonishment.

Charny arose and saluted the queen respectfully, who muttered between her teeth:

"Monsieur de Charny! Monsieur de Charny! here—with the king—at the Tuileries!" And then she added, in a low voice: "And I not know it!"

There was so much grief in the eyes of the poor woman, that although Charny had not heard the last words, he guessed them, and advanced two steps toward her.

She held out her hands as if she were going to him, but almost immediately put one on her heart, which doubtlessly beat violently.

Charny saw all. The king had, in the meanwhile, taken up the paper that had escaped from the queen's hands. He read what was written on this paper, but without being able to understand it. "What do these three words mean? 'Fly! fly! fly!' and this signature half written?"

"Sire," replied the queen, "they mean Monsieur de Mirabeau is already dead for the last ten minutes, and that this is the last advice he gives us."

"Madame," said the king, "the advice which he gives shall be followed, for it is good, and the moment is approaching when we must put it into execution."

Then, turning to Charny, "Count," he continued, "you can follow the queen to her apartments and tell her all."

The queen rose, looking now at the king, now at Charny, and addressed the latter:

"Come, Monsieur le Comte," said she.

And she went out as quickly as possible, for she could not have suppressed the various emotions within her a minute longer. Charny bowed to the king, and followed Marie Antoinette.

The queen entered her apartments, and sunk down on a sofa as she made a sign to Charny to fasten the door.

Scarcely was she seated before she sobbed.

She wept for weeping's sake. Her tears would have choked her else. She wept without speaking a word. Was it joy or grief? Something of each, perhaps.

When without saying anything, with more love than respect, Charny approached the queen, and drawing one of her hands from her face, he covered it with kisses, as he said:

"Madame, I assure you that since the day I took leave of you, a day has not passed but that I have occupied myself with you one hour even."

"Oh, Charny! Charny!" replied the queen, "there was a time when you were less occupied with me, but thought more."

"Madame," said Charny, "a great responsibility was laid on me by the king. This responsibility imposed silence on me until all was completed. It is finished to-day only. To-day I can see you again—can halt with you. Until to-day I could not even write to you."

"It is a great instance of loyalty this, which you have given, but I regret that you have done it at the expense of another sentiment."

"Madame," said Charny, "since I have received the permission of the king, allow me to inform you of all I have done for your safety."

He related all to her; how he had been sent to M. Bouille; how Count Louis had come to Paris; how he, Charny, had examined the route by which the queen must fly, and finally, how he came to announce to the king that there was nothing to prevent them putting the project at once into execution.

The queen heard Charny with great attention, and at the same time with profound gratitude. It seemed to her that devotion only could go so far. Love, an ardent and burning love, could only overcome these obstacles, and invent the means by which they were surmounted.

She let him speak to the end. Then, when he had finished, looking at him with a profound expression of tenderness, "You will then be very glad to save me, Charny?" she asked.

"Oh!" cried the count, "can you ask me that, madame? It is the dream of my ambition, and if I succeed, it shall be the glory of my life."

"I had rather it should be the recompense of your love," said the queen, sadly. "But n'importe. You wish, do you not, that this great work of saving the king, the queen, and the dauphin of France should be accomplished by you?"

"I only wait your assent to devote myself to it."

"Yes, I understand, my friend," said the queen, "this devotion ought to be free from every foreign sentiment, and every material affection. It is impossible that my husband, my children, can be saved by a hand which dare not extend itself to them to sustain them, if they should slip in this route we are about to travel together. I place their life and mine in your hands, my brother; but in your turn, will you not have pity on me?"

"Pity on you, madame?" said Charny.

"Yes; you would not that at this time, when I require all my strength, all my courage, all my presence of mind, you would not, I say, that all this should be lost, perhaps, for want of a pledged word? You would not, would you?"

Charny interrupted the queen. "Madame," said he, "I wish your majesty to be safe; I wish the good of France; I wish the glory of perfecting the work I have commenced; and I avow it to you, I am grieved to have such a small sacrifice only to offer you; I swear not to see Madame de Charny save with your permission."

And respectfully and coldly saluting the queen, he withdrew, without the latter, numbed by the accent with which he had pronounced these words, attempting to detain him.

But scarcely had Charny shut the door behind him, than, stretching out her arms, she cried, painfully:

"Oh! I had rather it had been I that he had sworn never to see, and that he had loved me as he loves her!"

CHAPTER XXV.

DOUBLE SIGHT.

On the 19th of June following, toward eight in the morning, Gilbert was walking at a great rate backward and forward in his rooms in the Rue St. Honoré, going from time to time to the window, and looking out like a man who expects some one with impatience, and whom he wishes to see arrive.

He held in his hand a paper folded in four, with the letters and seals shining through on to the other side, and that on which they were printed. It was, without doubt, a paper of great importance, for two or three times during these anxious minutes of waiting, Gilbert unfolded it, read it, unfolded it again, reread it, and refolded it only to open it and read it again.

At length the sound of a carriage stopping at the door made him run quickly to the window, but he was too late; he who had got out of the carriage was already in the passage.

"Bastien!" said he, "open the door for Monsieur le Comte de Charny, for whom I wait."

And a last time he unfolded the paper which he was in the act of reading, when Bastien, instead of announcing le Comte de Charny, announced M. le Comte de Cagliostro.

This name was at this time so far from the thoughts of Gilbert that he started as if thunderstruck.

He quickly refolded the paper, which he concealed in his pocket at the side of his coat.

"Monsieur le Comte de Cagliostro!" he repeated, quite astonished.

"Eh, mon Dieu! yes, myself, my dear Gilbert," said the count. "I am not the one you expect. I know well that is Monsieur de Charny, but Monsieur de Charny is engaged—I will tell you in what directly, so that he can not manage to be here within less than half an hour, and knowing this, I said, 'Since I am in this quarter, I will just step up and see Doctor Gilbert.' I hope, although not expected, that I am welcome, however."

"Dear master," said Gilbert, "you know that night and morning, at every hour, two doors are open to you here, that of the house and that of the heart."

"Thanks, Gilbert. I, too, perhaps, shall be called upon to show how much I love you, and should this day ever come, the proof shall not be wanting. Now, let us talk."

"And of what?" asked Gilbert, smiling. For Cagliostro's presence always brought something astonishing with it.

"Of what?" repeated Cagliostro. "Of that great topic of discussion, the king's departure."

Gilbert felt himself freeze from head to foot; but the smile did not disappear for a single moment from his lips.

"And as we shall have some of it, sit down," continued Cagliostro.

And Cagliostro sat down.

The first moment of terror past, Gilbert reflected that if it were chance that had brought Cagliostro to see him, it was at least a fortunate one. Cagliostro, not being in the habit of keeping secrets to himself, would, without doubt, relate all that he knew about the departure of the king and queen, which he had just mentioned.

"Well," continued Cagliostro, seeing Gilbert waiting, "it is then decided to start to-morrow."

"My dear master," said Gilbert, "you know I am in the habit of letting you talk to the end, and even if you err, there is always something for me to learn."

"And when have I been mistaken, up to now, Gilbert?" said Cagliostro. "Was it when I predicted the death of Favras, whom, up to the very last moment, I tried to save? Was it when I told you that the king himself was intriguing against Mirabeau, and that Mirabeau would not be minister? Was it when I told you that Robespierre would re-erect the scaffold of Charles I., and Bonaparte the throne of Charlemagne? As to this last you can accuse me of no error, because the time has not yet passed by, and, moreover, these things belong to the next century. And to-day, more than any one else, you know that I speak the truth when I say that, during to-morrow night the king will fly—for you are one of the agents."

"If it be so," said Gilbert, "you do not expect that I should avow it, do you?"

"And what need have I of your avowal? You know well that I am not only he who *is*, but more, that I am he who *knows*."

"But if you are he who knows," said Gilbert, "you know what the queen said yesterday, apropos of the refusal of madame to attend the Fête Dieu next Sunday, to Monsieur de Montmorin. I am sorry she will not go with us to St. Germain l'Auxerrois. She might well sacrifice her opinions for the king. So if the queen goes on Sunday with the king to the Church of St. Germain l'Auxerrois, they cannot go to-night, nor go on a long journey."

"Yes, but I know also," said Cagliostro, "that a great philosopher has said, 'Speech was given to man to conceal his thoughts;' and God is not so exclusive as to have given to man alone a gift so precious."

"My dear master," said Gilbert, "you know the history of the incredulous apostle?"

"Who began to believe when Christ showed him His feet, His hands, and side. Well, my dear Gilbert, the queen, who is in the habit of considering her ease, and who does not wish to undergo any deprivation during the journey, however short it may be, if the calculation of Monsieur de Charny is correct, the queen has ordered at Desbrosses, Rue Notre Dame des Victoires, a charming *necessaire* in silver-gilt, which is thought to be intended for her sister, the Archduchess Christine. The *necessaire*, bought yesterday morning, only was sent yesterday evening to the Tuileries. They are going in a large, roomy traveling-carriage, which will hold six people. It has been ordered of Louis, the first builder in the Champs Elysées, by Monsieur de Charny, who is at home at this very moment, paying him twenty-five louis, that is to say, the half of the sum agreed for. The report, also, of Monsieur

Isidor de Charny was not bad. Monsieur de Montmorin, without knowing what he signed, signed this morning a passport for Madame la Baronne de Korff, her two children, her two maids, her steward, and three servants. Madame de Korff is Madame de Tourzel, governess of the children of France ; her two children are Madame Royale and Monsieur the Dauphin ; her two women are the queen and Madame Elizabeth ; her steward is the king ; lastly, her three domestics who intend—habited as couriers—preceding and accompanying the carriage, are Monsieur Isidor de Charny, Monsieur de Malden, and Monsieur de Valory. This passport is the paper you held in your hand when I entered, that you folded and put in your pocket, and which is conceived in these terms :

" 'On behalf of the king.

" 'We command all to let pass Madame la Baronne de Korff with her two children, one woman, one valet de chambre and three servants.

" 'The Minister of Foreign Affairs,

" 'MONTMORIN.'

"Am I well informed, my dear Gilbert ?"

"Except a little contradiction between your words and the passport."

"Which ?"

"You said that the queen and Madame Elizabeth represented the two femmes de chambre of Madame de Tourzel, and I see but a single woman mentioned in the passport."

"Ah ! I see. Arrived at Bondy, Madame de Tourzel, who thinks to go to Montmedy, will be asked to descend. The queen will then become Madame de Korff, and then, as there will be only one woman, and she Madame Elizabeth, it would be useless to put two on the passport. Now, would you like more details ? I will give you some. The journey ought to have taken place before the 1st of June ; Monsieur de Bouille wished it much—he even wrote to the king about it in a very pressing letter, adding that the troops were being corrupted from day to day. By these words, 'being corrupted,' he meant that the army was beginning to understand its having to choose between a monarchy which had, for three centuries, sacrificed the people to the nobility, the soldier to the officer, and a constitution which proclaimed equality before the law, which recognized merit and courage. But the carriage and other things were not ready, and it was, therefore, impossible to start on the 1st of June ; this was a great misfortune, for since the 1st of June the army has become more corrupted, and the troops are ready to swear to the constitution. The departure was then fixed for the eighth ; but Monsieur de Bouille received notice of this date too late, and in his turn he was obliged to answer that he was not ready. Then the twelfth was chosen. They would have preferred the eleventh, but a woman, very democratic, and moreover, mistress of Monsieur de Gouvoin, aide-de-camp to Monsieur de Lafayette, Madame de Rochereul, if you would know her name, was in close attendance on the dauphin, and they feared she would see something and denounce them. On the twelfth the king perceived he had only six days to wait to get possession of a quarter of his yearly civil list—six millions. Peste ! you understand well the trouble of waiting those six days, my dear Gilbert. In brief, the departure was put off until Sunday, the nineteenth, at midnight ; but on the eighteenth a despatch arrived, putting off this departure until Monday, the twentieth, at the same hour, that is to say to-morrow evening. This, too, may have its own inconveniences. Monsieur de Bouillé had already sent his orders to the detachments, and now he must send counter orders. Take care, my dear Gilbert, take care ; all this wearies the soldiers, and makes the people think."

"Count," said Gilbert, "I shall not deceive you ; all that you have said is true. Now, tell me frankly, considering his personal danger, and that of the queen and his children, if the king would remain as king, man, husband, father, whether you do not think him justified in flying ?"

"Well, do you wish me to tell you one thing, my dear Gilbert ? It is not as a father ; it is not as a husband ; it is not as a man that Louis XVI. flies. It is not on account of the 5th of October that he leaves France. No; he is a Bourbon, and the Bourbons know how to look danger in the face. No; he leaves France on account of this constitution, which, at the instance of the United States, the National Assembly is about to form, without reflecting that the model it follows is adapted for a republic, and applied to a monarchy does not leave the king breathing room. No; he leaves France on account of that famous affair of the Knights of the Poignard, in which your friend, Lafayette, acted so irreverently toward the king. No, my dear Gilbert, you are honestly, frankly, a constitutional royalist—you believe in that sweet, consoling Utopia of a monarchy tempered by liberty. You should know one thing, and this is it—kings, in imitation of God, whom they pretend to represent on the earth, have a religion of their own—the religion of royalty; and the day on which the people prevented the king from going to St. Cloud, and that on which they expelled the knights of the Poignard from the Tuileries, this religion was touched, was broken in upon, and this is what the king cannot bear; that is the true abomination; this is why the king, who had refused to be carried off by Monsieur de Favras, and to save himself with his aunt, consents to fly to-morrow with a passport of Monsieur de Montmorin—who knows not for whom he signed it—under the name of Durand, and in the dress of a domestic; always reminding them, however—kings will be kings to the end—to put the red coat, embroidered with gold, that he wore at Cherbourg, into the portmanteau."

Gilbert resolved to speak frankly on the matter.

"Count," observed he, "all you say is true, I repeat. Now, why have you come to tell me this? Under what title do you present yourself to me? Do you come as a loyal enemy inviting me to battle, or do you come as a friend to aid me?"

"I come, my dear Gilbert, in the first place," said Cagliostro, kindly, "as the master comes to the pupil to say: 'My friend, you were wrong in attaching yourself to this falling ruin called monarchy. Men like you do not belong to the past or even to the present; they are the property of the future. Abandon what you do not believe in for what you know. Do not let fall the reality for the shadow; and if you do not become an active soldier of the revolution, let it pass by, and do not attempt to check it.' Mirabeau was a giant, but he failed."

"Count," said Gilbert, "I will reply to that on the day that the king, who has confided in me, shall be safe. Louis XVI. has taken me as a confidant, as an auxiliary, as an accomplice, if you please. I have accepted this mission, and will fulfil it openly. I am a physician, my friend, and to me the material health of my patient is an object of primary consideration. Now, answer me: In your mysterious plans and dark combinations, is it necessary that this succeed or fail? If you wish it to fail, say so, for it will be useless to go. Say, 'Do not go,' and we will remain, bend our heads, and await the blow."

"Brother," said Cagliostro, "if impelled by the God who has placed me on the route, it were necessary for me to strike those whom your heart loves, I would remain in the shadow, and ask but one thing of the superhuman power I obey; that you might be ignorant whence the blow was winged. No; if I do not come as a friend—I cannot be the friend of kings, whose victim I have been—I do not come as an enemy. I come with a balance in my hand, and say I have weighed the fortunes of the last Bourbon, and I do not believe his death is important to the cause. Now, God forbid that I who, like Pythagoras, think I have no right to take away the life of the merest insect, should destroy that of a lord of creation. There is none. But I come not only to say I will be neuter, but to offer you my aid if you need it."

Gilbert tried a second time to read the heart of Cagliostro.

"Good," said the latter, in resuming his tone of raillery; "now you doubt. Let us see, thou man of letters, dost not remember the story of Achilles' spear, that wounded and cured? I possess this lance. The woman who has passed as the queen in the shrubberies of Versailles, cannot she also pass for the queen in the apartments of the Tuileries, or on some route in the opposite direction to that which the true fugitive follows. Now, what I have just offered you is not to be despised, my dear Gilbert."

"Be frank, count, even to the end, and tell me with what object you have made me this offer."

"Why, my dear doctor, it is a very simple one; in order that the king may quit France, may go, and so that we may be able to proclaim the republic."

"The republic?" said Gilbert, astonished.

"Why not?" said Cagliostro.

"But, my dear count, I look around me in France, north and south, east and west, and I do not see a single republican."

"There you are mistaken. I see three. Petion, Camille Desmoulins, and your humble servant. Those you can see, as I do; but I see those you do not see, but whom you will see when the time appears. Then rely on me to produce a theatrical effect which will surprise you. I desire only that in the changes there may be no serious accident. Accidents always happen to the machinist."

Gilbert reflected for an instant. He then gave his hand to Cagliostro.

"Count," said he, "were I only concerned, were my life, my honor, reputation, and memory only at stake, I would accept at once. But as a kingdom, a king, a queen, a race, a monarchy are at stake, I cannot undertake to act for them. Remain neuter, my dear count; that is all I ask." Cagliostro smiled.

"Yes," said he, "I understand. Well, Gilbert, the man of the necklace is about to give you advice."

"Silence!" said Gilbert, "some one rings."

"What of it? You know that person is the Count de Charny. Both he and you may profit by my advice. Enter, count."

Charny, in fact, appeared at the door. Seeing a stranger when he expected to see Gilbert, he paused for a moment.

"This advice," said Cagliostro, "is this: Do without

two heavy carriages, and two striking likenesses. Adieu, Gilbert; adieu, count; and to use a common phrase, I wish you a pleasant journey. May God keep you in His holy charge."

The prophet bowed kindly and courteously to Charny, and retired. The count looked anxiously after him.

"Who is that man, doctor?" asked Charny, as soon as his steps were no longer heard.

"One of my friends, a man who knows, and who has promised not to betray me."

Gilbert hesitated a moment.

"He is the Baron Zanoni."

"Strange, I do not know the name; but it seems to me I remember the face. Have you a passport?"

"Here it is, count."

Charny took the passport, and became completely absorbed by the attention this important document required, and for the moment, at least, forgot Zanoni.

CHAPTER XXVI.

THE EVENING OF JUNE 20TH.

NOT without reason had distrust of Mme. Rochereul been exhibited. Though her service had ceased on the 11th, she had continued, somehow or other, to return to the capital, and had discovered, though the jewel-cases of the queen were in their places, that the diamonds were gone; they had, in fact, been given by the queen to her jeweler Leonard, who was to set out on the 20th, a few hours before his august mistress, with M. de Choiseul, commander of the first detachment of soldiers, posted at the bridge of Someville, who also had charge of the relays at Varennes, composed of six good horses, awaiting the final orders of the queen and king. It was, perhaps, indiscreet to trouble De Choiseul with M. Leonard, and imprudent to take a hair-dresser with her. Who, though abroad, could have dressed her hair as Leonard did? A hair-dresser who is a man of genius is not easily given up.

The consequence was that the chambermaid of the dauphin, not doubting but that the escape would be made on Monday, the 20th, at eleven o'clock, not only informed M. de Gouvoin of the matter, but Bailly also.

Lafayette had gone to find the king, and to have a frank explanation of the matter with him, simply shrugging up his shoulders.

Bailly had done better. While Lafayette became blind as an astronomer, Bailly became courteous as a knight; he even sent the queen the letter of Mme. Rochereul.

M. de Gouvoin, who was much interested, was very suspicious. Having learned all from his mistress, under the pretext of a military reunion, he had invited a dozen officers of the National Guard; he placed five or six as videttes at each door, and himself, with five majors, undertook the surveillance of the doors of M. de Villequer, which had been specially pointed out to him.

About the same hour, at No. 9 Rue Coq-Heron, in a room we are all acquainted with, sat on a sofa a young and beautiful woman apparently calm, but in fact deeply excited, who talked with a young man of twenty-three or four, clad in a vest of a courier, of chamois, pantaloons of leather, a pair of boots, and armed with a *couteau de chasse.*

The young woman insisted on something which the young man denied.

"But, vicomte, why, since during the last two months, he has come to Paris, has he not come himself?"

"My brother, madame, has often sent you messages."

"I know he has, and am grateful to him for doing so. It seems to me, though, that now he might have come himself."

"Madame, it was impossible, and therefore he sent me."

"And will your journey be long?"

"I do not know, madame?"

"I say so to you, count, because from your costume I think you are about to set out."

"In all probability, madame, I shall have left Paris at midnight."

"Do you go with your brother, or in an opposite direction?"

"I think, madame, that we go in an opposite direction?"

"Will you tell him that you have seen me?"

"Yes, madame; for from the anxiety he exhibited when he sent me to you, and his reiterated orders not to return until I had spoken to you, he would not pardon me for any act of omission."

The young woman passed her hands over her eyes and said, after a moment's reflection:

"Vicomte, you are a gentleman, and will understand all I say to you. Tell me, will you answer me as if I were really your sister, and answer me as if you spoke to God? Does Monsieur de Charny incur any serious danger in the journey he undertakes?"

"Who can tell, madame," said Isidor, seeking to elude the question, "where danger does, and does not exist? On the morning of the 5th of October, our poor brother George, had he been questioned, would have been confident that he saw no danger. On the next day he lay pale and dead at the queen's door. Danger, madame, in the age we are in, springs from the earth, and we often stand face to face with death without knowing why."

Andrée grew pale.

"Then his life is in danger, count?"

"I did not say so, madame."

"But you think so?"

"I think, madame, that if you have anything important to say to my brother, that the enterprise we are engaged in is serious enough for you to transmit *viva voce*, by me, your thought or wish."

"It is well, count. I ask but five minutes of you." She entered the chamber and closed the door behind her.

The young man looked anxiously at his watch.

"Quarter after nine," said he. "The king awaits us at half-past nine. Happily it is but a step to the Tuileries."

The countess did not, however, use as much time as she

asked. After a few moments she entered with a sealed letter in her hand.

"Vicomte, I confide this to your honor."

Isidor reached forth his hand to take the letter.

"Wait a moment," said Andrée, "and understand what I say; if your brother meet with no accident in the journey he meditates, nothing need be said but what I have told you, that I sympathize with his loyalty, respect his devotion, and admire his character. If he be wounded," Andrée's voice changed visibly, "ask him to permit me to join him, and if he grant me that favor, send me a message so that I may certainly know where to find him, for I will set out at once. If he be mortally wounded"—emotion almost stifled Andrée's voice—"give him this letter; if he cannot read it, do so for him, for before he dies I wish him to know the contents of this letter. Give me your word, vicomte, that you will do what I ask you."

Isidor, deeply moved as the countess was, gave her his hand.

"On my honor, madame," said he.

Isidor took the letter, pressed the countess's hand, and left.

Just as Isidor read this letter and placed it in his bosom, two men, dressed precisely as he was, passed him at the corner of the Rue Coquillière, and seemed to be going in the same direction; that is, toward the boudoir of the queen.

Both were introduced, and almost at the same time, by two different doors; the first introduced was M. de Valory.

A few seconds after, another door was opened, and M. de Valory saw another person enter. The two officers were unacquainted. Presuming, however, they were both called for the same purpose, they approached and bowed. Just then a third door opened, and Isidor de Charny appeared. He was the third courier, also unknown to the other two above, of the three who knew the other two. Isidor alone knew why they were sent for.

He was about to answer any questions which might be put to him, when the door opened and the king appeared.

"Messieurs," said Louis XVI., speaking to M. de Malden and M. de Valory, "excuse my having used you without permission, but I thought you were faithful subjects; you belonged to my guards. I wished you to go to a tailor, the address of whom I gave you, and each get a courier's dress, and to be to-night at the Tuileries at half-past nine. Your presence satisfies me that whatever be the question at stake, you will undertake what I request of you."

The two gardes de corps bowed.

"Sire, your majesty knows that you may command your nobles without consulting them, and dispose of their courage, life, and fortune."

"Sire," said De Malden, "my colleague, in replying for himself, has replied for me, and, I presume, for this gentleman also."

"The third gentleman to whom I would introduce you is the Vicomte de Charny, brother of him who was killed in the defense of Versailles at the queen's door. We are used to the devotion of families, and the thing is now so common that we often forget even to give thanks for them."

"From what the king says, I presume the Count de Charny is aware of the motive of our union. I am ignorant of it, and am anxious to learn it, sire."

"Messieurs, you are not ignorant that I am a prisoner of the commandant of the National Guard, of the maire of Paris, and of the National Assembly. Well, sirs, I have relied on you to rescue me from this humiliation, and enable me to resume my liberty. My death, that of the queen and her children, are in your hands. All is ready for our flight; contrive only to extricate us from this place."

"Sire," said the three young men, "give your orders."

"We cannot go out together, messieurs, as you see. Our common rendezvous is in the corner of the Rue St. Nicole, where the Count de Charny awaits us with a carriage. You, vicomte, will take charge of the queen, and answer to the name of Melchoir. You, Monsieur de Malden, will take charge of Madame Elizabeth and Madame Royale, and will be called Jean. You, Monsieur de Valory, will take charge of Madame de Tourzel and the dauphin and will be called François. Do not forget your names, and await other instructions.

The king gave his hand to each of the three young men, and left in the room three men ready to die for him.

M. de Choiseul had, on the previous night, told the king, from M. de Bouillé, that it would be impossible to wait later than twenty minutes after twelve for him, and that he had resolved on the 21st, if he had no news, to set out at 4 A. M., taking all the detachments with him to Dun, Stenay, and Montmedy. Choiseul was in his own house in Artois Street, where he awaited the final orders of the king, and as it was nine o'clock, he had begun to despair, when the only servant he had kept, who thought his master just about to set out for Metz, came to say a messenger from the queen wished to speak to him. He bid him come up.

A man entered with a round hat pulled over his eyes, and wrapped in an immense pelisse.

"Is it you, Leonard? I awaited you anxiously."

"If I made you wait, duke, it was not my fault, but the queen's, for she told me only ten minutes ago that I had to come to your house."

"Did she say nothing more?"

"Yes, duke. She bid me take these diamonds and bring you this letter."

"Now," said the duke, "arouse yourself, and tell me what the queen said."

"The queen said, in a low voice, 'Take these diamonds and hide them in your pockets. Take this letter to Monsieur de Choiseul, in the Rue d'Artois, but give it to him alone. If not you will find him at the house of the Duchesse de Grammont.' As I was leaving, the queen called me back. 'Put on a broad-brimmed hat and a large pelisse, that you may not be known, and obey Monsieur de Choiseul as if it were myself.' I went to my room, prepared myself, and came."

"Then," said M. de Choiseul, "the queen bid you obey me as herself?"

"These were the august words of her majesty."

Just then a servant came in and said the carriage was ready. M. le Duc de Choiseul made the hairdresser get into his cabriolet, and he set out at post haste for the barrier of Little Vellette.

CHAPTER XXVII.

THE DEPARTURE.

At eleven o'clock, at the very time when Mmes. du Touvres and Brennier, after having undressed and put Mme. Royale and the dauphin to bed, awoke and dressed them again, much to the mortification of the dauphin, who insisted on putting on boy's clothes instead of petticoats, the king and queen and Mme. Elizabeth received Lafayette and his aides-de-camp, Gouvoin and Romœuf. This visit was most annoying, especially when they took into consideration the suspicions they entertained of Mme. du Rochereul.

The queen and Mme. Elizabeth had, during the evening, gone into the Bois de Boulogne, and had returned at eight o'clock. Lafayette asked the queen if her promenade had been pleasant; but added that she was wrong to return so late, that the evening mists might hurt her.

"Mists in June!" said the queen, with a smile; "but unless one be manufactured expressly to conceal our flight, I do not know where, at this season, I could find a mist. I presume there is a report that we are about to fly."

"The fact is, madame, the report is more current than ever; and I have been told that it is to take place to-night."

"Ah! I bet that you received that intelligence from Monsieur Gouvoin," said the queen.

"Why from me, madame?" said the young officer, blushing.

"Because you have acquaintances in the palace. Monsieur de Romœuf has none; and I am sure he would be answerable for me."

"There would be no great merit in it, madame, as the

king has given his word to the National Assembly not to leave Paris."

It was the queen's turn to blush.

The subject of the conversation was changed.

At half-past eleven, Lafayette and his two aides took leave of the king. Gouvoin, yet unsatisfied, returned to his room in the château, where he found his friends on duty, and instead of relieving them, urged double diligence. Lafayette went to the Hôtel de Ville to make M. Bailly quiet, in case he should have felt any fear.

M. Lafayette having gone, the king and queen rang for their servants, and had the usual services rendered them, and then dismissed everybody.

The queen and Mme. Elizabeth dressed each other. Their dresses were as plain as possible. Their hats were very large, and concealed their faces.

When they were dressed, the king entered. He was clad in a gray coat, and one of those little bag-wigs called à la Rousseau. He wore short breeches, gray stockings, and shoes with buckles.

Eight days before, Hue, the valet, had, in precisely such a dress, left the door of M. de Villequier, who had emigrated six months before, and had gained the square of the Corvuses and the street of St. Nicaise. This precaution had been taken in order that people might be used to the dress, and that, if seen in the Tuileries, it might occasion no remark.

The three couriers were taken from the queen's boudoir, where they had been waiting, and they were taken through the salon into the room of Mme. Royale, who was there with the dauphin.

Once in M. Villequier's room it was easy to leave the palace. No one knew that the king had the keys, and there was no sentinel there. Besides, after eleven o'clock the sentinels in the courtyard were used to see many people pass.

There all arrangements were made.

The Vicomte de Charny, who had gone over the road with his brother, and knew the difficult and dangerous places, was to ride ahead and prepare the postilions, that there might be as little delay as possible.

M. de Malden and M. de Valory were on the seat and were ordered to pay the postilions thirty sous; ordinarily twenty-five was the price; but in consideration of the heaviness of the carriage, five were added.

The Count de Charny would be in the coach, ready to provide against all accidents. He would be well armed, and each of the couriers would find a pair of pistols in the carriage.

By paying well, it was hoped to reach Chalons in thirteen hours.

All this had been decided on between Charny and De Choiseul.

De Malden and Valory would pay. Charny, from the inside, would talk, if there was anything to be said.

All promised obedience. The lights were blown out, and they went to the room of M. Villequier.

It struck twelve as they passed the room of Mme. Royale. The Count de Charny must have been at his post an hour.

The king put the key in the door.

Steps and whisperings were heard in the corridor. Something strange was going on. Mme. de Tourzel, who lived in the château, and who passed to and fro so frequently that her presence would cause no surprise, offered to see what was the matter.

They waited motionless. Mme. de Tourzel returned and reported that she had seen M. de Gouvoin and several uniforms. It was impossible to leave this room unless it had some other outlet.

They had no light. A lamp was in the room of Mme. Royale, and Mme. de Tourzel lighted the candle, which had been blown out. For a long time the search was thought useless, but at last a little stairway was found leading to a small room on the ground floor. The door was locked. The king tried all his keys, but in vain. Charny tried to open it with his hunting knife. The bolt would not move. They had found an outlet, but were as closely confined as ever. The king took the lamp from Mme. de Tourzel's hands, and leaving all the rest in darkness, went back to his bedchamber, and thence to the forge. He took a bundle of lock-picks and came down. When he had reached the group, he had already made his choice. The lock pick the king had selected grated and slipped twice from the wards. The third time, however, the bolt turned, and all breathed freely.

Now the order of departure was to be regulated. Mme. Elizabeth went first, with Mme. Royale. Twenty paces after followed Mme. de Tourzel with the dauphin. Between them was M. de Malden, prepared, if necessary, to aid them. Tremblingly and timidly, these few grains detached from the royal chaplet, looking behind them for those they loved, descended and went into the circle of light formed by the lamp at the palace door. They passed the sentinel, who did not even seem to notice them. "Good," said Mme. Elizabeth, "we have already passed one difficulty." When at the wicket on the Carousel, they saw the sentinel crossing their path. When he saw them approach, he paused.

"Aunt," said Mme. Royale, "we are lost. That man sees us."

"It matters not. We will certainly be lost if we hesitate."

They continued to advance. When four paces from them the sentinel turned his back, and they passed on. Did this man know them ? Did he know what fugitives he suffered to escape ? The princesses thought so, and mentally gave a thousand thanks to their unknown preserver.

On the other side of the wicket they saw the uneasy face of the Count de Charny. He was wrapped in a full blue cloak, and wore a hat of oiled cloth.

"Ah !" said he, "here you are at last. And the king and queen ?"

"Are behind us."

"Come," said Charny. He took them rapidly to a carriage, which was waiting them in the Rue Nicaise.

A hack drove up to the side of the remise, as if to watch it.

"Well, comrade," said the hackman, as he saw Charny come up, "it seems you have a fare."

"Yes," said Charny.

He then said, in a low tone, to M. de Malden:

"Take this carriage and go at once to Porte St. Martin. You will recognize the vehicle that waits you without trouble."

M. de Malden understood, and got into the hack.

The driver thought his customer was some courier going to meet his master at the opera, and set out at once, making no remark, except about the price. He said:

"You know, sir, it is after midnight."

"Yes, be easy."

As, at that epoch, servants were sometimes more generous than their masters, the driver set out at a full trot, and without any observation but about the price.

Scarcely had he turned the corner of the Rue de Rohan, than by the same wicket which had given a passage to Mme. Royale, to Mme. Elizabeth, the dauphin, and Mme. de Tourzel, he saw advance, at a slow pace, like a clerk who had just left his office after a long and laborious day's work, a man in a great-coat, with the corner of his hat over his eyes, and his hands in his pockets. It was the king, followed by M. de Valory.

Charny advanced a few paces toward him. He had recognized the king, not by himself, but by his being accompanied by M. de Valory. He sighed with grief and almost with shame.

"Come, sire," murmured he.

Then, in a low tone, he said to M. de Valory:

"Where is the queen?"

"The queen follows with the vicomte."

"Come; take the shortest road and await us at Porte St. Martin. I will take the longest; the rendezvous is the carriage."

We will not attempt to describe the anxiety of the fugitives. Charny, on whom the responsibility rested, was almost mad.

The terror increased as they passed the carriage of General Lafayette all lighted up. It was entering the Carousel.

At the door of the court, the Vicomte de Charny gave his arm to the queen, and wished to turn to the left. The queen made him stop.

"Whither go you?" said she.

"To the corner of the Rue Nicaise, where my brother awaits us."

"Is the Nicaise on the river?" asked the queen.

"No, madame."

"Then your brother awaits you at the wicket toward the water."

Isidor would have insisted, but the queen appeared so sure of what she said that doubts entered his mind.

"My God, madame," said he, "every mistake is fatal."

"By the river-side. I am sure I heard by the river-side."

"Let us go thither, then, madame, but if we find no carriage, we will go at once to the Rue Nicaise."

The queen and Isidor crossed the openings one after the other, and also the three lines of sentinels. None thought of stopping them. What reason was there to believe that this young woman, dressed like a servant of a good house, and giving her arm to a young man in the livery of the Prince de Condé, was the Queen of France. They came to the river. The quay was deserted.

"It is, then, on the other side," said the queen. Isidor wished to retrace his steps. She seemed mad, though, and insisted on going to the other wicket. She dragged Isidor to the Port Royal. The bridge being crossed, the other side was found deserted as the first.

"Let us look down the street."

She forced him to go down the Rue de Bac. After going a hundred yards, she saw her error, and all panting, said:

"My strength begins to fail."

"Well, madame, do you still insist?"

"No," said the queen: "take me where you will."

"Madame, for Heaven's sake, have courage."

"Ah! I do not need courage, but strength." Then, turning back, she said: "It seems to me I shall never regain my breath. My God! my God!"

Isidor knew that breath was as much needed by the queen at this hour as it is to a wolf pursued by hounds. He paused.

"Get your breath, madame. We have time. I will answer for my brother; he will wait until morning."

She resumed walking, and retraced the previous unnecessary course she had taken.

Instead of returning to the Tuileries, Isidor passed through the gate into the Carousel; the immense square was crossed; until midnight, it was always covered with peddlers' stalls and with hackney coaches. It was nearly deserted and dark. The sound of wheels and of horses' feet, however, was heard. They had reached the gate at the head of the Rue des Echelles. It was evident that the horses, whose steps they heard, were about to pass in that direction. A light was seen, which doubtless was caused by the torches which accompanied the carriage. Isidor wished to pause; the queen hurried him on. Isidor rushed to the wicket to protect her, just as the torch-bearers appeared on the opposite side. He placed her in the darkest place, and stood before her. Even it, though, was for a moment inundated with the light of the torches. Amid them, in the rich uniform of general of the National Guard, was Lafayette.

At the moment the carriage passed, Isidor felt that a strong arm pushed him aside. This was the left arm of the queen. In her right hand she had a little bamboo cane with a gold head, such as was usually carried at that time by women. She struck the carriage wheels sharply, and said:

"So, jailer, I am out of your prison."

"What are you doing, madame? Why expose yourself to such danger?"

"I avenge myself. For that one would incur much danger."

When the last torch had passed, she rushed out, radiant as a child.

The queen had not gone ten steps from the wicket, when a man in a blue cloak, with his face hidden by an old cloth hat, seized her arm convulsively and dragged her toward a carriage which stood at the corner of the Rue Nicaise. This man was the Count de Charny. The vehicle was the one in which the royal family had been waiting for an hour.

All expected to see the queen arrive terrified, downcast, and overcome: she came, joyous and happy. The dangers she had run, the fatigue she had undergone, the time she had lost, all the consequences were forgotten in pleasure at the blow with the cane she had given the carriage of M. de Lafayette, and which she felt as if she had given the general himself.

Ten paces from the vehicle a servant held a horse. Charny pointed the horse to Isidor, who mounted and galloped away. He hurried on to Bondy to order post horses.

The queen got into the carriage in which the whole royal family already were. She sat down, took the dauphin on her knee, and the king sat by her; the rest of the family occupied the front seat.

Charny shut the door, and got on the box; and to divert the attention of spies, in case there should be any, went up to St. Honoré, down the boulevards to the Madeleine, and thence to Porte St. Martin. The carriage was there in waiting on a road leading to what was called La Voirie. The road was deserted.

The count sprung from the box and opened the door. In one moment the six persons in the carriage were put into the other. Charny then took the other vehicle and upset it in the ditch; he then returned to the carriage.

De Malden got up behind; M. de Valory sat with Charny on the seat. The carriage had four horses, and a clack of the tongue made them break into a trot. The driver moved rapidly. A quarter of an hour after the clock of St. Lawrence struck one. They set out for Bondy. The horses were harnessed, and waited outside of the stable.

On the other side of the road was a hired cabriolet all ready. In this were the two femmes de chambre of the dauphin and of Mme. Royale.

It had been agreed between the king and queen and Charny that at Bondy he would get inside of the carriage, and that Mme. de Tourzel would return thence to Paris. In this change, though, they had forgotten to consult Mme. de Tourzel. The king proposed the question. Mme. de Tourzel was devoted to the royal family, but as far as etiquette was concerned, was a perfect pendant to old Mme. de Noailles.

"Sire," said she, "it is my duty to watch over the children of France, and not to leave them for a moment without the express orders of your majesty. As the order has no precedent, I will not leave them."

The queen trembled with impatience. Two reasons excited her. She wished to have Charny in the carriage; as a queen, he insured her safety, as a woman she delighted to have him by her.

"My dear Madame de Tourzel," said the queen, "we are very grateful; but you suffer and exaggerate devotion. Remain at Bondy, and rejoin us wherever we be."

"Madame," said the old lady, "let the king order and I will obey, even though he place me on the roadside. An order of the king alone, however, can induce me to do so, and not only fail in my duty, but renounce my right."

"Sire," said the queen.

Louis XVI. did not dare to decide in so important a matter. He sought some exit, some mode of escape.

"Monsieur de Charny," said he, "can you not remain on the seat?"

"I can do anything the king wishes," said M. de Charny; "but I should have to remain there in my uniform of an officer, in which I have, for four months, traveled up and down this road. If I did not do that, I would have to wear my coat and hat, a dress which by no means suits so elegant an equipage."

Get into the carriage, Monsieur de Charny, get in ; I will hold the dauphin, and Madame Elizabeth will take Marie Theresa, and all will be right. We will only be a little crowded, that's all."

Charny awaited the king's decision.

"It is impossible, my dear," said Louis XVI. "Remember that we have ninety leagues to go."

Mme. de Tourzel stood up, ready to obey the king's order, if he should order her to get out. The king, however, did not venture to give it, so important do even the most trivial prejudices seem to people of courts.

"Monsieur de Charny, can you not replace your brother, and ride in advance to order the horses ?"

"I have already told your majesty that I am willing to do anything, but would suggest to the king that post-horses are usually ordered by a courier, and not by a captain of the navy. Such a thing might awake the suspicions of the post-agents and give occasion for much trouble."

"True," said the king.

"My God ! my God !" murmured the queen, impatient to the last degree. Then, turning to the count, she said : "Settle matters as you please, sir, but you must not leave me."

"It is my wish, madame, not to do so, but I see no way to avoid it but one."

"What is that ? Speak quickly," said the queen.

"Instead of getting either on the box or in the carriage, instead of riding in advance to return to Paris, and then ride back in the simple dress of a man riding post. Go on, madame, and before you have gone ten leagues, I will be within a hundred yards of your carriage."

"Then you return to Paris ?"

"Certainly ; but till you reach Chalons, your majesty has nothing to fear, and ere then I will have rejoined you."

"How, though, will you return to Paris?"

"On the horse my brother rode; he is very swift, and has had time to blow; in less than half an hour I will be there."

"Then?"

"Then, madame, I will put on a suitable dress, take a fast horse, and hurry on till I overtake you."

"Is there no other way?" said Marie Antoinette, in despair.

"None," said the king, "that I see."

"Then," said Charny, "let us lose no time."

The importance of the discussion made all forget to give to Isidor, De Malden, and De Valory the loaded pistols which were in the coach.

CHAPTER XXVIII.

THE ROUTE.

About eight in the morning the royal party reached a long ascent; on the right and left of the road was a wood in which the birds sung, and which the rays of a beautiful spring sun pierced with golden light. The postilion let his horses walk.

"Jean!" said the king, "open the door. I wish to walk, and I think the queen and children will not be sorry to do so likewise."

The postilion stopped. The door was opened, and the king, queen, and Mme. Elizabeth and children got out. Mme. de Tourzel was too feeble, and remained in the carriage.

The royal emigrants at once spread themselves along the road. The dauphin set to work to pursue butterflies, and Mme. Royale to gather flowers.

Mme. Elizabeth took the king's arm; the queen walked alone.

Presently a horseman appeared, a quarter of a league distant, wrapped in the dust raised by the horse's feet.

Marie Antoinette dared not say this was the Count de Charny. A cry escaped from her. She said :

"We will have news from Paris."

All turned round except the dauphin ; the careless child had just taken a butterfly, and cared nothing for the news.

The king, who was a little near-sighted, used his glasses.

"Ah ! it is, I think, Monsieur de Charny. Let us go on ; he will overtake us, and we have no time to lose."

The queen did not dare to say that the news brought by M. de Charny, at least, was worth waiting for. It was also a delay of but a few seconds. The postman evidently rode at speed.

He himself, as he drew near, evidently looked with great attention, and seemed not to understand why the huge carriage had placed its inmates on the roadside. He reached them just as the carriage reached the top of the rising, and paused.

"It is, indeed, Charny !"

He wore a little green frock with a full collar, a broad-brimmed hat with a steel buckle, a white vest, coated leather breeches, and military boots which reached the knee.

He sprung from his horse, and bowed before the king, and then turned and saluted the queen.

All grouped around him, except the two guards, who remained discreetly out of hearing.

"In the first place, sir, at two o'clock your flight was not suspected."

All breathed freely.

The king said to the guardsmen, "Draw near, gentlemen, and listen to Monsieur de Charny's news." He told them.

Many questions were asked.

Charny told how he had reached Paris and met a patrol, how he had been interrogated by it, and had left it fully convinced that the king was in bed and asleep.

He then told how, once in the interior of the Tuileries, calm as usual, he had gone to his room, changed his dress, and passed through the royal corridor, to satisfy himself that none suspected the escape, not even De Gouvoin, who had withdrawn the line of sentinels he had established around the king's room, and had sent away the officers and majors.

Charny had then taken his horse, which one of the servants, on duty for the night, had held in the courtyard, and thinking that at that hour it would be difficult for him to find a post-horse, had set out for Bondy. The unfortunate animal was almost broken down, but reached Bondy, and that was all the count cared for. He there got a fresh horse and rode on. Nothing else had occurred on the route.

They resumed their places, and Charny galloped by the side of the door.

At the next post station the horses were all ready, except one for Charny. Isidor had not ordered one, for he did not know that his brother was on horseback. They did not wait for the horse, but set out, and in five minutes after, Charny was in the saddle.

He had taken a relay at Montmirail, and thought that the carriage was a quarter of an hour in advance of him, when, at the turning of the street, his horse came directly on the carriage and the two guardsmen, who were seeking to mend a broken trace.

The count leaped from his horse, passed to the door, and advised the king to conceal himself and the queen not to be uneasy. He then opened a kind of box, forward, in which were placed all things likely to be made necessary by an accident on the road ; he found there a pair of traces, one of which he took.

The two guardsmen took advantage of the delay to ask for their arms, but the king positively objected. It was suggested that the carriage might be stopped, to which he said, that even in that case he would not have blood shed for him.

The trace was mended, the box shut, the guards and Charny were in their places, and they set out again. They had, however, lost half an hour, and at a time when the loss of a minute might be irreparable. At two they were at Chalons.

The king showed himself for a moment. Amid the groups formed around the door were two men who looked fixedly at him. One of the men left. The other approached the door, and said, in a low tone:

"Sire, do not expose yourself thus, or you are lost."

Then, speaking to the postilions, he said:

"Come, lazy bones, be quick! Is it thus you delay travelers who pay you thirty sous a station?"

He set to work himself; he was the post-agent. The horses at length were harnessed, and the postilions mounted.

In the interim, the man who had disappeared had gone to the maire, and told him that the king and all his family were at the post-house, and asked authority to arrest them.

The maire luckily was not much of a republican, and did not, besides, wish to assume so much responsibility. Instead of ascertaining the fact, he asked for all kinds of explanations, denied that it could be so, and reached the hotel just as the carriage drove off. They had, however, lost twenty minutes.

There was much alarm in the equipage. The horses kicking so unnecessarily recalled to the queen the sudden extinction of the four lights. As, however, they left the city, the king, queen, and Mme. Elizabeth said, "We are saved!"

A hundred paces further, a man appeared, rushed to the door, and said:

"Your measures are badly taken. You will be arrested."

The queen uttered a cry. The man rushed into a little wood and disappeared.

Fortunately they were but four leagues from the bridge of Someville, where Choiseul was with his dragoons. It was, however, three in the afternoon, and they were four hours behind time.

When M. de Choiseul reached the bridge of Someville, he found that his hussars had not yet arrived, but shortly after the trumpets and tramp of horses were heard. M. de Goquelot appeared. Choiseul had had the horses picketed out, had bread and wine given to the hussars, and then sat down himself with the colonel to dinner.

The news of M. Goquelot was not flattering. He had observed great excitement everywhere. For more than a year, reports of the king's flight had been circulated, not only in Paris, but in the country, and the detachments of different arms stationed at Ste. Menehould had excited suspicion. He had even heard the tocsin in a village near the road.

This was enough to take away even De Choiseul's appetite. After passing an hour at the table, he arose, and leaving the command of the detachment to M. Boudet, went to an eminence beyond the bridge, which permitted him to see the road for half a league.

He saw neither courier nor carriage. There was, however, nothing surprising in that, for De Choiseul could allow for petty accidents. He expected the courier in an hour, or an hour and a half, and the king in two or two and a half hours.

Nine passed, and he saw on the road nothing like the things he expected.

At half-past two there was no carriage. It will be remembered they had left Chalons only at three.

While, however, De Choiseul was thus waiting on the road, fatality had prepared at the bridge of Someville an event which had the greatest influence on the drama we relate.

Fatality had willed that a few days previous the peasants of an estate belonging to Mme. Elbœuf had refused to pay duties not redeemable. They had been menaced with troops. The federation, however, had borne its fruits, and the peasants of the villages in the vicinity had vowed to assist those of Elbœuf, if the threats were realized.

When they saw the hussars take their positions, therefore, the peasants thought they came with evil intentions. Couriers were sent to the neighboring villages, and about three the tocsin sounded throughout the whole city.

When he returned to the bridge, which he did immediately, Choiseul found his sub-lieutenant, M. Boudet, very uneasy. Muttered threats had been heard by the hussars, and the regiment at that time was one of the most detested of the French army. The peasants made mouths at them, and sung under their very noses this improvised song :

" Les hussards sont des Geux ;
Mais nous nous moquons d'eux." *

Other persons, too, who were more clear-sighted, began to say that the hussars were there not to enforce obedience from the peasants, but to await the arrival of the king and queen.

Four o'clock came without news. De Choiseul resolved, however, to remain ; but he ordered the horses to be put to his carriage, and took charge of the diamonds, sending Leonard to Varennes, and bidding him say at Ste. Menehould, to M. Dandoins—at Clermont, to M. Damas—and at Varennes, to M. Bouillé, the state of affairs.

Then, to soothe the excitement, he stated that he and his hussars were there not to repress the peasantry of Elbœuf, but to escort a large treasure which the minister of war had sent to the army.

The word treasure, though it soothed the excitement on one score, raised on the other much difficulty. The king and queen were also a treasure, and M. de Choiseul evidently waited for them.

After a quarter of an hour, M. de Choiseul and his troops were so pressed up that he could not keep his position, and if the royal party came, he, with his forty hussars, would be unable to protect them.

His orders were to keep the king's journey free from obstacle. Instead of protecting, however, his presence, was an obstacle.

The best thing he could do would be to retire, as he would thus leave the road free. He, however, needed a pretext.

* The hussars are beggars, but we laugh at them.

The post-agent stood in the midst of a crowd of five or six hundred persons, whom a trifle would make enemies of. He, like the others, stood looking with folded arms at M. de Choiseul.

"Monsieur," said the duke, "are you aware of any convoy of money having gone lately to the army at Metz?"

"Yes; this morning a hundred thousand crowns were sent, escorted by two gendarmes."

"Indeed!" said De Choiseul, amazed at his good fortune in receiving the news.

"Parbleu! it is true," said a gendarme. "Robin and I escorted it."

"Then," said the duke, turning to M. Goquelot, "the minister must have preferred another mode of escort, and our presence here is useless. I think we had best start. Hussars, bridle up!"

The hussars, who were uneasy enough, asked nothing better, and in a moment were bridled and mounted. M. de Choiseul placed himself in front, looked toward Chalons, and with a sigh, said:

"Hussars, by fours, break!"

He left Someville with his trumpets sounding, just as the clock struck four.

Two hundred paces from the village, De Choiseul took the cross-road to avoid Ste. Menehould, which he heard was in a great state of excitement.

Just then Isidor de Charny rode into the village, on a horse which had borne him four leagues in two hours. He inquired at the post-house, and learned that a detachment of dragoons had parted only a few minutes before. He ordered the horses, and hoping to overtake De Choiseul galloped rapidly after him.

The duke had left the main road and taken the cross-road just as Isidor entered the village; and the consequence was, the vicomte did not overtake him.

The carriage of the king came ten minutes after.

As De Choiseul had seen, the crowd was nearly dissipated.

The Count de Charny, aware that the first detachment of troops should be at the bridge of Someville, had been perfectly confident, and had not urged on the postilions, who seemed to have received the order to make the journey at a slow trot.

When he reached the bridge and did not see the cavalry of De Choiseul, the king put his head anxiously out of the carriage.

"For Heaven's sake, sire, do not show yourself! I will inquire."

He went into the post-house. In five minutes he returned, having learned all. The king saw that De Choiseul had retired to leave him a free passage. It was important to reach Ste. Menehould, in which place De Choiseul had, doubtless fallen back, and where he would find both the hussars and dragoons.

At the moment of departure, Charny approached the carriage.

"What does the queen order?" said he; "must I go in advance, or follow?"

"Do not leave us."

Charny bowed, and rode by the side of the carriage.

Isidor rode on, being unable to account for the solitude of the road, that was so straight that sometimes it could be seen for the distance of a league, or more, in advance.

He urged on his horse, and gained on the carriage more rapidly than he had done, fearing that the people of Ste. Menehould should suspect the presence of the hussars. He was not wrong. The first thing he saw was a great number of National Guards in the streets. They were the first he had met since he left Paris. The whole city seemed in motion, and on the opposite side of the town he heard the drums beat.

The vicomte rode rapidly through the streets, without appearing in the least uneasy about what was going on. He crossed the great square, and stopped at the post-house.

As he crossed the square, he noticed about a dozen dragoons in police caps seated on a fence. At a few paces from them, he saw, at a window of the ground floor, the

Marquis Dandoins, also in fatigue, and with a whip in his hand.

Isidor did not pause, and appeared to observe nothing. He presumed that M. Dandoins, aware of the king's couriers, would know him, and need no other hint.

A young man of twenty, with his hair cut à la Titus—as the patriots of that time wore it—with whiskers meeting under his chin, was at the door of the post-house.

Isidor looked for some one to speak to.

"What do you wish, sir?" said the man with the whiskers.

"To speak to the agent of the post."

"He is now absent, sir, but I, Jean Baptiste Drouet, am his son. If I can replace him, speak."

The young man laid an emphasis on his name, as if he were aware what a terrible celebrity it would obtain in history.

"I want six post-horses for two carriages which follow me—also a saddle-horse."

Drouet nodded an assent, and went into the yard.

"Postilions," said he, "six post-horses and a saddle-horse."

Just then the Marquis Dandoins came in.

"Monsieur," said he, "you precede the king's coach?"

"Yes, sir, and I am amazed to see you and your men in fatigue dress."

"We had not been warned, sir; and besides, very dangerous demonstrations have taken place around us. An attempt has been made to debauch my men. What must be done?"

"The king will soon pass. Watch his equipage, and be guided by circumstances, and set out half an hour after the royal family has gone, acting as a rear guard."

Then, interrupting himself, Isidor said:

"Silence! we are watched, and perhaps even heard. Go to your squadron, and do your best to keep your men faithful."

Drouet, in fact, stood at the door where this conversation took place. Dandoins left. Just then the sound of whips was heard at the door. The king's carriage had come. Curiosity attracted all the population around it.

Dandoins wished at once to tell the king why he and his troops were in fatigue uniform at the moment of his arrival, and advanced, cap in hand, and apologized with all possible respect.

The king showed himself twice or thrice.

Isidor, with his foot in the stirrup, stood by Drouet, who looked with profound attention into the carriage. During the previous year he had attended the federation, had seen the king, and recognized him.

On that day he had received a considerable sum in assignats; he had examined them one after another (they all had the king's likeness) to see if they were good, and he remembered the royal features. Something within him seemed to say, "That man is the king."

He took an assignat from his pocket, looked at it, and said:

"It is certainly he."

Isidor went to the other side of the carriage, and his brother covered the door at which the queen was sitting.

"The king is known," said he. "Hurry the departure of the carriage, and look at that tall, dark man. He has recognized the king, and is named Jean Baptiste Drouet."

"Very well," said Olivier; "I will take care. Go."

Isidor set out at a gallop to order horses at Clermont.

As soon as they were outside of the city, excited by the promises of MM. de Malden and De Valory, of a crown apiece, the postilions set out at a full trot.

The count had not lost sight of Drouet.

Drouet had not moved, but had spoken in a low voice to a stable-boy.

Charny drew near, and said:

"Monsieur, is there no horse for me?"

"One was ordered. But there are none."

"How—no horses? But that one which I see in the yard, Monsieur?"

"That is mine."

"Can you not let me have it, sir?"

"It is impossible. I have a journey of importance to make, which cannot be postponed."

To insist would arouse suspicions; to attempt to take a horse by force would be very dangerous.

Charny, however, thought of a way to arrange matters.

M. Dandoins had looked after the carriage until it turned the corner. He looked back.

"Eh," said Olivier, "I am the Count de Charny—I can get no horse—dismount a dragoon, and give me his charger. I must follow the king and queen; I only know De Choiseul's relay, and if I am not with them, the king must stop at Varennes."

"Count, I will not," said the marquis, "give you a dragoon's horse, but one of my own."

"I will take it. The fate of the whole royal family depends on the merest accident. The better the horse, the better the chance."

They crossed the street, and went to the marquis's quarters. Before he left, Charny bid a sergeant watch Drouet. The marquis, unfortunately, lived five hundred yards from the post-house. Before the horses can be saddled at least a quarter of an hour will have been lost. We say horses, for M. Dandoins had received an order to saddle up, and serve as a rear guard.

All at once Charny fancied that he heard voices shout, "The queen! the queen!"

He hurried out of the house, ordering Dandoins to send the horses to the post-house. The whole town was in a ferment; it seemed that it only waited for the king to leave to burst forth.

"The carriage which has just left is the king's," exclaimed Drouet, hurrying off. "The king, queen, and princess are in it." He mounted his horse. Many of his friends sought to retain him. Where goes he? what is he about? what is his plan?

"The colonel of the detachment of dragoons being there," he replied, in a low tone, "it was impossible to detain him without a collision, in which we might have been second best. What I did not do here, I will do at Clermont. Retain the dragoons, that is all."

He galloped after the king.

Then the report was spread that the king and queen were in the carriage that had just passed, and the noise arose which Charny heard.

The maire and municipality collected, and the dragoons were ordered to retire to their barracks until eight o'clock.

Charny has heard all. Drouet has gone, and he quivers with impatience.

Just then Dandoins came up.

"The horses! the horses! where are they?"

"They will be here directly."

"Are there pistols in the holsters?"

"Yes."

"Loaded?"

"I loaded them myself."

"Good! Now, all depends on your horse's speed. I must overtake a man who is a quarter of an hour in advance, and whom I must kill."

"How, kill him?"

"Yes, or all is lost."

"Mordieu! to horse, then!"

"Do not take any trouble about me, but mind your dragoons. Look, the maire harangues them; you have no time to lose."

Just then the servant came with two horses; Charny sprung on the first, took the bridle from the servant, and rode away after Drouet, without hearing Dandoins' adieu.

Those last words, however, were most important. They were, "You have taken my horse, count, and the pistols in the holsters are not loaded."

In the meantime, the carriage, preceded by Isidor, moved rapidly from Ste. Menehould to Clermont.

The day was declining; it had struck eight, and the carriage was on the high road through the forest of Argonne.

The queen now saw that Charny was not by her side; but there was no way either to slacken or to quicken the pace.

To explain events and to illustrate every point of this terrible journey, we must flit from one character to another. During this time, while Isidor preceded the carriage a quarter of an hour as a courier on the route to Ste. Menehould, and entered the forest of Argonne, and Drouet followed the coach, with Charny at his heels, Dandoins ordered boot saddle to be sounded.

Among the crowd were three hundred armed National Guards. To risk a battle—and all promised that it would be severe—would be to destroy the king. It would be better to remain, and thus restrain the people. Dandoins had a parley with them, and asked the leaders what they wanted, what they wished, and what was the meaning of these hostile demonstrations. In the meantime, the king would reach Clermont and find Damas with a hundred and forty dragoons.

Had he one hundred and forty dragoons, he would attempt something, but he had but thirty. What avail would they be against three or four hundred men?

He did parley. At half after nine the carriage, preceded by Isidor only a few hundred paces, reached Clermont.

It had been but an hour and a quarter going four leagues.

Outside of the city, Damas, who had been warned by Leonard, awaited them. He recognized Isidor's livery, and said:

"Excuse me, but do you precede the king?"

"Are you, sir, Count Charles de Damas?"

"Yes."

"I do. Assemble your dragoons and prepare to escort the royal carriage."

"Monsieur," said the Count de Damas, "there are rumors of insurrection which terrify me, and I own frankly that I cannot answer for the fidelity of my men if they recognize the king. All that I can promise is, when the carriage has passed, to follow it and close the road."

"Do your best, sir. Here is the king."

In the distance the royal carriage might be recognized by the sparks the horses' feet knocked from the stones of the road.

It was his duty to ride ahead and order the relays. Five minutes after, he was at the post-house. Almost at the same time came Damas and five or six dragoons. Then came the king.

The carriage followed Isidor so quickly that he had scarcely time to mount. The carriage, without being rich, was so remarkable that many persons began to collect.

Damas stood by the door of the house, pretending not to know the illustrious party.

Neither the king nor queen, however, could resist the desire to obtain information.

The king called Damas: the queen Isidor.

"Is it you, Monsieur Damas?" said the king.

"Yes, sire."

"Why are not your dragoons under arms?"

"Sire, your majesty is five hours behind the time. My squadron was mounted at four o'clock. I kept it waiting as long as possible, but the city began to get excited, and my men began to make some very troublesome conjectures. If the fermentation broke out before your majesty's arrival, the tocsin would have been sounded and the road closed. I then kept only a dozen men mounted, and made the others go to their quarters. I kept the trumpeters, though, at my own quarters, so that I could sound boot-saddle as soon as possible, if necessary. Your majesty sees I was right, for the road is now free."

"Very well, sir. You have acted prudently. When I am gone, sound the boot-saddle, and overtake me."

"Sire," said the queen, "will you hear what the vicomte says?"

"What does he say?" asked the king, impatiently.

"That you were recognized by the son of the post-agent at Ste. Menehould; that he saw this young man with an assignat in his hand examine your countenance and your likeness; that he told his brother, who is behind in the matter, that something serious had certainly taken place, or that Count de Charny would be here."

"Then, if we have been recognized, there is the more reason for haste. Monsieur Isidor, hurry up the postilions."

Isidor's horse was ready. The young man leaped into the saddle and cried out:

"Quick, to Varennes!"

M. Damas stepped back, and bowed respectfully to the king; the postilions started.

The horses had been changed in the twinkling of an eye, and they went like lightning.

As they left the city they passed a sergeant of hussars.

M. Damas had at first felt disposed to follow the carriage with the few men who were ready; the king, however, had given him other orders, to which he thought it his duty to conform. Some excitement also was observable in the city; the citizens going from house to house, the windows opening, and heads and lights being visible everywhere. Damas sought to prevent but one thing, the sounding of the tocsin, whither he went and watched the door.

Besides, he expected Dandoins every moment with his thirty men, which would reinforce him. All, however, appeared to grow calm; about a quarter of an hour after he went to the square, where he found his chief of squadron, M. de Norville, and asked him to get the men under arms. Just then they came to tell him that a non-commissioned officer, sent by Dandoins, waited with a message.

The message was that he must not expect M. Dandoins, who, with his troops, was retained by the municipality of Ste. Menehould, and also, this Damas knew already that Drouet had set out to overtake the carriages, which he probably had not been able to overtake, as he had not been seen.

This was the state of things when a non-commissioned officer of Lauzun's regiment was announced.

The message had been sent by the commander, M. de Rohrig, who, with young De Bouillé and De Raigecourt, commanded at Varennes. Uneasy at the lapse of hours without news, these gentlemen had sent to Damas for information.

"What was the condition of things at Varennes?" asked Damas.

"Perfectly quiet."

"Where are the hussars?"

"In quarters with their horses saddled."

"Did you meet any carriages on the road?"

"Yes; one with four and one with two horses."

"Those were the carriages you looked for; all is right," said Damas.

He went to his quarters and ordered boot-saddle. He prepared to follow the king, and defend him if necessary. Five minutes after, the trumpets sounded. All was well, except the incident which detained the troops of Dandoins. With his hundred and forty dragoons, however, he could do without his subordinate.

The royal equipage had turned to the left toward Varennes. It had been determined to change horses on the side toward Dun, and to reach it it was necessary to leave the road over the hills and take the one which led to the bridge. That being passed, to go beneath the tower to the place where De Choiseul's relays were, which were to be guarded by De Bouillé and De Raigecourt.

When at this difficult point they remembered that Charny was to guide the party through the streets to the post-house. The count had been there some days, and he had made himself familiar with every stone. Unfortunately, he was not there now.

The anxiety of the queen was doubled. Charny would have joined the carriage, had not some terrible accident befallen him.

As he approached Varennes, the king himself became uneasy. Relying on Charny, he had not even brought a map of the city. The night, too, was intensely dark, and lighted by the stars alone. It was one of those nights in which it was easy to become lost even in known localities, and for a better reason in strange places.

The order Isidor had received from Charny was to halt in front of the city. There his brother would relay, and, as we have said, resume charge.

As the queen, and perhaps Isidor as well, was uneasy about his brother, they had no hope, but that either De Bouillé or Raigecourt would meet the king outside of Varennes. They had been two or three days in the city, knew it, and would be guides. When, therefore, they reached the foot of the hill, and saw but two or three lights, Isidor halted, and looked around him, not knowing what to do. He saw nothing. He then called, in a low, and then in a loud voice, for MM. Bouillé and De Raigecourt. He heard the sound of the carriage-wheels as they approached, like distant thunder in sound. An idea occurred to him; perhaps they were on the edge of the forest. He entered and explored. He saw nobody. He had then one thing or the other to do; he must either go on or wait.

In five minutes the carriage had come. All asked at once:

"You have not seen the count?"

"Sire," said Isidor, "I have not; as he is not here, he must, while in pursuit of Drouet, have met with some accident."

The queen sighed.

"What must be done?" asked the king.

Speaking to the two guardsmen, he said:

"Gentlemen, do you know the city?"

No one did, and the answer was a negative.

"Sire," said Isidor, "all is silent and quiet. If it please your majesty to wait here ten minutes, I will enter the city, and find either Messieurs de Bouillé and De Raigecourt or the relays of Monsieur de Choiseul. Does your majesty remember the name of the inn where the horses were?"

"Alas! no," said the king; "I did, but have forgotten.

It matters not—go, and we will in the meantime search out some information."

Isidor hurried toward the city, and soon disappeared among the houses.

CHAPTER XXIX.

JEAN BAPTISTE DROUET.

THE words of the king, "We will get information here," were explained by the appearance of two or three houses on the right-hand side of the road. The nearest of these houses was opened at the sound of the approaching carriages, as they perceived by the light that shone through the doorway.

The queen descended, took the arm of M. de Malden, and went toward the house. But at their approach, the door was closed, yet not so quickly but that M. de Malden had time to dart forward before it was quite shut. Under the pressure of M. de Malden, although there was some resistance, the door opened.

Behind the door, and making an effort to close it, was a man about fifty, with his legs bare, and dressed in a robe de chambre and slippers. He cast a rapid look at the queen, whose countenance was visible by the light he held in his hand, and started.

"What do you want, sir?" he asked of M. de Malden.

"Monsieur," was the reply, "we do not know Varennes, and we beg you to be so good as to point out the way to Stenay."

"And if I do so," said the unknown, "and if they ascertain that I have given you the information, and if for giving you it I should be lost?"

"Ah! monsieur, should you run some risk in rendering us the service, you are too courteous not to oblige a lady wh finds herself in a dangerous position."

"Monsieur," replied the man, "the person who is behind you is the queen."

"Monsieur!"

"I have recognized her."

The queen, who had heard or guessed what had just passed, touched M. de Malden behind.

"Before going further," said she, "tell the king that I am recognized."

M. de Malden, in one second, had accomplished this commission.

"Well," said the king, "beg this man to come and speak with me."

M. de Malden returned, and thinking it useless to dissimulate, he said:

"The king wishes to speak to you, monsieur."

The man sighed, threw off his slippers, and with naked feet, in order to make less noise, advanced toward the door.

"Your name, monsieur?" asked the king at once.

"Monsieur de Préfontaine, sire," he replied, hesitatingly.

"What are you?"

"A major of cavalry, and Knight of the Royal Guard of the Order of St. Louis."

"In your double quality as major and Knight of the Order of St. Louis, you have twice taken the oath of fidelity to me; it is, consequently, your duty to assist me in the embarrassment I find myself in."

"Certainly," replied the major; "but I beg your majesty to make haste—I may be seen."

"And, monsieur, if you are seen," said M. de Malden, "so much the better. You will never have so good an opportunity again to do your duty."

The major, with whom this seemed no argument, uttered a kind of groan.

The queen shrugged her shoulders in pity and stamped her foot with impatience.

The king made a sign to her, and then, addressing the major, "Monsieur," he continued, "have you, by chance, heard speak of some horses that were waiting for a carriage, and have you seen any hussars stationed in the town since yesterday?"

"Yes, sire, horses and hussars are on the other side of the town; the horses at the Hôtel du Grand Monarque, the hussars probably in the barracks."

"Thanks, sir. Now go in; no one has seen you, and nothing will happen to you."

"Sire——"

The king, without listening any further, reached his hand to the queen to assist her into the carriage, and addressing the guards, who waited for his orders, "Gentlemen," said he, "forward to the Grand Monarque."

The two officers resumed their places, and cried to their postilions, "To the Grand Monarque!"

But at the same instant a kind of shadow on horseback darted from the wood, and riding across the road, "Postilions," said he, "not a step further!"

"Why so?" asked the postilions, astonished.

"Because you are conducting the king, who is flying from France, and in the name of the nation I order you not to stir."

The postilions, who had already made a movement forward, stopped, muttering, "The king!"

Louis XVI. saw the danger was great. "Who are you, sir," cried he, "who give your orders here?"

"A simple citizen; only I represent the law, and I speak in the name of the nation. Postilions, stir not. I order it a second time. You know me well—I am Jean Baptiste Drouet, son of the postmaster of Ste. Menehould."

"Oh! the miserable fellow!" cried the two guards, jumping down from their seats, with their couteaux de chasse in their hands. "It is he!" But before they had reached the ground Drouet had darted into the streets of the lower town.

"Ah! Charny, Charny!" murmured the queen, "what has happened to you?" She sunk into the bottom of the carriage, indifferent to what would take place now.

What had happened to Charny, and how had he let Drouet pass? Fatality!

The horse of M. Dandoins was swift, but Drouet had

already twenty minutes' start of the count. He failed in recovering these twenty minutes.

Charny drove the spurs into his horse; the horse bounded and went off at a gallop. Drouet, on his side, without knowing whether he was followed or not, went as hard as he could. He, however, had only a post-horse; Charny a thoroughbred. At the end of a league Charny had shortened the distance by a third. Then Drouet perceived he was pursued, and redoubled his efforts to escape. He had left so rapidly that he was without arms.

But the young patriot did not fear death, but he feared to be stopped. He feared the king would escape: he feared that this opportunity to render his name illustrious forever would escape him.

He had still two leagues to go before reaching Clermont, and it was evident that he would be overtaken at the end of the third league from Ste. Menehould. And yet to stimulate his ardor he heard the carriage of the king before him. He redoubled his spurring and whipping.

He was only three-quarters of a league from Clermont; but Charny was not more than two hundred paces behind him. Without any doubt, Drouet knew there was no post-house at Varennes, without any doubt the king was going on to Verdun.

Drouet began to despair. Before he could reach the king he would be overtaken himself. At half a league from Clermont he heard the gallop of Charny's horse nearly as well as that of his own.

All at once, as Charny was not more than fifty paces behind him, some returning postilions crossed before Drouet. Drouet knew that they were those who had conducted the king's carriage.

"Ah!" said he, "it is you. On to Verdun, eh!"

"What? On to Verdun?" asked the postilion.

"I said," repeated Drouet, "that the carriages you had just left have gone on to Verdun." And he passed, pressing his horse for a last effort.

"No!" cried the postilions, "on to Varennes!"

Drouet grave a cry of joy. He is safe, and the king is

lost. He darted into the forest of Argonne, all the paths of which he knew. In crossing the wood he would gain on the king. Besides, the darkness of the wood would protect him. Charny, who knew the country almost as well as Drouet, understood that Drouet would escape, and uttered a cry of anger. Nearly at the same time as Drouet, he pushed his horse into the open country that separated the road from the forest, calling out, "Stop! stop!"

But Drouet took care not to answer. He leaned over on the neck of his horse, exciting him with his spurs, whip, and voice. If he reached the wood, he was safe.

He reached the wood, but when he reached it he was only ten paces from Charny.

Charny seized one of his pistols, and pointing it at Drouet, "Stop," said he, "or thou diest!"

Drouet stooped still more over the neck of his horse, and pressed on. Charny pulled the trigger, but it missed fire.

Furious, Charny launched the pistol at Drouet, seized the second, dashed into the wood in pursuit of the fugitive, aimed at him betwixt the trees, but a second time the pistol missed fire.

Then it was that he remembered as he galloped away from M. Dandoins that he had heard him cry out something which he had not understood.

"Ah!" said he, "I have mistaken the horse, and without doubt he cried to me that the pistols were not charged. N'importe! I'll overtake this fellow, and, if necessary, will kill him with my hands."

And he continued the pursuit. But he had scarcely gone a hundred yards before his horse fell into a ditch. Charny rolled over his head, got up, jumped into the saddle again; but Drouet had disappeared.

And so Drouet escaped from Charny. So it happened that he crossed the high-road, like a threatening phantom, and commanded the postilions who were driving the king not to go a step further.

The postilions had stopped, for Drouet had ordered

them in the name of the nation, which had already commenced to be more powerful than the king.

Drouet had scarcely got into the streets of the lower town, before the galloping of an approaching horse was heard.

By the same street that Drouet had taken, Isidor appeared. His information was the same as that given by M. Préfontaine.

The horses of M. de Choiseul and MM. de Bouillé and Raigecourt were at the other end of the town, at the Grand Monarque. The third officer, M. de Rohrig, was at the garrison with the hussars. A waiter at a café, who was shutting up his establishment, had given him the information. But instead of finding the travelers, as he expected, full of joy, he found them plunged in the deepest grief.

M. de Préfontaine wept; the two guards threatened something invisible and unknown. Isidor stopped in the midst of his recital.

"What has happened, gentlemen?" asked he.

"Did you not meet in the street a man who passed you at full gallop?"

"Yes, sire," said Isidor.

"Well, that man was Drouet," said the king.

"Drouet!" said Isidor, with profound grief; "then my brother is dead!"

The queen shrieked, and buried her head in her hands.

There was a moment of inexpressible depression among these unfortunates, threatened with a danger unknown but terrible, and stopped upon the highway. Isidor recovered himself first.

"Sire," said he, "dead or living, do not think any more of my brother. Think of your majesty. There is not a moment to lose. The postilions know the Hôtel of the Grand Monarque. At a gallop, to the Hôtel of the Grand Monarque!" But the postilions did not stir.

"Don't you hear?" said Isidor.

"Yes."

"Well, then, why do you not start?"

"Because Monsieur Drouet has forbidden us."

"What! Monsieur Drouet has forbidden you? And when the king commands and Monsieur Drouet forbids, you obey Monsieur Drouet?"

"We obey the nation."

"Allons, gentlemen," said Isidor to his two companions, "there are moments when the life of a man is nothing. Each of you charge one of these men; I will charge this one. We will drive ourselves."

And he seized the nearest postilion by the collar, and put the point of his hunting-knife to his breast.

The queen saw the three knives sparkle, and uttered a cry.

"Gentlemen," said she, "gentlemen, pardon!" and then to the postilions, "My friends," said she, "you shall have fifty louis to divide among you now, and a pension of five hundred francs each, if you will save the king."

Whether they were frightened by the warlike demonstrations of the three young men, or whether they were sedduced by the queen's offer, the postilions recommenced their journey.

M. Préfontaine went into his house, trembling, and locked the door.

Isidor galloped before the carriage. He traversed the town and passed the bridge. Five minutes after they had passed the bridge they would be at the Grand Monarque. The carriage dèscended at a good rate the hill that conducted to the low town. But on reaching the entrance to the bridge they found one of the gates closed. They opened the gate; two or three wagons barred the passage.

"Come," said Isidor, jumping from his horse and pulling the wagons aside.

At this moment they heard the first beat of the drum, and the first clang of the tocsin. Drouet had done his work.

"Ah, fellow!" said Isidor, grinding his teeth, "if I find you!"

And by a great effort he pushed one of the wagons aside, as M. de Malden and M. de Valory did the other.

A third still remained in the way.

"Come! the last one!" said Isidor. And at the same time the wheels moved.

All at once, between the spokes of the third wagon, they saw the barrels of four or five muskets thrust. "A step further and you die, gentlemen!" said a voice.

"Gentlemen, gentlemen," said the king, "do not attempt to force a passage. I order you not!"

The two officers and Isidor drew back a step.

"What is it you wish?" asked the king.

At the same moment a cry of terror was heard from the carriage. Besides the men who intercepted the passage of the bridge, two or three others had glided behind the carriage, and the guns of several appeared at the door. One of these was directed against the breast of the queen.

Isidor saw all, seized the barrel, and knocked it up.

"Fire! fire!" cried several voices. One of the men obeyed. Happily his gun snapped.

Isidor raised his arm, and would have poniarded the young man, but the queen caught his arm.

"Ah, madame," cried Isidor, furiously, "let me charge these ruffians!"

"No, monsieur. Put up your sword. Listen."

Isidor half obeyed. He let his hunting-knife fall halfway down the scabbard.

"Ah! if I could meet Drouet!" he murmured.

"As for him," said the queen, in a low tone, and grasping his arm firmly, "as for him, I give you leave."

"Now, messieurs," repeated the king, "what is it you wish?"

"We wish to see the passports," replied two or three voices.

"The passports?" said the king "Go and fetch the authorities of the town, and we will show them to them."

"Ah! by my faith, good manners!" cried the man whose gun had already snapped, throwing himself toward the king. But the two guards threw themselves between him and the king and seized him. In the struggle the gun went off, but the ball struck no one.

"Halloo!" cried a voice, "who fired?"

The man whom the guard had seized cried:

"Help! help!"

Five or six other armed men ran to his assistance.

The two guards bared their hunting-knives, and prepared to fight.

The king and the queen made useless efforts to stop both parties. The struggle was about to commence—terrible, mortal, when two men suddenly threw themselves into the midst of the mêlée, one girdled with a tricolored scarf, the other dressed in a uniform.

The man with a tricolored scarf was Sausse, the procureur of the commune. The other in the uniform was Hannonet, commander of the National Guards. Behind them, lighted up by torches, were twenty guns.

The king saw in these two men, if not assistance, at least a guarantee.

"Gentlemen," said he, "I am ready to trust myself, and those with me, but defend us from the brutality of these people." And he pointed to the men armed with guns.

"Ground your arms, gentlemen!" said Hannonet. The men grumblingly obeyed.

"You will excuse me, monsieur," said the procureur of the commune, addressing the king, "but the report is spread that His Majesty Louis XVI. is fled, and it is our duty to see for ourselves if it is true."

"To see if it is true!" cried Isidor. "If it were true that this carriage contained the king, you ought to be at his feet. If, on the contrary, it only contains a private gentleman, why do you stop us?"

"Monsieur," said Sausse, continuing to address the king, "it is to you I speak; will you do me the honor of answering?"

"Sire," said Isidor, in a whisper, "gain time. Monsieur de Damas and his dragoons followed us, without doubt, and it will not be long before they arrive."

"You are right," said the king. Then, answering M. Sausse, "and if our passports are correct, you will let us, monsieur," said he, "continue our route?"

"Without doubt," said Sausse.

"Well, then, Madame la Baronne," said the king, addressing himself to Mme. de Tourzel, "have the goodness to seek for your passport, and give it to these gentlemen."

Mme. de Tourzel complied with what the king meant to say by the words, "have the goodness to *seek* for your passport." She commenced immediately to hunt up the passport, but in the pockets where it certainly was not.

"Ah!" said an impatient, threatening voice, "you know well you have no passports."

"Pardon, gentlemen," said the queen, "we have one, but, ignorant that we were going to be asked for it, Madame de Korff does not know where she put it."

A kind of humming went through the crowd, implying that they were not to be duped by any subterfuge.

"There is something more simple than all this," said Sausse, "Postilions, drive the carriage to my store. These ladies and gentlemen will come into my house, and there all can be put right. Forward, gentlemen of the National Guard; escort the carriage."

This invitation resembled an order too much for any one to gainsay it; and if they had attempted, they would probably not have succeeded. The tocsin continued to ring, the drum to beat, and the crowd to increase at each step.

More than a hundred persons accompanying the carriage remained on the outside of the house of M. Sausse, which was situated in a little square.

"Well," said the king, as he entered.

"Well, monsieur," replied Sausse, "we were speaking of the passport. If the lady who is said to be the mistress of the carriage will show hers, I will carry it to the municipality, where the council is sitting, and see if it is correct."

As in any case, the passport given by Mme. de Korff to Count Charny, and by Count Charny to the queen, was quite correct, the king made a sign to Mme. de Tourzel to give it up.

She drew this precious paper from her pocket and put it into the hands of M. Sausse, who bid his wife do the honors of his house to his mysterious guests, and left for the municipality.

As Drouet was present at the sitting, every one there was very excited. M. Sausse entered with the passport. Each knew that the travelers had been conducted to his house, and on his arrival curiosity made them silent.

He deposited the passport before the mayor.

We have already given the contents of this passport. After having read it, "Gentlemen," said the mayor, "the passport is perfectly good."

"Good?" repeated the eight or ten voices, with astonishment. And at the same time their hands stretched out to receive it.

"Without doubt, good," said the mayor, "for the king's signature is there." And he shoved the passport toward the stretched-out hands, which seized it immediately.

But Drouet nearly tore it from the hands that held it. "Signed by the king?" said he. "Well, so it may be; but is he one of the National Assembly?"

"Yes," said one of his neighbors, who was reading the passport at the same time as himself, and by the light of the candle, "I see the signature of the members of one of the committees."

"But," replied Drouet, "is it that of the president? And, besides all that," went on the young patriot, "the travelers are not Madame Korff, a Russian lady, her children, her steward, her woman, and three servants, but the king, the queen, the dauphin, Madame Royale, Madame Elizabeth, some great lady of the palace, three couriers—the royal family, in fact. Will you, or will you not, permit the royal family to leave France?"

The question was placed in its proper light; but, place it as you would, it was a very difficult one for the authorities of a third-rate town like Varennes to determine.

They then deliberated, and the deliberation promised

to be so long that the procureur determined to leave them to it, and return home.

The king advanced three steps to meet him. "Well," he asked, with an anxiety that he strove in vain to conceal, "the passport?"

"The passport," replied M. Sausse, "at this moment, I ought to say, has raised a great discussion at the municipality."

"And why?" demanded Louis XVI.; "they doubt its validity, perhaps."

"No; but they doubt its belonging really to Madame de Korff; and the rumor goes that it is in reality the king and his family that we have the honor to have within our walls."

Louis XVI. hesitated replying for a moment; then, determining all at once what to do:

"Yes, monsieur," said he, "I am the king; that is the queen; those are my children, and I beg you to treat us with the respect which the French have always shown their kings."

A great number of the curious surrounded the door. The words of the king were heard, not only within, but without too.

Unfortunately, if he who had just pronounced these words had said them with a certain dignity, the gray coat in which he was dressed, and the little peruke à la Jean Jacques that ornamented his head would not have corresponded with this dignity. To find a king of France in such an ignoble disguise! The queen felt the impression produced on the multitude, and colored to the very temples.

"Let us accept the offer of Madame Sausse," said she, quickly, "and go up-stairs."

M. Sausse took a light and went toward the stairs, to show the way to his illustrious guests.

During this time the news that it was really the king who was at Varennes, and who had said so with his own lips, flew through every street in the town. A man rushed into the municipality. "Gentlemen," said he, "the travelers stopping at Monsieur Sausse's really are the royal family. I heard the confession from the king's own mouth."

"Eh, bien, gentlemen," cried Drouet, "what did I tell you?"

At the same time a great hubbub was heard in the streets, and the tocsin continued to clang and the drums to beat.

A deputation of the commune soon arrived, who said to Louis XVI.:

"Since it was no longer doubtful that the inhabitants of Varennes had the happiness to possess their king, they came to take his orders."

"My orders!" replied the king. "Direct my carriages, then, to be got ready, so that I may continue my route."

No one knew what to reply to this demand of the municipal deputation. Just then the gallop of the horses of De Choiseul was heard, and the hussars were seen to draw up with bare blades in the square.

The queen became highly excited, and a ray of joy passed across her eyes. "We are saved!" murmured she, in the ear of Mme. Elizabeth.

"God grant it be so," said the pure-hearted, lamblike woman, who appealed to God under all circumstances.

The king arose and listened.

The municipal officers seemed uneasy.

Just then a loud noise was heard in the ante-chamber, which was guarded by peasants armed with scythes; a few words were interchanged, and then a contest ensued, and De Choiseul, bareheaded, and hat in hand, appeared at the door.

Above his shoulders was the pale head and resolute face of M. Damas.

In the expression of the two officers' faces there was such an air of menace, that the members of the commune separated, leaving an open space between the newcomers and the royal family.

When she saw De Choiseul, the queen crossed the whole length of the room, and gave him her hand.

"Ah, sir! is it you? You are welcome."

"Alas! madame, I have come very late."

"It matters not, you have come in good company."

"Madame, we are almost alone. Monsieur Dandoins has been detained with his dragoons at Ste. Menehould, and Monsieur Damas has been deserted by his men."

The queen shook her head.

"But," said De Choiseul, "where is Monsieur de Bouillé? where is De Raigecourt?"

M. de Choiseul looked anxiously around him.

"I have not seen those gentlemen," said the king, who had approached.

"Sire," said Damas, "I give you my word of honor, I believed they were killed in front of your carriage."

"What must be done?" said Louis XVI.

"Sire, I have forty hussars here. They have marched forty leagues to-day, but will go much further to serve you."

"But how?" asked the king.

"Listen, sire," said De Choiseul. "This is all that can be done: I have, as I said, forty hussars. I will dismount seven. You will mount one of the horses, with the dauphin in your arms, the queen will take a second, Madame Elizabeth a third, and Madame Royale a fourth. Mesdames de Tourzel, de Neuville, and Brennier, whom you will not leave, will mount the others. We will surround you with the thirty-three hussars, and cut our way through. Thus we shall have a chance of escape. Reflect, though, sire, if you adopt this course, you must do it at once, for in an hour, or half an hour, the soldiers will have left me."

M. de Choiseul awaited the king's orders. The queen appeared to like the project, and looked at Louis XVI. as if to question him. But he, on the contrary, seemed to shun the eyes of the queen, and the influence she could exert over him. At last, looking M. de Choiseul in the face. "Yes," said he, "I know well that there is a way, and only one, perhaps; but can you answer me that in this unequal contest of thirty-three men against seven or eight hundred, some shots will not kill my son, my daughter, the queen, or my sister?"

"Sire," replied Choiseul, "if such a misfortune happened, and happened because you had yielded to my counsel, I should kill myself before your majesty's eyes."

"Well, then," said the king, "instead of yielding to these wild projects, let us reason coolly."

The queen sighed, and moved two or three steps away. In this she did not feign regret. She met Isidor, who, attracted by the noise in the street, and still hoping that it was occasioned by the arrival of his brother, had approached the window. They exchanged two or three words, and Isidor left the room.

The king seemed not to have noticed what passed between Isidor and the queen, and said:

"The municipality refuses to let me pass. It wishes that I should wait here until the break of day. I do not speak of the Count of Charny, who is so sincerely devoted to us, and of whom we have no news, but the Chevalier de Bouillé and Monsieur de Raigecourt, left, as I am assured, ten minutes after my arrival, to warn the Marquis de Bouillé, and cause the troops to march, which were surely ready. If I were alone, I would follow your counsel and pass on; but the queen, my two children, my sister, and these two ladies, it is impossible to risk, especially with the few people you have, for I would not certainly go, leaving my three guards here." He took out his watch. "It is near three o'clock. Young Bouillé left at half-past twelve. His father has certainly formed his troops in echelons, one before the other. The first will be advised by the chevalier. They will arrive successively. It is only eight leagues from here to Stenay. In two hours or two hours and a half a man may easily get over the distance on horseback. Detachments will continue then to arrive throughout the night. Toward five or six o'clock the Marquis de Bouillé will be here in person, and then, without any danger to my family, without any violence, we will leave Varennes, and continue our way."

M. de Choiseul assented to the logic of this reasoning,

and yet his instinct told him that there are certain moments when it is not necessary to listen to logic.

He turned then toward the queen, and by his looks seemed to supplicate her to give him other orders, or at least to get the king to revoke those that he had already given. But she shook her head.

"I do not wish to take anything on myself," said she, "it is for the king to command, my duty is to obey. Besides, I am of the opinion of the king. It cannot be long before Monsieur de Bouillé arrives."

M. de Choiseul bowed, and drew some steps back, taking M. de Damas with him, with whom he wished to concert measures, and making a sign to the two guards to come and share in their councils, when a second deputation arrived, consisting of M. Sausse, M. Hannonet, commander of the National Guard, and of three or four municipal officers.

They caused their names to be announced, and the king, thinking that they came to say the carriages were ready, ordered them to be admitted.

The young officers, who interpreted every sign, every movement, every gesture, fancied they saw in Sausse's face something of hesitation, and in that of Hannonet a determined will, which seemed to them a good augury.

The king looked anxiously at the envoys of the commune, and awaited until they spoke to him. They did not speak, but bowed. Louis XVI. did not seem to mistake them. "Messieurs," said he, "the French people have only gone astray, for their love of their sovereigns is real. Weary of the perpetual outrages I have been subjected to in my capital, in the provinces, where the holy fire of devotion yet burns, I decided to withdraw. There, I am sure, I would find the love the people of France are wont to bear their rulers.

The envoys bowed again.

"I am willing to give my people a proof of my confidence. I have come to take hence a force, composed one half of troops of the line, one half of the National Guard, with which I will go to Montmedy, where I have determined to fix myself. The consequence is, Monsieur Hannonet, as commander of the National Guards, I wish you to select the troops who are to accompany me, and to have the horses put to my carriage."

There was a moment of silence, during which Sausse expected Hannonet to speak, and when Hannonet thought Sausse would speak.

Hannonet at last bowed. He said:

"Sire, I would obey the orders of your majesty, but for a clause which forbids the king to leave France, and all Frenchmen to aid him in doing so."

The king trembled.

"Consequently," said Hannonet, making a gesture to beseech the king to let him finish, "and consequently, the municipality of Varennes has resolved, before it suffers the king to pass, to send a courier to Paris, to ask the will of the National Assembly."

The king felt the sweat roll from his brow, and the queen bit her lips with impatience. Mme. Elizabeth clasped her hands, and looked to heaven.

"So, so, gentlemen," said the king, with that dignity which always came to his aid when forced to an extremity, "am I no longer able to go whither I please? If so, I am a more abject slave than the humblest of my subjects."

"Sire," said Hannonet, "you are still my master, but the humblest of all men, king or citizen, is bound by his oath. You made an oath. Sire, obey the law. This is not only a great example to follow, but to give."

The king saw that if, without resistance, he submitted to this rebellion—and such he thought it—of a village municipality, he was lost.

"Gentlemen," said he, "this is violence. I am not, though, so isolated as I seem. Before my door are forty faithful men, and around Varennes I have ten thousand soldiers. I order you, then, Monsieur Hannonet, commander of the National Guards, to have the horses at once put to my carriage. I order, and will have it so."

The queen drew near, and in a low tone said:

"Very well, sire; let us risk our lives, but not our honor."

"And if we refuse to obey your majesty, what will be the result?"

"The result will be that I will appeal to force, and that you will be responsible for the blood that will be shed, and which you really will have spilled."

"So be it, sire," said Hannonet. "Call your hussars. I will appeal to the National Guard."

He left the room. The king and queen looked at each other in terror, and the latter, seeing the danger of their position, hastily taking the dauphin, who was yet asleep, from his bed, went to the window, and throwing it open, said:

"Monsieur, let us show ourselves to the people, and ascertain if they be entirely gangrened. Let us appeal to the soldiers, and encourage them with our voices. That is as little as those who are ready to die for us can expect."

The king followed mechanically, and appeared with her on the balcony.

The square into which Louis XVI. and Marie Antoinette looked seemed a prey to the greatest agitation.

One half of the hussars of M. de Choiseul were mounted, and the others on foot. Those who were on foot were pulled about, lost, drowned amid the people, and suffered themselves, with their horses, to be taken anywhere. They were already won over by the nation. The others, who were on horseback, seemed submissive to M. Choiseul, who spoke to them in German; but they informed him that half of the troop had mutinied.

The cry of "The king! the king!" was at once uttered by five hundred mouths.

De Choiseul was desperate, and wished to die. He made one effort.

"Hussars," said he, "in honor's name, save the king!"

Just at that moment, surrounded by twenty armed men, a new actor appeared on the stage. Drouet came from the municipality, where he had resolved to stop the king's journey.

"Ah! ha!" said he, as he passed De Choiseul, "you would convey the king away! I tell you that if you do, you will take away only his body."

Choiseul advanced with his drawn sword. The commander of the National Guard was there, and said:

"Monsieur de Choiseul, if you come a foot nearer, I will kill you!"

Just then a man advanced whom no threat nor menace could induce to pause. It was Isidor de Charny. The man he looked for was Drouet.

"Back! back!" said he, driving his spurs into his horse; "that man belongs to me!"

He rushed on Drouet with his couteau de chasse.

When he was just within reach, two shots were fired, one from a pistol, and the other from a gun. The ball from the latter struck him in the breast.

The two shots were fired so near to him that the unfortunate young man was literally wrapped in flame and smoke. He reached out his arms, and, as he fell, exclaimed:

"Poor Catherine!"

Letting the couteau de chasse fall, he sunk back on the crupper of his horse, and thence to the ground.

The queen uttered a terrible cry. She had nearly let the dauphin fall from her arms, and rushed into a chair when she saw another horseman riding rapidly from Dun coming down the pathway Isidor had made in the crowd.

The king, when the queen had retired, turned and shut the window.

Not a few voices only cried, "Vive la Nation!" not a few hussars. The whole crowd did so. Only twenty hussars remained faithful, and they were the hope of the French monarchy.

The queen threw herself in a chair, and, with her hands over her face,.saw Isidor de Charny die, as she had seen George.

All at once a loud noise was heard, and she looked up.

We will not seek to tell what passed in the mind of the woman and the queen. Olivier de Charny, pale and bloody with the last embrace of his brother, stood at the door.

Somber and calm, he made a sign to the persons who were present, and said :

"Excuse me, messieurs ; I must speak to their majesties."

The National Guards sought to make him understand that they were there to keep his majesty from having any communication with any one else. Charny, however, folded his pale lips, knitted his brow, opened his frock, and showed a pair of pistols, repeating, at the same time, in a gentler but more positive voice than he had before :

"Gentlemen, I had the honor to tell you that I wished to speak to the king and queen alone." He, at the same time, made with his hand a gesture for all strangers to leave the room.

The voice, the power of Charny, exercised on himself and others, animated De Damas and the guardsmen, who resumed all their energy, and at once they drove the National Guards from the room.

Then the queen saw how useful such a man would have been in the carriage, had not etiquette demanded that Mme. de Tourzel should have been his substitute.

Charny looked around to see that none but the queen's faithful servitors were present, and approaching, said :

"Madame, I have seventy hussars at the gates, and can rely on them. What orders do you give ?"

"Tell me first, dear Charny," said the queen, in German, "what has happened ?"

The count made a gesture, which told the queen De Malden was there, and spoke German.

"Alas !" said the queen, "we did not see you, and thought you dead."

"Unfortunately, madame," said De Charny, "I am not dead, but"—and he spoke in deep sadness—"my poor brother is."

He could not restrain a tear. He said, however, in a low tone :

"My time will come."

"Charny, Charny, I ask, what is the matter ? Why did you leave me thus ?"

She then said in German:

"You treated us badly, especially ourselves."

Charny bowed. "I fancied," he said, "that my brother had told you why."

"Yes, I know; you pursued that wretch Drouet, and we at once saw trouble in the fact."

"I did meet with a great misfortune. In spite of every effort, I could not join him in time. A postilion, on the return, had told him that your majesty's carriage, which he had intended to follow to Verdun, had gone to Varennes. I then went in the wood of Argonne, and sought twice to shoot him, but the weapons were not loaded. I did not get my horse at Ste. Menehould, but used Dandoins' instead of mine. Ah, madame, about all this there was fatality. I followed him through the forest, but did not know the roads, while he was familiar with every by-path. The darkness every hour became more intense, and as long as I could see him or hear him, I followed him. At last light, and the sound of his horse's heels, passed away, and I found myself lost in the darkness of the forest. Madame, I am a man. You know me—I do not weep now, but then I wept tears of rage."

The queen gave him her hand. Charny bowed, and touched it with the tip of his lips.

"No one replied to me. I wandered all night, and at dawn I was at Genes, on the road from Varennes to Dun. Had you escaped Drouet, as he did me, this was impossible. You had passed Varennes, and it was useless for you to go thither. Not far from the city I met Monsieur Deslon and a hundred hussars. He was uneasy, but had no other news, except that not long before he had seen Messieurs de Bouillé and de Raigecourt flying across the bridge to tell the general what had gone on. I told Monsieur Deslon all; I besought him to come with me, with his hussars, which he did at once, leaving only thirty to guard the bridge over the Meuse. In half an hour we were at Varennes, and have come the whole distance, four leagues, in one hour. I wished to begin the attack at once, to charge everything, even if we found barricade on barricade. At

Varennes, however, we found some so high that it would have been madness to seek to pass them. I then tried to parley. There was an advance of the National Guards thrown out, and I asked leave to join my hussars with those who were in the city. This was refused. I then asked to send to the king for orders, and as they would have refused this, as they did the first request, I leaped my horse over the first barricade and also the second. Guided by the noise, I galloped up and reached the square just when your majesty had left the balcony. Now," said Charny, "I await your majesty's orders."

The queen clasped Charny's hand in her own.

She then turned to the king, who seemed plunged in a perfect state of torpor.

"Sire," said she, "have you heard what our faithful friend, the Count de Charny, has said?"

The king did not reply.

The queen then arose, and went to him.

"Sire," said she, "there is no time to be lost; for, unfortunately, we have already lost too much. Monsieur de Charny has seventy safe men, and asks for orders."

The king shook his head.

"Sire, for Heaven's sake give your orders."

Charny looked imploringly, while the queen besought him.

"My orders," said the king. "I have none to give. I am a prisoner. Do all you can."

"Very well," said the queen, "that is all we ask."

She took Charny aside. "You have carte blanche," said she. "Do as the king bids you—all you can."

She then said, in a low tone:

"Be quick, however; act with vigor, or we are lost."

"Very well, madame. Let me confer for a moment with these gentlemen, and what we decide on will be done at once."

De Choiseul came in. He had in his hand a bundle of papers wrapped up in a bloody handkerchief. He said nothing, but gave them to Charny.

The count at once understood that they were the papers found upon his brother. He took the bloody inheritance in his hand, and kissed it. The queen could not but sob. Charny did not change, but placed the pictures on his heart.

"Gentlemen," said he, "will you aid me in the last effort I shall make?"

"We are ready to sacrifice our lives," said all.

"Think you twelve men are yet faithful?"

"Here stand nine, at least."

"Well, I have sixty or seventy hussars. While I attack the barricades in front, do you make a diversion in the rear. I will then force the barricades, and with our forces united we will be able to carry off the king."

In reply, the young men gave Charny their hands.

He then turned to the queen, and said:

"Madame, in an hour I will be dead or your majesty free."

"Count," said the queen, "say not so. Liberty would be too dear."

Olivier bowed a reiteration of his promise, and without paying any attention to the fresh rumors and clamors which broke out, advanced to the door.

Just as, however, he advanced his hand to the key, the door opened and admitted a new personage, who was already about to mingle in the complicated intrigue of the drama.

He was a man of about fifty or fifty-two years of age, with a dark, stern look. His collar was turned back, his neck bare, and his eyes were flushed with fatigue. His dusty apparel showed that some great exertion had urged him to attempt a mad journey. He had a pair of pistols, and a saber hung to his belt. Panting and almost breathless when he opened the door, he seemed to be satisfied when he recognized the king and queen. A smile of gratified vengeance passed over his face, and without paying any attention to the minor personages who stood in the back part of the room, he reached forth his hand, and said:

"In the name of the National Assembly, all of you are my prisoners!"

With a gesture rapid as thought, M. de Choiseul rushed forward with a cocked pistol, and seemed ready to kill the newcomer, who exceeded in insolence and resolution all they had yet seen.

By a movement yet more rapid, the queen seized his hand, and said, in a low tone:

"Do not be too hasty, Monsieur de Choiseul. All the time we gain is gained, for Monsieur de Bouillé cannot be far."

"You are right, madame," said De Choiseul. He replaced his weapon.

The queen glanced at Charny, amazed that in this new danger he had not thrown himself forward. Strange it was, though, Charny did not wish the newcomer to see him, and, to escape his eye, retired to the darkest corner of the room.

The queen, however, knew the count, and did not doubt but that, as soon as he was wanted, he would emerge from that recess.

CHAPTER XXX.

ANOTHER ENEMY.

All this scene of M. de Choiseul menacing the man who spoke in the name of the assembly passed without his even seeming to remark that he had but narrowly escaped death. He seemed also to be occupied by a far more powerful sentiment than that of fear. There was no mistaking the expression of his face. He had the bearing of the hunter who sees before him the lion and lioness who has devoured his young.

The word prisoners, however, had aroused De Choiseul, and the king had sprung to his feet.

"Prisoners! prisoners! in the name of the National Assembly. I do not understand you."

"It is, however, easy to be understood," said the man.

"In spite of the oath you took not to leave France, you fled in the night, broke your word, betrayed the nation, and insulted the people. The nation has now appealed to arms, the people have risen, and through the mouth of one of the humblest, though not on that account the least powerful, says: 'Sire, in the name of the people and the National Assembly, you are my prisoner.'"

In the next room sounds of applause, accompanied by mad bravos, were heard.

"Madame," said De Choiseul whispering to the queen, "you will not forget that you stopped me. Otherwise you would not be exposed to such an offense."

"All this will be nothing," said she, "if we can but avenge ourselves."

"Yes," said De Choiseul, "but if we do not?"

The queen uttered a sad and melancholy sigh.

The hand of Charny passed over De Choiseul's hand, and touched the queen's.

Marie Antoinette turned quickly around.

"Let that man do and say what he will. I will take charge of him."

In the meantime, the king, completely overcome with the new blow which had been dealt him, looked with amazement at the somber personage who, in the name of the nation and the king, spoke so energetically to him. There was also some curiosity mingled with this feeling, for it seemed to Louis XVI., though he could not recall having seen him before, he knew that he had not met him for the first time.

"What do you want?" said he.

"Sire, I wish that neither you nor your family should leave France."

"And you have, doubtless, come with thousands of men to oppose my march?" said the king, who put on all his dignity.

"No, sire; but two have come—myself and the aide-de-camp of Lafayette. I am a mere peasant. The assembly, however, has published a decree, and confided its execution to me. It will be executed."

"Give me the decree," said the king.

"It is not in my possession; my companion has been sent by Lafayette and the assembly to have the orders of the king executed. I am sent by Monsieur Bailly, and also have come on my own account to blow out the brains of my companion if he should quail at all."

The queen, M. de Damas, and the others who were present, looked on with amazement. They had never seen the people, either oppressed or furious, asking mercy, except when murdering, and now, for the first time, saw it with folded arms, and heard it demand its rights.

Louis XVI. at once saw nothing was to be expected from a man of that temper, and wished to have done with him.

"Well," said he, "where is your companion?"

"Here, behind me."

As he spoke, he threw open the door, behind which stood a young man in the uniform of an officer of the staff, leaning against a window.

He also seemed to suffer much; but he suffered from want of strength, not from want of mental power. He wept, and had a paper in his hands.

It was De Romœuf, the young aide-de-camp of Lafayette, whom our readers will remember to have seen when Louis de Bouillé arrived in Paris.

De Romœuf, as may be deemed from the conversation he then had with the young royalist, was a true and sincere patriot. During the dictatorship, however, of Lafayette at the Tuileries he had been assigned to the care of the queen and with the charge of her excursions. He had always treated her with a respectful delicacy, which had often won the queen's thanks.

"Ah, sir," said the queen, painfully surprised, "is it you?"

With that painful sigh which indicated that a power almost invincible was falling, she said:

"Oh! I never would have believed it."

"It is well," said the other delegate. "It seems that I was right to come."

De Romœuf advanced slowly, with downcast eyes, holding his order in his hand. The king did not, however, permit the young man to present the decree; he advanced rapidly, and took it from his hands.

Having read it, he said:

"France now has no king!"

The man who came in with De Romœuf said:

"I know that well enough."

The king and the queen looked around, as if they would question him.

He said: "Here, madame, is the decree the National Assembly has dared to render."

With a voice trembling with indignation, he read the following words:

"The National Assembly orders the Minister of the Interior to send out at once couriers to the different departments, with orders to all civil functionaries and the officers of the National Guard, troops of the line, and the empire, to arrest any one, whoever he may be, seeking to leave the kingdom, and to prevent all exportation of property, arms, munitions, gold, and silver. In case these couriers overtake the king, or any members of the royal family, or those who have contributed to their escape, the said National Guards and troops of the line are ordered to use every effort to prevent the said escape, and cause the fugitives to cease their journey, and return, to submit themselves to the legislative assembly."

The queen heard all this with a kind of torpor; when he had finished, she shook her head, as if to arouse herself, and said, "Give it me!" As she reached forth her hand to receive the fatal decree, she said, "Impossible!"

While this was going on, the companion of M. de Romœuf, by a bitter smile, infused confidence into the National Guards and the patriots of Varennes.

The word *impossible*, pronounced by the queen, had made them uneasy, though they had heard every letter of the decree.

"Read, madame," said the king, bitterly; "if you doubt me, read, for it is signed by the president of the National Assembly."

"Who dared to write and sign such a document?"

"A noble, madame," said the king; "the Marquis de Beauharnois."

Is it not a strange thing, proving the mysterious union of the past with the present, that this decree, which arrested the flight of the king, the queen, and royal family, emanated from a man who, until then obscure, was about to unite himself in the most brilliant manner to the history of the nineteenth century?

The queen took the decree, and with wrinkled brows and contracted lips, read it again.

The king then took it and read it again. Having done so, he threw it on the bed, where insensible to all that was going on, slept the dauphin and Mme. Royale. That document, however, was decisive of their fate.

When she saw them, the queen could not restrain herself, but sprung up, and crushing the paper, threw it from her hands. She said: "Take care, sire. I would not have the paper sully my children!"

A loud cry was heard in the ante-chamber; the National Guards sought to enter the room occupied by the royal fugitives. The aide-de-camp of Lafayette uttered a cry of terror—his companion uttered one of rage.

"Oh!" said the latter, between his teeth, "the National Assembly—the nation, is insulted! This is well——"

Turning toward the crowd, already excited to the very acme of strife, and who stood around, armed with guns, scythes, and sabers, he said:

"Here, citizens, here!"

The latter, to enter the chamber, made a second movement, which was but the completion of the first. God only knows what would have resulted from these contests had not Charny, who from the commencement of the scene, had said only the few words we have recorded, rushed forward and seized the arm of the unknown National Guard, and said, just as the latter was about to place his hand on his saber:

"A word with you, Monsieur Billot, if you please."

"Very well, Monsieur de Charny; I also would speak to you."

Advancing toward the door, he said:

"Citzens, go for a moment. I have something to say to this officer; be easy, though, for neither the wolf, dam, nor cubs will escape us—I will be answerable for them."

As if this man, who was unknown to them as he was—except Charny—to king, queen, and all, had a right to give them orders, they withdrew, and left the room free.

Each one also was anxious to tell his companions what had taken place, and to advise them to be on their guard.

In the meantime, Charny said, in a low tone, to the queen:

"Monsieur de Romœuf, madame, is your friend. Do the best you can with him."

This was rendered especially the more easy, as when he came to the next room, Charny shut the door, and kept all, even Billot, from entering it. He stood with his back against it.

The two men on finding themselves *tête-à-tête*, looked at each other a few moments, but the look of the gentleman could not make the democrat lower his eyes—nay, more, it was Billot who first began to speak.

"Monsieur le Comte has done me the honor to announce that he has something to say to me. I will listen to anything he wishes to say."

"Billot," asked Charny, "how is it that I here find you charged with a mission of vengeance? I had thought you our friend—a friend of the other nobles, and, moreover, a good and faithful subject of the king."

"I have been a good and faithful subject of the king, and I have been not your friend—for such an honor was not reserved for a poor farmer like me—but I have been your humble servant."

"Well?"

"Well, Monsieur le Comte, you see, I am no longer anything of the kind."

"I do not understand you, Billot," replied the count.

"Why do you wish to understand me, count? Do I

ask you—I, the cause of your fidelity to the king, and the reasons for your great devotion to the queen? No; I presume that you have your reasons for acting thus, and that you are an honest and a wise man; that your reasons are good, or at least, according to your conscience. I have not your high position in society, Monsieur le Comte; I have not either your knowledge, but yet you know me to be, or have known me to have been, an honest and prudent man too. Suppose, then, that like you I have my reasons equally as good and equally according to my conscience?"

"Billot," said Charny, who was ignorant completely of any motives of hatred the farmer could possibly have against nobility or royalty, "I have known you—and it is not so very long since—very different from what you are to-day."

"Oh, certainly; I do not deny it," said Billot, with a bitter smile. "Yes, you have known me very different from what I am now. I am about to tell you, Monsieur le Comte, what I was—I was a true patriot, devoted thoroughly to two men and one thing. These two men were Doctor Gilbert and the king—this thing was my country. One day the agents of the king—and I confess to you," said the farmer, shaking his head, "that that first began the quarrel betwixt the king and myself—one day the agents of the king came to my house, and, half by force, and half by surprise, carried off a casket from me which had been intrusted to my care by Monsieur Gilbert. As soon as I was at liberty I started for Paris. I arrived there on the evening of the 13th of July, right in the midst of the commotions about the busts of the Duke of Orleans and Monsieur Necker. They carried these busts through the streets, crying, 'Vive the Duke of Orleans! Vive Monsieur Necker!' This was doing no great harm to the king, and yet all at once the soldiers of the king charged us. I saw poor devils who had committed no other crime than the crying long life to two men, whom they probably did not know, fall around me, some with their heads cut through with the sabers, and others with their breasts pierced by balls. I saw Monsieur de Lambesq, a friend of the king, pursuing, even into the Tuileries, women and children who had never uttered a word, and trample down under his horse's feet an old man of at least seventy. This made me quarrel with the king still more. Next day I called at the school of little Sebastian, and I learned from the poor child that his father had been sent to the Bastile by an order of the king, obtained from his majesty by a lady of the court. And I continued to say to myself that the king, who they pretended was so good, had, in the midst of this goodness, many moments of error, ignorance, and forgetfulness, and to correct, as far as in me lay, one of these faults that the king had committed in those moments of forgetfulness, ignorance or error, I contributed all in my power to take the Bastile. We arrived there ; it was not without trouble. The soldiers of the king fired at us and killed nearly two hundred men among us, and this gave me a fresh reason for not being of the opinion of all the world about this great goodness of the king ; but at length the Bastile was taken ; in one of the cells I found Monsieur Gilbert, for whom I had risked my life twenty times, and the joy of finding him again made me forget all these things. Besides, Monsieur Gilbert told me among the first, that the king was good, that he was ignorant of a great many of the shameful things that were done in his name, and that it was not to him they ought to be attributed, but to his ministers. And all that Monsieur Gilbert told me at this time was like Gospel—I believed Monsieur Gilbert ; and seeing the Bastile taken, Monsieur Gilbert free, and Pitou and I safe and sound, I forgot the firing in the Rue St. Honoré, the charging into the Tuileries, the hundred and fifty or two hundred men killed by the musketry of Monsieur le Prince de Saxe, and the imprisonment of Monsieur Gilbert on the simple asking of a lady of the court. But pardon, Monsieur le Comte," said Billot, interrupting himself, "all this does not concern you, and you have not asked to speak with me alone to listen merely to the thoughts of a peasant without education, you who are at the same time a great lord and a wise and learned man."

And Billot made a movement in order to put his hand on the lock and enter into the king's chamber again. But Charny stopped him.

In stopping him, Charny had two reasons. The first was to learn the cause of this enmity of Billot, which in such a situation, was not without its importance; the second was that he might gain time.

"No," said he, "tell me all, my dear Billot; you know the friendship that my poor brothers and I bore you, and that which you have already told me has interested me in the highest degree."

At the words, "my poor brothers," Billot smiled bitterly.

"Well, then," he replied, "I will tell you all, Monsieur de Charny; I especially regret that your poor brothers, above all, one—Monsieur Isidor—are not here to hear what I say."

Billot had pronounced the words, "above all, Monsieur Isidor," with such a singular expression, that Charny understood the emotions of grief that the name of his dearly loved brother awoke in his soul, and without answering anything to Billot, who was evidently ignorant of the misfortune which had happened to this brother of Charny, whose presence he desired, he made him a sign to continue.

Billot continued:

"So," said he, "when the king was on the way to Paris, I saw but a father returning to the midst of his children. I marched with Monsieur Gilbert, near to the royal carriage, making a rampart about those who were in it with my body, and crying at the very top of my voice, 'Long live the king!' That was the first journey of the king—that was. Blessings and flowers were showered around him, before, behind, on the road, under the feet of the horses, on the wheels of his carriage. On arriving at the Place of the Hôtel de Ville, the people perceived that he wore no longer the white cockade, and that he had not the tricolored one as yet. They cried out, 'The cockade! the cockade!' I took the one that was in my hat, and gave it him; he thanked me, and put it in his own, with great acclamation on the part of the people. I was drunk with joy at seeing my cockade on the hat of this good king, and I cried, 'Long live the king!' more loudly than ever. I was so enthusiastic about this good king, that I remained in Paris. My harvest was on hand, and required my presence; but, bah! what did I care about my harvest? I was sufficiently rich to lose one season, and if my presence was useful in any way to this good king, to this father of the people, to the restorer of French liberty, as, like ninnies, we called him at this time, it was better that I should remain in Paris than return to Pipelen. My harvest, that I had intrusted to the care of Catherine, was nearly lost. Catherine had, as it appeared, something else to attend to beside the harvest. Let us not speak any more of that. Yet they said that the king did not, so very frankly, accept the revolution; that he was constrained and compelled; that it was not the tricolored cockade that he would have liked to have borne in his hat, but the white one. Those who said this were calumniators, as was sufficiently well proved at the banquet of the body-guards, where the queen wore neither the tricolored cockade, nor the white cockade, nor the national cockade, nor the French cockade, but simply the cockade of her brother, Joseph II.—the Austrian cockade, the black cockade. Ah! I confess it, this time my doubts recommenced; but as Monsieur Gilbert had said to me, 'Billot, it is not the king who has done that, it is the queen, and the queen is a woman, and toward women we ought to be indulgent,' I believed it so well that when they came from Paris to attack the château, although I discovered at the bottom of my heart that those who came to attack the château, were not altogether wrong, I ranged myself on the side of those who defended it, so that it was I who went to wake Monsieur de Lafayette, who slept, poor, dear man, which was a blessing, and who brought him to the castle just in time to save the king. Ah! on that day I saw Madame Elizabeth press Monsieur de Lafayette in her arms; I saw the queen give her hand for him to kiss; I heard the king call him his friend; and I said to myself, 'Upon my word, it seems Monsieur Gilbert was right after all. Certainly, it cannot be from fear that a king, a queen, and a royal princess make such demonstrations as these, and if they do not share the opinions of this man, of what use can he be to them at this time; three personages like these would not condescend to lie.' This time again I pitied the poor queen, who was only imprudent, and the poor king, who was only weak. I left them to return to Paris without me. I was engaged at Versailles—you know in what—Monsieur de Charny."

Charny sighed.

"He said," continued Billot, "that this second voyage was not quite so gay as the first; they said that instead of blessings, there were curses; instead of vivats that there were cries for death; instead of bouquets of flowers being thrown under the feet of the horses, and on to the wheels of the carriage, that there were heads stuck on pikes. I knew nothing of all that; I was not there. I remained at Versailles. I still left the farm without a master. Bah! I was sufficiently rich after having lost the harvest of 1789 to lose that of 1790 too. But one fine morning Pitou arrived and told me that I was on the point of losing a thing which a father is never sufficiently rich to lose—this was my daughter."

Charny started.

Billot looked kindly at Charny, and continued:

"It is necessary to tell you, Monsieur le Comte, there is closely by us, at Boursonnes, a noble family, a family of great lords, a family powerful and rich. This family consisted of three brothers; when they were children, and came from Boursonnes to Villers-Cotterets, the youngest of these three brothers almost always did me the honor to stop at my farm; they said they had never tasted such good milk as the milk of my cows, and never such bread as the bread of my wife, and from time to time they added, I believed, poor simple ninny that I was, that it was in return for my hospitality that they had never seen such a beautiful child as my daughter Catherine. And I! I thanked them for drinking my milk, for eating my bread, and for discovering my daughter Catherine to be beautiful. What would you? I trusted in the king, who is to say, half German by his mother. I could easily then trust to them. Also, when the cadet who had quitted the country for a long time, and who was called George, was killed at Versailles at the door of the queen, while bravely doing his duty, during the night of the fifth of October, God only knows how much I was wounded by the blow that killed him. Ah! Monsieur le Comte, his brother has seen me, his eldest brother, he who did not come to the house, not because he was too proud, but because he had left the country at an earlier age even than his brother George; he has seen me on my knees before the body, shedding as many tears as he had drops of blood, at the bottom of a little green and humid court, where I had carried him in my arms. I believed him still alive, for, poor young man! he was not mutilated as his companions, Messieurs de Varicourt and Des Huttes, had been; I had as much of his blood on my clothes as there was on yours, Monsieur le Comte. Oh! it was the fine fellow whom I aways saw going to the College of Villers-Cotterets on his little gray horse, with his satchel in his hand—and it is true that in thinking of that time, if I could think of him, I should weep even now as you weep, Monsieur le Comte. But I think of another," added Billot, "and I cannot weep."

"Of another? and will you say then?" asked Charny.

"Wait," said Billot, "we shall arrive at that. Pitou had come to Paris, and he spoke two words that proved to me that it was no longer my harvest that was being risked, but my child. That it was not my fortune that was being destroyed, but my happiness. I left the king then at Paris. Although it was in good faith from what Monsieur Gilbert had told me, that everything would go well whether I was in Paris or not, and so I returned to the farm. I believed at first that Catherine was only in danger of death; she had the brain fever, was delirious, but what could I know ?—I The state in which I found her rendered me very uneasy, and I became more so when told by the doctor I must not enter her chamber until she was cured. Not enter her chamber ! Poor father ! I believed that I might listen at her door ; I listened then. Then I learned that she had nearly died, that she had the brain fever, that she was nearly mad because her lover had gone away. A year before I had gone away, too, and instead of becoming crazed, because her father left her, she smiled at my departure. But my leaving left her free to see her lover. Catherine recovered her health, but not her spirits. One month, two, three, six months passed, without a single smile lighting up the countenance on which my eyes were always fixed ; one morning I saw her smile, and I trembled ; her lover was about to return, since she could smile. In fact, next day a shepherd, who had seen him pass, announced to me that he had returned that very morning. I doubted not but that that very evening he would come to see me, or, rather, Catherine. So, when evening came, I loaded my gun and laid myself in ambush."

"Billot ! Billot !" cried Charny, "did you do that ?"

"Why not ?" said Billot. "I put myself in ambush to kill the wild boar that comes to turn up my potatoes ; the wolf that would feed on my flocks ; the fox that would devour my fowls, and why should I not lay in ambush to kill the man who comes to steal my happiness ; the lover who comes to dishonor my child ?"

"But, arrived there, your heart failed you, did it not, Billot ?" asked the count, quickly.

"No," said Billot, "not the heart, but the eye and hand ; a trace of blood, however, showed me that I had not quite failed, only you understand well," added Billot, with bitterness, "between a lover and a father, my daughter did not hesitate. When I entered Catherine's room, Catherine had disappeared."

"And you have not seen her since ?" asked Charny.

"No," replied Billot ; "but why should I see her ? She knows well that if I did see her I should kill her."

Charny made a motion which expressed both terror and admiration of the powerful nature thus exhibited before him.

"I went back," said Billot, "to my agricultural labors. What cared I for domestic troubles if France were happy? Was not the king treading in the footsteps of the revolution? Did he not see again the good king to whom I had given my cockade on the 16th of July, and the life of whom I had nearly saved on the 6th of October? How he would rejoice to see all France collected at the Champs de Mars, swearing like one man to the unity of the country? For a moment I forgot all, even Catherine. No, no, I never forgot her. He, too, swore. I thought he took the oath with a bad grace, and that he swore from the throne instead of at the altar of the country. Bah! though he swore, and that was all that was essential, for an oath is an oath without regard to locality, and honest men always keep them. The king then said, I will keep my oath. True, when I returned to Villers-Cotterets, as I had no longer anything to occupy me, my child being gone, I heard that the king wished to escape, through Monsieur de Favras, but that the affair was a failure. That the king wished to escape with his aunts, but that he failed; that he wished to go to St. Cloud, and thence to Rouen. The people, however, opposed it. I heard all this, but I did not believe it. Had I not with my own eyes seen the king at the Champs de Mars reach forth his hand? had I not with my own ears heard him take his oath to the nation? Could I not believe a king who, in the face of three hundred thousand citizens, had taken an oath, would keep it? Was it not probable? When, therefore, I went to the market of Meaux, I was amazed. I must tell you, I had slept at the post-house with one of my friends, to whom I had brought a heavy load of grain. I was awaked while the horses were being put to the carriage, to see the king, queen, and dauphin. I could not have been mistaken, for I had been used to see him in a carriage since the 16th of July, when I accompanied him from Versailles to Paris. Then I heard those gentlemen in yellow say,

'To Chalons.' I looked, and saw—whom? The man who had carried Catherine away, a nobleman who played the lackey by preceding the king's carriage."

As he spoke, Billot looked anxiously at the count to see if he knew that he spoke of his brother Isidor. Charny, however, wiped away the sweat which stood on his brow, and was silent.

Billot resumed:

"I wished to follow him; he was already far ahead: he had a good horse, was armed, I was not. One moment I ground my teeth at the idea of the king, who would escape from France, and the ravisher, who had escaped from me. But all at once I caught an idea. 'Hold!' said I, 'I also will take the oath to the nation, and now the king has broken his, shall I keep mine? My word! Yes, keep it. I am only ten leagues from Paris. It is three o'clock in the morning; on a good horse, it is a matter of two hours. I will talk this over with Monsieur Bailly, who appears to me to be of the party of those who keep their oaths instead of those who do not keep theirs.' This point determined, in order not to lose time, I begged my friend, the post-agent at Meaux—without, be it understood, telling him what I wanted to do—to lend me his uniform of the National Guard, his saber and pistols. I took the best horse in his stable, and instead of setting out for Villers-Cotterets, I went to Paris. I came just in time, for they had just heard of the flight of the king, and did not know whither he had gone. Monsieur de Romœuf had been sent out by Lafayette toward Valenciennes. See, though, what chance effects. He had been arrested at the barrier, and had obtained permission to be sent back to the National Assembly, whither he came just as Monsieur Bailly, who had been informed by me, described his majesty's itinerary, with all the particulars. There was then only an order to write, and the route to change. The thing was done in an instant. Monsieur de Romœuf set out to Chalons, and I was directed to accompany him, a mission which, as you see, I have fulfilled. Now," said Billot, with a moody air, "I have overtaken the king, who deceived me as a Frenchman, and I am easy; he will not, however, escape me now. I have now, count, to meet him who deceived me as a father, and I now swear he will not escape me."

"Alas! dear Billot," said Charny, with a sigh, "you are mistaken now."

"How so?"

"The unfortunate man of whom you speak has escaped you."

"Has he fled?" said Billot, with an expression of intense rage.

"No," said Charny, "he is dead."

"Dead!" said Billot, trembling, and wiping away the sweat from his brow.

"He is dead. This blood which you see, and which you just now compared to that which covered you at Versailles, is his. If you doubt me, go below and you will see his body in a little courtyard, like the one in which at Versailles you saw another who died for the same cause."

Billot looked at Charny, who spoke to him in the mildest voice, while two great tears stole down his haggard cheeks. He then exclaimed:

"Ah! then, that is the justice of God."

He rushed from the room, saying:

"Count, I believe your words, but I wish to see for myself if justice be done or not."

Charny saw him go, and stopping a sigh, wiped away a tear. Then, seeing that not a moment was to be lost, he rushed to the queen, and said:

"What about De Romœuf? He is our friend."

"So much the better, for nothing is to be expected from the other person."

"What is to be done?" asked the queen.

"Gain time until De Bouillé comes."

"But will he come?"

"Yes; for I will go for him."

"Oh!" said she, "the streets are full, you are known, and will not be able to pass. They will kill you, Olivier! Olivier!"

Charny did not answer, but with a smile opened the window, which locked into the garden, bid the queen a last adieu, and sprang to the ground.

The height was fifteen feet, and the queen uttered a cry of terror, hiding her face in her hands. The young men ran to the window, and by a cry of joy replied to the queen's alarm. Charny had leaped over the garden wall, and was hidden by it.

It was high time, for Billot just then appeared at the door of the room.

CHAPTER XXXI.

M. DE BOUILLÉ.

LET us see what, during this time of agony, the Marquis de Bouillé was doing.

At nine o'clock, that is to say, at the moment the fugitives approached Clermont, the marquis left Stenay with his son, and advanced toward Dun to be nearer the king.

When just a quarter of a league from that city, he feared lest his presence should be remarked, and hurried with his companions off the roadside, establishing himself in a ditch. He waited there. It was the hour when, in all probability, the courier of the king was to appear.

In such circumstances moments seemed hours and hours centuries. They heard the clock strike slowly, and with an impassivity which they would fain have attuned to the pulsation of their own hearts, ten, eleven, twelve, one, two, three.

Day dawned between two and three, during which time the slightest sound was observable, whether any one either approached or left them, and brought hope or despair.

The little band began to despair. M. Bouillé fancied that some grave accident had occurred, but being ignorant what, he resolved to regain Stenay; that being in the center of his command, he might provide against it as well as possible. He was only a quarter of a league distant, when M. de Bouillé looked back and saw the dust raised by the rapid approach of many horses. They paused and waited. As they came, they doubted no longer. The persons were Jules de Bouillé and De Raigecourt.

The little troop advanced to meet them. Every mouth then asked in each troop the same question, and each made the same reply, "What had happened?"

"The king had been arrested at Varennes."

The news was terrible. It was especially terrible, as the two young men who were at the Hôtel Grand Monarque, awaiting the king with the bags, suddenly found themselves in the midst of an insurrection, and compelled to fly without any exact news.

Terrible as it was, though, all hope was not lost. M. Bouillé, like all old officers who rely on discipline, fancied that every order had been executed.

If the king had been arrested at Varennes, the different posts which had been ordered to follow him had reached that city.

These were composed of thirty of Lauzun's hussars, commanded by De Choiseul.

The thirty dragoons of Clermont, commanded by Damas.

The sixty hussars of Varennes, commanded by MM. de Bouillé and de Raigecourt, whom the young men had not been able to inform of their departure, but who had remained under the command of De Rohrig.

True, they had not confided everything to De Rohrig, who was but twenty; but he would receive orders either from De Choiseul, Dandoins, or Damas, and would join his men to those who came to aid the king.

The king would then have with him sixty hussars, and a hundred and sixty or eighty dragoons.

This was force enough to repress the insurrection of a little town of eighteen hundred souls.

We have seen how events had marred the strategic calculations of M. de Bouillé. The security he felt was about to be attacked seriously. While De Bouillé and De Raigecourt were talking to the general, a horse approached at full gallop. He brought news. All looked, and recognized De Rohrig.

The general rode rapidly toward him. He was in one of those happy humors when a man is glad to have some one to find fault with.

"What does this mean, sir?" asked the general. "Why have you left your post?"

"Excuse me, general, by order of Monsieur Damas."

"Well, is Damas at Varennes with his dragoons?"

"He is at Varennes without any force but an officer, an adjutant, and three or four men."

"The others, though?"

"Would not march."

"And where is Dandoins, with his men?"

"They are prisoners at Ste. Menehould."

"But Choiseul and his men are there with his troops and yours?"

"The hussars of Choiseul have joined the people, and now shout, 'Vive la Nation!' My hussars are shut up in their barracks by the National Guard at Varennes."

"And you did not place yourself at their head, and charge the rabble? You did not hurry to your king?"

"You forget, general, that I had no orders, that Messieurs de Bouillé and De Raigecourt were my superiors, and that I was utterly ignorant that the king was expected."

"That is true," said De Bouillé and De Raigecourt, thus doing homage to truth.

"The first noise I heard," said the young subaltern, "I went into the street and inquired, and heard that a carriage, said to contain the royal family, had been arrested a quarter of an hour before, and that the inmates had been taken to the house of the procureur. There was a great crowd. The drums beat and the tocsin was sounded. Amid all this tumult, some one touched my shoulder, and I looked around. It was Damas with a frock over his uniform. 'Are you in command of the hussars of Varennes?' said he. 'Yes,' I replied. 'You know me?' 'You are Count Charles de Damas.' 'Well, get on horseback at once, and ride to Dun—to Stenay, and find the Marquis de Bouillé. Say Dandoins and his men are prisoners at Ste. Menehould, and that my dragoons have mutinied. Say Choiseul's men threaten to join the people, and that the king and royal family are prisoners, and that there is no hope but in him.' I thought that I could say nothing to such an order, but that it was my duty to obey it blindly. I got on my horse, and rode as rapidly as I could to this place."

"Did Damas say nothing more?"

"Yes, that he would use every means to gain time to enable you, general, to reach Varennes."

"Forward!" said the general; "each, I see, has done the best he could. Let us do our best, also."

Turning to Count Louis, he said:

"Louis, I remain here. These gentlemen will take the different orders I give. The detachments at Mouza and Dun will march at once on Varennes, and, taking possession of the passage of the Meuse, will commence the attack. Rohrig, give this order, and say they will soon be sustained."

The young man rode rapidly toward Dun.

M. de Bouillé continued:

"Raigecourt, go to the Swiss regiment of Castello, which is *en route* for Stenay. Wherever you find it, tell the state of affairs, and urge it on. Tell the commandant he must double its pace."

Having seen the young officer ride in an opposite direction to that De Rohrig had taken, he turned to his son:

"Jules," said he, "change your horse at Stenay, and go to Montmédy. Tell Klenglin to march his regiment of Nassau infantry to Dun, and go himself to Stenay."

The young man saluted and left.

"Louis," said De Bouillé, "the Royal Germans are at Stenay?"

"Yes, father."

"They were ordered to be ready at dawn."

"I gave the order to the colonel myself."

"Bring them to me. I will await them on the roadside.

Perhaps I may have other news. The regiment is true, think you ?"

"Yes, father."

"It is enough, then ; we will march on Varennes."

Count Louis set out. Ten minutes after he reappeared.

"The Royal Germans follow me," said he.

"You found them, then, ready to march ?"

"No. To my great surprise, the commandant must have misunderstood my order, for I found him in bed. He got up, however, and promised himself to go to the barracks to hurry their departure. Fearing that you would become impatient, I came to account for the delay."

"Very well," said the general, "he will come ?"

"He said that he would follow me."

They waited ten minutes, a quarter of an hour, and then twenty minutes, but no one came. The general became impatient, and looked at his son.

"I will go back, father," said he.

Forcing his horse into a gallop, he returned to the city. Long as the time appeared to General de Bouillé, it had been badly used by the commandant. Only a very few men were ready, and the young officer, complaining bitterly renewed the general's order, and on a positive promise of the commandant that the regiment would follow in ten minutes, he returned to his father.

As he returned, he observed that the gate he had passed four times was given in charge of the National Guard.

He waited again for five minutes, ten minutes, a quarter of an hour, but no one came. Nearly an hour had passed, and M. de Bouillé invited his son to go the third time to Stenay, and not to come back without the regiment. Count Louis left in a perfect rage. When he reached the square, his ill-temper increased. Scarcely fifty men were mounted.

He took those fifty men and occupied the gate, thus assuring himself free ingress and egress. He then went to the general, who yet waited for him, saying he was followed by the commandant and his soldiers.

He thought so; but it was not until he was about to enter the city for the fourth time did he see the head of the Royal Germans.

Under any other circumstances, M. de Bouillé would have arrested the commandant by his own men, but now he feared to offend the officers and soldiers. He, therefore, simply reproved the colonel for his dilatoriness, and harangued the soldiers. He told them for what an honorable duty they were intended, as not only the liberty, but the lives of the king and royal family were at stake. He promised the officer honors, the soldiers reward, and distributed a hundred louis to the latter.

The discourse and peroration produced the intended effect. An immense cry of "Vive le roi!" was heard, and the regiment at full trot set out for Varennes.

At Dun, guarding the bridge over the Meuse, was a detachment of thirty men which M. Deslon, when he left Charny, had posted there. The men rallied, and they moved on.

They had to travel eight leagues, through a mountainous country, and they could not march as rapidly as they wished. It was also necessary that the soldiers should be in a condition to stand a shock or a charge.

It was, however, evident that they were in a hostile country, for in the villages, on either side, the tocsin was heard, and in advance something like a fusilade. They still advanced.

At Grange le Bois a horseman, bareheaded, seemed to devour the road, and made frequent tokens of anxiety to meet them. The regiment quickened its pace.

This person was the Count de Charny. "To the king! gentlemen, to the king!" said he, lifting his hand and rising in his saddle.

"To the king!" cried the officers and soldiers.

Charny took his place in the ranks, and briefly exposed the state of affairs. The king, when the count left, was at Varennes. All, then, was not lost.

The horses are very much fatigued, but it matters not. The horses have had hay; the men are heated with the hundred louis of M. de Bouillé. The regiment advances like a hurricane, and cries, "Long live the king!"

At Cressy they met a priest. This priest is constitutional. He sees this regiment rushing toward Varennes. "Go, go!" said he. "Fortunately, however, you will come too late."

The Count de Bouillé hears and rushes on him with his saber uplifted. "Boy! boy!" said his father, "what would you do?"

The young count saw that he was about to kill an unarmed man, and that man, too, a priest. The crime was double. He took his foot from the stirrup and kicked the priest.

"You come too late," said the priest, as he rolled in the dust.

They continued their journey, cursing this prophet of misfortune.

In the meantime, they gradually approached the place where the shots were fired. M. Deslon and his seventy hussars were skirmishing with nearly the same number of National Guards. They charged the guard, dispersed it, and passed through.

There they learned from M. Deslon that the king left Varennes at eight in the morning. M. Bouillé took out his watch. It wanted five minutes of nine.

"Well, all hope is not lost. We must not attempt to go through the city. The streets will be barricaded. We will go around Varennes."

They turn to the right. The situation of the country makes the left impossible; they have the river to cross, but it is fordable.

They leave Varennes on the right, and ride through the fields. They will, on the road to Clermont, attack the escort, whatever be its force, and rescue the king or die.

Two thirds of the distance from the city, they come to the river. Charny dashes into it, followed by the De Bouillés. The officers come next, and then the troopers. The stream is hidden by the uniforms. In ten minutes all have crossed. The cool water has refreshed officers and men. They gallop on toward Clermont.

All at once Charny, who has preceded the regiment, pauses. He is on the brink of a masked canal, the top of the wall being level with the ground. This canal he had forgotten, though it was laid down in the map. It is several leagues long, and everywhere presents the same difficulties.

Unless crossed at once, it cannot be crossed at all. Charny set the example. He first rushed into the water. The canal is not fordable, but the count's horse swims toward the other shore. The bank, though, is steep, and the horse's shoes cannot take hold.

Two or three times Charny sought to ascend, but in spite of all the science of the rider, his horse, after desperate efforts, which were so intelligent as to seem almost human, slid back for want of a foothold for his feet, and fell back in the water, panting and nearly drowning. Charny saw that what his horse, a thoroughbred animal, could not do, four hundred troops horses dare not attempt.

He had failed, therefore. Fatality was too powerful. The king and queen were lost, aud he had but one thing left to do—die with them.

He makes a last effort, but which, like the others, is useless. He, however, contrives to bury his saber half its length in the glacis.

This saber remained there as a *point d'appui*, useless for his horse, but valuable to himself.

In fact, Charny deserts his stirrup and bridle; he leaves his horse to struggle in the water, and swims toward the saber; he seizes and grasps it, and after a few efforts, obtains a foothold.

He looked back and saw Bouillé and his son weeping with rage, the soldiers moody and motionless, seeing, after Charny's effort, how vain it would be for them to seek to cross what he could not.

M. de Bouillé wrung his hands in despair. He who had hitherto succeeded in every enterprise, all of whose deeds were crowned with success, who had acquired in the army the name of the "Happy Bouillé," said, sadly.

"Oh, gentlemen, tell me now if I am happy."

"No, general," said Charny, from the other bank, "but I will say that you have done all that man could do; when I say so, I will be believed. Adieu, general."

On foot across the fields, covered with mud, dripping with water, unarmed, for his pistols were wet, Charny took his way and disappeared among the trees, which, like advanced sentinels, appeared here and there on the road.

This road was that by which the king and royal family were being taken. He has only to follow to overtake them.

Before he did so, he looked back, and on the banks of the accursed canal saw Bouillé and his troop, who, though unable to advance, would not retreat. He made them one last signal, and then rapidly turning a corner, disappeared.

He had to guide him only the immense noise proceeding from the cries, shouts, and menaces of ten thousand men.

CHAPTER XXXII.

THE DEPARTURE.

LET us return to the house of M. Sausse.

Charny had scarcely touched the step, when the door opened, and Billot stood before him.

His face was dark; his eyes, the brows of which were corrugated by thought, were anxious and deep. He passed in review all the characters of the drama, but he could make but two observations:

The flight of Charny—it was evident. The count was not here, and M. Damas was closing the window. Billot looked around and fancied he saw Charny leap over the garden wall.

The agreement concluded between the queen and De

Romœuf, which the latter had pledged himself to, was, that he would remain neutral.

The room behind Billot was filled with many people, armed with guns, scythes, or sabers, whom one gesture of the farmer had driven out.

These men, by some magnetic influence, seemed impelled to obey the plebeian chief, in whom they saw a patriotism equal to their own, or, rather, a hatred not less intense.

Billot looked around him; as his eye met those of the armed men, he saw he could rely on them, even if things came to extremities.

"Well," said De Romœuf, "are they decided to go?"

The queen cast on Billot one of those oblique glances which would have pulverized those to whom she addressed them, had she, as she wished, been able to infuse into it the power of lightning.

Without a reply she sat down, taking hold of the arms of her chair, as if she wished to keep herself steady.

"The king requests a delay of a few moments," said De Romœuf; "no one has slept during the whole night."

"Monsieur de Romœuf," said Billot, "you know well enough that their majesties are fatigued, that they ask for delay because they expect Monsieur de Bouillé to arrive. Let, however, their majesties beware, for if they do not come willingly, they will be dragged by force."

"Villain!" said Damas, rushing toward Billot with his drawn sword.

Billot folded his arms. The fact was, there was no necessity for his defending himself. Eight or ten men rushed from the first to the second room, and Damas at once had ten different weapons at his breast.

The king saw that one word alone was necessary to insure the death of De Choiseul, Damas, the guardsmen, and the two or three officers and sub-officers with him.

"Very well," said he, "put horses to the carriage, and we will go."

Mme. Brennier, one of the queen's ladies, shrieked and fainted. The dauphin began to cry.

"Monsieur," said the queen to Billot, "you have no children, or you would not be so cruel to a mother."

Billot trembled, and with a bitter smile, said:

"No, madame, I have none."

He then said to the king:

"There is no need for your order; the horses are already harnessed."

"Well, bring them up."

"The carriage is at the door."

The king went to the window and saw that Billot told the truth. The uproar in the street had drowned the sound of the wheels.

The people saw the king. A loud cry, or, rather, menace, arose. The king grew pale.

De Choiseul approached the queen.

"What does his majesty order? Myself and my companions had rather die than witness what passes here."

"Do you think Monsieur de Charny is safe?" asked the queen, in a low but anxious voice.

"Yes, I am sure of that," said M. de Choiseul.

"Then let us go. For Heaven's sake, though, both on your account and on ours, do not leave us."

The king understood the queen's fears.

"Monsieur de Choiseul and Monsieur de Damas accompany us, but I do not see their horses."

"True," said De Romœuf, "we cannot keep those gentlemen from following the king and queen."

"These gentlemen can accompany the king and queen, if they can. Our orders relate to the king and queen, but have no relation to them."

The king said with more firmness than might have been expected from him:

"I will not go until those gentlemen have their horses."

"What say you to that?" said Billot, turning to his men.

"The king will not go until these gentlemen have their horses."

The men laughed.

"I will send for them," said De Romœuf.

Choiseul stepped in front of him, and said:

"Monsieur de Romœuf, do not leave their majesties. Your mission gives you some power over the people, and it will reflect credit on you if not a hair of the heads of their majesties be injured."

De Romœuf paused. Billot shrugged his shoulders.

"Very well; I am going," said he.

He advanced first. When at the door he turned.

"You will follow me, will you not?"

"Be easy," said the men, with a burst of laughter which indicated that in case of resistance no pity was to be expected from them.

They were so irritated that they certainly would have employed force against the royal family had any attempt at escape been made.

Billot did not have the trouble to come up-stairs again. One of the men stood at the window, and watched what was going on in the street.

"All is ready," said he; "come."

"Come," said his companions, with an accent which admitted of no discussion.

The king went first. Then came De Choiseul with the queen. Then came Damas, who gave his arm to Mme. Elizabeth. Mme. de Tourzel came next with the children, and after them the rest of the faithful group.

Romœuf, of the envoy of the National Assembly, was particularly charged with the care of the royal cortége.

It must, however, be said that De Romœuf himself needed looking after. It had been said that he had executed with great gentleness the orders of the assembly, and that he had covertly, if not openly, favored the escape of one of the king's most faithful servants, who had left, it was said, only to summon Bouillé to their aid.

The result was that when at the door, while the conduct of Billot was glorified by all the people, which seemed to recognize him as its chief, De Romœuf heard around him, on all sides, the words of aristocrat and traitor.

They got into the carriage in the same order in which

they descended the stairway. The guardsmen resumed their places on the seat.

Just as they came down, M. de Valory approached the king.

"Sire," said he, "my comrade and myself have come to ask a favor of your majesty."

"What is it?" said the king, amazed that he had yet any favor to dispose of.

"Sire, the favor, since we have no longer the honor of serving you as soldiers, is, that we may be near you as servants."

"Servants! Gentlemen, the thing is impossible," said the king.

M. de Valory bowed. "Sire," said he, "in the situation in which your majesty is, it is our opinion that such a duty would do honor to a prince of the blood; for so much better reason does it do honor to poor gentlemen like ourselves."

"Well, gentlemen," said the king, with tears in his eyes, "remain with us and never leave us."

Thus these two young men, making a reality of their livery and their factitious duties as couriers, resumed their places on the seats.

"Gentlemen," said the king, "I wish to go to Montmédy. Postilions, take me thither."

A cry, not from a single voice, but from the whole population, was heard. It shouted: "To Paris!"

After a moment's silence, Billot, with his saber, pointed out the road he wished them to follow, and shouted: "To Clermont!"

The carriage began to move.

"I call you to witness that violence is used against me," said the king.

The unfortunate king, exhausted by this exertion, which exceeded any one he had yet made, sunk back in the carriage between the queen and Mme. Elizabeth.

The coach rolled on.

CHAPTER XXXIII.

THE JOURNEY OF SORROW.

THE royal family continued on to Paris, making what we may call the journey of sorrow.

They advanced slowly, for the horses could not walk but as fast as the escort, which was in chief composed of men armed with scythes, forks, guns, sabers, pikes, and flails, the whole number being completed by an infinite number of women and children. The women lifted their children above their heads to show them the king was being brought back by force to his capital, and whom none had ever expected to see so situated.

They reached Clermont without seeing, though the distance was four leagues, any diminution in the terrible escort, those of the men who composed it, and whose occupations called them homeward, being replaced by others in the environs, who wished to enjoy a spectacle with which others had been satisfied.

Among all the captives of this traveling prison, two were most exposed to the anger of the crowd, and more completely the butts of its menaces; these were the unfortunate guardsmen on the box. Every moment—and this was one way to strike at the royal family, their persons having been declared by the National Assembly inviolable—at every moment bayonets were directed against their breasts, or some scythe, which might well have been that of death, was elevated above their heads, or else some lance glided like a serpent between the intervals to prick them, and was brought back quick as lightning to gratify its master by showing by its point that it had not been misdirected.

All at once they saw, with surprise, a man, bareheaded, without a hat, without arms, and with his dress all mud-stained, pierce the crowd, after having simply spoken respectfully to the king and queen, rush toward the box of the carriage, and take his place between the guardsmen.

The queen uttered a cry of joy. She had recognized Charny.

They reached Ste. Menehould at about two in the afternoon. The loss of sleep during the night of their departure, and the excitement they had gone through, had its effect on all, especially on the dauphin, who, at that place, had a violent fever. The king ordered a halt.

Perhaps of all the cities on the road, Ste. Menehould was the one most excited against the unfortunate family of prisoners. No attention was paid to the king's order, which was superseded by one from Billot to put horses to the carriage. He was obeyed.

The passage through the city was cruel. The enthusiasm excited by the appearance of Drouet, to whom the appearance of the prisoners was due, would have been a terrible lesson to them if kings could learn anything. In these cries, however, Louis XVI. and Marie Antoinette only saw a blind fury, and in these patriots anxious to save France they only saw rebels.

At the entrance into Ste. Menehould, the crowd, like an inundation, covered the whole plain, and could not cross the narrow street.

It burst around the two sides of the city, following the exterior contour; as, however, they only stopped at Ste. Menehould long enough to change the horses at the other side of the city, it crowded around the carriages more orderly than ever.

The king had fancied—and this idea, perhaps, alone had excited him to adopt a wrong course—that the people of Paris alone were enraged, and had relied on the provinces. He had not only alienated the country, but it was perfectly pitiless toward him. The country people had terrified De Choiseul at the bridge of Someville, had imprisoned Dandoins at Ste. Menehould, had fired on Damas at Clermont, and had killed Isidor beneath the king's eyes. All protested against his flight, even the priest whom the Chevalier de Bouillé had kicked from his horse.

They reached Chalons at a late hour. The carriage drove into the courtyard of the intendant, whither preparations had been ordered by a courier.

The courtyard was filled by the National Guard of the city and by spectators.

At the door where the tumultuous cortége had paused cries had ceased, and a kind of murmur of compassion was heard when the royal family left the carriage. They found a supper as sumptuous as possible, and with an elegance which astonished the prisoners.

Servants were in attendance, but Charny claimed the privilege for himself and the guardsmen to wait at table. Such a humiliation, which to-day would seem strange, was an excuse for Charny not to lose sight of the king, and to be prepared for any conjuncture.

The queen understood, though she had not even looked toward him nor thanked him with her hand, eyes, or by a word.

Charny knew the state of feeling in every village. Now, Chalons was an old commercial town, with a population of bourgeoisie, land-holders, and nobles. It was aristocratic.

The result was, that while at the table their host, the intendant of the department, bowed to the queen, who, expecting nothing favorable, looked anxiously at him.

"Madame," said he, "the young girls of Chalons wish to offer your majesty flowers."

The queen in surprise looked toward Mme. Elizabeth and the king. "Flowers?" said she.

"Madame," said the intendant, "if the hour be inconvenient and badly chosen, I will order that they be not admitted."

"No, no; do not say so. Girls—flowers—let them come."

The intendant withdrew, and a moment after, twelve girls, at from fourteen to sixteen years of age, the most beautiful that could be found, passed the ante-chamber, and stopped at the door.

"Come in! come in, my children!" said the queen, extending her arms to them.

One of the young girls, the interpreter, not only of her companions, but of their parents and the city, had committed to memory an address. She was about to repeat it, but when the queen offered her arms, at the sight of the emotion of the royal family she could but weep, and utter these words, which came from her lips in the deepest distress:

"Ah, your majesty, what a misfortune!"

The queen took the bouquet, and kissed the young girl.

Charny whispered in the king's ear: "Perhaps, your majesty, this city may be turned to advantage. Perhaps all is not lost, and with your leave given, I will descend and report to you what I have seen and done, perhaps."

"Go," said the king, "but be prudent. Did anything happen to you, I would never be consoled. Two deaths in one family, alas! are more than enough."

"Sire, my life, like the lives of my brothers, is your own!" He left. As he did so, however, he wiped away a tear.

The presence of the royal family only retained the apparent calmness of this firm-hearted man, and made him seem so much of a stoic. "Poor Isidor!" said he. He placed his hand on his breast, to see if he had still in his pockets the papers which De Choiseul had found on his brother, and which he proposed to read, at the first quiet moment, religiously, as if they had been a will.

Behind the young girls, whom Mme. Royale kissed like sisters, were their parents, almost all of whom were bourgeois or nobles. They came humbly and timidly to salute their sovereign.

In about half an hour Charny returned.

The queen had seen him go out and return, and her eye could not possibly read the reasons.

"Well?" asked the king, leaning toward Charny.

"All, sire, is well. The National Guard offers to-morrow to escort your majesty to Montmédy."

"Then you have decided on something?"

"Yes, sire, with the principal men. To-morrow, before leaving, the king will ask to hear mass, and they cannot refuse permission. It is a festival day. The king will find his carriage at the door of the church, and will enter it. *Vivats* will be heard, and the king will then order his carriage to be driven to Montmédy."

"It is well," said Louis XVI.; "and if the state of things does not change, all will be as you say; only do you and your companies go to sleep, for you will additionally need it to-morrow."

The reception of the young girls and their parents was not prolonged, and the king and royal family retired at nine o'clock.

When they retired, the sentinel at the door recalled to them that they were yet prisoners.

An hour afterward, having been relieved, the sentinel asked leave to speak to the chief of the escort, Billot.

He was supping in the street with the men who had come from the different villages on the route, and sought to induce them to remain until morning.

The majority of these men had seen what they wished—that is, the king—and each wished to keep the approaching holy day (Fête Dieu) in his own village. Billot sought to retain them, for he was uneasy at the feeling displayed by the aristocratic city.

They replied: "If we do not return to-morrow, who will make preparations for the festivals and place hangings before our houses?"

The sentinel surprised him in the midst of this conversation. They talked together in an animated manner. Billot sent for Drouet. The same whispered conversation was continued. Billot and Drouet then went together to the post-house, the master of which was a friend to the latter. Two horses were at once saddled, and ten minutes after Billot galloped toward Rheims and Drouet to Vitry-le-Français.

Day came, and not more than six hundred men remained of the escort. Those who did remain were the most outré, or the meanest. They had slept in the street on bales of straw, which had been brought to them, and when morning came, they saw half a dozen men in uniform enter the intendancy, and immediately after leave in haste.

There was a station of the guards of Villeroy in Chalons; and about a dozen of those gentlemen were in the city. They came for orders to Charny.

Charny bid them put on their uniforms and be at the church when the king should leave it. They went to prepare themselves.

As we have said, some of the peasants who, the previous evening, had escorted the king had not retired at night because they were worn out; in the morning, however, they began to reckon up the leagues. Some were ten, others fifteen from home. Two or three hundred set out in spite of the persuasion of their comrades.

Now they might rely on at least an equal number of National Guards devoted to the king, leaving out the officers, who were to be united into a kind of sacred battalion ready to set an example of exposure to all dangers.

At six in the morning the inhabitants who were most zealous were out, and in the courtyard of the intendancy. Charny and the guardsmen were with them. The king arose at seven, and said that he wished to attend mass. Nothing seemed to oppose the accomplishment of the wish.

The king seemed pleased; Charny, though, shook his head. Though he did not know Drouet, he knew Billot.

All seemed favorable, however. The streets were crowded, but it was easy to see the population sympathized with the king. While the blinds of the room of the king and queen were closed, the crowd, not to disturb them, had moved about quietly and calmly, lifting up its hands to heaven, and the four or five hundred peasants of the escort, who would not return home, were scarcely observable in its masses.

As soon, though, as the blinds of the royal chambers were opened, cries of "Vive le roi!" and "Vive la reine!" were uttered so energetically that the king and queen appeared at the balcony.

The cries were then unanimous, and for a last time the captive sovereigns seemed condemned to disappointment.

"Well," said Louis XVI. to Marie Antoinette, "all goes well."

She lifted her eyes to heaven, but made no reply.

Just then the ringing of the clock was heard. Charny tapped lightly at the door.

"Very well," said the king; "I am ready."

Charny glanced at the king, who seemed calm and almost firm. He had suffered so much that by suffering he seemed to have lost his irresolution.

The carriage was at the door. The king and queen were surrounded by a crowd at least as considerable as that of the previous evening. Instead, however, of insults, it demanded no favor but a word, a glance, or permission to touch the apparel of the king, or leave to kiss the queen's hand.

The three officers got on the box; the driver was ordered to proceed to the church, and did not hesitate. Who was to give a counter order?—the chiefs were absent. Charny looked round, and saw neither Drouet nor Billot. They reached the church.

Every moment the number of National Guards increased at the corner of every street; they joined the cortège by companies. At the church door Charny saw that he had six hundred men.

Places had been kept for the royal family beneath a kind of daïs, and though but eight o'clock, the priests began high mass. Charny saw it. He feared nothing so much as delay, which might be fatal to his hopes. He sent word to the priests that mass must last but a quarter of an hour.

"I understand," said the minister, "and I shall pray God to grant his majesty a prosperous voyage."

The mass lasted just a quarter, and yet Charny more than twenty times looked at his watch. The king could not hide his impatience, while the queen leaned her head on the prie-dieu. At length the priest turned and said: "*Ite, missa est.*"

As he left the altar, he turned and blessed the royal family, who bowed and answered in the response of the formula used by the priest, "Amen."

They went to the door; those who had come to hear mass knelt, and moved their lips, though no audible sound was uttered. It was easy to guess the prayers that trembled on their mute lips.

At the door were ten or a dozen mounted guardsmen. The royal escort had begun to assume colossal proportions; yet it was evident that the peasants, with their rude will, with their arms less mortal, perhaps, than those of the citizens, but more terrible in appearance—a third had guns and the rest pikes and scythes—might be a dangerous enemy.

Not without something of fear did Charny lean toward the king, and asking his orders, saying to encourage him: "Let us on, sire."

The king was decided. He looked out of the window, and speaking to those who surrounded him, said:

"Gentleman, yesterday at Varennes I was seized. I ordered them to take me to Montmédy, yet I was dragged toward a revolted capital. I was then amid rebels; to-day, faithful subjects surround me, and I order you to escort me to Montmédy."

"To Montmédy!" said Charny. "To Montmédy!" said the guardsman of Villeroy. "To Montmédy!" shouted the National Guards of Chalons, with one voice.

A chorus of "Vive le roi!" was heard.

Charny looked at the peasants, who seemed, in the absence of Drouet and Billot, to be commanded by the Garde Française, who had been on duty at the king's door. He followed, and made his men silently seem to obey, and suffering the whole National Guard to pass, forming his rude masses in the rear. Charny became uneasy, but, situated as he was, he could not prevent it nor ask for any explanation.

The explanation was soon given. As they advanced toward the gate of the city, it seemed to him that, in spite of the sound of the wheels and the murmurs of the crowd, a dull murmur was heard in the distance. He placed his hand on the knee of the guardsman by his side, and said: "All is lost!"

Just then they turned the angle of the wall. Two roads ended there, one of which led to Vitry-le-Français, and the other to Rheims. Down each of these roads, with drums beating and colors flying, advanced large bodies of the National Guards. One seemed to be composed of eighteen hundred, and the other of twenty-five hundred men, or of three thousand. Each seemed commanded by a mounted man. These horsemen were Billot and Drouet.

Charny had but to glance at them to see all. The absence of Billot and Drouet, hitherto inexplicable, was now plain enough.

They must have learned what was going on at Chalons, and had set out to Rheims and Vitry-le-Français to bring up the National Guards of those cities. Their measures had been so well arranged that both arrived at once. They halted their men on the square, closing it entirely. The cortége paused.

The king looked out of the window; he saw Charny standing, pale and with his teeth clinched, in the road.

"What is the matter?" asked the king.

"Our enemies, sire, have obtained a reinforcement, and now load their arms, while behind the National Guards of Chalons the peasants stand already loaded."

"What think you of that, Monsieur de Charny?"

"That, sire, we are between two fires. This is no reason why, however, you cannot pass, if you wish to do so; but, sire, whither your majesty will go I know not."

"Well," said the king, "let us return."

The young men on the seat sprang to the door, around which the guards of Villeroy collected. These brave and gallant officers asked nothing better than an opportunity to enter into a contest with their opponents. The king, however, repeated more positively the order he had given before.

"Gentlemen," said Charny, "let us return—the king will have it so;" and taking one of the horses by the bridle, he turned the heavy carriage around.

The royal carriage was driven sadly enough toward Paris, under the surveillance of those two men, who had forced it to resume its direction, until when, between Stenay and Dormans, Charny—thanks to his stature and the elevation of his seat—Charny saw a carriage, drawn by four post-horses, advancing rapidly. He perceived at once that this carriage either brought some important news or some distinguished individual.

When it had joined the advance guard of the escort, after the exchange of a few words, the ranks of the advance guard opened, and the men who composed it respectfully presented arms.

Three men descended from the carriage. Two of them were utter strangers to the royal escort and prisoners. The third had scarcely put his foot on the ground, when the queen whispered to the king:

"Latour Maubourg, the scapegoat of Lafayette!"

Shaking her head, she said:

"This presages nothing good."

The oldest of the three men advanced, and opening the door of the carriage, rudely said:

"I am Petion, and those two gentlemen are Barnave and Latour Maubourg. We are sent by the National Assembly to escort the king, and to prevent popular anger from anticipating justice. Sit closer together and make room for us."

The queen cast on the deputy from Chartres and his two companions one of those disdainful glances of which the daughter of Marie Theresa was so prodigal. Latour Maubourg, a courtier of the school of Lafayette, could not support her eye.

"Their majesties," said he, "are much crowded, and I will get into the next carriage."

"Go where you please," said Petion; "my place is in the queen's carriage, and thither I will go."

He got into the carriage.

The king, queen, and Mme. Elizabeth occupied the back seat. Petion looked at them, and said:

"As delegate of the National Assembly, the post of

honor belongs to me. Be pleased to sit on the other side."

Mme. Elizabeth arose and gave her seat to Petion, casting a look of perfect resignation on the king and queen.

Barnave stood outside, hesitating to enter a carriage in which seven persons were already crowded.

"Well, Barnave," said Petion, "will you get in?"

"Where shall I sit?" said Barnave, evidently much annoyed.

"Do you wish a seat?" said the queen, bitterly.

"I thank you, madame, but I will find a place with those gentlemen on the box."

Mme. Elizabeth drew Mme. Royale close to her, and the queen took the dauphin on her knees. Thus room was made for Barnave, who sat opposite to the queen with his knees close to her.

"Forward!" said Petion, without asking the king's consent. The procession started amid loud cries of "Long live the National Assembly!"

As soon as Barnave took his place opposite the queen, the king said:

"Gentlemen, I assure you I never intended to leave the kingdom."

Barnave, who was seated, arose and said to the king:

"Monsieur, is that so? That word will preserve France." He sat down.

Then something strange passed between that man, sprung from the bourgeoisie of a provincial city, and that woman, descended from one of the greatest thrones of the world.

They sought to read the hearts of each other, not as two political enemies who wish to search out state secrets, but like a man and woman who would penetrate the mysteries of love. Whence arose in the heart of Barnave that sentiment which the piercing eye of Marie Antoinette discovered after the lapse of a few minutes.

Barnave claimed to be the successor of Mirabeau. In his opinion he had already occupied his place in the tribune. There was one thing besides, however. In the opinion of all—we know how—Mirabeau had seemed to enjoy the confidence of the king and the favors of the queen. The one and only conference Mirabeau had ever enjoyed had been exaggerated into many, and from the known audacity of the great tribune, the queen had been represented as having yielded even to weakness. At this time it was the fashion not only to slander Marie Antoinette, but to also believe them.

Barnave was anxious to be the complete successor of Mirabeau ; that was his reason for being so anxious to be one of the envoys. He was appointed, and went with the assurance of a man who knows that if he cannot win a woman's love, he has the power at least to make himself hated.

All this the queen, with one rapid glance, at once saw. She also saw that Barnave paid great attention to her. Five or six times during the quarter of an hour, when Barnave sat in front of her, the young deputy looked carefully on the three men who were on the seat of the carriage, and from it he looked each time more bitterly at the queen.

Barnave knew that one of the three, he did not know which, was the Count de Charny, whom public rumor represented as the queen's lover.

The queen saw this. At once she acquired great power. She had detected the weak point in the cuirass of her adversary ; she had only to strike, and strike firmly.

"Monsieur," said she to the king, "you heard what the leader of our guard said ?"

"About what, madame ?"

"About the Count de Charny."

Barnave trembled. The queen did not fail to notice this tremor, for his knee touched hers.

"Did he not say that he was responsible for the life of the count ?" said the king.

"Yes, sire ; to the countess, too."

"Well ?" said the king.

"Well, sire, the Countess of Charny is my old friend. Do you not think that, on my return to Paris, I had best give De Charny a leave, so that he may visit his wife? He has run a great risk, and his brother has been killed for us. I think to ask him to continue his services would be cruel."

Barnave stared.

"You are right, madame," said the king; "but I doubt if the count will consent."

"Well, then, each of us will have done what is right; we will have offered, and De Charny refused. We have additional reasons to congratulate ourselves, as we did not bring the count with us. I fancied him safe in Paris, when all at once I saw him at the carriage door."

"True," said the king, "but it proves that the count needs a stimulus to induce him to do his duty."

Barnave was in one of those states of mind, when, to contend with an attractive woman, one would undertake a Herculean task with the certainty of being overcome. He asked the Supreme Being (in 1791 people did not ask God) to grant him some opportunity to attract the eyes of the royal scorner on him; and all at once, as if the Supreme Being had heard the prayer addressed him, a poor priest, who had watched by the roadside, drew near to obtain a better view, and lifting his eyes to heaven, said:

"Sire, God bless your majesties!"

The bearing of the old man, the prayer he pronounced, was replied to by the people with a roar, and before Barnave had aroused himself from his reverie, the old priest was thrown down and would have been murdered had not the queen, in terror, said:

"Monsieur, see you not what is going on?"

Barnave looked up, and at once saw the ocean beneath which the old man had disappeared, and which, in tumultuous waves, rolled around the coach.

"Wretches!" said he. He threw himself against the door, burst it open, and would have fallen, had not Mme. Elizabeth, by one of those motions of the heart, which were to her so prompt, seized his skirts.

"Tigers!" said he, "you are not Frenchmen, or

France, the home of the brave, has become the abode of murderers."

The people fell back, and the old man was saved.

He arose, saying: "You are right to save me, young man; I will pray for you." Making the sign of the cross, he withdrew.

The people suffered him to pass, overcome by the bearing and glance of Barnave, who seemed the statue of command.

When the old man had gone, the young deputy sat down simply and naturally, without showing any evidence that he believed he had saved a life.

"Monsieur," said the queen, "I thank you."

These words awakened an emotion in all Barnave's body. Beyond all doubt, never since he knew Marie Antoinette, had she been so attractive and beautiful.

He was ready to fall at her feet, but the young dauphin uttered a cry of pain. The child had annoyed the virtuous Petion by some trick, and the patriot had pulled his ear very sharply.

The king grew red with rage, the queen grew pale with shame. She reached out her arms and took the child from Petion's knees, and placed him on Barnave's.

Marie Antoinette wished to take him herself.

"No," said the dauphin; "I am very comfortable here."

Barhave had changed his position, so as to enable the queen to take the child if she pleased, but either from coquetry or policy, she suffered him to remain where he was.

Just then there passed through Barnave's mind something untranslatable; he was at once proud and happy.

The child began to play with Barnave's ruffles, with his sash and the buttons of his coat as a deputy. The buttons bore one engraven device, and occupied the dauphin's attention. He called the letters one by one, and then, uniting them, read these four words:

"Live free or die!"

"What, monsieur, does that mean?"

"It means, my fine fellow, that Frenchmen have sworn to have a master no longer. Do you understand that?"

"Petion!" said Barnave.

"Well," said Petion, as naturally as possible, "give another explanation of the device if you can."

Barnave was silent. The device on the night before seemed sublime—now it was cruel.

The queen wiped a tear from her eyes.

The carriage continued to roll through the crowd. They soon came to the city of Dormans.

Nothing had been prepared for the royal family. It was forced to descend at an inn.

Either by order of Petion or because the inn was really full, meager accommodations were found for the royal family, who were installed in three garrets.

When he left the carriage, Charny, according to custom, wished to approach the king and queen to receive their orders. A glance at the queen, however, bid him keep away. Though he did not understand the motive, the count obeyed it.

Petion had gone into the inn and taken charge of the arrangements. He did not take the trouble to come downstairs again, and a waiter came to say that the rooms of the royal family were ready.

Barnave was in a terrible state; he felt the greatest anxiety to offer the queen his arm, but he feared lest she who had so insisted on etiquette in the case of Mme. de Noailles would apply the same ideas to him. He waited, therefore.

The king got out first, leaning on the arms of the two guardsmen, De Malden and De Valory.

The queen got out and reached her arms for the dauphin, but, as if the poor child felt how necessary the flattery was to his mother, he said:

"No; I will remain with my friend Barnave."

Marie Antoinette made a sign of assent, accompanied by a sweet smile. Barnave suffered Mme. Royale and Mme. Elizabeth to get out, and then followed with the dauphin in his arms.

The queen ascended the tortuous and difficult stairway leaning on her husband's arm. At the first story she paused, thinking that twenty-steps were high enough. The voice of the waiter, however, was heard, saying, "Higher! higher!"

She continued to ascend.

The sweat of shame hung on Barnave's brow. "What, higher?"

"Yes," said the waiter. "This story contains the dining-room and the rooms of the gentlemen of the assembly."

Barnave became dizzy. Petion had taken rooms for himself and his colleagues on the first story, and had sent the royal family to the garret. The young deputy, however, said nothing; hearing, however, without doubt, the first outbreak of the queen when she saw the rooms of the second story had been occupied by Petion, while she had been sent to the third, he placed the dauphin on the landing.

"Mother," said the young prince to his mother, "my friend Barnave is going."

"He is right," said the queen, glancing around the room.

A moment after they announced to their majesties that dinner was served. The king came down, and saw six covers on the table. He asked why there were six.

"One," said the waiter, "is for the king, one for the queen, one for Madame Elizabeth, one for Madame Royale, one for the dauphin, and another for Monsieur Petion."

"Why not for Messieurs Barnave and De Latour Maubourg?"

"They were prepared, sir, but Monsieur Barnave ordered them to be removed."

"And left Petion's?"

"Monsieur Petion insisted on it."

At this moment the grave, more than grave face—austere—of the deputy of Chartres appeared at the door.

The king acted as if he were not there, and said to the boy:

"I sit at the table only with my family, and with those we invite. We will not sit down."

"I was aware," said Petion, "that your majesty had forgotten the first article of the rights of man. I thought, though, you would pretend not to do so."

The king seemed not to hear Petion, as he had not to see him, and bid the boy take away the plate. The servant obeyed, and Petion left in a perfect rage.

"Monsieur de Malden," said the king, "close the door, that we may be alone." De Malden obeyed, and Petion heard the door closed behind him.

The king thus dined *en famille*. The two guardsmen served as usual.

When the supper was over, and the king was about to rise from his chair, the door of the room opened, and their majesties were requested by Barnave to take the rooms on the first floor instead of their own.

Louis XVI. and Marie Antoinette looked at each other. They thought to assume dignity and repulse courtesy from one of the delegates to punish another was best. That would have been the king's wish, but the dauphin ran forward, and cried:

"Where is my friend Barnave?"

The queen followed the dauphin, and the king the queen. Barnave was not there.

Twice or thrice on the road the queen had remarked the profusion of flowers in the gardens. The room of the queen was filled with the most magnificent spring flowers, and at the same time the open windows brought perfumes too strong to escape. The mousseline curtains only prevented any indiscreet eye from watching the august prisoners. This was Barnave's work.

In the meantime, what had become of Charny?

Charny, we have seen, in obedience to a sign from the queen, had withdrawn, and had not reappeared.

Charny, whose duty bound him to the king and queen, was pleased to receive this order, the cause of which he did not ask, for it gave him time to think. For three days he had lived so rapidly, he had, so to say, lived so much for others, that he was not sorry to leave their griefs and think of himself.

Charny was a noble of other days. He was, above all things, a man of family. He worshiped his brothers, the father of whom he really was. When George died, his grief had been intense; he had, however, been able to kneel by his body, in the dark and somber courtyard of Versailles, and expend his grief in tears; at least, he had another brother, Isidor, to whom all his affection took wing; Isidor, who, if possible, had become dearer to him than ever during the three or four months which preceded his departure, and since he had been the means of communication between himself and Andrée.

We have sought, if not to explain, at least to describe, the singular mystery of the separation of certain hearts which absence seemed to animate, rather than cool, and which, in separation, find a new ailment to sustain them. The less Charny saw of Andrée the more he thought of her, and to think of Andrée was to love her.

When he saw Andrée—when he was by her—he seemed to be by a statue of ice, which the least ray would melt, and which, when in the shade, feared, as a statue really of ice might, the approach of a ray. He was in contact with her cold, icy bearing, with her grave and veiled words, beyond which he saw nothing.

As soon, however, as he left her, distance produced its ordinary effect by extinguishing the two rare tints, and dimming the outlines, which were too defined. Then the cold bearing of Andrée became animated—her regular, measured voice became sonorous and animated—the drooping eye was uplifted, and shed a humid and devouring flame—a secret fire seemed to animate the statue, and through her alabaster bosom he saw the circulation of the blood and the beating of her heart.

Ah, in these moments of absence and solitude, Andrée was really the queen's rival. In the darkness of those nights, Charny fancied that the door of his room opened, and the tapestry uplifted, while, with murmuring lips, she approached his door with opened arms. Charny then opened his arms, and called to the sweet vision. Charny then sought to press the phantom to his heart, but, alas! it escaped him. He embraced only a void, and from his dream shrunk back into cold and sad reality.

Isidor then became dearer than George had ever been. Both had died for that fatal woman, for a cause full of abysses. For that same woman, into the same abyss, Charny, too, would certainly fall.

Well, for two days since the death of his brother—since the last embrace of his blood-stained arms—since he had pressed his pale lips, warm with his last sigh—M. de Choiseul had given him the papers he had found on Isidor's person, yet he had scarcely time to think of his own sorrow.

The signal of the queen to keep away he had received as a favor and accepted with pleasure. He at once sought for some place aside, where, in the reach of the royal family, if they should will, he might yet be alone with his sorrow and isolated with his tears. He found a garret vacant near the stairway, where De Malden and De Valory watched.

There he sat alone. He took the bloody papers from his pockets, the only relics of his brother. With his head resting on his hands—with his eyes fixed on the letters in which the thoughts of one no more continued to live—he suffered for a long time silent tears to course down his cheeks. He sighed, looked up, shook his head, and opened a letter. It was from Catherine.

For several months Charny had suspected a liaison between Isidor and the farmer's daughter. When at Varennes, Billot undertook to tell him all the details. Not until that time did he suffer it to assume its due importance in his mind. This importance was increased by reading the letter. Then he saw the mistress's claim was sanctified by that of the mother, and Catherine expressed her love in such simple terms that the whole life of the woman could not but be an expiation of the fault of the girl.

He opened a second and a third, all of which spoke of the future, of happiness, of maternal joy, of the fears of a loving heart, of the same regrets, griefs, and contrition.

All at once, amid these letters, one struck him. The writing was Andrée's. It was addressed to him. To the letter a sheet of paper, folded square, was fastened by a wax seal, which bore Isidor's arms.

This letter of Andrée's, addressed to him, and found among Isidor de Charny's papers, appeared so strange that he opened the note before he touched the letter itself. The note had been written by Isidor in pencil, beyond doubt, on some inn table, while his horse was being saddled, and was as follows:

"This letter is addressed, not to me, but to my brother, Count Olivier de Charny. It is from his wife, the countess. Should any misfortune befall me, the person who finds this paper is requested either to send it to the count, or return it to the countess.

"I received it from her with the request that, if in the enterprise he was engaged in, no accident should befall him, that I would restore the letter to the countess.

"If he were wounded severely, but without danger, to beg him to permit his wife to join him.

"If he were mortally wounded, to give him the letter, if he could read it, or, if not, to read it myself to him, that he might know the secret it contained.

"If this letter be sent to my brother, as doubtless it will be, he will act as his sense of propriety directs.

"I bequeath to his care Catherine Billot, who is living with my child in the Ville d'Avray.

"ISIDOR DE CHARNY."

At first the count seemed entirely absorbed by the letter. His tears, checked for a moment, began to flow again, until at last he looked at the letter of his wife. He looked long at it—kissed and placed it to his heart, as if it could thus communicate the secret it contained. He then read, twice or thrice, his brother's letter.

He shook his head and said, in a low tone:

"Have I the right to read it? I will, however, ask her to permit me to do so."

As if to encourage himself in this resolution, he said, two or three times, " No, I will not."

He did not; but day found him seated at the table, devouring with his eyes the letter which was yet humid with his kiss, so often had he pressed it to his lips.

All at once, amid the noise which always precedes a departure, he heard the voice of De Malden calling for the Count de Charny.

" Here I am," said the count.

Placing the letter of poor Isidor in his pocket, he kissed the sealed one, again placed it on his heart, and descended rapidly. He met Barnave on the stairway, who asked after the queen, and who was looking for De Valory to obtain orders in relation to the departure.

It was easy to see that Barnave had not slept any more than De Charny had.

As they entered the carriage, the king and queen saw that they had around them only the population of the city come to see them set out, and an escort of cavalry.

To this they were indebted to Barnave. He knew that on the previous day, the queen, forced to travel slowly, had suffered with heat, with dust, and been annoyed by the menaces uttered against the guardsmen and the faithful subjects who came to pay their respects to her. He pretended to have received news of an invasion, that De Bouillé had entered France with fifty thousand Austrians, and that every man with a gun, pike, scythe, or other weapon should march against him. The whole population heard this and retraced its steps.

In France, at that time, foreigners were really hated so intensely that all this animosity was transferred to the queen, merely because she was a stranger.

Marie Antoinette guessed whence came this new *kindness*; we used the word kindness, and there is no exaggeration in doing so. She glanced her thanks at Barnave.

Just as she was about to take her seat, she looked around for Charny. He was already in his seat; but, instead of sitting as he had done between the guardsmen, he insisted on yielding to De Malden the less dangerous place he had previously occupied. Charny longed for a wound to permit him to open the letter of Andrée. He did not see that the queen sought to catch his eye.

The queen sighed deeply. Barnave heard her. Anxious to know why, he paused on the steps.

"Madame," said he, "I observed yesterday that you were crowded in this berlin. One less will accommodate you. If you wish, madame, I will get into the next carriage with Latour Maubourg, or accompany you on horseback."

When Barnave made this offer, he would have given half of his life, and it was not long, to have it refused. It was:

"No," said the queen; "remain where you are."

The dauphin just then reached out his little hands to the young deputy: "My friend, Barnave, Barnave! You must not go."

Barnave, perfectly delighted, resumed his seat. When in the carriage the dauphin went from the queen's knee to his.

As the queen put him down she kissed his cheeks. The humid touch of her lips yet remained on the velvet cheek of the child. Barnave looked at them as Tantalus did at the fruits which hung before him.

"Madame," said he to the queen, "will your majesty deign to permit me to kiss the cheek of the prince, who, guided by the instinct of childhood, deigns to call me his friend?"

The queen smiled, and nodded an assent. The lips of Barnave were then imprinted on the trace which the lips of the queen had left so ardently that the child uttered a cry. The queen did not lose one item of all this.

Thanks to Barnave, the carriage now traveled two leagues an hour.

They paused at Château Thierry for dinner.

The house at which they stopped was near the river, in a charming position, and belonged to a wealthy female dealer in wood, who, on the previous night, had sent one of her clerks on horseback to offer hospitality to the delegates of the National Assembly and to the king and queen. Her offer was accepted.

The moment the carriage stopped, a crowd of eager servants pointed out to the august prisoners an altogether different reception from that they experienced at Dormans. The king, queen, Mme. Royale, and Mme. Elizabeth were each conducted to different rooms, as also were the dauphin and Mme. de Tourzel, and every arrangement made for all to be able to pay the most minute attention to their toilet.

Since she left Paris, the queen had met with nothing like this. The most delicate habits of the women were caressed by this aristocratic attention, and Marie Antoinette, who appreciated such cares, asked to be permitted to thank her hostess.

About four o'clock in the afternoon they reached Meaux, and stopped in front of an episcopal palace, which was occupied by a constitutional bishop who had taken the oaths. This they saw later, from the manner in which he received the royal family.

At first the queen was surprised at the somber appearance of the building she was about to enter. Nowhere could a princely or religious palace be found, its melancholy appearance more calculated to afford a shelter for the misery that sought for a refuge in it. She glanced across this lugubrious place, and finding it attuned to her own feelings, looked around for some arm to lean on while she entered the palace. Barnave was there alone.

The queen smiled. "Give me your arm, monsieur, and deign to be my guide through yon old palace."

Barnave approached rapidly, and gave his arm to the queen with mingled respect and anxiety.

She hurried Barnave through the rooms of the palace. One who looked after her floating form might imagine that she fled, for she looked neither to the right nor to the left. Almost panting, she at last paused in the chamber of the great preacher, and saw, to her surprise, a female picture before her. She looked up mechanically, and read these words: "Madame Henriette."

Barnave felt her tremble, though he did not know why. "Does your majesty suffer?" asked he.

"No," said the queen; "but that picture, Madame Henriette."

Barnave saw what passed in the poor woman's heart. "Yes," said he; "poor Madame Henriette of England, not the widow of the unfortunate Charles I., but the wife of the careless Duke of Orleans. Not she who had nearly died of cold in the Louvre, but the one who died at St. Cloud, and sent Bossuet this picture."

After a moment of hesitation, he said:

"I wish it were the portrait of the other."

"And why so?" asked the queen.

"Because certain mouths alone can give certain advice, and those mouths are those which death has closed."

"Can you not tell me, sir, what the mouth of the widow of Charles I. would advise?" asked the queen.

"If your majesty order, I will try."

"Do so."

"'Ah! sister,' that mouth would say, 'see you not the resemblance between our fates? I come from France, you from Austria. To the English, I was a stranger as you are to France; I might have given my husband good advice; but I kept silence or advised him wrongly; instead of uniting the people, I urged him to war, and brought him to march on London with the Irish Protestants; I not only kept up a correspondence with the enemy of England, but went twice into France to bring foreign soldiers into the kingdom. At last——'"

Barnave paused.

"Go on," said the queen, with a dark brow and compressed lip.

"Why should I continue, madame?" said he, shaking his head sadly. "You know the end of that bloody story as well as I do. Yes, I will continue and tell you what this portrait of Madame Henriette says to me, and you shall tell me if I am mistaken. 'The Scotch betrayed their king, the king was seized as he was about to cross to Paris. A tailor took him, a butcher conducted him to prison, and a publican presided at the court of justice, and that nothing might be wanting, a disguised hangman struck off the head of the victim before the judge who reviewed the whole trial.' This is what the portrait of Madame Henriette says to me; am I right? My God, I know that as well as any one; I know more; I know that nothing is wanting in the resemblance. We have our seller of beer of the faubourgs, only, instead of calling him Cromwell, we call him Santerre; we have our butcher; instead of Hamilton, he is called what? Legendre, I believe; instead of calling him Pridge, they call him—that I do not know. The man is so insignificant that I do not even know his name, nor do you either, I am sure; but ask him, he will tell you; the man, I mean, who conducted our escort, a peasant, a villain. This, this is what Madame Henriette tells me. And what is your answer?"

"I answer, poor, dear princess, it is not advice you give me, it is history—a history completed. Now, now, let me hear your advice."

"Oh! this advice, madame," said Barnave, "if you will only not refuse to follow it, shall be given by the living a well as the dead?"

"Living or dead, let those who ought to speak, speak. Who says if the advice is good we shall refuse to follow it?"

"Eh, mon Dieu! living or dead have one but advice to give."

"What?"

"Make the people love you."

"And it is an easy thing to make the people love you?"

"Ah! madame, this people are more yours than mine; as a proof, when you first came to France, they adored you."

"Oh, monsieur, you are speaking of that very fragile thing—popularity."

"Madame, madame," said Barnave, "if I, unknown, leaving an obscure sphere, have obtained this popularity, how much easier must it have been for you to preserve it, how much easier to reconquer it! But no," continued Barnave, growing animated, "no; what have you trusted your cause, the cause of monarchy, the most holy, most beautiful of causes, to? What voice, what arm has defended it? Never was seen such ignorance of the times, never such complete forgetfulness of the genius of France. I—I who have solicited the mission of going before you on your return, I whom you see, I who speak to you, how many times—mon Dieu! how many times have I been on the point of opening myself to you to devote myself to——"

"Silence!" said the queen; "some one comes; we will talk of all this, Monsieur Barnave. I am ready to see you, to hear you, and follow your counsels."

"Ah, madame! madame!" cried Barnave, transported.

"Silence!" repeated the queen.

"Your majesty is served," said the domestic, appearing on the threshold, whose step they had heard.

They passed into the salle à manger. The king had arrived there by another door. He had conversed with Petion during the time Barnave had been speaking to the queen, and he seemed in better spirits. The two guards waited, claiming, as always, the privilege of attending on their majesties. Charny, the most distant of all, was in the embrasure of a window.

The king looked round, and making good use of the time he was alone with his family, the two guards and the count, "Gentlemen," said he to the latter, "after supper I wish to speak with you. You will follow me, if you please, to my apartment."

The three officers bowed.

The dinner commenced as usual. But though dressed, this time, in the palace of one of the first bishops of the kingdom, the table was as badly served this evening at Meaux as it had been well served in the morning at the Château Thierry.

The king, as usual, had a good appetite, and eat a good dinner, in spite of the poorness of the fare. The queen only took two fresh eggs. The dauphin, who had been ill since the evening, had asked for some strawberries. Since the evening, all those to whom he had addressed himself had answered, "There are none!" or "We cannot find any!"

And yet on the road he had seen the children of the peasants eating quantities which they had gathered in the woods.

This desire, which the queen was unable to satisfy, had made her sad, so that when the child, refusing everything that was offered him, asked again for strawberries, the powerless mother's eyes filled with tears.

But at this moment the door opened and Barnave appeared with a plate of fresh strawberries in his hand.

"The queen will excuse me," said he, "if I enter thus, and the king will also be so good as to pardon me, I hope, but many times during the journey I have heard Monsieur le Dauphin ask for strawberries. I found this plateful on the bishop's table, and brought them for him."

"Thanks, my dear Barnave," said the young dauphin.

"Monsieur Barnave," said the king, "our dinner is not very tempting, but if you will take some you will give both the queen and myself great pleasure."

"Sire," said Barnave, "the invitation of the king is an order. Where does your majesty wish me to sit?"

"Between the queen and the dauphin," said the king.

Barnave sat himself down, mad at the same time with love and pride.

Charny looked on this scene without the least jealousy rising in his heart. Looking at the poor butterfly that was about to burn his wings at the royal light, he said:

"Another one lost! It is a pity; he is worth more than the rest."

And then, reverting to his incessant thought: "This letter! this letter!" murmured he. "What can there be in this letter?"

After supper, the three officers, according to the orders they had received, ascended to the chamber of the king.

When the young man had entered, "Monsieur de

Charny," said the king, "will you shut the door, so that we may not be disturbed? I have something of the utmost importance to communicate to you. Here, gentlemen, at Dormans, Monsieur Petion has proposed to me to let you escape in disguise; but the queen and I are both opposed to it, fearing lest it be a trap and that they would only separate you from us in order to assassinate you, or deliver you up to some military commission which would condemn you to be shot. We, the queen and I, have taken upon ourselves to reject this proposal, but to-day Monsieur Petion has returned to the charge, pledging his honor as a deputy, and I thought it best to let you know what he fears and what he proposes.

"Here are the words of Monsieur Petion, 'Sire, there is not, at the time of your re-entrance into Paris, any security for the three officers who accompany you. Neither I, Monsieur Barnave, nor Monsieur de Latour Maubourg can answer for their safety, even at the risk of our lives."

Charny looked at his two companions; a smile of contempt passed over their lips.

"Afterward," said the king, "hear what Monsieur Petion proposes. He proposes to procure for you three dresses as National Guards, to cause the doors to be left open for you to-night, and give each of you an opportunity to fly."

Charny consulted his companions again, but the same smile was the response.

"Sire," said he, addressing the king, "our days have been consecrated to your majesties, you have accepted them, and it will be easier for us to die for you than to be separated; do us the honor, then, to treat us to-morrow as you did yesterday, nor more, nor less. Of all your court, of all your army, of all your guards, you still have three faithful hearts left; do not take away the only glory of their ambition, that of being faithful to the end."

"It is well, gentlemen," said the queen, "we agree; only you understand from this moment that all is common with us; you are no longer servants, but friends. I will not ask you to give your names; I know them; but"—

she drew her tablets from her pocket—"but give me those of your fathers, your mothers, your brothers, and your sisters; it may happen that we may have the misfortune to lose you without sinking ourselves; then it shall be my duty to tell them of their misfortune to these cherished beings, and to offer at the same time to relieve it as much as lies in my power. Allons, Monsieur de Malden, allons, Monsieur de Valory, say boldly, in case of death, and we are all so near the reality that we ought not to shudder at the word, who are the relations, who are the friends whom you would recommend to my care?"

M. de Malden mentioned his mother, an elderly, infirm dame, dwelling on a small property in the neighborhood of Blois; M. de Valory recommended his sister, a young orphan, who was a pupil in a convent at Soissons.

Certainly the hearts of these two men were strong and full of courage, and yet, while the queen was writing down the addresses of Mme. de Malden and Mlle. de Valory, neither could restrain their tears.

The queen also was obliged to stop writing, and draw out her handkerchief and dry her eyes.

Then, when she had written the addresses down, she turned to Charny.

"Alas! Monsieur le Comte," said she, "I know that you have no one to recommend to my care; your father, your mother are dead, and your two brothers."

The queen's voice failed her.

"My two brothers have had the good luck to die for your majesty, madame," added Charny, "but the last one who died left a poor child, whom he confided to me by a testament I found upon him. This young girl he took from her own family, whence she can expect no pardon. As long as I live, neither she nor her child shall want for anything; but your majesty has said, with an admirable courage, that we are all confronting death, and if death should strike me, the poor girl and her child would be without resources. Madame, deign to put on your tablets the name of an unfortunate peasant, and if I have, like my two brothers, the happiness to die for my august master and noble mistress, bestow your gratitude on Catherine Billot and her child. They will both be found in the little village of Ville d'Avray."

Without doubt, the picture of Charny dying in his turn, as had already died his two brothers, was a spectacle too terrible for the imagination of Marie Antoinette, for she turned back with a feeble cry, let her tablets fall, and went tottering toward a chair.

The two guards started toward her, while Charny, taking up the royal tablets, wrote on them the name and address of Catherine Billot, and placed them on the chimney-piece.

The queen made an effort to recover herself. The young men, then, knowing the necessity there was for her being alone after such emotion, drew back in order to leave the room.

But she, stretching her hand toward them, "Gentlemen," said she, "you will not leave me without kissing my hand?"

The two guards advanced in the same order that they had given their names and addresses: M. de Malden first, then M. de Valory. Charny approached her last. The hand of the queen trembled as she awaited the kiss for which certainly she had offered the two others.

Next day, at the very moment of departure M. de Latour Maubourg and Barnave, ignorant, without doubt, of what had passed the previous evening betwixt the young men and the king, they renewed their arguments in favor of dressing these two young men as National Guards; but they refused, saying that their place was on the seat of his majesty's carriage, and that they could put on no other dress than that which they had dressed themselves in at his command.

Then Barnave wished that a plank, passing from the right to the left of the seat of the carriage, should be attached to that seat, so that two grenadiers could sit on this plank and guarantee, so far as in them lay, the safety of these two obstinate servants of the king.

At ten in the morning they quitted Meaux; they were

about to enter Paris, from which they had been absent five days.

Five days! What a great deal had passed in these five days!

Scarcely were they a league from Meaux than the cortège assumed an aspect more terrible than it ever had. All the population of the neighborhood of Paris joined it, Barnave had wished to make the postilions go at a trot, but the National Guard of Claye barred the road, presenting the points of their bayonets.

Soon the crowd was such that the carriages could hardly move. The insolent curiosity of the people followed the king and queen even into the corners of the carriage, where they had retreated. Men mounted up the steps and thrust their heads into the carriage; some hung on in front and others behind.

It was a miracle that Charny and his companions were not killed twenty times. The two grenadiers could not parry all the blows; they begged, they prayed, they commanded even in the name of the assembly; but their voices were lost in the midst of the tumult and noise.

An advance guard of more than two thousand men preceded the carriage; more than four thousand followed it. At its sides the crowd increased at every instant.

The carriage drove along under a burning sun, and through a cloud of dust, of which each particle seemed of glass. Two or three times the queen turned round and cried.

They reached Villette. The sidewalks were covered so thickly that it was impossible to move on them. The doors, the windows, and roofs of houses were crowded with spectators.

The trees bent down under the weight of their living fruit. Every one kept his hat on.

Since the previous evening, the following notice had been placed on the walls of Paris:

"If any one salutes the king, he will be beaten.

"If any one insults him, he shall be hung."

All this was so terrible that the commissioners did not

dare to pass through the Faubourg St. Martin. They resolved then to enter by the Champs Elysées, and the cortège going round Paris passed along the outer boulevards.

This would make the punishment three hours longer, and this punishment was so unsupportable that the queen begged they would take the shortest way, even if it were the most dangerous.

Twice had she attempted to draw down the blinds, and twice had the groanings of the crowd made her raise them.

On arriving at the barrier, the king and queen saw an immense mass of men, stretching as far as the eye could reach, silent, gloomy, threatening, with their hats on their heads. What was more dreadful, certainly more painful, than all this was a double rank of National Guards, with arms reversed in sign of grief, at the gates of the Tuileries.

It was a day of grief, great grief, mourning for a monarchy of seven centuries.

They took an hour to go from the Barrier to the Place Louis XV. The horses bent under their burdens—each carried a grenadier.

On debouching into the Place Louis XV. the king perceived that they had bandaged the eyes of his ancestor.

"What do they mean by that?" the king asked Barnave.

"I do not know, sire," answered the latter.

"I know," said Petion; "they wish to express the blindness of the monarchy."

During the progress, in spite of the escort, the commissioners, the placards forbidding the king being insulted under pain of being hung, the people three or four times broke through the line of grenadiers—a feeble barrier to this element to which God had forgotten to say, as to the sea, "Thus far and no further shalt thou go!"

Once the crowd pressed so that they broke one of the windows of the carriage.

"Why are you breaking the glass?" cried ten furious voices.

"Look, gentlemen," said the queen, "look at the state

my poor children are in." And wiping the perspiration from their faces, " We choke ! " said she.

" Bah ! " replied a voice, " that is nothing ; we shall choke you in another way. Be quiet ! "

And a stone broke the windows into shivers.

Yet in the midst of this terrible spectacle, some episodes would have consoled the king and queen if their minds had been as impressible for what is good for them as that which was evil.

In spite of the placard which forbade the king being saluted, M. Guilhenny, member of the assembly, uncovered when the king passed, and as they wished to make him put on his hat again, he said :

" Who dare reprove what I have done ? "

At the entrance of the bridge twenty deputies were assembled to protect the king and the royal family. Then came Lafayette and his staff.

" Oh ! Monsieur de Lafayette ! " cried the queen, as soon as she saw him, " save the guards ! " This cry was not useless, for danger was approaching, and the danger was great.

During this time, a scene in which there is some poetry was passing at the doors of the château.

Five or six ladies of the queen, who, after the flight of their mistress, had quitted the Tuileries, believing that the queen herself had left them forever, wished to re-enter to receive her majesty.

" Away ! " cried the sentinels, presenting the points of their bayonets at them. " Slaves of the Austrians ! " growled some, showing their poniards.

Then, crossing before the bayonets of the soldiers, and braving the threats of the women, the sister of Mme. Campan made some steps forward. " Listen," said she ; " I have been attached to the service of the queen since I was fifteen. I served her while she was powerful ; she is unhappy now—should I abandon her ? "

" She is right ! " cried the people. " Soldiers, let her pass ! "

And at this order, given by a master whom none could

resist, the ranks opened, and the ladies passed. A moment afterward the queen could see them waving their handkerchiefs from the windows.

And still the carriage went, pushing before it a crowd of people, and a cloud of dust, even as a vessel the waves of the ocean, and a cloud of foam.

At last the carriage stopped. They had arrived at the steps of the great terrace.

"Oh, gentlemen!" said the queen again, but this time addressing herself to Petion and Barnave, "the guards! the guards!"

"Have you no one, madame, to recommend more particularly to me than these gentlemen?" asked Barnave.

The queen looked at him fiercely with her clear eyes.

"No one!" said she.

And she allowed the king and the children to go out first.

The ten minutes which passed next—we do not except even those in going to the scaffold—were certainly the most unhappy of her life.

She was convinced—not that she should be assassinated—to die was nothing to her, but that she should either be delivered up to the people as a laughing-stock, or that she would be shut up in a prison, the door of which would only open through an infamous action.

As she put her foot on the steps of the carriage, protected by the arch of iron that was formed above her head, by the order of Barnave, the guns and the bayonets of the National Guards dazzled her so that she believed she was about to fall backward.

But as her eyes were about to close, in that last look of agony when one sees all, she thought she saw immediately in front of her that man—that terrible man—who at the Château de Taverney had in so mysterious a way raised for her the veil that shrouded the future—that man that she had only seen once since, in returning from Versailles on the 6th of October; that man, finally, who only appeared but to foretell great and sudden catastrophes, or at the very hour when these great catastrophes were accomplished.

After she was perfectly certain that she was not mistaken, she closed her eyes, which as yet had hesitated, strong in opposing realities; but inert and powerless before this sinister vision, she uttered a loud shriek and fell down.

It seemed to her as if the earth had gone from under her feet, and then the crowd, the trees, the burning sky, the immovable château seemed to turn with her; vigorous arms, however, seized her, and she felt herself borne off amid the cries, growlings, and noise. At this moment she believed she heard the voice of the guards who cried out, trying to turn the anger of the people upon them, hoping thus to turn it aside from its true inclination. For an instant she reopened her eyes and saw the unhappy occupants of the seat of the carriage, Charny pale and beautiful as ever, struggling alone against ten men, the lightning of the martyr in his eyes, the smile of disdain upon his lips. The looks of Charny were fixed upon the man who had raised her up from the midst of the crowd; she recognized with terror the mysterious being of Taverney and of Sèvres.

"You! you!" she cried, trying at the same time to repulse him with her rigid hands.

"Yes, I!" murmured he in her ear. "I have need of thee yet to push monarchy down into its last abyss, and so I save thee!"

This time it was more than she really could support; she uttered a piercing cry, and fainted.

During this time the crowd was trying to cut MM. de Charny, de Malden, and de Valory in pieces, and to carry Drouet and Billot in triumph.

CHAPTER XXXIV.

THE CHALICE.

WHEN the queen revived, she found herself in her bedchamber, in the palace of the Tuileries. Mme. de Misere and Mme. Campan, her two ladies-in-waiting, were at her side. Her first expressed wish was to see the dauphin.

He was in his chamber, and in his bed, watched by Mme. de Tourzel, his governess.

This assurance did not suffice the queen; she arose immediately, and, all in disorder as she was, she ran to the apartment of her son, where she remained a long time with her eyes fixed upon him, leaning on the post of the bedstead, and looking at him through her tears.

The terrible words that that mysterious being had said to her in his low but sweet voice murmured incessantly through her ear, "I have need of thee to push monarchy down into its last abyss, and so I save thee!"

Was it, then, true? Was it really she who was pushing monarchy toward the abyss?

It seemed that it must be so, since her enemies watched over her clay, leaving her to work out its destruction, which she was accomplishing better than themselves.

At last she shook her head, and returned to her own apartments. Barnave had been twice to bring her the news.

Since their arrival at the barrier, Charny and his companions had formed a plan. This plan had for its object the taking away, in relieving themselves from them, a part of the dangers too that threatened the king and queen. It was arranged, consequently, that as soon as the carriage stopped, one should cast himself to the right, the other to the left, and the one seated in the middle should go forward, dividing in this fashion the crowd of assassins, and making them follow in three opposite directions; perhaps they thought there might thus be a way left clear for the king and queen to reach their apartments.

We have said that the carriage stopped near the great terrace of the castle. The haste of the murderers was so great that in throwing themselves before the carriage two of them were dreadfully wounded. For an instant longer the two grenadiers stationed on the seat were able to guard the three young officers, but being themselves soon torn down to the ground, they left them to their own resources.

This was the moment that they selected. All three darted off but not so rapidly, nevertheless, as not to overturn five or six men who had mounted on the wheels and steps in order to tear them down from their seats. Then, as they had imagined, the anger of the people was divided in three directions.

When scarcely on the ground, M. de Malden found himself under the axes of two sappers. The two axes were raised, and only sought for means to strike him. He made a violent and rapid movement, by which he escaped from the two men who held him by the collar in such a manner that in a second he stood alone.

Then, crossing his arms, "Strike!" said he.

One of the axes remained raised. The courage of the victim paralyzed the assassin. The other fell, thirsting for blood, but in falling it encountered a musket, which turned it aside, and the point only reached M. de Malden's neck, making a slight wound.

Then the multitude opened, and he passed along with head hung down; but after a few paces he was received by a group of officers, who, wishing to save him, conducted him toward the National Guards, who had made the way safe for the royal family from the carriage to the château. At this moment General Lafayette perceived him, and pushing his horse toward him, he seized him by the collar and drew him toward his stirrups, so as in some measure to cover him with his popularity; but M. de Malden recognized him, and cried:

"Leave me, sir; give all your attention to the royal family, and leave me to the mob."

M. de Lafayette left him, perceiving a man who was seizing the queen, and rushed to her aid.

M. de Malden had been tossed about in every direction, attacked by some, defended by others, and at length had reached, covered with bruises, wounds, and blood, to the gate of the château; there an officer seeing him about to yield, seized him by the collar and drawing him toward him, cried:

"It would be a pity that such a miserable being should die so pleasant a death; it would be necessary to invent some punishment for a brigand of this kind. Deliver him up to me, then; I'll take him in charge."

And, continuing to insult M. de Malden, saying to him: "Come, rascal! come here! You'll have to deal with me now!" he had got him by this time drawn to a darker entrance into the palace, where he said to him: "Save yourself, sir, and pardon the stratagem I was obliged to use to get you out of the hands of these wretched fellows."

M. de Malden had glided up the staircases of the château, and had disappeared.

Something of the same kind had happened to M. de Valory; he had received two severe wounds upon his head. But at the very moment when twenty bayonets, twenty sabers, were raised to kill him, Petion had darted forward, and thrusting the assassins back with all his strength, "In the name of the National Assembly," he cried, "I declare you unworthy of the name of Frenchmen, if you do not disperse at once, and if you do not deliver up this man! I am Petion!"

And Petion, who, under a rude exterior, concealed great honesty of purpose, a courageous and loyal heart, presented, as he said these words, such a glorious appearance in the eyes of the murderers, that they had drawn back and abandoned M. de Valory. He sustained him, for, stunned by the blows he had received, M. de Valory could hardly support himself, and conducted him to the National Guards, and placed him under the care of the aide-de-camp, Mathieu Dumas, who answered for his safety and protected him to the château.

At this moment Petion had heard the voice of Barnave. Barnave was calling him to his assistance, finding he could not protect Charny. The count, seized by twenty men, cast down, dragged in the dust, had got up again, snatched a bayonet from a gun, and assailed the crowd around him. But he would have fallen in this unequal contest if Barnave, and then Petion, had not run to his assistance.

Half an hour had scarcely elapsed since the queen had been put in possession of these details, when the valet de chambre announced M. de Comte de Charny; and the latter appeared in the entrance of the doorway, lighted up by the reflection of the golden rays of the setting sun.

He, like the queen, had employed the time which had elapsed since his entrance into the château in removing the traces of his long journey and the terrible conflict in which he had been engaged. He had put on his old uniform—that of a captain of a frigate.

Never had he been so elegant, calm, and handsome; and the queen could scarcely believe that this was the same man who, but one short hour before, had barely escaped being cut to pieces by the people.

"Oh! monsieur," cried the queen, "it is necessary to tell you how uneasy I have been about you, and how I have sent in every direction to obtain some news of you."

"Yes, madame," said Charny, bowing, "but believe that I did not retire before being assured by some of your ladies, that you yourself were safe and well."

"They say you owe your life to Monsieur Petion and Monsieur Barnave, and do I owe to the last this new obligation?"

"It is true, madame, and I owe double thanks to Monsieur Barnave; for not wishing to leave me when I had reached my chamber, he has had the goodness to inform me that you were anxious about me on the way hither."

"About you, count? And in what way?"

"But in exposing to the king the inquietudes you chose to think your ancient friend would experience at my absence, I am far from believing like you, madame, in the earnestness of these inquietudes; but yet"—he stopped, for it seemed to him that the queen, already very pale, had become paler still.

"But—yet——" repeated the queen.

"Yet," continued Charny, "without accepting, in every sense, the permission which your majesty had the intention to offer to me, I believed that, assured as I am of the safety of the king and yourself, madame, and that of the august children, that it is right I should bear the news of my safety to Madame la Comtesse de Charny in person."

The queen placed her left hand on her heart, as if she wished to reassure herself that her heart had not ceased to beat, and in a voice nearly choked by the dryness of her throat, "But it is just, monsieur, that I am only surprised that you have waited so long before fulfilling this duty," said the queen.

The queen forgets that I pledged my word not to see the countess without her permission."

"And you have come to ask for this permission?"

"Yes, madame," said Charny, "and beg your majesty to give it me."

"Without which, in the anxiety you are in to see Madame de Charny, you will even go, will you not?"

"I believe that the queen is unjust to me," said Charny. "At the time I left Paris, I thought I was leaving it for a long time, if not forever. During the journey, I did all that it was in my power to do for the success of the journey. It was not my fault, that your majesty remembers, if I have not, like my brother, left my life at Varennes, been cut to pieces on the road or in the gardens of the Tuileries. If I had had the joy of conducting your majesty beyond the frontier or the honor of dying for you, I should have exiled myself or have died without seeing the countess. But I repeat to your majesty, on my return to Paris, I cannot put on the woman that bears my name—and you know how she bears it, madame—this mark of indifference not to give her some intelligence of myself; above all, my brother is no longer there to take my place. For the rest, Monsieur Barnave has deceived himself, or it was your majesty's opinion the day before yesterday."

"You love this woman, then, sir," said the queen, "about whom you make such a complaint so coolly?"

"Madame," said Charny, "it will soon be six years since you yourself, at a moment when I did not dream of such a thing, because for me there existed but one woman on earth, and this woman God had placed in so high a position that I could not obtain her—it is six years since you gave me in marriage Mademoiselle de Taverny, since you made her my wife. During those six years my hand has not twice touched hers, without necessity; I have not addressed her ten times, and ten times we have not certainly interchanged a look. My life has been occupied, filled, filled with another love, occupied with a thousand cares, a thousand labors. I have lived at the court, traversed the world—blindfolded on my part with the thread that the king has been willing to confide to me; and I have neither counted the days, months, nor years; the time has passed so much the more rapidly, owing to my being so much occupied with all these affections, cares, and intrigues I have just mentioned. But it has not been thus with the Countess de Charny, madame, since having had, without doubt, the misfortune of displeasing you, she has lived alone, isolated, lost in this pavilion of the Rue Coq-Heron; this solitude, this isolation, this abandonment she has accepted without complaint, because, with heart free from love, she feels not the want of the same affections as other women do; but what she will not accept, perhaps without complaint, will be my forgetfulness of duties and attentions so very simple."

"Eh, mon Dieu! monsieur," cried the queen, "you are pretty well occupied with what Madame de Charny will think or not think of you, according as she sees you or not. Before taking all this trouble, it would be as well, perhaps, to ascertain whether she thought of you at the time of your departure, or whether she dreams of you in the hour of your return."

"I do not know whether the countess dreams of the

hour of my return or not; but I am sure she thought anxiously of the hour of my departure."

"You saw her, then, before you left?"

"I had the honor to tell your majesty that I had never seen the Countess de Charny since I pledged my word to the queen not to see her."

"Then she has written to you?"

Charny kept silent.

"Let us see!" cried Marie Antoinette; "she has written to you. Say so if she has."

"She sent a letter for me to my brother Isidor."

"And you had read this letter? What did she say, what could she write? Ah! she has spoken against me? Well, in this letter she says? Speak, then; you see I am impatient!"

"I cannot repeat to your majesty what she has said to me in this letter. I have not read it."

"You have torn it up!" cried the queen, joyously. "You threw it into the fire without reading it! Charny, Charny, if you have done so, you are the most loyal of men, and I am wrong, and have lost nothing!"

And the queen stretched out both her arms toward Charny, to call him to her. But Charny remained in his place.

"I have not torn it, I have not thrown it in the fire."

"But then," said the queen, falling again into her chair, "how is it that you had not read it?"

"The letter was not to have been given to me by my brother unless I was mortally wounded. Alas! it was not I who was about to die; it was he. When he was dead, they brought me his papers; among these papers were the letters of the countess and this note. Take it, madame."

And Charny presented to the queen the billet written by Isidor, and annexed to the letter.

During this scene which we have just related, night had come on.

"Lights!" said she, "at once."

The valet de chambre went out; there was a moment

of silence, when nothing was heard but the loud breathing of the queen, and the beatings of her heart.

The valet de chambre entered with two candelabra, which he placed on the chimneypiece.

The queen would not even give him time to retire, and while he withdrew and shut the door, she approached the chimneypiece with the billet in her hand. But she looked at the paper twice without seeing anything.

"Oh!" murmured she, "it is not paper, it is flame." And passing her hand over her eyes, as if to restore to them the faculty of seeing, which they seemed to have lost, "My God! my God!" said she, stamping her foot with impatience.

At length, by strength of will, her hand ceased to tremble, and her eyes began to see. She read in a rough voice, and which had nothing in common with her usual voice:

"This letter is addressed, not to me, but to my brother, Comte Olivier de Charny; it is written by his wife, the Countess de Charny."

The queen stopped some seconds, and then continued:

"If anything should happen to me, those into whose hands this paper may fall are begged to hand it to the Comte de Charny, or send it to the countess."

The queen stopped a second time, shook her head, and continued:

"Add to this the following recommendation."

"Ah! the recommendation!" murmured the queen; and she passed her hand again over her eyes.

"If the enterprise in which the count is engaged should succeed without any accident, return the letter to the countess."

The voice of the queen panted more and more as she read.

She continued:

"If he should be grievously wounded, but without danger of death, beg him to accord the favor to his wife of answering it."

"Oh! it is clear!" lisped the queen. Then, in a voice nearly unintelligible:

"Lastly, if he should be so severely wounded that death is certain, give him this letter, and, if he cannot read it himself, read it for him, that before he expires he may know the secret that it contains."

"Well, do you deny it now?" cried Marie Antoinette, in gazing at the count with a vexed look.

"What?"

"My God! that she loves you?"

"Who? I? The countess loves me? What do you say, madame?" cried Charny, in his turn.

"Oh! unhappy one that I am, I speak the truth!"

"The countess loves me? I? Impossible!"

"And why? I love you well; I——"

"But if the countess has loved me for six years, the countess would have told me—would have let me perceive it."

The moment had come for poor Marie Antoinette in which she suffered so much, that she felt the need of driving away, like a poniard, the sufferings from her heart.

"No!" cried she, "she could not let you perceive anything. She would not say anything to you; but if she had said nothing, let you perceive nothing, it was because she knew well she could not be as your wife."

"The Countess de Charny could not be as my wife?" repeated Olivier.

"It was," said the queen, intoxicated more and more with her own grief, "it was that she knew well that there was between you a secret that would destroy your love."

"A secret that would destroy our love?"

"It was that she knew well, at the very moment she spoke, you would despise her."

"I despise the countess?"

"In proportion as we despise the young girl who is a woman without spouse, a mother without husband."

It was Charny's turn to become pale, and to seek a shelter behind the nearest chair.

"Oh, madame, madame," said he, "you have said either too much or too little, and I have the right to ask an explanation of you."

"An explanation, monsieur, of me—of the queen—an explanation?"

"Yes, madame," said Charny, "and I demand it."

At this moment the door opened.

"Who wants me?" asked the queen, impatiently.

"Your majesty," replied the valet de chambre, "said that you always wished to see Doctor Gilbert."

"Well?"

"Doctor Gilbert has the honor to present his humble respects to your majesty."

"Doctor Gilbert!" said the queen. "Are you sure it is Doctor Gilbert?"

"Yes, madame."

"Oh! let him come in! let him come in, then!" said the queen.

Then, turning toward Charny: "You wish for an explanation about Madame de Charny," said she, raising her voice. "Look; ask Doctor Gilbert for an explanation; he is the best person to give it to you."

During this time Gilbert had entered. He had heard the words Marie Antoinette had spoken, and he remained immovable at the threshold of the door.

As for the queen, throwing back to Charny the note of his brother, she made some steps toward her dressing-room; but, more rapid than she was, the count barred the passage and seized her by the robe.

"Pardon, madame," said he; "but this explanation—it ought to take place before you."

"Monsieur," said Marie Antoinette, with set teeth, "you forget, I believe, that I am the queen!"

"You are an ungrateful friend who calumniates her friend; you are a jealous woman who insults another woman, the wife of a man who, for the last three days, has risked his life twenty times for you; the wife of Count de Charny. It is before you who have calumniated her, who have insulted her, that justice shall be done her. Sit down then there, and listen!"

"Well, let it be so!" said the queen. "Monsieur Gilbert," continued she, making a bad attempt to smile, "you see what monsieur wishes?"

"Monsieur Gilbert," said Charny, in a tone full of courtesy and dignity, "you hear what the queen orders?"

Gilbert stepped forward and looked sadly at Marie Antoinette. "Oh, madame, madame!" murmured he.

Then, turning toward Charny: "Monsieur le Comte, what I have to tell you is the shame of a man—the glory of a woman. An unhappy man, a peasant, loved Mademoiselle de Taverney. One day he found her—she had fainted—and without respect for her youth, her beauty, her innocence, the miserable being violated her; and it was then that the young girl was a woman without spouse—mother without husband. Mademoiselle de Taverney is an angel. Madame de Charny is a martyr!"

Charny wiped away the perspiration that trickled down his face.

"Thanks, Monsieur Gilbert!" said he.

Then, turning to the queen: "Madame," said he, "I was ignorant that Mademoiselle de Taverney had been so unfortunate—I was ignorant that Madame de Charny was so respectable—without which, I beg you will believe me, I should not have been six years without falling on my knees before her, and adoring her as she deserves to be adored."

And, bowing before the stupefied queen, he left, without the unhappy woman daring to make a movement to detain him. He heard only her cry of grief, as she saw the door shut between him and her.

Then she understood that it was upon this door that the hand of the demon of jealousy would come and write, as upon that of hell, these terrible words:

"LASCIATE OGNI SPERANZA!"

CHAPTER XXXV.

GIVE LILIES.

LET us tell what became of the Countess de Charny, while the scene we have described took place between the count and queen—the scene which we have described, and which crushed so painfully a long series of griefs.

In the first place, to us who know the secrets of her heart, it is easy to see what she suffered on account of the absence of Isidor.

She trembled because the great project would be either an escape or a failure. If it succeeded she knew well enough the devotion of the count to his sovereigns, to be aware that, when they were in exile, he would never quit them. If it failed, she knew Charny's courage well enough to be sure that he would struggle to the last moment, as long as hope remained, and even when it was gone, against any imaginable obstacles.

As soon as Isidor had bid her adieu, the countess had her eye constantly open to seize every light, her ear constantly attentive to perceive every noise.

On the next day, she, with the rest of the people of Paris, learned that the king and royal family had left Paris during the night. No accident had made the departure remarkable. As there was a flight, Charny knew of it, and had therefore left her.

She uttered a profound sigh—knelt and prayed for a happy return.

Then for two days all Paris remained mute and silent, and without an echo. On the morning of the third day, an echo pervaded all Paris. The king had been arrested at Varennes.

M. Bouillé, it was said, had followed and attacked the royal escort, and after the contest had retired, leaving the king in the hands of the people.

Charny had participated in this contest, she knew. He would be the last to retire, if he had not remained on the field of battle.

Then it was said that one of the three guardsmen, who had accompanied the king, had been killed.

Then the name transpired ; but none knew if it were Count Isidor or Olivier de Charny.

For the two days during which this question was undecided, she suffered inexpressible anguish.

At last the return of the king and royal family was announced for Saturday, the 26th.

Calculating time and space by the ordinary measure, the king should be in Paris before noon. If he came by the most direct route, he would enter Paris through the Faubourg St. Martin.

At eleven o'clock, Mme. de Charny, in a costume of the greatest simplicity, and with a veil over her face, went to the barrier. She waited until three.

At that hour, the first waves of the crowd passing before her announced that the king was going around Paris, and would enter the city through the Champs Elysées.

She had to pass through the whole city, and pass through it on foot. None dared to drive through the compact crowd which filled the streets. Never, since the taking of the Bastile had the boulevard been so encumbered.

Andrée did not hesitate, but crossing the Champs Elysées, was one of the first to reach the barrier. She waitedthere three hours—three mortal hours !

At last the cortége appeared ; we have described how and in what order it marched. Andrée saw the carriage pass. She uttered a cry of joy, for she saw Charny on the seat.

A cry which seemed an echo to her own, had it not been a cry of grief, replied. Andrée hurried toward the side whence came the cry. A young girl was struggling in the arms of three or four persons who sought to assist her. She seemed the prey of violent despair.

Perhaps Andrée would have bestowed more attention to the young girl if she had not heard muttered around her all possible imprecations against the three men who sat on the royal coach.

The wrath of the people would be expended on them. They would be the rams to replace the great royal sacrifice ; they would be torn to pieces as soon as the carriage approached and halted. Charny was one of the three men.

Andrée resolved to find out what she should do in order to enter the garden of the Tuileries. She had to pass around the whole crowd to go to the bank of the river—that is to say, along the Quai de la Conference, and, if possible, reach that of the Tuileries.

After many attempts, and running the risk of being crushed twenty times, she passed the gate. Such a crowd, however, pressed around the place where the carriage was to stop that she could not reach the front rank. Andrée thought that from the terrace above the water she would be able to see everything, though the distance would be too great to enable her to distinguish anything certainly and surely. It matters not ; she would see and hear as well as she could ; and that was better than not seeing or hearing at all.

She then ascended the terrace on the bank of the river. She could see the seat of the coach, Charny and the two guardsmen.

Had she but known that at that very moment Charny pressed her letter to his bosom, and his thought offered her the last sigh which he would ever exhale !

At last the carriage paused, amid cries, howlings, and clamors. Almost immediately there was a loud cry around the carriage, a great motion and tumult. Bayonets, pikes, and sabers were lifted ; one might almost think a harvest of steel rising after a storm. The three men were thrown from the seat, and disappeared as if they had been cast into a gulf. There was such an excitement in this multitude that its outer ranks were pushed back and broke against the wall sustaining the terrace.

Andrée was wrapped in a veil of anguish ; she saw and heard nothing. She cast herself panting, with outstretched arms and inarticulate sounds, amid the terrible concert composed of maledictions, cries, and blasphemies.

She could no longer render an account of what passed; the earth turned, the heaven became red, a murmur like that of the sea sounded in her ears. She then fell, half fainting, and seeing that she lived because she suffered.

An impression of freshness recalled her to consciousness. A woman applied a handkerchief dipped in the water of the Seine to her brow, while another applied a bottle of Seine water to her face.

She remembered that the second woman was the one whom, like her, she had seen dying at the barrier, and by the unknown bonds of grief seemed attached to her.

When she returned to herself, the first words were: "Are they dead?"

Compassion is quick-sighted. Those who surrounded Andrée at once understood that she referred to the three men, the life of whom had been so cruelly menaced.

"No," said they, "they are saved."

"All three?"

"Yes."

"Oh, Lord be praised! Where are they?"

"They are at the palace."

"At the palace? Thanks."

And lifting herself up, shaking her head with a wild eye, the young woman left by the gate on the bank to re-enter by the wicket of the Louvre.

She fancied that on that side the crowd would be less compact, and she was right. The Rue des Orties was almost empty. She crossed the corner of the Place du Carrousel, and hurried to the gate. The porter knew the countess, for he had seen her go in and out during the two or three days after the return to Versailles. He had then seen her leave to return no more, on the day she had taken Sebastian away.

The keeper of the gate promised to obtain information for her. Passing through the interior corridors, he soon reached the center of the castle. The three officers were saved, and M. de Charny had gone safely to his room. A quarter of an hour after he left his room in the uniform of a naval officer, and had gone to the queen where he was.

Andrée gave her purse to the man who had given her such good news, and panting and overcome, asked for a glass of water.

Charny was saved.

She thanked the good man, and returned to the Rue Coq-Heron. When there, she had sunk, not on a chair or a sofa, but on her prie-dieu.

She did not pray with her mouth. There are moments when gratitude to God is so great that words fail us. Then the arms, eyes, body, and heart all rush to Heaven.

She was plunged in that happy ecstasy when she heard the door open; she returned slowly, not understanding this earthly noise which came to seek her in the depth of her reverie.

Her femme de chambre was standing lost in obscurity. Beside the woman stood a shadow of undecided form, but to which her instinct at once gave a name.

"Monsieur le Comte de Charny," said the femme de chambre.

Andrée wished to look up, but her strength failed her, and she sunk again on the cushion, and half turning round rested her arms on the front of the prie-dieu.

Andrée made a sign which the woman understood. She got out of the doorway to suffer Charny to pass, and closed the door.

Charny and the countess were alone.

"They told me that you had come home, madame; am I not indiscreet in having followed you so closely?"

"No," said she, with a trembling voice, "no, sir; you are welcome. I was so uneasy that I went out to ascertain what was going on."

"You went out long since?"

"In the morning. I went first to the Barrière St. Martin, and to the Champs Elysées; there I saw—I saw ——" She hesitated. "I saw the king and royal family; I saw you, and I was for the time comforted; I was afraid that you would be in danger in your descent from the carriage. I then went into the garden of the Tuileries. Oh! I thought I would die."

"Yes," said Charny, "the crowd was very great; you must have been almost crushed and stifled."

"No," said Andrée, shaking her head; "it was not that; at last I inquired and learned that you were saved. I returned here, and you see I was thanking God on my knees."

"As you are on your knees, madame, I beg you will not rise until you have prayed God for my poor brother."

"Isidor! Ah!" said Andrée, "then it was he, poor young man." She let her head fall on her two hands.

Charny advanced, and looked with an expression of deep sadness and melancholy at the chaste and tearful creature. His heart was filled with commiseration, mildness, and pity. He felt, also, something like a repressed desire to explain himself. Had not the queen said, or, rather, suffered to escape her, that she loved him?

Her prayer being finished, the countess turned around.

"He is dead!" said she.

"Dead! yes, madame, like poor George, for the same cause, and discharging the same duty."

"And amid the great grief caused by a brother's death, you had yet time to think of me?" said Andrée, in a voice so feeble that her words were scarcely intelligible.

"Madame," said he, "did you not charge my brother with a commission for me—with a letter?"

"Monsieur!" said Andrée, shuddering.

"After the death of poor Isidor, his papers were given to me, and among them your letter."

"You read it?" said Andrée, hiding her face in her hands. "Ah!"

"Madame, I was to know its contents only in case I was wounded, and you see I am safe and sound."

"Then the letter?"

"Is, here, untouched, as you gave it to Isidor."

"Oh!" murmured Andrée, taking the letter, "you have acted well, or, rather, cruelly."

Charny opened his arms, and took the hand of Andrée

with both of his. Andrée sought to withdraw hers. Charny insisted, and uttered a sigh almost of terror. Powerless, however, herself, she left her damp, humid hands in Charny's.

Then, embarrassed, not knowing how to extricate herself from the glance of Charny, which was fixed on her as she knelt at the prie-dieu, she said:

"Yes, I understand, and you have come to give me the letter."

"For that purpose, madame, and also for another; I have, countess, to beseech you to pardon me."

Andrée's heart beat quickly; it was the first time he had preceded the word countess by madame.

He pronounced the whole phrase with an intonation of infinite sweetness.

"Pardon from me, count! Why, for what?"

"For the manner I have acted toward you for six years."

Andrée looked at him with great surprise. She said:

"Did I ever complain, monsieur?"

"No, madame; because you are an angel."

Andrée's eyes became suffused in spite of herself, and the tears quivered on her lids.

"You weep, Andrée?" said Charny.

"Ah!" said Andrée, bursting into tears, "forgive me, sir, but I am not used to hear you speak thus."

She threw herself on a sofa and hid her face. After a moment she withdrew her hands, shook her head, and said:

"Really, I am mad!"

She paused; while her hands were before her face, Charny had knelt before her.

"You at my feet? you on your knees to me?" said she.

"Did I not say, Andrée, that I had come to beg your pardon?"

"On your knees! at my feet!" said she, as if she would not believe the impression received from her own senses.

"Andrée," said Charny, "you withdrew your hands."

He reached out his hand again to the young woman. She shrunk back, however, with an expression of terror.

"What means this?" said she.

Andrée placed her hand on her heart, and uttered a cry. Then, rising, as if a spring had been beneath her feet, and clasping her temples in her hands, she said:

"He loves me! he loves me!" repeated she; "it is impossible!"

"Say, Andrée, that it is impossible for you to love me, but not for me to worship you."

She looked down on Charny, as if to be sure that he spoke the truth; the great black eyes of the count told much more than his words had said. Andrée, who might have doubted his words, could not doubt his looks.

"Ah!" murmured she, "my God! my God! was ever any one so unhappy as I am?"

"Andrée," said Charny, "tell me that you love me, or, if not, say at least that you do not hate me."

"I! hate you?" said Andrée.

And then her calm, limpid eyes suffered a double light to escape them.

"Oh, sir, you would not be unjust—to take for hatred the feeling you inspire me with."

"If it be not hatred, Andrée, if it be not love, what is it?"

"It is not love, for you will not suffer me to love you. Did you not hear me say just now that I was the most unfortunate being alive? And why is it not permitted you to love me? Did you not hear me say just now that I was the most unfortunate woman on earth?"

"And why may you not love me, Andrée, when I love you with all my heart?"

"Ah! I would not have you do that, because I dare not say why," said Andrée, wringing her hands.

"But," said Charny, speaking in a yet kinder tone, "if what you will not and cannot, another person has told me."

Andrée placed her hands on Charny's shoulder.

"Ah!" said she, frightened.

"What if I knew?" said Charny.

"My God!"

"And if, on account of that very misfortune, I thought you more interesting, if that very misfortune made you more attractive, and induced me to tell you that I loved you?"

"If so, sir, you would be the noblest and most interesting of men."

"I love you, Andrée," said Charny. "I love you! I love you!"

"Oh!" said Andrée, looking to heaven, "I did not know there could be such joy in the world!"

"But tell me, Andrée, that you love me!" said Charny.

"No, no; I dare not; but read this letter, which was to be given only at your death."

She gave him the letter he had returned to her.

Andrée covered her face with her hands, while Charny broke the seal of the letter, read the first lines, uttered a cry, and then clasped Andrée to his heart.

"Since the day you saw me, for six years. How, oh, blessed creature! can I atone for the sufferings I have caused you?"

"My God!" said Andrée, bending like a reed beneath the weight of such happiness, "if this be a dream, let me never awake, or die when I do."

And now let us forget the happy to return to those who suffer, who struggle, or who hate, perhaps, their evil fate, will forget them, as we have.

CHAPTER XXXVI.

THE GROUND FLOOR OF THE TUILERIES.

BEHIND a door of a dark room opening on a dark corridor, on the ground floor of the Tuileries, a woman stood, with a key in her hand, apparently fearful lest her step should awaken an echo.

Did we not know this woman, it would be difficult for us

to recognize her, for, besides the obscurity, which even in the broad daylight, pervades a corridor, it is now night, and either intentionally or not, the wick of the only lamp has almost disappeared, and seems ready to become extinct.

The second room of the suite only is lighted, and the woman leans against the door nearest the corridor.

Who is that woman?

Marie Antoinette.

Whom does she wait for?

Barnave.

Proud child of Marie Theresa, who would have told you, on the day of your arrival in France, when you were crowned Queen of France, that a time would come when, hidden behind the door of your chamber-maid, you would await with anxiety the coming of a little Grenoble lawyer, after having caused Mirabeau to wait so long and deigned to receive him only once?

Let us not, however, be mistaken, for merely from motives of policy did you receive Barnave; your suspended respiration, your nervous motions, your trembling hand cannot be referred to the heart. Pride alone is concerned.

We say pride, for in spite of the countless persecutions to which the king and queen have been subjected during their return, it is clear that life is sweet, and that the question is summed up in these few words: "Will the fugitives lose the remnant of their power, or will what they retain be swept away?"

Barnave was coming to tell the queen all that had taken place on the 5th.

All seemed to anticipate some great event.

The king also had awaited Barnave in the second of Mme. Campan's rooms, and had been informed of Gilbert's coming; and to hear more at ease, had retired to his room, leaving Barnave with the queen.

About nine, a step was heard in the passage, and a voice heard to exchange a few words with the sentinel, and a young man appeared at the end of the corridor in the uniform of a subaltern of the National Guard. It was Barnave.

The queen opened the door, into which Barnave glided, after having very carefully looked behind it.

The door closed, and without a word having been exchanged, the sound of the turning of a key in the wards of the lock was heard.

The heart of each beat with equal violence, though from very different sentiments. The heart of the queen from the hope of vengeance, that of Barnave from the desire of love.

The queen hurried into the second room, in search, so to say, of light. When there she sunk on a chair.

Barnave paused at the door and looked round the room. He expected to find the king, who had been present at all the other interviews of the queen and himself.

The room was unoccupied except by the pair; and for the first time since his fall in the garden of the palace of the Bishop of Meaux, he was *tête-à-tête* with Marie Antoinette.

"Monsieur Barnave," said the queen, "I have been waiting two hours for you."

"I wished, madame, to come at seven; then, however, it was too early, and I met Monsieur Marat; how can such a man dare to approach your palace?"

"Monsieur Marat!" said the queen, as if she looked into her memory. "Is he not a man who writes against us?"

"Who writes against everybody. His viper's eyes followed me until I disappeared behind the grating of the Feuillants."

"I heard that to-day we won a victory in the assembly?"

"Yes, madame, we won a victory in the assembly, but were defeated in the Jacobins."

"My God!" said the queen, "I do not understand this. I thought the Jacobins belonged to you, to Lameth and Dupont, and did what you wished?"

Barnave shook his head sadly. "Once," said he, "that was the case; a new spirit, however, now influences the assembly."

"Orleans?" asked the queen.

"Yes, madame, the present danger is from that source."

"Danger? Have we not avoided it by to-day's vote?"

"Understand me, madame; for to understand our danger it is necessary to avoid it. The vote of to-day declares, 'if a king retracts his oath, if he attacks or neglects to defend his people, he abdicates and becomes a simple citizen, liable to be accused for all that occurs after his abdication.'"

"Well," said the queen, "the king will not retract his oath, he will not attack his people, and if they be attacked, he will defend them."

"Yes, madame; but this vote leaves an opening to the Orleanists and revolutionists. The assembly did not act against the king, but merely took preventive measures against a second desertion, leaving the first. Do you not know what Laclos, the agent of the duke, proposed this evening at the Jacobins?"

"Something terrible! What else could be expected from the author of 'Liaisons Dangereuses'?"

"He requested that a petition be circulated in Paris, and throughout France, in favor of deposing his majesty, and promised to obtain ten million signatures."

"Ten millions! Good God! are we so hated that ten million Frenchmen would reject us?"

"Madame, majorities are easily had."

"Was the proposition successful?"

"It created some discussion. Danton sustained it."

"Danton? I thought he was our friend. Montmorin speaks of a place of *avocat* to the king, given to or sold to this man."

"Montmorin is deceived. If Danton belongs to any one, it is to the Duke of Orleans."

"And did Robespierre speak? He, I am told, is beginning to acquire great influence."

"Yes; he did not approve of the petition, but of an address to the people of the province."

"But Robespierre must be disposed of, as he begins to acquire such influence."

"No one has or can ruin him, madame. He is for himself. He has some idea, some utopia, a phantom, an ambition, perhaps."

"What ambition can we not gratify? Does he wish to be rich?"

"No."

"To be minister?"

"He may wish to be more."

The queen looked at Barnave with terror.

"It ever seemed to me that the post of minister was the highest to which any of my subjects could pretend."

"If Robespierre looks on the king as deposed, he no longer regards himself as a subject."

"What does he desire, then?" asked the queen, with terror.

"These are times, madame, when men aspire to new political titles in place of old ones which have been effaced."

"Oh, yes! I can understand that the Duke of Orleans aspires to be regent. His birth calls him to such a post; but a little country lawyer——"

The queen forgot Barnave occupied exactly that position.

Barnave did not notice the slight, either because he did not remark it or had the courage to pretend not to do so.

"Marius and Cromwell, madame, emerged from the people."

"Marius and Cromwell—alas!" said the queen; "when I heard those names, in my childhood, I never fancied they would be so terrible in my ears. But let us return to the subject we have left. Robespierre, you say, opposed the scheme of Laclos, which Danton sustained."

"Yes; but at that moment there came in a band of the every day bathers of the Palais Royal, a troop of women controlled by Laclos, and the vote was not only passed, but at eleven to-morrow the Jacobins are to hear the petition at the Palais Royal, and will proceed to sign it on the altar of the country, thence to be sent to the provincial societies, to be signed by them."

"And who is to draw up the petition?"

"Danton, Laclos, and Brissot."

"Three enemies!"

"Yes, madame."

"But what are the constitutionalists about?"

"Well, madame, they have resolved to-morrow to risk all for all."

"They cannot act with the Jacobins."

"Your wonderful comprehension of men and things, madame, shows you the state of affairs."

"Yes, guided by Dupont and Lameth, your friends will to-morrow leave your enemies. They will oppose the Feuillants to the Jacobins."

"What are the Feuillants? Excuse me, but so many new words are introduced into politics, that each demands a question."

"Madame, the Feuillants is a great building near the riding-school, and, therefore, near the assembly, and which gives the name to the terrace of the Tuileries."

"Who compose the club?"

"Lafayette and the National Guards—Bailly and the municipality."

"Lafayette? Think you you can rely on him?"

"I believe him sincerely devoted to the king."

"Devoted as the woodman is to the oak he fells. Bailly—go on; I have no cause of complaint against him. I will even say more: he gave me the name of the woman who informed of our intention to escape. But Lafayette?"

"Your majesty will have an opportunity of judging."

"Yes, it is true," said the queen, looking painfully back, "Versailles! Well, this club—what will it propose? what will it do? what is its power?"

"An enormous power, since, as I told you, it controls the National Guard, the municipality, and a majority of the assembly which vote with us. What will remain to the Jacobins? Five or six deputies, perhaps Robespierre, Petion, Laclos, the Duke of Orleans, three heterogeneous elements, who will only be able to disturb the new members, and a herd of noisy barkers who will make a noise, but who have no influence."

"I trust so. But what will the assembly do?"

"Reprove Bailly for his hesitation and delay. The consequence will be that Bailly, like a good clock being well wound up, will keep time. But I see it is time for me to retire, yet it seems that I have much more to tell your majesty."

"I, Monsieur Barnave, can say nothing more than tell you how grateful we and our friends are for your goodness in exposing yourself to so much danger for us."

"Madame, danger is a game by which I profit, whether beaten or successful in it, if the queen but reward me with a smile."

"Alas! sir," said the queen, "I have forgotten how to smile almost. But you have been so kind, that I will try to recall the time when I could, and promise that my first smile shall be yours."

Barnave placed his hand on his heart and bowed. He then begged to retire.

"When shall I see you again?"

"To-morrow," said Barnave, seeming to calculate, "is the petition, and the first vote on it. In the evening, madame, I will come to tell you what has taken place in the Champs de Mars."

He left.

The queen returned sadly to the king, whom she found pensive as herself. Dr. Gilbert had left him, and given him the same information Barnave had imparted to the queen.

They had but to exchange a glance to see that each saw how somber things were.

The king had just written a letter. Without speaking, he gave it to the queen. It was one to Monsieur, authorizing him to ask the intervention of Austria and Prussia.

"Monsieur," said the queen, "has done me much harm, hate, and would do more wrong; as he has the king's confidence, however, he has mine."

Taking a pen, she heroically wrote her name by the side of the king.

Let us now follow Dr. Gilbert to the Tuileries.

The queen expects him, and as he is not Barnave, she is not in Mme. Campan's room on the ground floor, but in her own apartments, seated on a chair, with her head leaning on her hand.

She awaits Weber, whom she sent to the Champs de Mars upon hearing a discharge of musketry there which caused her great uneasiness. The journey to Versailles had taught her much; until then the revolution had seemed to her only a maneuver of Pitt and an intrigue of Orleans. She thought Paris immoral and under bad conduct, but used to say, "the honest country." She had seen the country; it was more revolutionary than Paris.

The assembly was old, decrepit, and stupid in adhering to the promises Barnave had made in its name. Besides, was it not about to die? The embraces of a dying thing are not healthy.

The queen waited for Weber most anxiously. The door—she looked anxiously to it; but instead of the broad Austrian figure of her foster-brother, she saw the austere face of Gilbert.

The queen did not like him; for his royalism was accompanied by such well-defined constitutional theories that she thought him a republican; she had, though, a certain respect for him. She would send for him neither in a physical nor moral crisis, but on this occasion she felt his influence.

As she saw him she trembled. They had not met since the return from Varennes. "Is it you, doctor?" murmured she.

Gilbert bowed. "Yes, madame, it is I. I knew that you expected Weber, and I can give you the news he would bring more precisely than he can. He was on the bank of the Seine, where there was no murder. I was on the other."

"Murder? What has happened, sir?" asked the queen.

"A great misfortune. The court party has triumphed."

"The court party has triumphed! Call you that a misfortune, Doctor Gilbert?"

"Yes; because it has triumphed by one of those fearful measures which destroy the conqueror, and which result to the benefit of the conquered."

"What has happened?"

"Lafayette and Bailly have fired on the people, and consequently can no longer be of use to you."

"Why?"

"They have lost their popularity."

"What did the people on whom they fired?"

"Signed a petition for the deposing——"

"Of whom?"

"Of the king."

"And you think to fire on them was wrong?" asked the queen, with a sparkling eye.

"I think it would have been better to convince than to shoot them."

"Of what would you convince them?"

"Of the king's sincerity."

"The king is sincere."

"Excuse me, madame. Three days ago I left the king. All the evening had been passed in an effort to make him understand that his true enemies are his brothers, Monsieur de Condé and the emigrés. On my knees I besought him to break off all connection with them, to adopt the constitution frankly, except those articles which are impossible. The king was convinced; at least I thought so, and was good enough to promise to have done with the emigration; yet behind my back, madame, the king signed, and caused you to sign, a letter to Monsieur, in which he was authorized to say to the Emperor of Austria and the King of Prussia——"

The queen blushed like a child taken *flagrante delicto*, and looked down. She, however, recovered herself soon.

"Have our enemies, then, spies in the king's cabinet?"

"Yes, madame; and it is this which makes every error on the king's part as dangerous as it is."

"But the letter was written by the king's own hand,

and as soon as it was signed by me, was sealed and given to the courier who was to bear it."

"True, madame."

"The letter was read?"

"The courier was arrested."

"We are, then, surrounded by traitors?"

"All men are not like the Charnys."

"What mean you?"

"Alas! madame, I wish to tell you one of the fatal auguries of the fall of kings is when they drive from them men they should attach to their fortunes by chains of adamant."

"Monsieur de Charny was not driven away; he left us. When kings become unfortunate, no tie suffices to retain men as friends."

Gilbert looked at the queen, and shook his head, and said:

"Do not let us thus calumniate Charny, madame, or the blood of his brothers will shout from the tomb that the Queen of France is ungrateful."

"Monsieur!"

"Madame, you know I speak the truth; that in the time of real danger Monsieur de Charny will be where duty calls him—where the peril is greatest."

The queen looked down. At last she said:

"You did not, I suppose, come to talk to me about Monsieur de Charny?"

"No, madame; but ideas, like events, are sometimes so linked together by invisible threads, that those are exposed which should remain in the secret places of the heart. No, I came to speak to the queen, excuse me if I spoke to the woman; I am ready to repair my fault."

"What have you, monsieur, to say to the queen?"

"I wished to show her the situation she, France, and Europe occupy. Madame, in your hands is the future of the world. You play with it, as with cards. You lost the first trick October 6th; your courtiers think you have won the second. The next trick will be *la belle*, and the stakes, which are throne, liberty, perhaps life, are all lost."

"And," said the queen, haughtily, "think you, sir, such a fear will induce us to pause?"

"I know the king is brave; he is the descendant of Henry IV. I know the queen is heroic, she is the granddaughter of Marie Theresa. I will, therefore, seek only to convince them; unfortunately, I fear I shall never be able to impart my ideas to either."

"Why take such trouble, then, sir, if you think it will be useless?"

"To do my duty, madame. Believe me, it is pleasant in stormy days as ours, at every effort, to say, 'I did my duty.'"

The queen looked Gilbert in the face.

"Monsieur, first of all, do you think it is yet possible to save the king?"

"I do."

"And royalty?"

"I hope so."

"Well, sir," said the queen, with a sigh of intense sadness, "you are more happy than I, for I fear both are lost, and I contend only to fulfil my ideas of duty."

"Yes, madame, I see; but because you wish a despotic monarchy, and an absolute king; like a miser who does not know, even when in sight of a shore which will restore him more than he loses, how to sacrifice a portion of his treasures, you sink yours, being borne down by the weight. Do as the prudent sailor does: throw the past aside, and strive for the future."

"To do so would be to break with the kings of Europe."

"True; but it is to make an alliance with the French people."

"The French people cannot contend against coalition."

"Suppose you had at its head a king. With a king really attached to the constitution, the French people would conquer Europe."

"An army of a million of men would be needed for that."

"Europe, madame, is not to be conquered by a million of men, but by an idea. Plant on the Rhine and on the Alps two tricolored flags with the inscription, 'War to tyrants!' and 'Liberty to peoples!' and Europe is conquered."

"Really, there are days when I am inclined to think the wisest become mad."

"Madame, you do not know what France now is in the eyes of nations, France, with some individual crimes—some local excesses, which do not, however, sully her white robe or her purity—virgin France is the goddess of liberty. The whole world loves her. The Pays Bas, the Rhine, Italy, with her minions—invoke a blessing on her. She has but to cross the frontier, and millions will fall down before her. France, with liberty in her hands, ceases to be a nation, but is immutable justice—eternal reason. Madame, madame, take advantage of the fact that it is not yet entered into violence; for if you hesitate too long, these hands she extends to you will be turned against herself. Belgium, Germany, Italy, watch each of her movements with joy. Belgium says, 'Come!' Germany says, 'I follow!' Italy exclaims, 'Save me!' Far in the north, an unknown hand wrote in the cabinet of the great Gustavus. 'No war with France.' None of those whom you call to your aid are prepared for war. Two empires hate us deeply. When I say empires, I mean an empress (Catherine) and a minister (Pitt). They are powerless, though. At this moment Russia holds Turkey under one of her claws and Poland under the other. Two or three years will be required to digest one and devour the other. She urges the Germans on and offers them France. She shames the inactivity of your brother Leopold, and points to the occupation of Holland by the King of Prussia, on account of a simple insult to his sister. 'Forward!' says Russia; but Leopold does not obey. Mr. Pitt is now swallowing India, and, like a boa-constrictor, suffers from laborious indigestion. If we wait, he will attack us, not by foreign, but by civil war. I am aware this Mr. Pitt you fear dreadfully; that when you think of him you grow pale. Would you strike him to the heart? Make France a republic with a king. What are you doing, though, madame? What does your friend, the Princess de Lamballe? She tells England, where she represents you, that the only ambition of France is to obtain the *magna charta,* and that the revolution, guided by the king, is reacting. What says Pitt to these advances? That he will not suffer France to be a republic; that he will save the monarchy. All the caresses and persuasions of Madame Lamballe have not induced him to promise that he will save the monarch; for he hates him; he hates the constitutional and philosophic Louis XVI., who contended with him for India, and wrested America from his grasp. Pitt desires only that history may make a pendant to Charles I."

"Monsieur," said the queen, in terror, "who unfolds all this to you?"

"The men who tell me what the letters of your majesty contain!"

"Have we, then, no thought not theirs?"

'I have told you, madame, that the kings of Europe are wrapped in a net in which those who would resist strive in vain. Do not you, madame, advance the ideas you seek to repress, and that net will become your armor. Those who hate will become your defenders, and the invisible poniards that menace you will become sabers to strike your enemies."

"But those whom you call our enemies are kings, and our brothers."

"Madame, call the French your children, and see what the value of your diplomatic brethren is. Does not some fatal stain, too, seem to rest on all these kings? Let us begin with your brother, Leopold. Is he not worn out at forty by the Tuscan harem he transported to Vienna? and does he not reanimate his expiring faculties by the murderous excitements he prepares for himself? Look at Frederic! look at Gustavus—the one died, the other will die, without posterity; for, in the eyes of all, the Prince Royal of Sweden is the son of Monk, and not of Gustavus.

Look at the King of Portugal, with three hundred nuns! at the King of Saxony, with his three hundred and fifty bastards! Look at Catherine, the northern Pasiphæ, whom a bull would not satisfy, and who has three armies of lovers! Madame, madame, do you not see that all these kings rush to suicidal ruin? You, instead of going with them, should advance to universal empire!"

"Why, then, Monsieur Gilbert, do you not say this to the king?"

"I do, I do! He, though, like you, has his evil genii, which come to undo all that I accomplish."

Then, with profound melancholy, he continued:

"You have Mirabeau; you have Barnave; you will use me after them, and, like them, amid all, will be said."

"Monsieur Gilbert," said the queen, "I will seek the king, and return."

Gilbert bowed. The queen passed through the door which led into the king's room.

The doctor waited ten minutes, or a quarter of an hour—a half hour, and at last a door on the other side opened.

An usher, having looked carefully around, advanced toward Gilbert, made a masonic sign, and handed him a letter. He left at once.

Gilbert opened the letter, and read:

"You lose time, Gilbert; for at this moment the queen and king listen to Monsieur de Breteuil, who brings them this advice from Vienna:

"To treat Barnave as they did Mirabeau, to gain time, to swear to the constitution, and execute it liberally, so as to show that it cannot be executed. France will grow cold and become tired. The French are volatile, some new whim will seize them, and the revolution will be forgotten.

"If liberty does pass away, we will have gained a year or two, and will be ready for war.

"Leave, then, those two beings called in derision king and queen of France, and hurry to the hospital of Gros Caillon. You will find there a dying man less fatally affected, though, than they, for you may save him, while without doing them any good you *may* be borne down, down, by their fall."

The note had no signature, but Gilbert recognized Cagliostro's hand.

At that moment Mme. de Campan entered from the door of the queen's room, and handed Gilbert this note:

"The king asks Doctor Gilbert to write down his political plan as he explained it to the queen.

"The queen, being detained by a matter of importance, regrets that she will not be able to return to Monsieur Gilbert. It is useless, then, for him to wait longer."

Gilbert thought for a moment, and shook his head.

"Mad! mad!" said he.

"Have you nothing to say to their majesties, monsieur?" said Mme. de Campan.

Gilbert gave the letter without a signature he had just received, and said:

"Only this."

He left.

CHAPTER XXXVII.

NO MASTER! NO MISTRESS!

On the next day, the assembly received a report from the maire of Paris, and from the commandant of the National Guard. All were anxious to be deceived, and the comedy was easily played.

The assembly thanked them for an energy they had no idea they had employed, and congratulated them for a victory each deplored from the bottom of his heart, and thanked God from the bottom of its heart, that at one blow both the insurrection and the insurgents had been crushed.

According to these felicitations, the revolution was terminated. It was just beginning.

In the meantime, the old Jacobins, judging the morrow

by the yesterday, fancied they were attacked, pursued, tracked up, and prepared to find pardon for their real importance in a feigned humility. Robespierre, yet alarmed at having been nominated as king, instead of Louis XVI., drew up an address in the name of the present and absent.

In this address he thanked the assembly for its generous efforts, its wisdom, firmness, vigilance, and impartial and incorruptible justice.

How was it possible for the Feuillants not to regain courage, and think themselves powerful, when they thus saw the humility of their adversaries.

For a time they thought themselves masters not only of Paris, but of France.

Alas! the Feuillants did not understand the state of things; when they left the Jacobins, they had merely formed an assembly which was a double of the real one. The similitude between the two was such that in the Feuillants, as in the chamber, none was admitted except on condition of paying taxes, being an active citizen and eligible of voting for electors.

The people then had two chambers instead of one. This was not what it wanted. It wished a popular chamber, to be not the ally, but the enemy of the assembly, which would not reconstruct, but destroy royalty.

The Feuillants did not, then, in any respect, satisfy the public. The public, therefore, at once abandoned them.

By crossing the street they lost all popularity.

In July there were out of Paris, four hundred societies. Three hundred corresponded with both Jacobins and Feuillants, one hundred with the Jacobins alone.

As the Feuillants grew weak, the Jacobins rebuilt themselves under the guidance of Robespierre—the most popular man of France.

What Cagliostro had written to Gilbert about Barnave was accomplished.

Perhaps we will also see it fulfilled in relation to the little Ajaccio Corsican.

The time for the termination of the National Assembly

came. It struck slowly, it is true, like the life of an old man which slowly drops away.

Having taken three thousand votes, the assembly had finished the revision of the constitution.

This constitution was an iron cage, in which it knew not how the king had been shut up. The fact that the bars were gilded did not make it the less a prison.

The royal will was powerless, for it had become a wheel which received, instead of giving, motion. All the power of resistance which Louis XVI. had was in the veto, which suspended for three years the execution of any decrees which did not please the king. The wheel then ceased to turn, and the whole machine was stopped.

This *vis inertiæ* being left aside, the royalty of Henry IV., of Louis XIV., all power of action of those great monarchs was gone.

The day on which the king was to swear to the constitution drew near. England and the emigré wrote to him:

"Die if it be needed, but do not degrade yourself by that oath!"

Leopold and Barnave said:

"Swear, and let any one keep his oath who can."

The king terminated the discussion by this phrase:

"I declare that I do not see consistency or amity enough in the constitution; as opinions, however, I will consent, and experience shall decide."

It remained to be determined where the constitution should be presented to the king, at the Tuileries or in the assembly. The king said he would swear to the constitution where it was voted.

The appointed day was the 13th of September.

The assembly received this communication with unanimous applause. The king went thither.

In an outbreak of enthusiasm, Lafayette proposed an amnesty to all who were accused of having favored the king's flight. It was acceded to by acclamation. The cloud which had darkened the prospects of Andrée and Charny was dissipated.

A deputation of sixty members was appointed to thank the king for his letter.

The keeper of the seals hurried to tell the king of the vote.

On the same morning, the assembly had abolished the Order of St. Esprit, authorizing the king alone to wear the cordon, which was the evidence of the high nobility.

The deputation found the king wearing only the star of St. Louis, and as Louis XVI. knew the effect which the absence of the *cordon bleu* would produce, he said:

"Gentlemen, this morning you abolished the Order of the St. Esprit, preserving it for me alone. As an order to me has no value except that it gives me the power of communication, henceforth I look on it as abolished for me also."

The queen, dauphin, and Mme. Royale stood near the door. The queen was pale, and quivered in every nerve. Mme. Royale, already proud, passionate, and violent, was haughty, and seemed not only to be aware of what passed, but to foresee future indignities. The dauphin was careless as a child, and looked like a human being inserted in a group of statuary.

The king, a few days before, had said to Montmorin:

"I know I am lost; all that is now done for royalty is for my son."

Louis XVI. replied, with apparent sincerity, to the reply of the deputation; when he had done, he turned to the dauphin and royal family.

"My wife and children," said he, "partake of my sentiments."

Yes, they did; for when the deputation retired, they drew together, and when they had looked after it anxiously, Marie Antoinette placed her white and marble-cold hand on the king's arm, and said:

"These people will have no more king. Stone by stone, they tear down the monarchy, and of those stones build a tomb for us."

She was mistaken, poor woman! She was to have a pauper's grave, not even a tomb.

She was not, however, wrong about the attacks on the royal prerogative.

M. de Malouet was president of the assembly, and was a royalist. He, however, thought it necessary to consult the assembly as to the manner in which the oath should be administered, and whether it would be seated, or stand during the ceremony.

"Seated," was heard from all sides.

"And the king?" said De Malouet.

"Standing and uncovered," said a voice.

The assembly trembled.

This voice was isolated, but clear, strong, and vibrating. It seemed the voice of the people, uttered alone for greater distinctness. The president grew pale.

Who pronounced those words? Came they from the hall, or from the galleries? It mattered not; they were so powerful that he had to reply.

"Gentlemen," said he, "there is no circumstance in which the assembly of the nation does not recognize the king as its chief. If the king stand, I propose that the assembly hear the oath in the same attitude."

The voice then said:

"I propose an amendment which will suit everybody. Let us order that it be permitted to Monsieur de Malouet, and those who prefer it, to hear the king kneeling; let us, though, maintain the proposition."

The proposition was lost.

On the next day the king was to swear. The hall was full, and the galleries crowded with spectators. At noon the king was announced.

He spoke erect, and the assembly heard him standing. The discourse having been pronounced, the constitution was signed, and all sat down.

The president, Thouret, arose to pronounce his discourse; but, after the two or three first phrases, seeing that the king did not rise, he resumed his seat. The galleries applauded, and the king evidently grew pale.

He took his handkerchief from his pocket, and wiped

the perspiration from his brow. The queen, in a closed box, witnessed the ceremonial. She could bear no more, but arose, went out, closed the door, and returned to the Tuileries.

She returned without speaking a word, even to her most intimate friends. Since Charny had gone her heart absorbed poison, but did not emit it.

He returned half an hour after.

"The queen?" asked he.

They told him where she was.

An usher wished to walk before him. He put him aside by a sign, and appeared at the door of the room where she was.

He was so pale, so overcome, that the perspiration hung in large drops on his brow. The queen, when she saw him, arose and shrieked:

"Sire," said she, "what has happened?"

Without speaking, the king sunk into an armchair, and sobbed.

"Madame, madame!" at last said he, "why would you be present at this session? Why would you be a witness of my humiliation? Was it for this, under the pretext of being a queen, that I brought you to France?"

Such an explosion from Louis XVI. was the more painful, because it was rare. The queen could not resist, and running to the king, threw herself at his feet. Just then the door opened, and she turned around. Mme. Campan had come in.

The queen reached out her hand, and said:

"Leave us, Campan, leave us."

Mme. de Campan did not misconceive why the queen wished her to go. She retired respectfully, but standing behind the door, heard the unfortunate couple long exchanging phrases broken by sobs. At last they calmed their sobs, and were silent. After half an hour the door opened, and the queen herself called Mme. de Campan.

"Campan," said she, "give this letter to Monsieur de Malden. It is addressed to my brother Leopold. Let him set out at once for Vienna, which he must reach before the news of to-day. If he need two or three hundred louis, give them to him. I will return them."

Mme. de Campan took the letter and left. Two hours after, M. de Malden set out for Vienna.

The worst feature of all this was that they had to seem happy and joyous.

During the rest of the day a tremendous crowd filled the Tuileries; at night the whole city was illuminated. The king and queen were invited to show themselves in the Champs Elysées, escorted by the aides-de-camp and chiefs of the Parisian army.

Scarcely had they appeared than cries of "Vive le roi!" "Vive la reine!" arose. After an interval the cries ceased. It was where the carriage had halted.

"Do not believe them, madame," said a stern-looking man of the people, who stood by with folded arms. "Vive la nation!"

The carriage was slowly driven on, but the man who had spoken placed his hand on the carriage door, and whenever the cry of "Vive le roi!" was heard, or "Vive la reine!" shouted "Vive la nation!"

The queen returned with her heart crushed by the constant and heavy blows which were launched on her by anger and hatred.

Representations were organized at the different theaters, at the opera, the Comedie Française, and the Italians.

At the two first there were Galies, and the king and queen were received with unanimous applause. When they sought to do the same thing at the last, they had been anticipated; the people had taken all the pit.

They saw that at that place things would not go on, and that there would probably be trouble during the evening. The fear became certain when they saw who filled the pit.

Danton, Desmoulins, Legendre, Santerre occupied paramount seats. When the queen entered the box the galleries sought to applaud. The pit hissed.

The queen looked with terror at the gaping crater before her. She saw the flame of eyes flashing with hatred and menace.

"What have I done?" said she, seeking to hide her trouble with a smile. "Why do they detest me so violently?"

All at once her eyes rested with terror on a man who leaned against one of the columns on which the boxes rested.

It was he of Tavernay, of Sèvres, of the garden of the Tuileries. It was he of the menacing words and mysterious and terrible actions.

When her eyes had once rested on him, she could not look away. He exerted the fascination of the serpent over her.

The play began. The queen made an effort, and broke the charm, so as to be able to turn away and look at the stage.

"Evenements Imprévus" of Gretry were played.

All the efforts of Marie Antoinette to divert her attention, however, were vain; for the mysterious man used a magnetic power more mighty than her will, and she could not but turn and look in one direction.

The stare—motionless, sardonic, and mocking. It was a painful impression, internal and fatal. It was to one awake what the nightmare is to one asleep.

A kind of electricity floated through the hall. These two influences could not but meet and crash, as in an August day two clouds come together and hurl forth lightning if not bolts. The occasion came.

Mme. Dagazon, a charming woman, who gave her name to a peculiar line of business, had a duo to sing with the tenor, in which were these words:

"*Ah! comme j'aime ma maitresse.*"

The brave woman rushed to the front of the stage and opened her arms, reached them forth to the queen, sung the verses, and gave the fatal challenge.

The queen knew the tempest was come; terror-stricken, she turned aside, and her eyes fell involuntarily on the man who leaned against the column. She saw him make a sign, which the whole pit obeyed as an order.

With one voice, it cried out:

"No master! no mistress! Liberty!"

To this the galleries and boxes replied:

"Vive le roi! Vive la reine! Long live our master and mistress!"

"No master! no mistress! Liberty! liberty! liberty!" howled the pit.

After this double declaration of war, the strife began. The queen shrieked with terror, and closed her eyes. She could no longer look at this demon, who seemed the god of disorder, the spirit of destruction.

The officers of the National Guard then surrounded her, making a rampart of their bodies, and took her away.

In the corridor she heard the same cries.

"No master! no mistress! no king! no queen!"

They took her to her coach. She had fainted away.

She never went to the theater again.

September 30th. The Constitutional Assembly declared that it had fulfilled its functions, and closed its sessions.

The following is the result of its labors, during a session of two years and four months:

The complete disorganization of the monarchy.

The organization of popular power.

The destruction of all ecclesiastical and military privileges.

The issue of one hundred million assignats.

The mortgage of the national property.

The recognition of freedom of worship.

Abolition of monastic vows.

Abolition of lettres de cachet.

Equality of right of office.

Suppression of internal custom-houses.

The establishment of the National Guard.

The adoption and ratification of the king.

CHAPTER XXXVIII.

THE FAREWELL OF BARNAVE.

On the 2d of October, that is to say, two days after the dissolution of the assembly, at the hour of his usual rendezvous with the queen, Barnave was introduced not on the ground floor of Mme. de Campan, but in the room called the great cabinet.

On the evening of the day when the king swore to the constitution, the sentinel and aide-de-camp of Lafayette disappeared from the interior of the castle, and if the king had not regained his power, he had at least regained his liberty.

This was small compensation for the humiliation of which he had complained so bitterly to the queen.

Without being received publicly, and with all the preparation of a public audience, Barnave was not on this occasion subjected to the precautions which hitherto had made his presence at the Tuileries necessary.

He was pale, and seemed very sad; his sadness and pallor struck the queen.

She received him standing, though she knew the respect the young lawyer held her in, and that if she sat down, he would not do what President Thouret had when he saw that the king did not rise.

"Well, Monsieur Barnave, are you satisfied?" said she. "The king has followed your advice, and sworn to the constitution."

"The queen is very kind," said Barnave, bowing, "to say my advice. Had it not been both the advice of the Emperor Leopold and of Prince Kaunitz, perhaps, your majesty had hesitated to accomplish this great act—the only one which, perhaps, can save the king, if the king——"

Barnave paused.

"Can be saved. Is not that, monsieur, what you wished

to say ?" said the queen, meeting the doubt courageously, and we may add with the daring which was peculiar to her.

"God grant, madame, that I may never be the prophet of such misfortune. Yet on the point of leaving Paris, of being separated forever from the queen, I would neither have her majesty despair nor yield too much to illusion."

"You leave Paris, Monsieur Barnave ? You leave us ?"

"The assembly, madame, to which I belonged, is over, and as it has been determined that no member of the assembly, which established the constitution can belong to the legislative assembly I have no longer a motive to remain in Paris."

"Not even if you could be useful to us, Monsieur Barnave ?"

Barnave smiled sadly.

"Not even for that purpose, for from yesterday I shall be able to do you no good."

"Sir," said the queen, "you have too lowly an estimate of yourself."

"Alas ! madame, I have tried and found myself weak. I have weighed and found myself light. What was my power, and what I wished the monarchy to use as a lever ? My influence was my power over the Jacobins ; it was a popularity laboriously, painfully acquired. The assembly, though, is dissolved ; the Jacobins are Feuillants ; and I am afraid the latter made a great mistake when they left the old club ; in fine, madame, popularity."

Barnave smiled more sadly than he had at first.

"In fine, my popularity is gone."

The queen looked at Barnave, and a strange glance like one of triumph passed over her eyes.

"Well, sir," said she, "you see that popularity may be lost."

Barnave sighed.

The queen saw that she had committed one of those little cruelties which were habitual to her.

The fact was, Barnave had so completely lost his popularity that he had been forced to bend his head to Robespierre, and to whom was the fault of this to be attributed? Was it not to that fatal monarchy, which dragged all that it touched into an abyss, into which it was itself hurrying, to that terrible destiny which made Marie Antoinette, as it had done of Marie Stuart, an angel of death devoting all those to whom it appeared to the tomb?

Then, to a degree, she retraced her steps, and regretting that Barnave had replied by a simple sigh when he might have said, "For whom have I lost my popularity, unless for you?" she resumed:

"But, Monsieur Barnave, you will not go?"

"Certainly," said Barnave, "if the queen bid me stay, I will, as a soldier, remain under the flag, though he have permission to go and guard it in battle. But, if I remain, madame, do you know what will happen? Instead of being weak, I shall be a traitor."

"How so, sir?" said the queen, slightly wounded. "Explain, I do not understand."

"Will the queen permit me to show her not only the situation in which she is, but in which she will be?"

"Do so, sir; I am accustomed to measure abysses, and had I been liable to vertigo, would long ago have cast myself headlong."

"The queen, perhaps, looks on the assembly which has just expired as her enemy."

"Let us make a distinction, Monsieur Barnave; in that assembly I had friends. You will not, however, deny that the majority of the assembly was hostile to royalty."

"Madame," said Barnave, "the assembly never attacked either you or the king but once. That was when it declared that none of its members could belong to the corps legislative."

"I do not understand this, sir. Explain it to me," said the queen, with a doubt.

"Easily enough; it wrested a buckler from the arms of your friends."

"And it seems to me also a sword from the hands of my enemies."

"Alas! madame, you are mistaken. The shaft was winged by Robespierre, and all that comes from him is terrible. He throws you unknown into the first assembly. You knew in the old one whom to contend with; in the corps legislative you have a new study to make. Observe, too, madame, in excluding all of us, Robespierre forced France into the alternative of receiving our superiors or our inferiors. There is nothing above us; the emigration has disorganized everything, and if there was a noblesse in France, the people would not select its representatives from it. The new assembly, then, will be democratic; there will be shades in that democracy, that is all."

The queen's countenance showed that she followed with attention what Barnave had said, and beginning to understand, she began to be afraid.

"Listen," said Barnave; "I have seen these deputies; for, during the last three or four days, they have begun to collect at Paris; I saw those from Bordeaux. They are almost men of unknown names, but who are anxious to be conspicuous—apart from Condorcet, Brissot, and some others, the oldest is scarcely thirty years old. Age is driven away by youth, which dethrones tradition. Away with white hairs; new France will be ruled by black."

"Think you, sir, we have more to fear from those who are about to come than from those who have gone?"

"Yes, madame; the newcomers have instructions to make war on nobles and on priests. They say nothing as yet about the king, but time will show. If he be content with the executive, however, perhaps all will be pardoned—that has passed."

"How!" said the queen, "pardon the past? I presume the king has the right to pardon."

"That is exactly what people will never understand again—especially the people who are coming, madame, and you will have evidence of it. They will not even keep up the hypocritical pretenses of those who are going. They, like one of my confrères, Vergniaud, a deputy from La Gironde, will look on the king as an enemy."

"An enemy?" said the queen, in amazement.

"Yes, madame," repeated Barnave, "an enemy; that is to say, the voluntary or involuntary center of all our internal and external enemies. Alas! yes; it must be owned that the newcomers are not altogether wrong who believe they have discovered a truth, and who utter aloud what your bitterest adversaries dare not whisper."

"Enemy?" repeated the queen; "the king the enemy of his people? That is a thing, Monsieur Barnave, you not only never can convince me of, but you cannot make me understand."

"Yet it is true, madame; he is an enemy by nature and by temperament; yet three days ago he accepted the constitution. Did he not?"

"Yes. Well?"

"Well, when he returned hither, the king had almost died of anger, and this evening he wrote to the emperor."

"But how, think you, can we bear such humilities?"

"Ah, madame, he is an enemy, and fatally, an enemy. He is, besides, a voluntary and an involuntary enemy; for, educated by Monsieur de la Vauguyon, the general of the Jesuitical party, the heart of the king is in the hand of the priests, who are the enemies of the nation; involuntary enemy, because he is the compulsory chief of the reaction. Suppose, even, that he remains in Paris; he is at Coblentz with the emigration, in La Vendée with the priests, in Prussia with his allies, Leopold and Frederic. The king does nothing. I admit, madame," said Barnave, sadly, "that he does nothing. Not being able to use him, however, they use his name. In the cottage, in the pulpit, in the castle, he is the poor, good king, the holy king; so that a terrible revolt to the reign of the revolution is threatened; madame, it is the revolt of pity."

"Indeed, Monsieur Barnave, do you tell me these things? and were you not the first to pity us?"

"Yes, madame, yes; I did and do pity you sincerely. There is, however, a difference between me and the persons of whom I speak. They, by their pity, destroy; I would save you."

"But, sir, among those, as you say, who come to wage

war on and to destroy us, is there aught predetermined on?"

"No, madame; and I have, as yet, only heard of vague expressions. The suppression of the title of 'majesty' in the first session; instead of a throne an armchair, on the seat of the president."

"See you in that anything worse than Monsieur Thouret taking his seat because the king did?"

"It is, at least, one step forward, instead of in the rear. This, then, madame, is alarming; Lafayette and Bailly will be dismissed."

"Well," said the queen, "I do not regret them."

"You are wrong, madame; they are both your friends."

The queen smiled bitterly.

"Your friends, madame; perhaps your best friends. Be careful of them. If they have preserved any popularity, be not slow to use it; for it will pass away, madame, as mine has."

"And beyond all that, monsieur, you show me ruin. You conduct me to the very crater, make me measure its depths, but do not tell me how to avoid it."

For a moment Barnave was silent.

Then, uttering a sigh:

"Madame," said he, "why were you arrested at Montmédy?"

"Good!" said the queen, "Monsieur Barnave approves of my flight to Varennes."

"I do not, madame; for the situation in which you are now is the natural consequence of it. As its results, though, have been such, I am glad that it did not succeed."

"Then, to-day, Monsieur Barnave, a member of the National Assembly, delegate of that assembly with Petion and Latour Manbourg, to bring back the king and queen to Paris, deplores that they are not in a foreign land."

"Let us understand each other, madame. He who deplores that is not a member of the assembly, not the colleague of Petion and of Latour Maubourg, but poor Barnave, your humble servant, ready to sacrifice his life for you, and life is all that he possesses."

"Thanks, sir!" said the queen. "The accent in which you speak proves that you would keep your word. I hope, though, such devotion never will be necessary."

"So much the worse for me, madame," said Barnave.

"How, so much the worse?"

"Yes, fall or not, I had rather have died fighting, as I see I shall, than in the depths of Dauphiny, where I shall be useless to you; but yet will make vows and prayers for the most beautiful woman that ever lived—for the most tender and devoted mother—for the queen. The same faults which have created the past will prepare the future. You will rely on an assistance which will never come, or which will come too late. The Jacobins will seize on the power of the legislative assembly; your friends will leave France to avoid persecution, and those who remain will be arrested and imprisoned. I will be one of them; for I will not fly. I will be judged—condemned. Perhaps my death will be useless to you, or even unknown; should you hear of it, I will have been of little use to you, and you will have forgotten the few hours during which I hoped to serve you."

"Monsieur Barnave," said the queen, with great dignity, "I am ignorant what fate is in store for the king and myself. All I know is, that the names of those who have served us are scrupulously inscribed in my memory, and that neither their good nor ill fortune will be strange to us. What, though, Monsieur Barnave, can we do for you?"

"You, madame, personally, can do much. You can show that I have not been entirely without value to you."

"What can I do?"

Barnave knelt.

"Give me, madame, your hand to kiss."

A tear rushed to Marie Antoinette's dry eyelids. She gave the young man her white, cold hand, which had been kissed by the lips of the two most eloquent men of the assembly, Mirabeau and Barnave.

Barnave merely touched it. The poor madman was afraid if he kissed it he would never be able to tear his lips away.

Then, rising, he said :

"Madame, I have not pride enough to tell you, 'The monarchy is safe ;' but I say, if it be lost, one who never will forget their kindness will fall with it."

He bowed and withdrew.

Marie Antoinette looked after him with a sigh, and when the door was closed, said :

"Poor hollow nut ! it needed but a little time to reduce you to a mere shell."

THE END.

www.ingramcontent.com/pod-product-compliance
Lightning Source LLC
Chambersburg PA
CBHW032301020726
47495CB00001B/194

* 9 7 8 1 4 3 4 4 0 5 4 1 8 *